REUNION

Susannah ran the brush through her hair one last time, then took the lamp to the bedside table and placed it next to her gun. She'd sleep until first light, then, with or without help, she was going out again to search for Conor.

She heard a sound outside the door and froze. There was a soft knock. She reached for the gun.

"Susannah."

Her heart started pounding in wild joy. She hurried to the door, then paused with her hand on the key. What if her mind was playing tricks on her?

The knock sounded again. "Susannah, it's Conor."

There was no mistaking his voice. With a glad cry, she turned the key and flung the door open.

He stood there, tall and handsome, his hat in one hand, his rifle in the other. "I'm back," he said.

"I'm glad."

As he watched, an enchanting smile lit up her face. Her eyes were very green, and it seemed to Conor that they were shining. Her beauty took his breath away.

"Are you going to come in?" Susannah asked quietly.

He nodded and stepped into the room, leaning his rifle against the wall. The lamp spread its warm, welcoming light over the bed, the inviting bed, with the blankets pulled back. Suddenly he felt awkward and shy. He watched as Susannah locked the door. "Your uncle's papers, they—"

"I don't care about my uncle's papers." Susannah took his hat from his hand and tossed it toward the chairs. Conor watched in surprised silence as the hat hit the edge of one seat and fell to the floor. He looked back at Susannah when she moved against him and put her arms around his neck.

"I prayed for the chance to tell you I love you," she whispered. "I thank God I got it."

DISCOVER DEANA JAMES!

CAPTIVE ANGEL   (2524, $4.50/$5.50)
Abandoned, penniless, and suddenly responsible for the biggest tobacco plantation in Colleton County, distraught Caroline Gillard had no time to dissolve into tears. By day the willowy redhead labored to exhaustion beside her slaves . . . but each night left her restless with longing for her wayward husband. She'd make the sea captain regret his betrayal until he begged her to take him back!

MASQUE OF SAPPHIRE   (2885, $4.50/$5.50)
Judith Talbot-Harrow left England with a heavy heart. She was going to America to join a father she despised and a sister she distrusted. She was certainly in no mood to put up with the insulting actions of the arrogant Yankee privateer who boarded her ship, ransacked her things, then "apologized" with an indecent, brazen kiss! She vowed that someday he'd pay dearly for the liberties he had taken and the desires he had awakened.

SPEAK ONLY LOVE   (3439, $4.95/$5.95)
Long ago, the shock of her mother's death had robbed Vivian Marleigh of the power of speech. Now she was being forced to marry a bitter man with brandy on his breath. But she could not say what was in her heart. It was up to the viscount to spark the fires that would melt her icy reserve.

WILD TEXAS HEART   (3205, $4.95/$5.95)
Fan Breckenridge was terrified when the stranger found her near-naked and shivering beneath the Texas stars. Unable to remember who she was or what had happened, all she had in the world was the deed to a patch of land that might yield oil . . . and the fierce loving of this wildcatter who called himself Irons.

Available wherever paperbacks are sold, or order direct from the Publisher. Send cover price plus 50¢ per copy for mailing and handling to Penguin USA, P.O. Box 999, c/o Dept. 17109, Bergenfield, NJ 07621. Residents of New York and Tennessee must include sales tax. DO NOT SEND CASH.

JESSICA WULF

THE MOUNTAIN ROSE

ZEBRA BOOKS
KENSINGTON PUBLISHING CORP.

ZEBRA BOOKS are published by

Kensington Publishing Corp.
850 Third Avenue
New York, NY 10022

First Printing: August, 1994

Printed in the United States of America

ACKNOWLEDGEMENTS

There are a few people I wish to acknowledge for their contributions to this book:

My editor, Beth Lieberman, for her unerring instincts, gentle guidance, and endless patience.

John LeBow, D.O., for his medical expertise, and his very entertaining way of sharing that knowledge with me.

Karen Karsh Daugherty, for kindly agreeing to talk with me about what it is like to be blind.

The members of my critique group: Barbara, Denée, Margaret and Mary. Your heroic efforts to read my manuscript before its deadline are appreciated more than I can adequately express, as are your excellent observations and suggestions. Thank you.

My dear friend Sandie, whose no-nonsense attitude toward life and stubborn determination to fight for what is right was the inspiration for Alexandra's personality.

My mother, Sharlene, and my husband, Drew, for their loving support and encouragement (and cooking and housecleaning!) while I wrote this book.

And finally, I'd like to acknowledge a very special little girl named Suzie, to whom this book is dedicated. You didn't let the dream die.

—J. W.

One

"Not much farther, girls," Susannah Duncan called to the pair of sweating mares as the animals strained to pull the old farm wagon up the steep incline. Her voice was low and musical, with a soft accent that declared her Southern upbringing. She pushed a stray wisp of golden hair back under the confines of her wide-brimmed felt hat, then returned her gloved hand to the reins. The wagon was not overfull, but the trip had started at first light; it was now early afternoon, and the grade proved difficult for the tired horses.

At the sound of a bark, Susannah looked down from the high seat to see her big black dog trotting beside the wagon. "Where have you been, Jesse?" she affectionately demanded. "Chasing rabbits?" The dog's sides heaved and his tongue was hanging, but he managed an answering bark.

Susannah laughed. "I know you want a ride, but you'll have to wait until we reach that dip up ahead; I'll not stop the horses on this incline."

Jesse barked again and kept pace with the wagon. Susannah finally pulled on the reins, bringing the team to a stop in the shade. She set the brake and, before she climbed down, took her hat off and laid it on the wagon seat. The cool breeze felt good on her forehead. She bent to greet the dog.

"You rascal," she said with a smile as she scratched his ears.

"You like living up here much more than in Grandmother's fancy house in Charleston, don't you?" She straightened, then pulled loose hairpins from her untidy hair. Thick, golden tresses fell to her waist, releasing a faint scent of lavender. While her fingers absentmindedly combed the shining lengths, she let her eyes wander with appreciation over the vista around her.

The day was clear and cool, the sky a brilliant blue above the surrounding mountains. The breeze rustled through the plentiful pine trees, filling the air with their distinctive fragrance. An abrupt drop-off on the east side of the road gave her a clear view of a small valley nestled between the peaks, breathtaking in its beauty. Several hundred feet below her, a swift-running river rushed along at the bottom of the mountain, in a hurry to get to the plains so many miles to the east.

Susannah deftly twisted her hair into a simple bun at the back of her head and secured the arrangement with the hairpins. "I love it here, too, Jess," she admitted to the resting dog. She glanced up over the wagon, where the whispering trees marched off to timberline, remembering her discussion with Mr. Jackson at the land office that morning. He told her no one had yet staked a claim on the valley, because no evidence of gold or silver deposits had been found there. That was fine with her. The greed for those two metals led men to do terrible things to the land, and sometimes to each other.

She moved around to face the horses. "Who cares about gold or silver, Minnie? Do you, Muffin? I'd raise horses in a valley like this." Her gaze fell on her hands as she adjusted the harness. The elegant and expensive leather riding gloves she wore had been intended for genteel jaunts in the park, not for driving a farm wagon.

Susannah shook her head in wry amusement. A year ago she had lived in Charleston, South Carolina, attending balls and soirees, accompanied by her wealthy grandmother. Colorado Territory had been a mystical place, belonging to another world.

Now she and her father and her little sister lived here, in her uncle's small, snug cabin high on Blue Mountain. She had traded satin ball gowns for practical wool dresses and learned to cook and clean, and even to manage a team of draft horses. Her grandmother would be appalled.

Minnie nudged Susannah's shoulder with her soft muzzle.

"When we get home, you can each have one of those dried apples I bought today, as soon as you cool down," Susannah promised with a smile. "And you won't have to pull this old wagon into town for a few weeks at least." Muffin answered with a quiet nicker; then both mares pulled away and looked up the road, their ears cocked. Susannah kept one hand on the harness and turned; she heard the sound of approaching horses. Jesse moved to her side and sat, his ears up, his nose quivering inquisitively.

"Who would be way up here?" Susannah murmured uneasily.

Her question was answered a minute later when a group of riders raced around the bend toward her. She recognized the lead man. Jesse growled low in his throat. "Easy, boy," Susannah whispered, although she shared Jesse's apprehension.

The horsemen slowed, then pulled to a halt.

"Lookee who's here, Kyle!" one of the men shouted. "If it ain't Miss Duncan herself!" The scruffy cowboy grinned, showing broken, yellowed teeth. "We was jist a'callin' at yore place, and you wasn't there, and now here you are!"

Susannah coughed as dust swirled around her. She glared up at the leader. "What are you doing out here, Kyle? You're a long way off your brother's land."

"It's like Harry said, Susannah. We come calling." Kyle Banning pushed his hat back on his head, revealing unkempt black hair. His small brown eyes insolently roamed over her.

Susannah bristled at his insulting perusal. "I don't know why you bothered. No one at my place wants to see you." Her tone was contemptuous. "I'm surprised Fletcher trusted you out of his sight."

Kyle flushed. At the sound of a snicker, he glanced threateningly at his men. It grew ominously quiet.

"Your pa wasn't too nice at first, either, but I taught him some manners," Kyle snapped. He closed one hand into a fist. "I can do the same for you."

The man called Harry laughed out loud. Susannah tightened her hold on the harness as a cold dread wrapped its fingers around her heart. A picture of her gentle, aging parent filled her mind. Had they hurt her father? And what of her little sister? Had her father been able to hide the child from these men?

"If you laid a hand on my father, so help me, Kyle, you'll regret it." Her fear-tinged anger made her voice harsh.

"You shouldn't talk nasty to me, Susannah. You should be very, very nice." He motioned to one of the men.

Susannah recognized the man as Ben Hollister, Fletcher Banning's foreman. He circled behind the wagon, dismounted, and tied his horse to the tailgate. She whirled to face Kyle again. "I don't know what your game is, Kyle Banning, but I'll not play. You just keep on going to wherever you were going, and I'll be on my way."

"Fletcher wants to see you, Susannah, so we're all going the same way."

Susannah's hands found her hips. "No, we are not. I told your brother last fall I would not welcome his attentions. I've not changed my mind."

Kyle urged his horse closer to her and leaned down. "Maybe that's because I'm more to your liking. You'd welcome my attentions, wouldn't you?" He reached out to catch a stray golden curl that waved in the breeze.

Susannah could not suppress a scornful laugh as she jerked away from his hand. "Why on earth would I welcome the attentions of an arrogant, gunslinging bully?" She moved around her team and whistled for Jesse, then looked at Ben Hollister. "Get your horse away from my wagon," she ordered. At the sound of a gun being cocked, her gaze flew back to Kyle.

He had urged his mount closer yet. His face was mottled with fury; his eyes seemed to blaze. He held one of his two pistols. The barrel of the drawn gun rested on his saddle horn. "Fletcher wants to see you, and I'm taking you to him," he repeated through clenched teeth.

"And are you going to shoot me if I refuse?" Susannah asked derisively as she gathered her skirts and placed one foot on a wheel spoke. Her eyes fell on the rifle that waited in a slot next to the brake handle. It was time to put an end to this nonsense.

"Not you, dear Susannah. I'll shoot your dog." He aimed his weapon at Jesse. Jesse bared his teeth and growled.

Susannah stopped cold. One look at Kyle's face told her he would not hesitate to do as he threatened. "Let's go, then," she snapped. She stepped onto the spoke.

Kyle waved his gun at her. "Ben'll drive. You get in the back."

She balanced on her precarious foot rest and defiantly stared at him, her chin high. "I'll drive my own wagon."

"Damn you, stop arguing with me!" Kyle returned his gun to its holster and leaned out of the saddle. His hand closed on her upper arm with cruel strength as he jerked her off the wagon wheel. "Get in the back *now!*"

Susannah hit the ground hard, the wind knocked from her lungs. Stunned, she gasped for air. Jesse moved to stand protectively at her side and snarled a warning. Kyle's nervous mount danced dangerously close to her head.

Ben helped Susannah to her feet. "It would be best if you obey him, Miss Duncan," he said in a low tone.

Kyle stepped down from his saddle and handed the reins to Harry. He advanced on Susannah and without warning slapped her across the face. Pain exploded along her jaw. She staggered back against Ben. Jesse growled and barked his protest.

"Damn it, Kyle, what the hell are you doing?" Ben cried. He steadied Susannah and whipped a handkerchief from his pocket to dab at the blood that had appeared at the corner of her mouth.

"Shut up, Ben." Kyle's voice was ugly with rage. He shook a finger in Susannah's face. "Don't disobey me again." He pulled her from Ben's grasp and wrapped an arm around her waist, forcing her against the length of his body. "Get up on the seat, Ben. I'll keep Miss Duncan company." He moved toward the wagon.

"Let go of me!" Susannah struggled against him, kicking and clawing. Kyle grabbed a handful of her hair and yanked her head back to a painful position.

"Kyle, don't mess with her," Ben warned from the seat. "Mr. Banning wants her for himself, and he's not going to be happy if you ruin her."

Kyle stopped and glared at Ben. His hold on Susannah tightened. "Are you gonna try and stop me, Ben?" He kicked at the snarling, barking dog.

Susannah frantically searched the faces of the surrounding men for any sign of sympathy; she found none. Harry had a look of gleeful anticipation on his face while the other two men simply looked nervous. There would be no help from any of them.

"I will if I have to," Ben answered, one hand moving to rest on the butt of his gun. "Mr. Banning pays me to do as he says."

"I'm a Banning, too, or have you forgotten that?" Kyle demanded. "Fletcher isn't here now, so I'm the boss. My big brother always takes the best of everything for himself. This time, I'll beat him to it." He ran one hand over Susannah's breast. She squirmed in revulsion. "I'll have the best first." Kyle's voice had become bitter and determined. "Harry, you shoot Ben if he does anything except turn this wagon around and drive real slow. All Fletcher said was to bring her, and that's what I'll do." He pulled Susannah one step closer to the wagon. Jesse snagged his pant leg, and Kyle shook him off with a curse.

Harry drew his gun. "It's true, Ben. Mr. Banning didn't say nothing 'bout not touchin' her. Since I ride with Kyle here, I gotta do as he says."

"You're crazy, Harry, and so's Kyle. Fletcher'll kill you both." Ben took up the reins. "And I don't like being party to rape."

"Just drive," Kyle commanded between gritted teeth. He turned his attention to Susannah. "Damn you, stop fighting me!"

"I'm not getting in the wagon with you, Kyle Banning," Susannah vowed breathlessly. "You'll not have me." Her flailing fist found his lip with enough strength to bloody it at the same time her booted foot landed on his shin. One of the men chuckled. Susannah twisted away from her tormentor just as Jesse sank his teeth into Kyle's calf. The dog retreated to Susannah's side, his lips drawn back, a menacing growl coming from his throat.

"You bitch!" Kyle swore as he touched his bloody lip. "You and that damned dog!" He whipped one of his pistols from its holster and, before Susannah's horrified eyes, took aim at Jesse.

"No!" Her anguished scream reverberated down the valley. She threw herself at Kyle, desperately grabbing for the gun. "Jesse! Home!" she cried. The pistol fired and missed one of the men by a narrow margin.

"Damn, Kyle, control her!" the man shouted as his horse sidled dangerously close to the edge of the road.

Kyle struck Susannah on the head with the barrel of his gun, again knocking her to the ground. Jesse stood over her protectively, growling. Blood coursed down her cheek, and her vision blurred, but she had the strength to scream one more time, "Go, Jesse! Home!"

The dog would not leave her. Determined to shield him, Susannah struggled to her knees as the shots rang out. She heard a yelp. Kyle laughed, a harsh, humorless sound, then returned the gun to its holster. He grabbed Susannah's upper arms and dragged her to her feet. The sleeves of her simple dress were no protection against the brutal grip of his fingers as they dug into her flesh. She did not notice the pain. Her eyes wide with horror, she watched her dog roll down the steep hill toward the river. Jesse came to a stop against a boulder near the water and lay still.

Grief and rage exploded from Susannah in a tortured cry that echoed off the surrounding peaks. She became like a wild thing, scratching, clawing, biting, kicking. For all his superior strength and size, Kyle could not subdue her. The riders hooted and cheered, laughing at Kyle and encouraging him.

Susannah butted his face with her head and jerked away. A wave of dizzy exhaustion washed over her; she sank to her knees at the edge of the road. Her breath seemed to tear through her lungs. She pushed her tangled hair from her eyes and stared at Kyle. His expression was one of shock as he touched his bleeding nose, a nose curiously bent to one side. Had she done that?

A strange detachment filled her. The wind felt cold now. She raised a trembling hand to her chest. The front of her dress had been torn to the waist, exposing her chemise. No wonder she was cold. Kyle's hand moved from his face toward his pistol in what seemed to her a very slow motion. She stared into his eyes and knew he would kill her. With an eerie smile, she pushed herself over the edge of the road.

"No!" cried Ben helplessly as he watched Susannah tumble down the steep mountainside.

She slammed into rocks and small bushes and still forced herself on. At last she reached the bank of the swift river and lay there on her back, breathless. The pins had come from her hair, and she pushed loose strands away from her eyes. She wearily searched the rim of the road far above. The group of men stood in a line, staring down at her. One of them started a careful descent. A shot whistled over her head and another ricocheted off a boulder near her hip, but she could not move. She recognized the gunman as Kyle, and as she watched, Ben took Kyle's gun from him and knocked the younger man to the ground.

Susannah turned her eyes to the river. Sunlight danced on the rushing waters. The river beckoned, like a long-lost friend, its steady, comfortable roar blocking all other sound. She glanced back once more to see the man gaining on her, then inched into the river. The icy water was both a shock and a relief to her battered body. She gratefully gave herself up to the power of the current and was swept away.

Across the valley, Conor O'Rourke stood in the stirrups and swore as he watched the woman go into the water. Her anguished scream had shattered the quiet of the afternoon and had drawn his attention a few minutes earlier. Frustrated and outraged, he had observed the entire scene with the aid of his telescope, helpless to do anything. His marksmanship was of no use at such long range. Now she had gone into the river. It was an effective escape, but one that could kill her.

He swung the lens to the spot where the dog had come to rest. Either he had the wrong boulder, which he doubted, or the animal had moved. With another curse, Conor slammed the expandable telescope down against his gloved palm. The instrument obediently shortened, and he returned it to its beaded leather case. Maybe he could help the woman now. He'd look for the dog later.

One hand whipped his rifle from its scabbard in a practiced, fluid motion, and he let his horse have its head. "Let's go, Charlie," he said in a low voice. The animal carefully picked its way over a slide of loose shale. When they reached the protection of the trees, Conor took up the reins again and urged the horse down across the mountain at an angle. They neared the river's edge. His anxious gaze swept the water, gauging the speed of the current. The woman could not have gone by yet.

A quick look around assured him that none of her pursuers were in the area. He returned the rifle to its scabbard and jumped off his mount, letting the reins hang. His duster flapped against his legs as he ran up the shore. His eyes continued their search. It was not easy going. Shrubs grew around rocks and small trees, and the ground was rough and uneven.

A movement across the water caught his eye. A large black dog made its way along the opposite bank. Conor grinned. That dog had grit. He watched the animal carefully then, for it seemed to have spotted something. The dog ran into the water and swam to a formation of rocks in the middle of the river. The woman was there, clinging to one of the rocks. The dog scrambled onto a long-dead tree trunk wedged between two boulders and barked excitedly. The woman's head moved.

Conor watched them, his mind racing. He whistled for his horse, who obediently trotted to his side. His eyes did not leave the woman as he stripped the hat from his head and the duster from his back and threw them aside, then tore the rope from its ties on the saddle. He waded into the freezing water as far as he could go and still keep his footing.

The dog barked. Conor twirled the rope over his head and threw it. Too far! Cursing, he pulled it in, then threw it again. The line slapped the water next to the woman, but the current took it out of her reach. She looked back and saw him for the first time. Her eyes widened in fear.

"No!" he shouted. "I'm not one of them!" He worked feverishly to pull in the rope. "Let me help you!"

The woman pushed away from the rock into the current. Without hesitation, the dog joined her.

"Damn, damn, damn!" Conor swore as he staggered back toward the shore, looping the line. He ran along the edge of the water, following the bobbing heads until they were swept out of sight around a bend. Still he struggled on, his frozen feet beyond feeling, his breath tearing at his lungs. He rounded the bend with a rare prayer on his lips.

Conor almost fell to his knees in surprise and relief when he saw the dog towing the woman into the shallow waters of a small eddy, the material of her burgundy skirt held fast in its teeth. The hound looked up with a snarl, then went deeper into the water and nudged her shoulder with its nose. She floated on her back, her eyes closed, her lips blue, her long hair resting on the water in a graceful swirl. Conor threw the rope to the shore and started toward them, one hand outstretched. The dog braced itself, head lowered threateningly, teeth bared. It growled a warning. Conor slowed his walk. He noticed blood on the dog's side.

"Easy, boy." His voice was soothing. "I won't hurt your lady."

The dog growled again. Conor stopped. "Let me help you, boy," he pleaded. He began to move. The animal eyed him warily, a low rumble coming from its throat. Conor was close enough to touch the woman now, but he did not try to do so. He reached across her and waited. With caution, the dog sniffed his outstretched hand, then took the woman's torn sleeve between its teeth and pulled her toward the shore. Conor bent to help. From behind, he wrapped his arms around her ribs and eased her out of the water. He sank back to a sitting position on the grassy bank, pulling her across his lap. She gave a weak cough. A small amount of water escaped from her lips, but she did not awaken. The exhausted dog dropped to the sand and rested its head on her thigh.

Reaction and cold set in. Conor began to shake, and held the woman tightly to his chest. He rocked back and forth, his eyes closed in silent thanksgiving, but only for a few minutes. He supported her shoulders with one arm and gently brushed her wet hair away from her white face. She was young and pretty, and slender, almost to the point of being thin. He wondered what color her eyes were. A terse smile of admiration spread across his grim features at the memory of her battle with the man on the road. She sure was a spunky little thing. He grasped her chin and gently shook it.

"Miss, can you hear me?" His hand moved to pat her cheek. "Miss, wake up." The woman groaned and coughed again. The dog lifted its head and watched her.

Conor scanned the opposite side of the river. The road was hidden from view by trees on the far bank, but if those men were looking for her, and followed the riverbed as he had done, they would soon be discovered. He had to get her out of sight and away from there.

He eased out from under her and laid her back on the grass, then ran his hands over her body in a quick search for obvious injuries. No bones were broken, as far as he could tell, although she had a wound on her head that oozed blood. He was grateful the cold water had slowed the bleeding. His jaw tightened at the sight of scratch marks on her throat and chest; the river had not torn the bodice of her dress. Her wet, clinging chemise did little to hide her breasts, with their darker, cold-tautened peaks, from his view. Self-consciously he pulled the sides of her bodice together and covered those soft mounds as best he could.

Conor carefully picked her up and carried her a short distance, then lowered her to the ground behind a thick bush, out of sight of the far bank. The dog followed and again lay down next to his mistress.

"Lie still, boy," Conor said. Dark blood mixed with the animal's wet black fur on one side. The dog warily eyed him as he examined the long wound that ran the length of the animal's ribcage. "You were lucky," Conor said as he patted the dog's head. "The bullet didn't get past your ribs."

The woman curled onto her side and coughed again, harder this time. Then it seemed she could not stop coughing. Conor pushed her onto her stomach and pressed rhythmically on her back until more water came from her mouth. The coughing

eased. He sat back on his heels and watched as she curled up
again and lay qui , her body racked with violent shivering.

"I've got to get my horse. Will you be all right for a few
minutes?"

She nodded, not opening her eyes.

Conor grabbed his rope, then made his way through the trees,
back in the direction from which he had come, listening intently
for any sound of pursuit from across the river. His boots squished
as he walked, and he could not suppress an occasional shiver.
The water had been icy cold from the spring run-off of melting
snow, and now the sun had disappeared behind a threatening
bank of dark clouds. He found Charlie where he had left him.
Conor praised the horse for staying put as he tied the rope to
the saddle. It only took a few minutes to locate his hat and duster,
put them on, then lead the horse back to the woman's side. She
appeared to be sleeping.

He knelt beside her and patted her cheek. "Come on, miss,
wake up," he pleaded. "You've got to help me get you in the
saddle."

A frown creased her brow. "I'll try," she whispered. Conor
helped her to a sitting position, then stood and lifted her to her
feet. He steadied her and pulled on the reins to bring Charlie
closer. She sagged against the horse as Conor placed one of her
feet in the stirrup. He guided her hands to the saddle horn. She
tightly grasped it.

"When I tell you to, push up into the saddle," he instructed.
He grabbed her narrow waist with both hands. "Now!" As he
lifted her, she hopped off the ground and weakly swung her right
leg out. Conor shifted one hand to her thigh and pushed it over
the horse's back, then returned his hand to her waist. He held
her firmly as she settled in the seat. She turned her head to look
at him, her hair falling in a bedraggled curtain around her face.

"Thank you," she whispered.

Conor pushed the long strands back over her shoulder.

"You're welcome," he answered as his eyes locked on hers. His breath caught. Her large eyes, rimmed with thick dark lashes, stood out dramatically against her pale face. Their unusual gray-green color reminded him of the sea off the coast of southern Virginia on a stormy afternoon. His fingers tightened on her waist for a moment, then he blinked and released her, stepping back from the horse.

The woman's head dropped against her chest, but she stayed in the saddle. Her skirt bunched around her thighs, exposing legs whose shapely outline was easy to see through her wet drawers and stockings. She shivered uncontrollably. Conor shrugged out of his duster and threw the garment over her shoulders, then vaulted up behind her and wrapped an arm around her waist. Low thunder rumbled across the sky.

Conor glanced up at the leaden clouds. The wind had picked up in the last few minutes. "Come on, dog," he said, and guided the horse up the hill. The dog followed.

The rain had started by the time Conor pulled the horse to a stop a half an hour later outside a natural cave carved into the mountain. He slid from the horse and caught the woman as she fell off. She moaned, but her eyes did not open. Conor carried her inside the cave and laid her on the ground next to the remains of a fire. She curled up again, pulling the duster more tightly around her. The dog crept in and took his usual place at the woman's side. The rain fell harder now.

Conor coaxed the horse just inside the cave, out of the worst of the weather, then worked feverishly to build up the fire. He laid good-sized rocks close to the flames and set a battered coffeepot and a stew pot of water on to boil. He stood still for a moment and watched the rain pour from the sky in the usual fierce fashion of a high-country storm. Any tracks they had left would be washed away. Hopefully her attackers would assume the current of the river had carried the woman downstream. He glanced back at her.

She looked so small and vulnerable, wrapped in his duster. Even through the coat, he could see the shivers rock her body. The first thing he had to do was get her warm, and that meant getting her out of her wet clothes. And himself as well, he thought grimly as a deep shudder ran through his weary body.

With his hands, he dug a long, shallow hollow out of the soft sand next to the fire, then kicked the heated rocks from the perimeter of the blaze into it and covered the stones with a dry blanket. After he took a knife from one boot and stuck the blade in the sand next to the fire, he removed his wet footgear and stripped out of his clothes and into his only other pair of clean pants. Keeping his gunbelt near, he turned his attention to the woman.

"We have to get you out of these wet clothes," he said softly as he pushed her onto her back. There was no response. Her long lashes rested on cheeks so pale that he could see the bluish paths of the blood vessels under her skin. The wound on her head had grown into a nasty welt, the top of it scraped and still lightly bleeding; one section was cut deeply enough to warrant stitches. A bruise darkened her jaw, and one corner of her mouth was swollen. His hands clenched and unclenched. He longed to meet the man who would hit a woman.

"Miss, we have to take your clothes off," he repeated as he gently shook her shoulder, a note of desperation creeping into his voice. Again, she did not respond. He pulled the duster open and laid his ear against her breast. His shoulders sagged with relief at the faint but steady sound of her heart. She was either deeply asleep or unconscious, which was not surprising, considering her injuries.

"I hope you'll forgive me," he muttered, and matter-of-factly set to the task of removing her clothes. One by one, the wet feminine articles were hung to dry at various points along the cave wall until all that covered her was her chemise and drawers. He knew he would have to get even those wet garments away from her skin, but he was reluctant to do so. It didn't seem right. A fine sweat broke out on his upper lip.

Conor reached for the small clean towel he used for washing and turned back to her. The full sight of her affected him like a blow. A sudden, almost painful fire deep in his gut reminded him that it had been a long time since he had been with a woman. His breath caught in his throat, and he sat back on his heels, clutching the towel tightly in one hand.

She was lovely, beyond anything he had ever seen. The damp cotton undergarments could not hide the exquisite contours of her body. Her breasts were high and full, in perfect proportion to her narrow waist and slender hips. Her long legs tapered to small feet that were cold to his touch. He frowned at the bruises on her shapely arms and marveled at her delicate hands. She turned her head. A grimace of pain flashed across her beautiful face.

With a twinge of guilt, Conor mentally shook himself. He applied the towel to one of her arms, then the other, hoping she would awaken before he was forced to remove her last defenses. His wish was granted. Her eyes fluttered open. She rolled her head from side to side.

"I'm glad you're awake, miss," he said, feeling awkward and embarrassed. "We need to get these wet, uh, things off you."

Her glazed eyes seemed to finally focus on him. "What did . . . you say?"

Conor plucked at the strap of cotton over her shoulder. "You must take this off. You'll never get warm if you don't."

She frowned and crossed her arms over her breasts. "No." Her eyes traveled his naked chest, taking on a scared, hunted look.

"There's no other choice, miss," Conor said firmly. "You must trust me." He yanked the blanket from the rocks and held it up in front of his face. "You take them off, or I will." He dropped the blanket enough to peek over it. "I mean it." The blanket covered his eyes again.

She pulled the blanket from his grasp and struggled to cover herself with it. Conor helped her, then turned away to tend the fire, trying not to let his wayward gaze return to her intriguing wiggling. A hand holding the crumpled chemise snaked out from under the blanket, then disappeared when he took it. The drawers soon followed. Her movements ceased. Exhaustion covered her pale face as completely as the blanket covered her body.

"I'm sorry for this," Conor said, his voice soft with sympathy. After a brief hesitation, he put his hands on one of her blanket-covered legs and began to rub briskly.

She started. "What are you doing?" she cried. She pushed weakly at his arm.

"You have to get dry and warm, and this is the fastest way to do it." His tone brooked no argument. She fell back on the duster and said no more. She flinched when his hands rubbed the blanket over her stomach, and her eyes flew open when he touched her covered breasts; but she did not protest. Conor pulled her to a sitting position and guided her arms into the sleeves of his last clean shirt. She allowed the blanket to drop to her waist and buttoned the shirt with shaking fingers, then lay back down.

"I have no other dry clothes, so there's nothing for your legs." When she did not respond, Conor moved away from her. The rocks in the hollow had cooled enough for him to touch; he tossed them against the far wall of the cave. He pulled the blanket from her legs and spread it in the now warm hollow, then carried her there and wrapped the blanket around her. She sighed and her eyes drifted closed.

"I'm going to tend to your head," Conor said.

There was no response.

Conor pulled the pot of warm water from the fire, dipped the corner of a clean rag into it, and gently washed the blood from her head. "I'm sorry," he whispered when she moaned. Whatever she had hit her head on had split the skin. On either side of the inch-long gash, he twisted thin strands of hair, then tied the twists together, effectively closing the wound. He laid a hand on her forehead.

"There's nothing else I can do for now, miss," he said softly. She shifted. The dog moved closer to the woman. Conor rinsed the rag and cleaned the blood from the dog's side. "I don't think stitches would help much, boy, any more than I think you'd let me sew you up, and your hair isn't long enough to tie like I did your lady's. I'll keep the wound clean and we'll see how you do." He scratched the dog's ears.

The horse nickered. "I know, Charlie, I know," Conor muttered. He shook the sand from his duster and draped it over a rock, then saw to the horse, removing the saddle and brushing him down. After wrapping another blanket around his shoulders, he poured himself a badly needed cup of old, too-hot, too-strong coffee and settled next to the fire, his eyes on the storm outside.

Conor watched the rain fall for some time, making sure the fire stayed high. The smoke gathered in the cave and stung his eyes, but he was grateful for the warmth. He glanced back at the woman. The blanket did not hide her shivering. She tossed her head and moaned. He set the tin cup down. There had to be some way to get her warm.

He uncovered her and lay beside her, propped on one elbow. Her eyes fluttered open, and he was struck again by their unusual color. She stared at him in confusion and fear. One small hand came up to rest against his naked chest, her fingers touching the edge of the large scar that covered the front of his left shoulder.

"I haven't . . . the strength to fight you," she whispered. "Please . . . don't harm me."

Conor's features softened in sympathy. "I won't," he assured her. She nodded almost imperceptibly as her eyes closed. Her hand fell. She offered no protest when Conor turned her on her side so that her back was nestled against his chest, her legs next to his. He pulled the second blanket over them, then wrapped his arms around her and held her close, trying without much success to keep from noticing how good she felt. The dog moved up and snuggled next to her thighs. After a few minutes the violence of her shivers eased and she seemed to relax. The rain continued to fall with a comforting sound. The flames of the fire crackled and popped, and Charlie contentedly nickered. Man, woman and dog fell into an exhausted sleep.

Two

"What do you mean, *you lost her?*" Fletcher Banning thundered. An expertly tailored, very fashionable suit covered his stocky frame. Streaks of premature gray at his temples contrasted with his dark hair and full mustache, giving him a distinguished air. He looked older than his thirty years.

Kyle avoided the furious gaze of his brother and tried to ignore the throbbing pain that radiated from his bent and swollen nose. "She fell into the river, Fletcher. She was swept away. We searched for miles downstream, but she's gone, probably dead."

The door to the office quietly opened and closed again. Ben Hollister removed his hat and waited. Fletcher acknowledged him with a curt nod, then stalked back and forth in front of the massive marble fireplace. "I don't understand how she could fall in the river," he muttered.

"Excuse me, Mr. Banning, but she didn't *fall* in the river," Ben interjected sharply. Kyle flashed him a hate-filled look.

Fletcher did not miss the look. His eyes narrowed as he advanced on Kyle. "So once again, little brother, you haven't been completely honest with me? How disappointing! And this was such a simple assignment." He stopped in front of Kyle, very close, not taking his eyes from his brother's face. "Please tell me what happened to Susannah, Ben." Kyle looked down at the floor.

"We ran into her on the way back from Duncan's. I guess she'd been to town for supplies. She didn't want to come with us, but Kyle made her. She *threw* herself in the river to get away from your brother! He was gonna take her right there in the wagon bed, though I warned him not to. He had that fool Harry hold a gun on me. I gotta hand it to that gal, though, Boss. She did all right for herself. She's the one that broke Kyle's nose. But then he tried to shoot her, and I had to take his gun."

"Did the river get her?"

Ben nodded. "I think so. We searched all over. Either she snagged on something on the bottom or she was carried down-river, God only knows how far."

"I told you she was lost," Kyle said defensively. Then his body jerked back as Fletcher planted his fist in Kyle's belly, followed by a swift uppercut to the jaw. Kyle dropped like a stone and curled up on the carpeted floor, his arms wrapped around his middle. He moaned.

"You assaulted her? The woman I intended to have as my wife?" Fletcher fell on his brother, his hands at the younger man's throat. His fingers tightened. "Damn you to hell, Kyle!"

Kyle clawed at Fletcher's hands. His face turned red, and horrible choking sounds escaped from his mouth.

"Susannah was pure and perfect, Kyle, the only woman I've ever met worthy to be my wife. And you dared to touch her!" Fletcher's fingers tightened even more. Kyle's hands fell away and his eyes rolled up in his head.

Ben had watched the proceedings up to this point with casual disinterest, but now he spoke. "I told Kyle you'd kill him, Mr. Banning, but are you sure you want to do that?" When Fletcher did not respond, Ben stepped over and touched his shoulder. "Mr. Banning, you're killing him."

Fletcher sagged. He released his brother and accepted Ben's assistance in standing. The wild look in his eyes faded as he stared down at Kyle; he casually straightened his cravat.

Kyle's hands flew to his throat. He dragged air into his tortured lungs. The sound was not pleasant.

Fletcher flicked a speck from his immaculate cuff. "You meant to defile her, Kyle, and I won't forget it. I told you my plans are very carefully laid, and you interfered with them. I can't afford that, nor will I allow it." He stormed to the office door and jerked it open. "Harry!" he bellowed.

The cowboy came running down the hall from the porch, his battered hat in one hand. "Yessir, Mr. Banning?"

Fletcher waited until Harry entered the room, then sent him flying back out into the hall with a well-aimed fist to the jaw. Fletcher's angry voice further assaulted the unfortunate cowboy.

"I know you haven't worked for me for very long, so you'll get off easy this time! But if you ever disobey Ben again, by anyone's word other than my own, *especially that of my worthless brother,* I'll have you shot for insubordination!"

Harry struggled to his feet, wiping at the blood that ran down his chin. "Y-yessir, Mr. Banning. It won't happen again."

"My men ride for me, and for me alone, and Ben is my right-hand man. When he speaks, he speaks for me. He will be obeyed. If those terms are not acceptable to you, gather your gear and get out now."

"No, sir, I mean, yessir, that'll be fine. I ride for you, sir."

"Good. Now get this useless cur from my sight." Fletcher waved at his brother, still lying on the floor. "Take him up to his room and have our sister see to him."

Harry cautiously entered the office again and helped Kyle rise.

"Someday I'll kill you for this, Fletcher," Kyle rasped, hatred flashing from his dark eyes.

"No, you won't," Fletcher said calmly as he settled into his chair. "You don't have the guts. You fancy yourself the fastest gun alive, and maybe you are. But you're stupid, Kyle, impulsive and stupid. You're a bully who hides behind those guns, and someday you'll pick on the wrong man. You'll run into someone who is smart as well as fast, and smart will win every time." He pulled a pile of papers closer and perused them, then continued speaking without looking up. "The next time you interfere with my plans, I *will* kill you, regardless of the promise I made to Mother." He motioned toward the door with one hand. "Now get out."

Harry draped one of Kyle's arms over his shoulders and led him into the hall. Ben pushed the door closed and crossed the room to take a chair in front of the desk.

"Well?" Fletcher asked, his eyes still on the papers.

"We went to old man Duncan's, just like you said. Walt wasn't there, but his brother Thomas was. He told us Walt had gone down to Denver." Ben paused. "But I don't think he did. I think old Walt's dead, Mr. Banning."

Fletcher looked up in surprise, his full attention now riveted on his foreman. "Why?"

"Saw a rock-covered mound off under the trees, with a cross over it. You know Walt was doing poorly last fall. Someone didn't survive the winter up on that mountain. I'd bet it was him."

"Did you ask Thomas about the grave?"

Ben shook his graying head. "Didn't want to in front of the others. Far as I could tell, Kyle and that fool Harry didn't notice it. Neither did Roberto or Shorty. I didn't want them getting wind of it 'til I talked to you. If Walt Duncan is dead, no one knows yet."

Fletcher leaned back in his chair. "Good thinking. This may turn out to be very advantageous for me. Did you talk to Thomas about the wisdom of selling to me?"

"I tried to. He wasn't in the mood to listen. Then Kyle roughed him up."

Fletcher's eyes narrowed. "How badly?"

Ben looked down at the hat he held in his hands. "Bad, Boss. You know how Kyle gets sometimes. I finally stopped him, but it took a while. He even hit me." He touched the new bruise on his cheek.

"Is Thomas Duncan dead?"

"He wasn't when we left, but I don't know that he'll pull through. He's an old man, like his brother was. Kyle really laid into him."

Fletcher braced his elbows on the armrests and made a tent of his fingers, then swiveled the chair around to gaze out the window. Rain ran down the glass in little rivers, and a loud clap of thunder echoed around the house. "Perhaps my hot-headed little brother has done me some good, after all," he mused. "If Walter is dead, and Thomas does not survive, and the river truly did kill Susannah, the Duncan mine will be auctioned off. This may all work out for the best."

A frown furrowed Ben's weather-beaten brow. " 'Scuse me, Boss, but I thought you wanted to marry Susannah Duncan. Surely you aren't glad she's dead."

Fletcher turned around to once again face his foreman. "No, not glad. She was a lovely woman, with the proper social background, even if she was a Southerner. She would have made a perfect wife, especially for a man of my ambition. The right mate is imperative." He sighed. "But she was a stubborn, independent woman, and resistant to my overtures. While her refusal of me only made her more enticing, in the end I would've had to break her. I'm not sure I'd have had the time for that now." His shoulders lifted in a careless shrug. "There will be another woman. Perhaps I'll travel to England when this matter with Duncan's mine is settled, and find a blue-blooded wife."

Ben did not comment.

Fletcher rose from his chair and leaned against the heavy curtain at one side of the rain-streaked window. On a clear day, the window perfectly framed Blue Mountain across the valley. "It's only a matter of time, Ben," he said almost dreamily. "Colorado will be admitted to the Union as a state, and I intend to be one of her first two senators. Who knows where I'll go from there? President perhaps? But to do that, I need money, because money buys power. I need the Duncan mine! That old bastard's claim lies right over the biggest silver lode in the territory; I'm *sure* of it! If he and all his kin are dead, there are no heirs. I'll drop the lawsuit I filed against him and simply have the claim title transferred to me, before anyone knows what's going on. Jackson's still the assessor, isn't he?"

Ben stood up. "Yes, sir."

"Pay him a visit. Make sure he's still my man. And don't tell a soul about Walter Duncan. We'll just keep it to ourselves for a while. In a day or two I want you to go back and make sure our friend Thomas is dead. Search the place from top to bottom. I want that original claim deed! If you can't find it, burn the cabin to the ground."

"Yes, sir, Mr. Banning." Ben moved to the door and reached for the handle just as the door flew open. He stepped back in surprise. "Hello, Miss Victoria."

A young woman stormed into the room, ignoring the foreman. Ben quietly took his leave.

"What is it, Victoria?" Fletcher demanded. "I have business matters to attend to."

"I've just seen Kyle," she said heatedly. "This time you went too far, Fletcher. He's really hurt! You nearly strangled him, and you broke his nose!"

"No, sister dear, you have it wrong. I did nearly strangle him, but Susannah Duncan broke his nose, when he tried to rape her."

Victoria paled. After a confused moment, she planted her hands on her hips. "I don't believe you," she snapped. "Kyle would never rape anyone, and certainly not *her.* He can't stand her! Besides, no woman is strong enough to hurt Kyle like that!"

"Well, it doesn't matter now, because we have reason to believe Susannah is dead, drowned in the river."

Victoria's large brown eyes widened; then a satisfied smile

curved her thin lips. "Good," she announced, crossing her arms over her chest. "Now you can't marry her. I don't know why you wanted to in the first place, other than to get her uncle's mine. She wasn't that pretty, and her clothes were awful. I hated her! And you don't need her anyway. I can be your hostess when you go to Washington, Fletcher." Her hands dropped to smooth the skirt of her costly silk day gown.

Fletcher laughed out loud. "Don't be ridiculous, Victoria! You? My hostess?" He came from behind the desk and circled his sister, examining her with a critical eye. "I think not. You are but sixteen, and you've no education or manners."

"Send me to one of those fancy finishing schools back east, Fletcher," Victoria pleaded. "I can learn education and manners."

"Perhaps so," Fletcher mused. Hope flared in Victoria's eyes, then faded quickly at his next words. "But your beauty is non-existent." He derisively lifted a limp strand of dark hair from her shoulder, his cruel gaze raking her thin form. "And your figure is dismal. No amount of schooling will change that. You won't do at all."

Victoria's face blanched. She bit her bottom lip to keep it from trembling and blinked at the tears in her eyes.

"Now go, silly girl. You are as useless as our idiotic brother." Fletcher impatiently waved her away and returned to his chair.

Victoria whirled and ran to the door. "I hate you, Fletcher Banning!" she cried fiercely. "I hope Kyle does kill you!" She rushed through the door and slammed it behind her.

Fletcher did not look up from the column of figures he was examining. He merely shook his head in disgust and cursed his dead parents for ever bringing his brother and sister into the world.

Conor stirred, roused from the depths of a pleasant dream. The soothing sound of falling rain reached his ears, and his arms tightened around the woman he held. *The woman he held?* His eyes flew open; then he relaxed when he remembered the events of the day. He and the woman both lay on their sides, their legs curled together, her back and bottom snuggled against his chest, stomach and hips. Her shivering had stopped. He raised up on one elbow and looked down at her. She seemed to be sleeping peacefully now. The black dog nestled close to her stomach.

Conor blinked and rubbed a hand over his eyes. What was he going to do with the woman? God only knew how serious her head injury was. If she did not fully awaken, and soon, he would need to get her to a doctor.

He eased out from under the blankets and tucked them securely around her. The dog watched him, but soon settled back down and closed its eyes. Conor stroked the animal's head, then stood and stared out the mouth of the cave. The rain still fell, softly now. He could tell by the amount of light that it was late afternoon. A shiver ran through him. It was damp and cool in the cave. The horse nickered.

"Well, Charlie, we've got our hands full," Conor muttered. He fingered his shirt hanging on the wall; it had not dried, and the woman was wearing his only other shirt. He thought for a minute and searched through his saddlebags, finally finding a worn, long-sleeved miner's shirt that he usually used to dry the dishes. He shrugged into the garment, then pulled a clean pair of socks over his cold feet. His boots were still wet, also. It would do no good to put them on. He sighed and reached for a frying pan. His rumbling stomach reminded him that he had eaten breakfast long ago.

The smell of frying bacon soon filled the cave. Conor pulled half a loaf of sourdough bread from a flour sack. The bread was a luxury, one he had indulged in when he had passed through Georgetown the day before. Georgetown! That gave him an idea of where he could turn for help.

He was in this area because he had promised his cousin he

would look up her old friend, a woman named Susannah Duncan. From the directions a bartender in Georgetown had given him, the Duncan homestead was not far. He had intended to call on the Duncans tomorrow, before he left for Pueblo and the job he had lined up with Charles Goodnight. He broke off a piece of the bread and soaked it in the bacon grease, then popped it in his mouth.

The Duncans probably knew who this woman was. Surely they would help care for her. His gaze fell on her. Some food would do her good. He noticed that the dog was awake. "I'll feed you, too," Conor assured the animal.

He moved to the woman's side and rolled her onto her back. "Wake up, miss," he said as he shook her shoulder. She moaned and turned her head. Conor brushed the hair away from her face. "You need to eat something."

Her hand moved to touch the bruise on the side of her forehead. She winced and opened her eyes, then closed them again. Finally she looked up at him, her lovely eyes clouded with pain and confusion.

Conor smiled. "Well, hello," he said softly.

"Who are you?" she whispered, her eyes closing again. "Where am I?" The dog sat up and watched her.

"You're in a cave. I brought you here after I fished you out of the river, with the help of your dog. My name is Conor O'Rourke." He settled back on his heels.

"Do I know you?" The woman's forehead wrinkled in bewilderment.

"Not before today."

"Oh, God!" she suddenly cried. "The river!" She tossed her head, and her fingers plucked at the blanket. "They shot my dog!"

"Shh, shh, miss, it's all right." Conor moved to a sitting position and put an arm under her shoulders, then pulled her up to rest against him. "Don't get yourself all worked up. Your dog's right here. He's hurt, but not badly. He's got grit, like you do."

Her eyes flew open and fell on the dog. "Oh, Jesse!" The dog licked her face, his tail thumping. She put her arm around the animal's neck and hugged him tightly. Suddenly she stiffened. "I have to get home." She pulled away from Conor and sat up. With a moan, she leaned forward, her face in her hands.

Conor grabbed her shoulders and forced her back down to the blanket. "Take it easy, miss. What's your name?"

"Susannah Duncan," she answered weakly.

Conor's eyes widened in surprise. "You're Susannah Duncan?"

She nodded, her pale features suddenly wary. "Do you work for Banning?" she whispered fearfully.

Conor shook his head, his mouth twisted in a wry smile. "No, Miss Duncan, I don't. I don't know anyone named Banning."

"I have to get home," Susannah repeated.

"You aren't going anywhere for a while," Conor said firmly. "I'm sure your head hurts something fierce, and you're probably dizzy, and a little sick as well."

"But I have to get home!" She struggled against him. "I have to be certain my father is all right!"

"Your father can take care of himself, I'm sure." Conor held her down until she lay still. He stood and walked around the fire. "You need to eat something. Are you thirsty?" He reached for the canteen that lay against the far wall of the cave. When he turned back to her, his eyes widened in astonishment.

Susannah had managed to gain her feet and now leaned against the rock wall. Her golden, almost-dry hair fell in wild disarray to her waist. His shirt covered her only to mid-thigh, and could not hide the trembling of her long, lovely legs. She took a determined step toward the mouth of the cave.

With a curse, Conor dropped the canteen and darted around the fire to her side, just in time to catch her as she fell forward.

He lifted her into his arms and returned her to the makeshift bed, then pulled the blankets over her.

"You can't walk or ride right now. You have to rest, Miss Duncan. You'll do your father no good like this."

Susannah clutched frantically at his shirt. "Then you have to go. Please!"

Conor shook his head. "I can't leave you alone."

"You have to!" she cried. "Jesse can stay with me. I think they hurt my father, Mr. O'Rourke. He's an old man, and not well. And my sister is there. Maybe they found her. God only knows what they did to them. I beg you, sir!" She grabbed his hand. Her desperate grip was surprisingly strong. "Please!"

Conor looked into her tear-filled eyes. Something in those gray-green depths tugged at his heart. He sighed. "I'll go on one condition."

"Anything," Susannah whispered fervently.

"That you *promise* to wait here." Conor's voice was firm. "Jesse will stay with you, and I'll leave you my rifle. But you must wait here."

She relaxed her hold on his shirt and nodded. "I promise."

"And you must eat something."

Again she nodded. "I'll try. Do you have something I can feed my dog?"

Conor stood and waved toward the frying pan. "Just what we have, but he's welcome to it. Bread and bacon, and some grease. There's also some terrible coffee. I'll set it all close to you." He threw more wood on the fire, then sat down and reached for his boots. A grimace twisted his face as he forced his feet into the damp, stiff leather; he truly hated to wear wet boots. He snatched up the knife and inserted it into his right boot.

"There's plenty of wood. Try to keep the fire up. You must stay warm," he said.

"I will."

"Are you familiar with rifles?" At her nod, he continued.

"Mine is a lever-action Winchester, very easy to use. Hopefully, you won't need it." He arranged everything beside her, then threw the still-damp saddle blanket over Charlie's back. "How do I get to your place?"

"Follow the river road up the mountain, past where you found me. There's a cutoff to the right that leads up another narrow valley. Just follow it. You'll see Uncle Walter's cabin on the left, in a stand of aspen." Her voice had faded to a whisper. Conor glanced back at her as he hefted the saddle. Her eyes were closed again.

He finished saddling the horse in silence. After checking his pistol and strapping the gunbelt around his hips, he shrugged into the duster and put his hat on. He led the horse toward the mouth of the cave, then paused when she spoke.

"Find my sister, Mr. O'Rourke. My father will have hidden her. Don't let anyone see her. No one knows about her. We've kept her hidden to keep her safe." She did not open her eyes. Jesse lay next to her, watching him intently.

"What's your sister's name?"

"Lily Carolina. My father's name is Thomas."

"I know."

Susannah's brow furrowed in confusion. "How did you know that?"

He did not answer her question. "I'll find them. You just rest."

"Thank you," she whispered.

Conor led Charlie out into the drizzle, then climbed into the saddle and guided the horse down toward the river.

It took Conor almost an hour to reach the cabin. The rain had stopped, but a brisk wind had come up. He pulled the collar of his duster more tightly around his neck and surveyed the area. As Susannah had said, the cabin was nestled in a stand of still-naked aspen at the far edge of a long meadow, and commanded an impressive view of the narrow mountain valley. He could make out the entrance to a mine a short distance up the hill behind the cabin. A pair of horses stood by a corral that had been built among the trees to one side of the small structure. They were hitched to an old farm wagon. The two horses looked back over their shoulders at him; one whinnied a welcome.

Conor eased his pistol from the holster, then nudged Charlie forward. He stopped the horse in front of the cabin and listened for a moment, eyeing the many tracks and the few small splotches of blood on the ground.

"Hello the house!" he shouted.

There was no answer. He slipped from the saddle and cautiously approached the closed door. Blood was smeared on the wood as well. Someone had been hurt. Standing off to one side, he knocked. A bullet tore through the top of the door. Conor cocked his pistol as a man's voice came from inside.

"If you ride for Banning, leave now or I'll kill you."

Conor had to strain to hear the words. He wondered who Banning was. "I don't ride for Banning!" he called. "I've come to see Thomas Duncan."

There was a bout of coughing, then the voice continued. "State your business, mister."

"I'm coming in, Mr. Duncan." Conor released the hammer and returned his pistol to its holster. He reached for the door latch. "I mean you no harm, sir. My hands are raised. Don't shoot." He stepped into the dim cabin, his arms held wide to the sides.

"Light the lamp on the table . . . so I can see you." The weak voice came from the corner behind the door. Conor saw the gleam of a rifle barrel pointed toward him. He obeyed the command, and in a moment, light filled the small, tidy room. The big stone fireplace on the left was flanked on both sides by two stacked beds, while a small cookstove rested next to the right wall. A few shelves held an assortment of supplies, dishes and pots, as nails along the back wall above a trunk held a few clothes. One of four chairs that circled the cloth-covered table in the center of the room lay on its side, the only thing out of place.

Conor closed the door and straightened the chair before he turned toward the corner. A man sat on the floor, slumped down, his rifle still aimed. Because of his own shadow, Conor could not see much of the man, but he could tell the man's hair was white, and that an equally white mustache covered his upper lip.

"Who are you?" Thomas demanded, then was seized by another fit of coughing.

Conor waited until the coughing passed. "My name is Conor O'Rourke, Mr. Duncan. Your daughter Susannah sent me."

At that, the rifle barrel fell to rest on the man's thigh. "She's safe, then?"

"Yes, sir, for now. But she's very worried about you. How are you?"

"Not good, son. The bastards . . . have killed me." He coughed again, weakly this time. "Where is she? When the horses brought the wagon back without her, I was afraid . . . they'd gotten her."

Conor crouched down. The sight of the man's battered face filled him with anger. "They did get her, Mr. Duncan." The older man's eyes widened fearfully. "But she fought them off and got away. You would have been proud of her."

Thomas nodded. "She's a real fighter . . . my girl is. What happened?"

"She threw herself down the mountain into the river. I saw the whole thing from across the valley. She and the dog are at my camp. I don't know what's going on, but I do know she doesn't want those men to find her."

"Why didn't she . . . come with you?"

"She's pretty banged up, Mr. Duncan. Some bad bruising, and a nasty bump on her head. She couldn't walk or ride, although she tried. She was determined to get to you and her sister."

"She told you about . . . Lily Carolina?"

Conor nodded. "In case something had happened to you. She wanted me to know to look for her sister." He paused. "She said you hide her from other people to keep her safe."

Thomas looked up at him. "It was my brother's idea. He said there was no telling how far . . . Banning would go to get this claim, and he didn't want anyone knowing about . . . my little girl until things were settled."

Conor noticed a trickle of blood at the corner of Thomas's mouth. "You're hurt, Mr. Duncan. Let me see to you."

Thomas shook his head. "It's too late for me, son." He shifted his position in a futile attempt to get comfortable.

"At least let me get you to the bed," Conor argued. When Thomas did not object, Conor took the rifle from the man's hand and set it on the table. He then lifted Thomas to a standing position and half-guided, half-carried the tall, thin man to one of the lower beds. Thomas's breath came in short gasps.

"He stove in my ribs . . . Mr. O'Rourke. I'm bleeding inside, and badly. There's nothing . . . anyone can do."

Conor knelt near the bed and, with gentle care, ran his hands over Thomas's ribs. One side of the man's chest was lower than the other; it did not move when he took a breath, signaling a collapsed lung. Thomas Duncan had been brutally, horribly beaten. Certain the man had suffered other internal injuries as well, Conor sat back on his heels in helpless frustration. "Who did this?" he demanded.

"Kyle Banning . . . murdered me, but his brother Fletcher calls the tune." Thomas raised his head and stared at Conor, his old eyes blazing. "You have to protect my daughters from the Bannings, Mr. O'Rourke. You must . . . take them away from here. My brother died in February; there's no one else . . . to help."

"Please don't upset yourself, Mr. Duncan," Conor pleaded. He heard the warning bells go off in his mind, felt the walls going up around his heart. He couldn't be saddled with two females now. Not now. Not ever. His guilty gaze met Thomas's knowing one. He had the uneasy feeling Thomas could read his thoughts.

Thomas fell back on the pillow. "Lily Carolina," he called weakly. "Come out, child."

Puzzled, Conor looked around the room. A scratching sound came from the direction of the fireplace. A small, square section of the floor moved. Conor leaned over and lifted the piece away. A tiny hand reached from the hole. He grasped it and helped a little girl climb out; the child clutched a china-faced cloth doll in her free hand. She pulled away from him and stood there hesitantly, staring straight in front of her.

Conor caught his breath. Lily Carolina was as beautiful a child as Susannah was a woman. He guessed her to be about five years old. She wore a simple blue dress covered with a white yoke apron. Her blond hair, so like her sister's, lay in tousled ringlets around her shoulders. A blue bow hung dispiritedly at the end of one curl. Her small, angelic face carried a dirt smudge on one cheek, and her eyes were blue. Conor blinked. He realized there was something strange about those pretty blue eyes. They never moved.

"Papa?" she whispered.

"I'm here, darling, in your bed. Come to me, and mind the floor trap."

Conor watched in amazement as the girl held a hand out and carefully placed one foot in front of the other until she had crossed the short distance to her father's side.

"Who's here, Papa? Where is Susannah? And Jesse?"

Thomas pulled his daughter to a sitting position next to him. "There's a very nice man here named Conor O'Rourke, who is going to take you to your sister and Jesse. I want you to mind what he says, Lily Carolina." Thomas stared into Conor's eyes as he spoke, daring him to contradict his word.

"Are you coming, too, Papa?"

"No, child . . . I can't." He was interrupted by a spell of coughing. More blood ran down his chin. "I'm going to join your mother and Uncle Walter."

Lily Carolina's bottom lip trembled. "Can Susannah and I go with you?"

With obvious effort, Thomas raised a hand and touched his daughter's cheek. "Not now, honey, although one day you will. I want you . . . to go with Mr. O'Rourke. He and your sister will take care of you."

Lily Carolina buried her face in the front of her father's shirt. "I don't want to go without you, Papa," she whispered.

Thomas closed his eyes and tenderly held his child against his broken chest, one hand stroking her hair. "I know, baby, I know."

Conor looked away, clenching one hand into a fist and releasing it, over and over.

"Mr. O'Rourke."

When Conor turned back to the bed, Thomas reached for his hand and grasped it tightly. His dying eyes shone with desperation. "I beg you, sir. Let me die in peace, knowing my daughters are safe."

Conor dropped his eyes. Powerful emotions battled within him. He had seen other men die. He had seen the death-bright eyes, the fear, the acceptance, the peace. He had been responsible for some of those deaths, during the long and terrible War Between the States. But only once before had a dying man affected him so deeply. Only once before had anyone asked so much of him. He did not know if he had any more to give.

"Mr. Duncan," he began helplessly, raising sad eyes to the man on the bed. "I have a job waiting for me with Mr. Goodnight in Pueblo. He's expecting me now."

Thomas's fingers tightened even more. "I beg you," he whispered.

Conor's shoulders sagged. He nodded.

"Swear it," Thomas insisted fiercely.

"I swear I will protect your daughters to the best of my ability, Mr. Duncan." Conor's voice was firm. "I'll care for them and see them settled in a safe place, far from the reach of the Bannings."

"Thank you, sir, with all my heart." Thomas released Conor's hand, drawing in a shaky breath. "Now you must go."

"Let me see to your horses first." Conor stood up. "They're still harnessed to the wagon."

"Take them. I'll not be needing them."

"Not tonight, sir. It'll be dark soon. I'll come back in the morning."

Thomas nodded. "As you wish. I'll say goodbye to my child."

Conor nudged the section of floor into place with his foot and left the cabin. Although the cloud cover remained, he could tell the sun had already dropped behind the mountaintops. They would be lucky to get back to the cave before dark. His gaze took in a grave off under the trees. He stared at it thoughtfully for a moment, then continued on to the wagon. It did not take him long to care for the gentle mares. He released them into the corral, gave them both a quick brushing, checked their water, then gave each a measure of oats from the covered bin he found in a lean-to at the back of the cabin. As he passed the wagon on the way back to the cabin, he noticed a barrel marked "Apples" and a box of other supplies. He grabbed the box and carried it inside.

"These supplies were in the wagon, Mr. Duncan," he said as he set the box on the table. "There's also a barrel of apples."

"Take them," Thomas rasped. "You'll . . . be needing them. Lily Carolina, please go outside for a minute."

"Yes, Papa." The child left her father's side, again with one hand out in front of her, and cautiously made her way to the open door. She stepped outside.

Thomas weakly motioned to Conor with one hand. "Come here."

Conor approached the bed and sank down on one knee.

"You see now why Lily Carolina needs protection, Mr. O'Rourke."

"Yes, sir."

"She said she hurt her hand going into her hidey-hole when you came. I couldn't see anything wrong, but you may want to keep an eye on it. It's her left hand. Now, both of the girls keep their clothes in the trunk. Take . . . everything." Blood ran from his mouth in a thin, steady stream. He pointed with a shaking finger toward the fireplace. "There, on the mantel. Lily Carolina's books. They'd be difficult . . . to replace." He grimaced in pain.

"Mr. Duncan, please rest," Conor implored. "We'll be fine. You don't need to be telling me this."

"I do," Thomas insisted. "The Bannings could come back. And I won't be here . . . tomorrow. Now listen to me."

Conor leaned forward.

"This claim belonged to my dead brother, and Banning . . . wants it. Susannah and Lily Carolina are Walter's . . . only heirs now, so it will rightfully be theirs. My brother . . . kept a lot of his papers with a friend of his . . . Fannie Hodges, in Denver, for safekeeping." Thomas clutched at Conor's sleeve. "Walter was convinced there's gold . . . on this claim. He never cared about the silver, if there is any. This perhaps worthless mine . . . is my daughters' only heritage. I want Banning defeated, but not at the cost of my daughters' lives . . . or yours." His grasp weakened and he paused to catch his breath.

"Is there anything I can get you?" Conor asked gently.

Thomas thought for a moment. "Walter kept a bottle of whiskey . . . on that shelf over by the stove, next to the tobacco tin.

I never was . . . much of a drinking man, but a shot sounds good to me now."

Conor quickly located the half-pint bottle. It was almost full. He pulled the cork with his teeth and spit it out, then placed the bottle next to Thomas's hip and guided the older man's hand to the neck.

"Thank you, Mr. O'Rourke. Now look in Lily Carolina's hidey-hole. Under the floorboard . . . to the left. There's a deep shelf dug into the earth." Thomas brought the bottle to his lips with a shaking hand. A quantity of the liquid ran down his chin, but he managed a swallow.

Conor pulled the knife from his boot and pried the square of floorboard free. He found the shelf, but had to stretch out flat to reach all the way to the back. His searching fingers closed on a soft leather bag, and then another. One bag was larger and heavier. He held them both up.

Thomas nodded in approval. "The big one is . . . Walter's stash. He eked a living out of this old mine, but only that."

Conor opened the bag. It was nearly filled with gold, both nuggets and flakes. "There must be a couple of hundred dollars worth here," he commented. He pulled the strings of the bag tight and slipped it inside his shirt.

Thomas nodded again. "Not a lot, but enough . . . to keep you and the girls going for a while. The other is Susannah's dowry. Don't let her sell . . . any more of it. That's for when she weds."

Curious, Conor opened the second, lighter bag. At first he could see nothing. He turned the bag upside down and was astonished when assorted jewels spilled into his hand.

"From her late mother," Thomas explained. "Violette . . . came from a wealthy family, from whom we are now . . . estranged." A sudden fear leapt into the older man's eyes. He reached toward Conor with a shaking hand. "I have no choice . . . but to trust you, sir." His hand fell to his side.

"And you can, Mr. Duncan." Conor returned the sparkling treasure to its bag and put it inside his shirt. His knife went back into his boot, and he replaced the piece of floorboard.

"Thank you. There's one more thing, Mr. O'Rourke." He pulled a thin cord from his shirt and yanked until the leather snapped. He held out his hand. "Give this . . . to Susannah."

Conor accepted it and saw that the cord threaded a small gold band.

"It was her mother's wedding ring," Thomas said.

"I'll see she gets it." Conor tucked the ring into his pants pocket.

"Now you must . . . get back to Susannah." Thomas's face twisted in a sad smile. "How I hate to leave my daughters! I don't know what waits for me . . . on the other side of the River Jordan, but I hope my Violette . . . is there. I've missed her terribly. If there is any help we can offer you . . . from wherever we are, you'll have it."

Conor looked at the floor, deeply touched by Thomas's words. "Thank you, sir."

"Now send in . . . my child."

Conor went outside. The little girl waited patiently a short distance away. "Your father would like to see you," he said softly. He took her hand and led her back inside. As father and daughter spoke, Conor stuffed what food and supplies he could into a large burlap sack. He carried the sack and a handful of Lily Carolina's books out to his horse.

Back inside, he formed two blankets and an armload of clothes from the trunk into a roll and hauled it out. He tied the roll behind the cantle, then looked up at the sky. It was almost dark. He returned once again to the cabin. Thomas was helping Lily Carolina button her cloak.

Conor laid wood on the hearth, then set a match to the kindling. The flame roared to magnificent life, filling the small cabin with comforting heat and light. He stood by the fireplace and waited.

"Kiss your father, child," Thomas gently commanded. Lily Carolina leaned forward and found his face with her hand, then kissed him. Tears sparkled in Thomas's eyes. "You and your sister must never forget how much your mother and I love you both."

"No, Papa, we won't," Lily Carolina whispered.

"Trust Mr. O'Rourke and do as he tells you. Go to your sister now, Lily Carolina. And go with God."

Conor blinked at the last words. His cousin had called those very words to him as he had left her so long ago. The memory brought a powerful pang of loneliness.

Lily Carolina straightened and reluctantly turned away from the bed. Tears welled in her unseeing eyes. One small hand clutched her doll, the other out in front of her. Conor stepped into her path and reached for her searching hand. She clung to him.

" 'Bye, Papa," Lily Carolina said sorrowfully.

"Goodbye, honey," Thomas whispered. His tears now ran down the side of his face and soaked the pillow.

Conor swung the child up into his arms and took her out to the horse. "I'm going to put you in the saddle, Lily Carolina, and you must sit very still for just a minute." He settled the little girl on the leather and guided her hand to Charlie's mane. "My horse's name is Charlie, and he's real nice. You just hold on to him. He won't move." He eyed the doll she held so tightly. "Can your doll ride in my saddlebag with your books, where she'll be safe?"

Lily Carolina hesitated, then, with great reluctance, held out the doll. "Her name is Amy," she offered shyly.

Conor tucked the doll in the saddlebag. "Amy will be fine. Now wait here. I'll be right back."

"Yes, sir."

Conor retraced his steps into the cabin. "Is there anything else I can do for you, Mr. Duncan?"

Thomas shook his head. "You've already done more . . . than I dared hope."

"Let me at least make you a little more comfortable." Conor removed the man's boots, then spread a bearskin over his legs. He positioned another pillow under Thomas's head. "That might make it easier to breathe," he commented.

Thomas nodded his thanks and held out his hand. "I regret that I will not . . . get a chance to know you better. I think I would have liked you."

Conor smiled as he shook Thomas's hand. "And I, you, sir." He moved to the table and picked up the rifle. He checked the chamber and returned to the bed, laying the weapon along Thomas's right side. "That's in case any varmints come calling. I'll be by tomorrow, Mr. Duncan, like I said, and check on you and the stock."

"I won't be here, son. If you'll bury me . . . next to my brother, I'd appreciate it."

"I will, sir. Would you like me to leave the lamp burning?"

"Yes. I want to see Violette . . . when she comes for me. She promised . . . she'd come for me."

Conor nodded in understanding, then made his way to the door and stepped outside. He turned and reached for the latch.

"Thank you again, Conor O'Rourke."

"You're welcome, Thomas Duncan. Goodbye, sir." He closed the door.

"Goodbye," Thomas whispered to the empty room.

Three

Conor held Lily Carolina before him in the saddle, snuggled securely against his chest. They were on the final approach to the cave, but night had fallen, and the moon was not yet up. Charlie carefully picked his way up the dark mountainside. The little girl had not said a word since they left the cabin. Conor was wondering if she had fallen asleep when she spoke.

"Are we almost there, sir?"

"Yes, we are. I see the firelight just ahead. Can you smell the smoke?"

"Yes, sir." She sounded tired and scared.

A few yards from the cave, Conor slipped from the saddle and dropped the reins. "You and Charlie wait here for a minute," he whispered. "I'm going to make sure everything is all right." He pulled his pistol and silently approached, listening intently. No sound reached his ears except the crackling of the fire. He peered into the cave. Susannah sat against the rock wall, wrapped in a blanket, her eyes closed. Jesse lay next to her, his head up, watching. The fire burned warm and high. Conor returned his pistol to the holster.

"Susannah," he called. "We're here." She stirred and looked at him. He raised a hand in greeting, then retraced his steps and led Charlie to the mouth of the cave.

"Susannah?" Lily Carolina said uncertainly as Conor lifted her from the saddle.

"I'm here," Susannah answered. Conor set the child at her side. She nestled Lily Carolina against her, holding her tightly.

"Where's Jesse?"

"He's here, too." Susannah eyed the dog and patted the blanket next to her sister. Jesse obediently moved closer. "If you reach behind you, you'll feel him."

Lily Carolina flung out her arm and caught a handful of fur. "Hi, Jesse," she sighed, then snuggled back against her sister.

"Your father said she might have hurt her hand," Conor commented as he set the sack of supplies next to the fire.

Susannah's discolored brow furrowed in concern. "Are you hurt, honey?"

"I fell when I got back in the hidey-hole. Papa couldn't help me." Lily Carolina's voice was muffled against Susannah's body. She lifted her arm again. "Now my hand hurts."

Susannah took her sister's tiny hand and carefully examined it. "Your wrist is a little swollen. You probably sprained it."

Conor hunkered down beside them, pulling off his gloves. "Let me see." Lily Carolina's hand looked ridiculously small in his. He gently probed the swollen wrist. "Can you move your fingers?"

Lily Carolina wiggled her fingers. "It hurts," she said plaintively.

"I'm sure it does. I'll wrap a cold, wet rag around it. That should make it feel better and help take the swelling down." He straightened.

Lily Carolina scooted down until her head rested on her sister's lap. Susannah absentmindedly stroked the child's tangled hair and watched as Conor carried the awkward roll of clothes and blankets to the back of the cave.

After a moment, she spoke, her voice somber. "What of my father?"

"Papa's sick," Lily Carolina interjected hoarsely, her young voice tremulous with anxiety. "He said he couldn't come with us because he was going with Mama, and we can't go with him."

"Shh, shh. It's all right." Susannah's fearful gaze did not leave Conor's face.

Conor returned to Susannah's side with a blanket in hand. He glanced meaningfully at Lily Carolina. "We'll talk about your father later," he said quietly as he tucked the warm wool around the child. "I'll be right back." He pulled a small towel from where it hung off an outcropping of rock and eased around the horse at the mouth of the cave.

A minute later he returned, wringing the now dripping towel. With Susannah's help, he wrapped the towel securely around Lily Carolina's wrist.

"It's cold," the child weakly protested.

"I know, but it will help," Conor assured her. He tied a thin strip of leather around the towel to hold it in place. "Wait just a minute and see if the pain doesn't lessen."

"Yes, sir."

Conor sat back on his heels, surveying his two patients. "I think we all could use something to eat," he announced.

"Don't forget Jesse," cautioned Lily Carolina. She yawned.

"I won't," Conor promised. He pulled his saddlebags from Charlie's back and fished in one until he found the doll. "Here's Amy," he said as he handed the doll to Lily Carolina. "She might be cold."

Lily Carolina snuggled the doll under the blanket. "I'll keep her warm." Her eyes closed.

Conor took off his duster and hat, then sat cross-legged by the fire, drawing the burlap sack close. Susannah remained quiet. He removed articles from the sack, avoiding her eyes. "Your father sent along these supplies, including your uncle's gold and your dowry." He worked the small leather bags from his shirt and tossed them toward her feet. "Clothes for you and your sister are wrapped in that blanket yonder if you want to change."

Susannah blushed at the memory of how she came to be wearing nothing but a man's shirt. Hopefully Conor would be enough of a gentleman to never mention that he had taken most of her clothes off. "Thank you," she said as she self-consciously smoothed the blanket that covered her legs. She wearily leaned her head against the rough stone wall and watched Conor arrange the fire to accommodate a collapsible iron spit he pulled from his saddlebag.

It was as though she saw him for the first time. She had known he was tall and lean, but now she realized he was also a handsome man in many respects. The thin material of his worn shirt outlined the contours of his shoulders and chest. A fleeting, disturbing memory teased a corner of her mind; she knew what he looked like without that shirt on. She knew his chest was nicely muscled, and covered with soft brown hair, and that he had a scar high on one shoulder. When had she seen him without his shirt? An involuntary sigh escaped her. There was so much about this day she did not remember, or understand. The questions tumbled around in her head. Could she trust this man? Why was he so willing to help her? What would he want in return? And where had she heard his name before?

When no answers came, she continued her silent, wary examination of him as he moved around the small cave, organizing the supplies. His broad shoulders tapered down to a flat belly and narrow waist and hips. His dark brown, shoulder-length hair framed a clean-shaven, strong-jawed face, and his eyes were a somehow familiar, arresting shade of blue.

"I know only one other person with eyes as blue as yours," she blurted out without thinking. Conor looked at her in surprise. She blushed again.

His lips curved in a smile that lit up his tired features. "And who would that be?" He broke bits of dried jerky into a stewpot of water.

"A very dear childhood friend of mine. She lives up in Wyoming Territory now, married to a rancher."

"And her name is Alina Gallagher Parker."

Susannah's eyes widened in amazement. "How do you know that?"

Jesse inched closer to the fire as Conor pulled a wrapped rabbit carcass from the bag of supplies. The dog rested his head on his paws, his eyes not moving from the unlucky rabbit.

"Alina is my cousin," answered Conor.

Relief washed over her. "That's why your name is familiar! She mentioned you in her letters." She looked at Conor with renewed interest, knowing she could trust him.

"She probably did. Alina writes a lot of letters." Conor shook his head, bemused. "I stayed with the Parkers for over nine months. It's actually because of Alina that I'm here. She asked me to look you up if I got down this way." He unwrapped the rabbit and arranged it on the spit.

"I can't believe it," Susannah marveled. "Do you think she knew I was in trouble? She knows things sometimes."

"Sometimes she does, but she didn't say anything about you being in trouble. She knew you'd lost your mother a while back, and that you and your father had come out here."

"From her letters, she sounds very happy."

Conor nodded. "She is. She married a good man." He stirred the jerky broth with his knife.

Susannah looked down at her sister and pushed fine golden curls away from Lily Carolina's cheek. The child did not stir. "She's asleep, Mr. O'Rourke." Susannah's voice had dropped. "Please tell me about my father."

Conor sighed as he glanced at the sleeping child; then he met Susannah's worried gaze. "He was dying, Miss Duncan," he said gently. "He may be gone already. There was nothing I could do."

He steeled himself against the sudden, terrible anguish in her lovely eyes, eyes that became more green than gray as they filled with tears.

"But where is he? Why didn't you bring him?"

"He's still at the cabin. He was in a lot of pain, and I think the trip would have killed him before we could have gotten here. I'm sorry."

"So you left him there to die all alone?" she demanded in an angry whisper. A tear trailed down one cheek.

Conor's mouth tightened. He stood up and returned to the horse. "I didn't want to, Miss Duncan, but I had to. I did everything I could to make him comfortable." He pulled the saddle from Charlie's back and set it on the ground. "I couldn't leave you alone all night, and we didn't know if the Bannings would return. Your father wanted me to get Lily Carolina away from there. I'll go back and check on him in the morning." He removed Charlie's sweat-damp saddle blanket and draped it over a boulder, then retrieved a brush from his saddlebag.

"I'll go with you."

"Maybe. We'll see how you feel." He ran the brush over Charlie's back with long, smooth strokes.

"I *will* go with you, Mr. O'Rourke," Susannah insisted.

Conor rolled his eyes in exasperation. Was the woman going to argue with him about everything? He glanced back at her. She stared at him, her lips pressed together in determination, her pale features hard. The bruise on her forehead had spread down to encircle her eye. Another, darker, bruise stood out in stark relief along her jaw. Conor's teeth clenched in reaction to the vivid reminders of the violence she had suffered. She had a right to be a little testy, he decided. He resumed the brushing, his voice as calm as his strokes. "We have only one horse, Miss Duncan, and we can't leave Lily Carolina here alone. We'll decide what to do in the morning."

Susannah made no comment.

When Conor was finished with the brush, he led Charlie off a short distance to a small, grass-covered clearing. He remained there for a few minutes, his thoughts in a turmoil. The bitter accusation in Susannah's eyes was hard to bear. With a frown, he reviewed the events at the cabin. There had been no other choice but to leave Thomas Duncan alone, as much as he had hated to do so. Thomas himself had known he was dying, had insisted that he be left alone until Violette came for him. Suddenly Conor remembered the ring in his pocket. How had he forgotten to give Susannah the ring?

"You wait here, Charlie," he ordered unnecessarily, knowing the horse would not wander off as long as the reins hung to the ground. He retrieved the small ring from his pocket, then returned to the cave.

He crouched down next to Susannah. "Your father wanted you to have this, and he said to remind you that he and your mother will always love you," he said softly, holding out his hand.

Susannah accepted the ring. Her eyes filled again as she slipped the narrow band on the third finger of her left hand. A falling tear splashed the gold as it sparkled in the firelight. She impatiently wiped her eyes. Jesse sat up and sniffed her face. His nose touched her cheek.

Conor straightened. "Charlie—he's my horse—may need a drink. I'll take him to the creek," he said quietly. Susannah nodded without looking at him. He watched her for a moment, his heart gripped by a deep, sympathetic sadness. He knew what it was to be orphaned. It hurt no matter how old a person was. He awkwardly patted Susannah's shoulder, then left her.

Susannah stared at the fire, numb with shock and pain. She could not believe that she would never see her father again, that Thomas was gone, just as her mother was. She and Lily Carolina were now alone in the world, with no one to turn to. Her gaze fell on her sleeping sister, and her heart lurched. What would they do? Where would they go? How could they fight the Banning brothers alone?

She dropped her aching head into her hand, but jerked back when she touched the wound. Not only did it hurt, but it felt very strange. With care, she ran her fingers over the curious ties. What had Conor O'Rourke done to her hair? She sighed and watched the dancing flames. Surely the handsome cowboy would help them. He wouldn't just leave them. Maybe they could go to Wyoming Territory and stay with Alina and her husband, at least for a while.

Her jaw tightened. But not until the Banning brothers were hanged for their crimes against her family. Only then would she ask Conor O'Rourke to take them to Wyoming.

Dinner was a simple, mostly silent affair. Lily Carolina awakened long enough to eat a small amount of the rabbit and to drink some of the broth. Conor removed the towel from the child's arm for the night, commenting that he agreed with Susannah's diagnosis of a bad sprain. He then fashioned a bed from the several blankets they now had while Susannah pulled a fire-warmed nightdress over her sister's chemise and drawers. They snuggled together with the child between them and Jesse at their feet. It was late May, but the nights were still very cold in the high country.

Although she was exhausted, Susannah slept fitfully. Each time she moved, an ache or pain somewhere on her body awakened her. Distorted, terrifying dreams plagued her when she did manage to drop off. Finally, the pale light of dawn brightened the sky outside the cave, and she gave up trying to sleep. She heard Conor ease from the blankets and leave the cave. When he returned a few minutes later, she lay still and watched as he built up the fire and prepared for his trip down the mountain.

Finally he looked at her. "Good morning," he said quietly.

"Good morning," she whispered, not wanting to awaken her sister.

"I'm returning to the cabin alone," he announced.

Although Susannah desperately wanted to see her father, she could not summon the strength to even raise her head from the blankets. "Very well." She noticed the surprised lift of Conor's eyebrows when she did not argue with him.

He gave Jesse the last of the rabbit, which the dog carried farther back in the cave and chewed on with relish.

"There's a can of peaches here by the fire, and I made fresh coffee. The rifle is in the same place." He hesitated. "Please don't try to follow me, Miss Duncan."

"I won't." Her voice sounded hoarse and weak even to her own ears.

Conor frowned. He moved to her side and crouched down. "How do you feel?"

"Tired," she sighed. "And stiff. It hurts to move."

"I'm sure it does, after the fall you took yesterday. Just rest. I'll be back as quickly as I can."

"Tell Papa we love him."

Conor nodded and left. Depressed and in pain, Susannah stared at the fire for a long time, listening to the crackling of the flames and the sound of Jesse crunching the rabbit bones. After a while, the dog returned to her side and lay down with a contented sigh. Her eyes drifted closed and at last she fell into an exhausted sleep.

Conor guided Charlie down the mountain, deep in thought. Hopefully Lily Carolina's wrist was only sprained, but what if it was broken? What if Susannah had internal injuries they weren't aware of? The vision of her tumbling down the mountain, dragging herself into the fast-moving river, flashed in his mind. Between Kyle Banning and the unforgiving mountain, she had been beaten almost as badly as her father. Conor's jaw tightened. He hoped he would have the pleasure of meeting Kyle

Banning one day. He wanted to explain, preferably with his fists or his gun, how he felt about men who beat on women and old men.

He approached the cabin with the same caution he had used the day before. From the tracks in the yard, he could tell no one had been there since he and Lily Carolina had left. He stepped down from the saddle and knocked on the door.

"Mr. Duncan. It's Conor O'Rourke, sir. I'm coming in." There was no answer, but Conor had not expected one. He let himself in. The fire had died down, and the oil lamp on the table was about to go out. Thomas Duncan lay on the bed, much as Conor had left him, except for the expression on his still face. His eyes were closed, and his lips curved in a small smile under the white mustache. His bruised features wore such a peaceful look that even Conor's hardened heart was comforted. The man was no longer in pain, physical or otherwise. The Bannings of the world would not hurt him again.

Conor gently removed the rifle from under Thomas's hand, wondering if Violette had come for her husband. He did not consider himself a religious man, and did not often think of what would happen when Death finally found him. But Thomas had fervently believed that Violette would be waiting for him, and Conor took solace in Thomas's belief.

"I hope she was there for you, sir," he said quietly as he pulled the almost full whiskey bottle from Thomas's side. "I'll bet she was, judging by the smile on your face." He set the blood-smeared bottle on the table and blew out the flickering lamp on his way out the door.

The sun had just climbed up over the mountaintops, spreading its golden warmth across the little valley. The light touched on the waving grasses and colorful, early-season wildflowers, and on the pine trees and aspen that swayed in the breeze. Conor could hear the trickle of a stream from somewhere nearby, and he breathed deeply of the fresh, early morning air.

Such a beautiful place, he thought. This valley, and the mountainside on which he and the cabin stood, had represented one man's dreams of gold, another man's hopes for a safe home for his daughters. Now both men, brothers, were dead, their dreams and their hopes dead with them.

He took off his duster and tied it behind the cantle of his saddle, knowing from experience that digging a grave was hot work, even on a cool morning. With a sigh, he trudged back to the rude stable, where he remembered seeing a shovel the day before.

"I'll take care of you when I'm done with this," he said to the two mares who pushed their heads over the fence and gazed at him with interest. One nickered in response. His eyes fell on the opening to the mine farther up the hill. A crudely lettered sign was nailed to the overhead support beam. It read "Lucky Lucy." He reached for the shovel, wondering who Lucy was.

By the time an hour had passed, Conor had dug the grave and gathered a pile of good-sized rocks from around the entrance to the mine. He returned to the cabin and brought Thomas's body outside. It took only a moment to straighten the dead man's clothes, and although he ridiculed himself mentally for it, Conor carefully washed the blood and grime from Thomas's old face. "No one should be buried with a dirty face," he muttered as he wrapped a blanket around the body. "And I'm sorry I don't have a pine box for you."

After he lowered Thomas Duncan to his final resting place next to his brother, Conor filled in the grave and covered it with the rocks. From two sturdy sticks and a strip of leather he fashioned a rough cross, then used one of the rocks to pound the simple marker into the ground at the head of the grave. He swept his hat from his head, wiping his forehead with a gloved hand. His eyes wandered the mountainside as he searched for something to say. Finally he spoke.

"I didn't know you long, Thomas Duncan, and I'm not too

good with words, but I feel I ought to say something over you."
He hesitated, then continued. "I suspect you were a good man,
who loved his wife and daughters, and you didn't deserve to die
the way you did. Like I promised, I'll see to your daughters, and
maybe I can do something to see that justice is served to the
men responsible for your death. I hope you and Violette are
together again. Amen." Conor was quiet for a minute, then
added, "Susannah said to tell you that she and Lily Carolina
love you." He shrugged. "That'll have to do," he said under his
breath as he put his hat back on.

In another hour he had one mare loaded with more clothes,
supplies and tools, while the other bore the weight of the trunk,
which was counter-balanced with the barrel of apples. Perhaps
when he had the Duncan sisters settled, he would come back for
the wagon, the furniture, and the rest of the household goods.
As he passed the wagon on his final trip from the stable, he
noticed a woman's broad-brimmed felt hat on the seat. No doubt
it belonged to Susannah. Conor looped the hat string over his
saddle horn and took one last look around.

The little homestead was peaceful and quiet. Dappled sunlight
moved in changing patterns over the two graves under the trees.
He found it hard to believe violent death had come calling in
such a beautiful place, and only yesterday. *Our lives are like the
elusive gold Walter Duncan hunted for,* Conor thought cynically.
*A flash in the pan. One day you're alive, loving, doing what
needs doing; the next day you're gone, and except for a fresh
mound of dirt, the place looks the same.* After a moment, he
shook his head, as if that would clear the morbid thoughts from
his mind. Once in the saddle, he urged Charlie down the mountain, leading the other two horses. He did not look back.

The usual afternoon clouds were gathering when he and the
horses made the final ascent to the cave. Again, he covered the
last few yards on foot, his gun drawn. Jesse growled, unseen
and threatening.

"Mr. O'Rourke?" Lily Carolina's voice trembled. "Is that you, sir?"

"Yes, honey, it is," Conor answered as he holstered his pistol. Jesse came up to him, his tail wagging. Conor patted the animal's head and entered the cave. The air felt cool and damp. The fire had died down to a glowing bed of coals. Lily Carolina sat on the blankets next to Susannah, wearing a plaid wool dress, her doll in her lap, one tiny hand resting on her sister's arm. Her tousled curls fell around her shoulders, and her unseeing eyes looked huge in her pale little face.

Conor knelt down next to the child and placed a comforting hand on her shoulder. "How are you? Does your hand still hurt?"

"Yes," Lily Carolina admitted. "And I'm thirsty."

"I'll get you some water." Conor slipped out of his duster and took his hat off. His eyes fell to Susannah. Her thick, golden hair spilled out from underneath the blanket, and her eyes were closed. "Do you know how long your sister has been asleep?"

"A long time." Lily Carolina patted Susannah's arm, an awkward and somehow endearing gesture. "She was awake before, but now she won't wake up."

Alarmed, Conor pulled the blanket from Susannah's shoulders and rolled her onto her back. She wore a simple green dress, one that resembled the burgundy dress she'd been wearing when he found her, except this one was not torn down the front. He ripped his gloves off, then placed a hand on her forehead. Her skin felt normal, but a faint sheen of perspiration covered her face and throat. Her breathing seemed shallow, its pattern irregular.

"Miss Duncan," he said urgently. He shook her shoulders. She rolled her head and moaned.

"What's wrong, Mr. O'Rourke?" Lily Carolina cried, her hands groping the air.

Conor looked at the terrified child and mentally kicked himself. He caught her uninjured hand and pulled her into a close embrace. "It's all right," he crooned. "I'm sorry I scared you."

Lily Carolina clung to him. "Is Susannah sick?" she asked mournfully.

"No. She bumped her head yesterday, and it's making her sleep a lot."

"Is she going with Mama, like Papa did?"

"No," Conor repeated firmly.

As if she heard him, Susannah opened her eyes. She frowned and moved a hand to her forehead, flinching when she touched the tender skin. Her pain-clouded eyes focused on Conor. "I must have fallen asleep," she murmured. Her gaze moved to her sister. "How are you, sweetie?"

Lily Carolina scooted from Conor's lap to snuggle at Susannah's side. "Thirsty, but Mr. O'Rourke said he'd get me some water. You slept a long time, Susannah. I couldn't wake you."

Conor pulled the blankets over the child. Before he could move toward the canteen, Susannah grabbed his arm in a frantic grip. "Did you just get back?" she whispered.

He read her true question in her eyes. "Yes," he answered as he covered her hand with his. He sorrowfully shook his head. "I'm sorry."

Her fingers tightened even more on his arm. Her eyes filled with tears just before she closed them, and one tear slipped out to trail down the side of her face into her hair. She released Conor and wrapped both arms around her sister.

"I'll get some fresh water," he said. When Susannah did not respond, he grabbed the coffeepot and hurried to the creek, apologizing to the patient horses on the way back to the cave. He dropped to his knees at Lily Carolina's side, filling a cup with the cold, clear water. Susannah rose up on one elbow, took the tin cup from him and guided it to her sister's mouth. Lily Carolina drank deeply, then fell back on the blanket.

Conor gently examined the child's injured wrist. "The

swelling hasn't gone down," he commented, his forehead wrinkled in a frown. He laid his forefinger across Lily Carolina's palm. "Grab my finger, honey, and squeeze it."

Lily Carolina's small fingers closed slightly; her little face puckered. "I can't," she whimpered. "It hurts."

"It's all right," Conor assured her. He stroked the tiny fingers. Was it his imagination, or had they begun to swell also? And they were very cold, with a blue tinge around the delicate little fingernails.

Susannah raised frightened eyes to Conor. "Do you think it's more than a sprain?"

"It could be. We'll keep an eye on it." He noticed the paleness of Susannah's face, the trembling of her hand. "How do you feel?"

Susannah took her weight off her elbow and sat up. "My head hurts something awful," she admitted, "and my stomach doesn't feel too well, either."

"You may have a concussion." He pushed her tangled hair back over her shoulder. "Can you feel your breath in your lungs?" She looked at him, her brow wrinkled in confusion. He could not resist the temptation to smooth the wrinkles away. His fingers were gentle on her bruised skin. "You inhaled some of the river water, Miss Duncan. You're at risk for pneumonia." Her eyes widened. "You don't have a fever," he assured her. "That's a good sign. Can you feel your breath?"

She concentrated for a moment. "No."

"Good."

Thunder rumbled outside.

Conor thought of the horses, and of all the supplies strapped to their backs. Reluctantly he stood up. Jesse took his place on the blankets.

"I have to see to the horses," Conor said.

"Horses? There's more than one?" Susannah slumped a little, her head resting on one hand.

"Your horses. I brought them with me this time."

Susannah looked up, her pale face suddenly alight with happiness. "You found them? Where? Are they all right?"

"Their names are Minnie and Muffin," Lily Carolina interjected helpfully. She stifled a yawn.

Conor arched an eyebrow and smiled. "Minnie and . . . Muffin are fine. They were at the cabin yesterday, still hitched to the wagon. When they came home without you, your father knew something had happened."

Her face sobered. "Poor Papa. I'm sure he was terribly worried."

"He was."

"Thank you for easing his fears, Mr. O'Rourke." Susannah took a sip of the water remaining in Lily Carolina's cup. "Minnie has a white blaze on her forehead, and Muffin doesn't, just so you can tell them apart."

Thunder rumbled again.

"I'd best get to it," Conor commented, and left the cave. The sky was dark and threatening, and once again the wind had come up. A few raindrops were already falling.

A short time later, he had the two mares unloaded and coaxed into the back reaches of the cave. He brought Charlie in and, for now, left him saddled. A loud crack of thunder startled them all, and the sky seemed to open in a tremendous downpour. Conor built up the fire, then returned to Susannah's side to find that she was again sleeping, as was Lily Carolina. He settled against the rock wall, his brows drawn together in worry.

For the next several hours, the rain fell and Conor watched Susannah. The firelight played over her face, touching her skin with gold. She seemed to drift in and out of sleep, sometimes moaning and tossing her head, sometimes lying so still that he checked to make sure she was breathing.

Darkness fell, and the rain lightened. Susannah woke up, aching and groggy. When she awakened her sister, Lily Carolina sat up and wrapped her arm around Jesse. The child began to softly cry.

"What's wrong, sweetheart?" Susannah kissed her sister's forehead. Conor looked up in concern from the pot of beans he was stirring.

"My hand really hurts, Susannah," Lily Carolina wailed. "And I want Papa."

Susannah gathered the little girl into her arms. "I know, Lily Carolina. I want Papa, too. But he can't be here right now. He wishes he could be, but he can't. I'm here, and so is Mr. O'Rourke. We'll take care of you." Susannah's sad eyes met Conor's.

After a rude meal of beans and soda crackers, of which none of them ate much except for Jesse, Lily Carolina settled into an uneasy sleep, her injured wrist cradled next to her stomach.

Susannah leaned her head against the rock wall. Her face was drawn with pain and fatigue, the bruises standing out in the flickering firelight. "Something is really wrong with her wrist. It's getting worse." Her voice sounded tired and flat.

"I know. I think it's broken, and I don't dare try to set it. There are too many small bones in there." Conor rubbed his eyes. Susannah's condition seemed to be worsening, as well. For the first time, he acknowledged his very real fear for the Duncan sisters. He had no way of knowing if Susannah had suffered internal injuries, and there was the possibility that her head injury was more serious than it looked. And gangrene could set in if proper circulation was not restored to Lily Carolina's hand, and soon. "You both need medical attention, Miss Duncan."

Susannah met his troubled gaze with bleary eyes. "I know."

"If we're lucky, the Bannings think you're dead. And if I understood your father correctly, no one knows of Lily Carolina's existence. It'll be dangerous to take you to town, but we have no choice. Do you know of a doctor, one we can trust?"

Susannah struggled to think around the terrible ache in her

head. She longed to snuggle back down under the blankets with Lily Carolina and sleep. Finally she shook her head. "I know very few people in Georgetown, Mr. O'Rourke. We got here last fall just before the snows came, and spent the winter snowbound on the mountain. I've only been to town a few times, and we didn't need a doctor then."

Conor stood up and glanced thoughtfully to the mouth of the cave. The rain had stopped. "There was a house at the edge of town, kind of sitting off by itself. I think I saw a sign on the porch advertising the services of a physician named Alex Kennedy. Have you heard of him?"

Again Susannah shook her head.

"Good. Let's hope he hasn't heard of you, either. And until we know where the doctor's loyalties lie, don't mention the Bannings."

"I don't understand."

"From what your father told me, the Bannings are powerful."

Susannah nodded. "And rich. And ruthless."

"Powerful men always have allies, especially in a small town. We don't know if the doctor is for the Bannings or against them, or indifferent. For now, we'll say as little as possible about what happened." He grabbed his rifle from where it rested against the wall and checked the cartridge chamber. "I'd like to keep the Bannings from learning that you're alive, at least for a while, for your protection as well as Lily Carolina's."

They both looked at the sleeping child. Susannah nodded again in weary agreement.

Conor slid the rifle into the scabbard, then took his duster from the rock over which it was draped. He helped Susannah to her feet and settled the duster on her shoulders. She worked her arms into the sleeves. The garment was ridiculously big for her. As he adjusted the collar, she swayed against him. His arms went around her. "A little dizzy?" he asked sympathetically.

"I guess so."

"Just rest and I'll get everything ready." He guided her to a sitting position next to her sister. "We're taking only one horse, so we can't carry much."

She watched as he grabbed his saddlebags. "Why only one?"

"Because your horses might be recognized. They'll be fine here tonight, and I'll come back and see to them in the morning."

In addition to Lily Carolina's doll, Conor stuffed nightdresses and a change of clothing for each of them into the saddlebags. He arranged the leather bags behind the saddle, then led Charlie outside, coming back a minute later for Susannah. With a supportive arm around her waist, he took her to the horse and helped her up into the saddle. She grabbed the pommel and held on tightly. Conor watched her in concern. He laid his hand on her thigh without thinking.

"Are you going to be all right?"

"I have to be, don't I?" She tried to smile.

He squeezed her leg in encouragement. "I'm going to put Lily Carolina in front of you, and I'll lead Charlie. Just holler if you need to rest, or if you think you're going to fall. We'll take it as slow as we have to."

Susannah gritted her teeth and nodded. Conor disappeared into the cave and emerged a moment later with the blanket-wrapped child in his arms. Lily Carolina did not make a sound while he positioned her in front of Susannah, although Conor knew she was awake. After a moment's hesitation, he looped his rope around them both, securing them to the saddle. He handed Susannah her hat and watched as she tightened the string under her chin.

"Are you ready?" he asked.

"Lead on, Mr. O'Rourke." She wrapped her arms around her little sister, her lips trembling in a brave smile.

Conor stared at her for a moment, struck anew by her spirit and courage. She was seriously injured and ill, yet throughout the ordeal of the past two days, her major concern had been for her father and her sister. She even thought of her dog and her horses before herself. An unfamiliar ache formed in his gut, one that he reluctantly acknowledged as an aching need to protect her and make her well.

With an effort, he tore his eyes away and looked up at the dark sky as he adjusted his own hat. A pale gray area in the inky blackness indicated the position of the moon, but the cloud cover made it impossible to see the bright orb itself, or to take advantage of its light. The wind whipped the tops of the trees, spraying him with drops of water from the wet branches. The rain would start again, and soon; he would bet on it.

"Come on, dog," he called to the waiting Jesse. "Let's get your ladies to town." Jesse barked and eagerly ran to his side, and the little party set off down the mountain.

Four

"Alex. Kennedy, Physician." In the dark, Conor could just make out the words on the sign nailed to the wall of the small wooden house. He stood on the covered porch, holding Lily Carolina with one arm while he pounded on the door with his free hand. The rain had started again when they were about a mile from town, and the drenched child was shaking with cold. He glanced anxiously over his shoulder at Susannah. She was still in the saddle, but now that he had loosened the rope, he was afraid the next gust of wind would blow her to the ground. He hit the door again.

A light appeared and shone through the window. At last the door opened. Without a word, Conor handed Lily Carolina to the astonished woman who stood there, then returned to Susannah's side. She put a hand on his shoulder and slid into his arms. He carried her up onto the porch and through the door the woman held open.

"In there, to your left," the woman instructed as she bumped the front door closed with her hip. She followed Conor into the room, set Lily Carolina on a chair by the door, and hurried to light another lamp.

Conor carefully laid Susannah on the examining table in the middle of the room. The pungent, antiseptic odor of carbolic acid assailed his nostrils, bringing a flash of memory of another sickroom, in another life. It was a smell he had hoped never to encounter again. Susannah moaned and shifted on the table. Conor blinked, forcing the memory away.

"We need the doctor, ma'am," he said as he loosened Susannah's hat string and pulled the hat off. He brushed away the wet hair clinging to the side of her pale face.

"I am the doctor," the woman said briskly. She pushed back the sleeves of her dark wrapper. "Alexandra Kennedy, at your service. Now, what is troubling this young woman?"

Conor looked up in astonishment. *A female doctor?* He saw a tall, thin woman whose auburn hair was pulled back in a long braid. A satin brocade wrapper of dark blue covered her nightdress, tied at her narrow waist. The fine lines around her clear blue eyes were the only indication that she had probably passed her thirtieth birthday. The doctor washed her hands in a basin, then turned to Susannah, drying her hands on a towel. Her eyes narrowed at the sight of Susannah's bruised face.

Dr. Kennedy waited a moment longer, then snapped, "If you prefer a male physician, you'll have to go farther into town. Dr. Pollok has offices at the corner of Rose and Alpine." She threw the towel onto the bureau next to the lamp and put her hands on her hips. "If my services will do, you must tell me what is wrong with the lady. Make up your mind, sir. It's very late."

"She bumped her head," Lily Carolina offered in a small, weary voice. "And I hurt my hand."

The doctor glanced at the child as Conor spoke. "Susannah has a head wound. She's dizzy, and has been sleeping a lot, sleeping heavily. And we think Lily Carolina's wrist is broken."

Susannah tried to sit up. "See to her first," she begged, waving a shaky hand toward her sister. "She's in a lot of pain."

Conor gently pushed her back down on the table. "So are you. Let the doctor decide what to do."

Dr. Kennedy knelt at Lily Carolina's side. "Let me see your wrist, honey."

Lily Carolina worked her left hand from under the wet blanket and held it out in the direction of Dr. Kennedy's voice, several inches above the doctor's waiting hand. The doctor frowned, then looked at Conor.

"She's blind, ma'am."

Dr. Kennedy's eyes widened and she turned back to the child. She gently took Lily Carolina's cold little hand in hers. "How did you lose your eyesight, honey?" she asked kindly as she moved Lily Carolina's fingers with care.

"I got real sick, ma'am, and when I got better, I couldn't see anymore." She winced when the doctor moved her thumb.

"And how long ago was that?"

Lily Carolina's brow wrinkled. "I don't know, ma'am. It was when we still lived in South Carolina."

"A little over a year ago," Susannah said wearily from the table.

Dr. Kennedy placed Lily Carolina's hand in her lap and stood up. "How old are you?"

"I'm five," Lily Carolina announced, a touch of childlike pride creeping into her tired voice.

"Such a big girl!" Dr. Kennedy marveled. "I'll bet that if you try real hard, you can keep your arm still, can't you?"

Lily Carolina nodded vigorously. "Yes, ma'am."

The doctor laid her hand on the child's head. "Good girl." She moved to the bureau and glanced over her shoulder at Conor as she opened one of the drawers. "What is your name, sir?"

"Conor O'Rourke."

"Do you have dry clothes for the child?" She searched through the drawer.

"Yes, ma'am, out in my saddlebags."

"And for your wife?"

His wife? Susannah's startled eyes met his. She raised her hand to him. The lamplight winked off her mother's wedding band. Conor took her hand and opened his mouth to correct the doctor, then paused. Perhaps it was best for the time being to act as if they were married; they would not have to divulge Susannah's last name.

"Yes, ma'am," he answered. Susannah started. He touched his forefinger to her lips and slightly shook his head in silent warning. She stared at him for a moment, then nodded.

"Is Jesse still outside?" Lily Carolina asked.

"Yes, he is," answered Conor. "The dog," he added at Dr. Kennedy's questioning look.

She waved a hand toward the door as she advanced on Susannah with a stethoscope. "Bring him inside, but not in here. The parlor will be fine, across the hall. Then I need you to get some water on to boil, Mr. O'Rourke." She pulled the sides of the duster open and unbuttoned Susannah's dress to the waist. "The kitchen is at the back of the house. You'll find everything you need."

"Yes, ma'am," Conor answered again. He touched Lily Carolina's cheek as he passed her chair on his way outside. Jesse waited patiently by the door. After retrieving his saddlebags and rifle from his equally patient horse, Conor returned to the porch. "Come on, boy," he said. The dog trotted inside, following him, then veered through the door to the examination room and joyously poked Lily Carolina with his nose. His tail wagged, creating an arc of fine droplets.

The little girl giggled and reached across her lap with her right arm to pat the dog's head. "You're wet!" she whispered. "And you're not supposed to be in here."

Conor rested his rifle against the wall and leaned through the doorway to grab the dog by the scruff of the neck. "Come on, Jess," he ordered. Jesse obediently accompanied Conor through the double doors of the darkened parlor across the hall. Light from the lamp on the side table in the hallway showed the position of the furniture in the room. "Now stay here," Conor instructed. He groaned and rolled his eyes as Jesse shook himself thoroughly, sending a spray of water over the upholstered camel-backed sofa. The dog circled twice and contentedly settled on the rug in front of the cold fireplace. "I won't tell if you won't," Conor muttered to the dog. He backed out of the room and returned to the examination room.

"Before you go to the kitchen, help me get this coat off her," said Dr. Kennedy. Conor dropped the saddlebags next to Lily Carolina's chair and moved to assist the doctor. He eased Susannah to a sitting position.

"Is her wrist broken?" whispered Susannah.

"Yes, Mrs. O'Rourke, it is. I'll see to her as soon as I know your condition." Dr. Kennedy pulled the sleeve of the duster from Susannah's arm. "Mr. O'Rourke, while I examine your wife, get the child into dry clothes. Use extreme caution with her injured wrist. You'll find a chamber pot, if she needs it, in the bathing room, which is to the left of the kitchen."

Conor stared at the doctor, a dull blush creeping up his neck, then glanced at the calm child on the chair. Hours had passed since they had left the cave. She probably did need to use the pot.

"Mr. O'Rourke." Dr. Kennedy's sharp voice brought his eyes back to hers. Her brows were drawn together in a puzzled scowl. "We can lay your wife down now." Conor guided Susannah's shoulders back to the table and pulled the duster out from under her. He squeezed her hand in encouragement, then took the damp garment to the hall and hung it on a coat tree near the front door.

The doctor spoke again. "There are dry towels on that shelf there by the door. Go on now. See to your child."

Conor sighed as he grabbed a towel. Careful with her arm, he lifted Lily Carolina from the chair and made his way to the dark kitchen. Jesse silently followed.

"Sit here for just a minute, Lily Carolina," he said as he settled her into a chair. The light from the lamp in the hall reflected off the glass chimney of another lamp that sat on a doily in the center of the table. Conor found an iron matchbox nailed to the wall above the imposing cast-iron stove and lit the wick.

The light showed a clean, cozy room, dominated by the dining table he now could see was made of polished oak. Four beautifully carved chairs accompanied it. Cheerful red gingham curtains framed a window over the tin sink sunk into a long counter along one wall, and woven rag rugs dotted the clean wooden floor. It was a comfortable room, still carrying the faint, delicious scent of whatever Dr. Kennedy had cooked that evening. Conor was amazed to find that even the stove was spotless. He stoked the coals and added a few pieces of wood. Judging from the weight of the cast-iron kettle that sat on top of the stove, it was full. He positioned the kettle over a burner.

"Can Jesse stay with me?"

At the sound of Lily Carolina's voice, Conor turned to face her. Jesse sat at the child's side. Her tiny hand rested on top of the dog's wet head.

"Yes, I guess he can, for now." Conor dumped the clothing from his saddlebags onto the table. He sorted through the garments until he found Lily Carolina's little nightdress. It was dry, but felt cold to the touch. He draped it over the back of a chair he pulled close to the stove, then looked at her, his hands on his hips. "Do you have to go?"

"Yes, sir."

"Then I guess we'd better go." He picked her up and settled her on one arm, grabbing the lamp with his free hand. "You just stay right where you are, Jesse," Conor warned the interested dog. "We don't need your help." He crossed the kitchen and, with one foot, pushed open the door to a small room that contained little besides a large bathing tub and the pleasing aroma of scented soap. He spied the chamber pot in the corner. As he set Lily Carolina on her feet, a thought came to him. "I guess with that bum arm, you'll be needing some help, won't you?"

"Yes, sir."

Conor put the lamp on a shelf near the door, trying to resist the blush that heated his face again. After checking to be sure the china pot was empty and clean, he picked it up and was startled to find that it was cold. Why was that so surprising? he wondered. It was cold in this room. He rubbed the rim with his hands to warm it at least a little bit, then set it at his feet. "I don't know much about helping little girls in these matters, so you'll have to tell me what to do, Lily Carolina."

"I will," she said as she lifted her skirt with her good hand. "First we have to get my drawers down."

Between the two of them, they managed to see to her needs. When she was finished, Conor ushered her back into the kitchen with a sigh of relief. He positioned the child on the rug in front of the stove. "Now we'll get you dry and warm," he said.

He knelt by her side and with great care for her arm eased her out of her wet clothes. Naked, she looked even smaller, and very vulnerable. A sudden, fierce wave of protective tenderness washed over Conor as he wrapped the towel around Lily Carolina's shivering little body. He wanted to gather the child in his arms and keep her safe from the world. Conor shook his head at the surprising and unfamiliar feeling; he must be more tired than he thought. He began to carefully rub her soft skin.

"Lily Carolina, we're going to play a game."

"We are?" The weary child perked up. "But I can't play hard because I'm not supposed to move my arm."

Conor smiled. "You won't have to use your arm." He slipped the warmed nightdress over her head. "Do you remember those bad men who came to your house and hurt your father?"

"Yes, sir," Lily Carolina whispered solemnly.

He turned her to face away from him and applied the towel to her long hair. "Those same bad men hurt Susannah, too."

"Is that how she bumped her head?"

"Yes. I don't want those men to find Susannah, or you, so we're going to hide from them."

"Like hide-and-seek?"

"Yes, something like that. We are going to hide here in the doctor's house for a while, and pretend we're a family. I'm the papa, Susannah is the mama, and you are our little girl. Do you think you can do that?"

Lily Carolina nodded. "And Jesse is our dog!" she added triumphantly.

"Yes, he is." Conor patted her hand.

Lily Carolina turned toward him, her forehead puckered in a frown. "But what about my own papa?" The sadness on her face tore at Conor's heart. He put an arm around her shoulders.

"If your papa were here, he would be the papa, Lily Carolina. But he can't be here right now."

"Will he feel bad if I call you 'Papa'?"

"I don't think so, because it's only a game."

"Who will the doctor be?"

"For now, the doctor isn't going to play. We have to try and fool her. So you must be very careful what you say to the doctor, Lily Carolina. If we don't fool the doctor, the game will be over."

"I'll be *very* careful," Lily Carolina promised. "And so will Jesse."

Conor gave the child a quick hug. "That's my girl," he said, then stood up. He took Susannah's nightdress from the table and hung it over the chair where Lily Carolina's had been a few minutes earlier. "How about if you and Jesse wait in the parlor until the doctor is ready to fix your arm?"

"All right," Lily Carolina answered.

Conor eyed the wet dog, remembering the spray Jesse had sent over the sofa. "But first we'd better dry him off." He threw the damp towel over the patient dog's back and rubbed vigorously. Jesse did not resist the toweling, and even seemed to enjoy it. When Conor was finished, the dog shook again. Conor was relieved there was no resulting shower. As he draped the towel over a chair, he spied Lily Carolina's doll lying among the clothes on the table. He grabbed the doll and turned to the child. "Are you ready?"

"Yes, sir." Lily Carolina clapped her hand over her mouth. "I mean, Papa," she said with a giggle.

Conor's heart lurched at the word while his mind rebelled against it. He could not get attached to the Duncan sisters, he warned himself as he stared at the lovely child. Her little mouth curved in a smile, her damp curls fell around her shoulders, her tiny bare feet peeked out from the hem of her white nightdress. She was so innocent, so trusting!

"I'm going to pick you up now, honey. Watch your arm."

He carried her to the parlor and settled her on the sofa, then pulled a knitted blanket from a quilt rack by the window and tucked its warmth around the child.

"Your face is scratchy," Lily Carolina commented.

"I do need a shave," Conor admitted.

"And your hair is *wet.*"

"That's because I was outside and it's raining," he said as he tapped her nose with his forefinger. "Your hair is wet, too."

Lily Carolina giggled. "Not as wet as yours."

"No, I guess not." Conor smiled. "Here's Amy." He put the doll in her searching hand. "Lie down if you feel sleepy. We'll be right across the hall."

"Yes, sir." Lily Carolina yawned. "Mr., uh, Papa?"

He reached out to touch her cheek. "What is it?"

"Will it hurt more when the doctor fixes my wrist?" Her voice sounded young and scared.

Conor grimaced, filled with sympathy for the child. Praying that the doctor had ether or laudanum, he said, "I don't think so, Lily Carolina. I know your wrist hurts something awful now. But Dr. Kennedy is a good doctor, and she'll make it better."

"Will you and Susannah be with me?"

"I promise we will." Conor leaned down and kissed her forehead. "I'll go check on Susannah now. And try to remember to call her 'Mama' when the doctor is around."

"Yes, sir." Lily Carolina carefully lay down on her right side, protecting her left arm, while Jesse curled up on the floor in front of the sofa. Conor smiled at the picture the girl and the dog made in the dim light, then crossed the hall to the open door of the examination room.

Susannah sat on the edge of the examination table. The top of her dress was bunched around her waist, exposing her chemise and her arms. She looked up and saw Conor standing in the door, with unmistakable interest shining in his blue eyes. She felt the heat of a blush color her cheeks. How dare he stare like that? She moved to cross her arms over her breasts, then glanced at Dr. Kennedy, who was working on something at the bureau. Surely the doctor would find it strange that a "wife" would be so uncomfortable in her underthings in the presence of her "husband." *And he knows it,* she fumed as she glared at Conor, forcing her hands to remain in her lap.

"How is Lily Carolina?" she demanded.

Conor stepped farther into the room. "She's dry and resting in the parlor." He hesitated. "She's a brave little thing. She's in a lot of pain, but she doesn't complain." He looked at the doctor. "I hope you have something to use for the pain when you set her wrist. Lily Carolina is afraid it'll hurt."

Dr. Kennedy nodded. "I do. Please get me that hot water, Mr. O'Rourke, and bring Susannah's nightdress."

"Yes, ma'am." He smiled at Susannah in what he hoped was an encouraging way and returned to the kitchen. The room no longer looked neat and orderly. With a sigh, Conor quickly stuffed the clothes that were strewn over the table into his saddlebags and hung the bags on a chair. He draped the warmed nightdress over one shoulder and was reaching for the steaming kettle when Dr. Kennedy stormed into the room.

"What happened to your wife?" she hissed.

"Excuse me?" Conor was taken aback by the fury in the woman's eyes.

Her hands found her hips. "You heard me, Mr. O'Rourke. How did she come to be injured?"

How much could he tell her? Conor wondered despairingly. What had Susannah told her? "She fell and hit her head on a rock," he hedged.

Dr. Kennedy glared at him, her piercing blue eyes seeming to bore right through him. He shifted his feet uncomfortably, but met her gaze.

"And how did the child break her wrist?" the doctor demanded.

"She fell down a hole and landed wrong," Conor answered truthfully.

Dr. Kennedy stiffened. "I don't believe you." Her voice was low with contempt. "But we'll talk of it later. Your wife has fainted. Bring that kettle and come with me." She spun on her heel and marched down the hall.

Conor stared after her for a minute. Susannah had fainted? And why was the doctor so upset? He grabbed the kettle and followed her.

The doctor stopped at one side of the examining table and tossed her long braid back over her shoulder. From the outline of Susannah's body through the sheet that now covered her, Conor could tell that all her clothes had been removed.

He set the kettle on the bureau and made his way to the opposite side of the examining table. He gazed down into Susannah's white face. The bruises stood out in stark relief. Her lips were touched with blue, and her breathing seemed shallow. "What happened? Why did she collapse?" he asked worriedly.

"She is chilled, exhausted, and she has a head injury. I'm only surprised she didn't faint before now."

The anger in the doctor's voice burned Conor's ears. He slowly raised his head and met her eyes. "What is the problem, Doctor, aside from her injuries?" he asked quietly.

"Your wife has been abused," she snapped.

"I know that."

Dr. Kennedy seemed taken aback at his words, but only for a moment. She lowered the sheet to expose Susannah's upper arm and pointed to the bruises there, bruises that only could have been made by a man's fingers pressing into the tender flesh. She waved at the scratches on Susannah's throat and chest, then over her sheet-blanketed form. "Her body is covered with bruises, Mr. O'Rourke. Are you responsible for this?"

Conor could only stare as the doctor's meaning sank in. "Are you asking if I *beat* her?" he demanded incredulously.

"Yes, sir, I am."

He stiffened. His eyes narrowed when he met Dr. Kennedy's accusing gaze. "No, ma'am, I did not. I told you she fell and hit her head, which, I'll admit, is only part of the truth. She was accosted by a group of thugs and threw herself down a mountainside into the river to escape them. I found her like this two days ago, and have done everything in my power to help her. And I don't appreciate your accusation."

"Why did you not tell me the truth?" the doctor demanded.

"We're new to this area, and I don't know you. Under the circumstances"—he waved a hand at Susannah—"perhaps you can understand my caution."

Dr. Kennedy shrugged, but the resolute set of her thin shoulders did not relax. "We'll see what your wife says when she wakes up, Mr. O'Rourke. And what of the child?"

Something in Conor exploded. "I told you what happened to the child, Doctor." The words came out in an outraged, dangerous whisper.

Susannah frowned and opened her eyes to find Conor and Dr. Kennedy glaring at each other above her.

"What happened?" she rasped. "What's going on?"

"You fainted, and Dr. Kennedy thinks I beat you and broke Lily Carolina's wrist." Conor turned away from the table, running his hands through his hair in angry frustration. "That's what's going on."

Her eyes wide with horror, Susannah clutched the sheet to her chest and sat up. "Oh, no, Doctor, that's all wrong. You must believe me." She reached for Dr. Kennedy's arm with a shaking hand. "He saved our lives. Lily Carolina and I would be dead if not for . . . Conor." She gulped, thankful that "Mr. O'Rourke" had not slipped out.

Dr. Kennedy's tense features softened. "You're not just saying that to protect him?"

"I swear," Susannah breathed. The doctor helped her lie back down and pulled the sheet up over her shoulders.

"I apologize, Mr. O'Rourke."

Conor turned to find Dr. Kennedy looking at him. He did not answer.

"It was obvious that Susannah had been abused. Since you were so evasive with your answers, I assumed it was by you. I was wrong."

Conor sighed and nodded, feeling very tired all of a sudden.

"Go get out of those wet clothes, Mr. O'Rourke, or you'll be needing my services as well." Doctor Kennedy spoke over her shoulder as she poured hot water into the basin.

Conor glanced at the clock ticking softly on the bureau. It was almost two o'clock. A clap of thunder rumbled outside, and the rain continued to beat against the side window. He shook his head. "I need to see to my horse, ma'am."

"There's a stable out back. You'll find a lantern on the front porch, hanging by the door. Help yourself to the grain bin." She turned to face them. "I don't have a hospital here, but I do have an extra room. The two of you can use it for a few days. If you don't mind, I'd like to have the child sleep with me, at least for a day or two. I'll be using a little ether to help her with the pain when I set her wrist, and I want to keep an eye on her. She may feel ill afterward, and she will most certainly be groggy."

"Thank you, Doctor," Susannah murmured.

"Yes, thank you," Conor repeated. "For everything."

"You're welcome, both of you. Now let's get moving. We still have to see to your daughter."

Conor clapped his wet hat on his head, then stepped out into the storm. He lit the lantern and felt a twinge of guilt when he saw Charlie still waiting patiently in the downpour. The animal nickered a welcome. "Come on, boy. I'm sorry about this." He grabbed the reins with his free hand and led the horse around the side of the house. "I'm sorry about all of this," he muttered.

Susannah listened to the sound of Dr. Kennedy's light steps climbing the stairs. She again sat on the edge of the padded, oilskin-covered table, but was now dressed in her clean night-dress. The bandage the doctor had wrapped around her head felt heavy and awkward. Her gaze traveled the neat examination room with as much interest as her pounding head and aching heart would allow, while her nose wrinkled at the strange smell of antiseptic.

A tall cabinet with glass doors held labeled bottles of all shapes and sizes. The window between the cabinet and the bureau was draped with heavy curtains closed against the night. A mantel clock, a water pitcher, a shiny metal basin, and a black leather physician's bag sat on top of the bureau, along with the lamp and a neat row of matching porcelain apothecary jars. The sound of pounding rain against another curtained window told Susannah from which direction the wind was blowing. She looked back over her shoulder and saw a small pot-bellied stove in one corner, and a large rolltop desk in the other. The towel- and blanket-laden shelves lining the wall by the door completed the furnishings.

It was a clean, orderly room. She felt safe here, and was assured that Dr. Kennedy would take good care of Lily Carolina.

Susannah's stomach suddenly knotted. Would the doctor have been able to help her father, if they could have brought him in time? A fresh wave of raw, tearing grief roared over her, causing her to drop her chin to her chest and wrap her arms around herself. *Oh, Papa.* She rocked silently, her anguish too terrible even for tears. The abyss yawned before her. If she jumped in, or fell in, if she started to cry, she would never be able to stop. She would cry for the rest of her life.

The stable was small, but clean and uncluttered. Another horse, a fine dappled gray mare, snorted a greeting. "Hello, yourself," Conor said as he stroked the animal's forehead. He led Charlie to the only other stall and quickly stripped the saddle and blanket from the horse's back. He draped them over the top of the stall fence, then lifted a brush from a nail on the wall.

"I never asked for this, you know," he informed the silent horses. "I didn't ask to be responsible for Susannah and Lily Carolina, but what was I to do? I couldn't deny a dying man's request." The brush traveled over Charlie's back in long, rhythmic strokes. "And the doctor thought *I* beat Susannah." He shook his head in disgust. The brush pushed the water from Charlie's tail. "Tomorrow I'll bring the mares and the rest of the supplies down, and once I know Susannah will recover, I'm leaving. I need to get to Pueblo and see if I still have a job."

Even as the words left his mouth, he knew they weren't true. He'd given his word to Thomas Duncan that he would see Susannah and Lily Carolina safely settled, far from the reach of the Bannings, and he would. With a weary sigh, he returned the brush to its nail. He gave each horse a measure of oats, offered Charlie some water from the gray's bucket, then headed back toward the house.

A shudder ran through Conor's chilled body as he hung his dripping hat from a low hook on the coat tree. Some coffee or a stiff shot of whiskey would be welcome. He moved quietly to the doorway of the parlor. Lily Carolina and Jesse had not changed their positions. With a satisfied nod, he backed away and turned to cautiously look into the examination room.

Once again, Susannah sat on the edge of the table, this time dressed in a high-necked white nightdress. A bandage of the same color had been wrapped around her bowed head, as her arms were wrapped around her middle. Her hair, now woven into a long, thick braid, fell forward over one shoulder. There was no sign of Dr. Kennedy.

"Hello," he said softly.

Susannah did not move for a moment, then, with visible effort, lifted her head and looked at him. "Did you check on Lily Carolina?" Her voice was strangely hoarse.

"Yes." Conor stepped farther into the room, shocked by the ravaged expression on her face, by the terrible anguish in her eyes. "She and Jesse are both sleeping in the parlor. Susannah . . ." Her Christian name slipped out.

"Is your horse all right?"

"He's fine, and much happier now. Where is the doctor?"

"Upstairs, preparing our room." Her arms fell so that her hands rested in her lap. She dropped her head for an instant, then faced him again. It was as if a curtain had come down over her eyes. Where there had been raw, pulsing agony a moment earlier, he found only numb fatigue. As he watched, her brows drew together. "Why do you want her to think we are married?" she asked dully.

"We don't know how she feels about the Bannings. I didn't want to tell her your last name, not yet."

"I don't like it. I don't want to lie to her. She's been good to us." She twisted the gold ring on her finger.

Conor ran his hands over his wet hair. "I know. I don't like it either. But we can't risk it, Miss Duncan. Not yet. The Bannings have already killed your father. We must wait until we know more."

Susannah stared down at her hands, tightly clasped in her lap. "I suppose that makes sense, for now. But you cannot sleep with me, Mr. O'Rourke. It wouldn't be proper."

Conor refrained from pointing out that he had already slept with her in the cave. "We'll see what accommodations the doctor offers."

Her head snapped up and she glared at him. "Mr. O'Rourke—"

Footsteps sounded on the stairs. Conor placed a finger on his lips. "You'd best call me 'Conor,' " he whispered. Susannah's intriguing eyes flashed at him, but she made no comment.

Dr. Kennedy briskly swept into the room. "Did you find all you needed for your horse, Mr. O'Rourke?"

"Yes, ma'am, I did, and thank you. What is Susannah's prognosis?"

The doctor ignored his question and fixed him with a quizzical stare. "Mrs. O'Rourke told me you tended her head injury."

"Yes, ma'am."

"How did you know to hair-tie a scalp wound?"

"My mother taught me."

"You did well. Aside from your mother, have you had medical training?"

Conor shrugged. "A little. Why?"

"Your knowledge of medical terms and procedures is unusual and impressive for someone not engaged in the medical profession." She moved to Susannah's side. "As I told your wife, the bruises and scratches will heal; it's her head we have to keep an eye on. I don't think she has a concussion, but she'll have a bad headache for several days, and it's possible she will experience confusion and temporary loss of memory. We can only wait and see." She patted Susannah's hand and smiled. "She told me of your concern about pneumonia. I agree that so far there is no sign of it. If nothing develops in the next day or two, we can safely assume she is out of the woods in that regard. Now, young lady, you must get to bed, and I must see to your daughter's wrist."

"Please let me stay, Doctor," Susannah begged. "I couldn't sleep anyway, knowing you were working on her."

"Very well, but you must sit on that chair and be quiet, and you must warn us if you are going to faint again." Her eyes suddenly widened. "Mrs. O'Rourke, is there any possibility you are pregnant?"

Susannah glanced at Conor, surprised to see that his face was as red as she knew hers was.

"Come, come, Mrs. O'Rourke. It's good to see some color in your cheeks, but not like this. There's no reason to be embarrassed." She looked at Conor and put her hands on her hips. "Nor you, Mr. O'Rourke. Intimate relations between a man and a woman, as well as the workings of both the male and female body, are completely natural." She turned back to Susannah. "I must know if there is a chance, my dear. After the injuries you've suffered, your baby could very well be in danger, if indeed you are pregnant."

Behind the doctor's back, Conor spread his arms and shrugged, indicating to Susannah that she was on her own. She faced the doctor and shook her head.

"I can't be, Doctor," she said firmly.

"How do you know for sure?" the doctor pressed.

Susannah dropped her eyes. What could she say? She glanced again at Conor. His handsome features seemed tense and rigid. *He'd better not laugh,* she thought peevishly. "We haven't been, uh, intimate, since my last cycle." Her face felt like it was on fire.

"Good," Dr. Kennedy said with satisfaction. "Then all we have to do is watch your head." She motioned to Conor. "Move her to the chair."

Conor stepped forward. Susannah was relieved to find nothing but concern in his eyes. He easily lifted her up and carried her to the chair, then left the room, only to reappear a moment later with Lily Carolina in his arms. He laid the child on the table.

"Where's Susannah?" she asked sleepily.

Conor eyed the doctor, who was rummaging in her medicine cabinet. He hoped she hadn't heard Lily Carolina's use of Susannah's name.

"Your mother is by the door, on that chair you sat on earlier."

"I'm right here, honey," Susannah assured her, then saw a movement out of the corner of her eye. She turned to find Jesse standing at the door. "Lie down, boy," she whispered. Jesse inched closer to her and obeyed, resting his head on his paws.

Dr. Kennedy laid thin pieces of wood and a bandage roll on the end of the table near Lily Carolina's feet, then retrieved a bottle and a cloth from a shelf in the cabinet. "Mr. O'Rourke, please wash your hands. I'll need your assistance."

Conor moved to the basin, pushing his sleeves back.

"Is it going to hurt?" Lily Carolina asked, her young face tense with fear.

"Not much, honey," soothed the doctor. "Your father is going to place a cloth over your nose and mouth, and all you have to do is breathe. It will smell funny, but it won't hurt you. You'll just sleep. When you wake up, your arm will be all wrapped up so it can get better." She handed Conor the cloth and the bottle.

"All right." Lily Carolina closed her eyes.

"Do you understand what you need to do?" Dr. Kennedy asked Conor in a low voice.

"Yes, ma'am. I've used ether before."

"Somehow, I'm not surprised." She washed her own hands. "You won't need much. Just a few drops at a time, and only as she needs it."

Conor nodded. He pulled the glass stopper from the bottle and stood at Lily Carolina's head, the cloth poised and ready.

Susannah's heart pounded in fear. "Is ether safer than laudanum?" she asked hesitantly.

"I prefer it," Dr. Kennedy answered. "I won't keep laudanum, or any derivative of opium, in my house, and everyone in town knows it. It's very addictive, and I don't want some crazed addict breaking in here looking for it. The only time I'll use laudanum is when a patient is terminally ill and in great pain. Then I send to Denver for it." She glanced at Susannah. "Ether is very safe, Mrs. O'Rourke. Your daughter will be fine."

But Lily Carolina was so small! Susannah prayed the doctor knew what she was doing.

At Dr. Kennedy's signal, Conor spoke to Lily Carolina in a comforting tone. "I'm going to put the cloth over your nose now, honey. Just breathe. That's right, darling girl. Don't worry. I won't let anything happen to you."

At his words, Susannah leaned her head against the wall. Why did she find his reassurances so comforting? She hardly knew the man, yet on some deep level she trusted him.

Conor and the doctor worked efficiently and well together. Lily Carolina moaned only once, and soon her hand, wrist and lower arm were wrapped in a neat splint. When Conor moved the cloth from her face, the child turned her head, but she did not awaken.

"It will take several weeks for the break to mend," Dr. Kennedy cautioned. "She'll be in the splint for at least a month and a half."

"How soon will she wake up?" Susannah asked.

"Any time. Ether wears off quickly. Or she could sleep through the night. I'm sure she's exhausted." Dr. Kennedy washed her hands one last time, then turned to Susannah as she dried them. "Sometimes a patient will feel nauseated, sometimes not. If she awakens and feels all right, I'll give her a little whiskey in some warm milk to help her sleep. She needs the rest." The doctor put a hand to the small of her back and stretched. "You did very well, Mr. O'Rourke. Thank you for your help."

Conor did not take his eyes from Lily Carolina. "It was nothing." He stroked the sleeping child's cheek. She was so beautiful and innocent! He hated that her young life had already known so much pain and loss. He raised his eyes to Susannah.

She was stunned by the sadness she read on Conor's face. How could he have come to care for Lily Carolina so quickly? Susannah looked at her sister, and knew how. Her heart lurched with love for the little girl. An orphaned little girl who was now her responsibility.

"Up to bed with you, Mrs. O'Rourke." Dr. Kennedy's tone made it clear no argument would be tolerated. "Mr. O'Rourke, please bring the child." The doctor took Susannah's arm and guided her up the stairs. They waited on the landing until Conor topped the stairs.

"In there." The doctor waved at one of two doors. "She'll sleep on the far side of the bed."

Conor turned to the left and entered a cozy room. The lamp on the mirrored bureau was turned low, the soft light touching a comfortable-looking bed with the bedclothes pulled back and the pillows fluffed. He walked around to the far side and laid Lily Carolina on the sheet, then pulled the bedclothes up to her neck. Impulsively he bent and placed a kiss on her soft cheek. The child did not stir.

"She'll be fine," Dr. Kennedy assured him from the door. "I'll take good care of her. Now let's get your wife to bed."

Conor followed the two women into the other room. While the doctor settled Susannah in the double bed, he looked around. The furnishings were simple, but comfortable. A lamp with a painted glass chimney rested on a stand next to the bed, and a china pitcher and basin graced the top of a two-drawer bureau along the opposite wall. Wool curtains of solid forest green hung at each of the two windows. The bed boasted a tall headboard and footboard of oak, and was covered with an intricately designed patchwork quilt. He felt something brush his leg and looked down. Jesse stood beside him.

"The dog is welcome to sleep in here," Dr. Kennedy commented as she came around the bed. "I checked his wound earlier, while you were out with your horse. He'll have a scar, but he seems to be healing nicely; I don't think stitches are necessary."

"Thank you, Doctor," Conor responded.

The doctor hesitated, eyeing him sharply, then Susannah. "You're not evading the law, are you?"

"No, ma'am, we're not," Conor answered. "But we'd appreciate it if you'd keep our presence unknown for a while. The men who attacked Susannah are around here somewhere."

Dr. Kennedy crossed her arms over her chest, her eyes narrow with suspicion. "How do you know that, Mr. O'Rourke? I thought you were new to the area."

"Susannah said they weren't traveling with any gear, ma'am. No bedrolls, no pack animals. They couldn't have come far."

Susannah nervously watched from the bed, anxious to see if the doctor accepted Conor's explanation.

Dr. Kennedy stared at him a moment longer, then relaxed and shook her head. "I sure would like to know exactly what happened to all of you," she said as she moved to the door.

"Someday we'll tell you the whole story," Susannah promised wearily, trying to keep her relief from being too evident. How her head hurt! She sighed and closed her eyes.

"Mrs. O'Rourke, you just get some sleep. You're exhausted." The doctor's eyes traveled over Conor, then she left the room without a word. She returned in a moment and handed him a man's floor-length robe. "Get out of those wet clothes, Mr. O'Rourke, and put this on." Conor accepted the garment. "It belonged to my father," she explained at his questioning look.

She turned away. "Then come to the kitchen. I don't know about you, but I could use some coffee and a smoke." She disappeared down the stairs.

Conor stared after her. Had he heard her correctly? Had she said *a smoke?* At any rate, the coffee sounded good. He shrugged and closed the door.

the front door. "Everyone up to bed now. Lindy, you go get Miss Lucy into bed. I'll walk Susannah to hers." She disappeared into the kitchen.

Conor felt a little foolish. And Robert? He was watching him with a mix of wry amusement and something else. Something he couldn't quite name. Guilt?

Five

Conor glanced at Susannah as he tossed the robe on the bed. She lay quietly, her eyes closed. Had she fallen asleep? He sat on the edge of the bed and tugged off his boots. As usual of late, they were soaking wet. He stood up, pulling the worn undershirt over his head in one swift movement. The damp garment joined the boots on the floor.

His gaze returned to Susannah. He unbuckled his gunbelt and hung it over the corner of the tall headboard. As he watched, she shifted her position. A grimace of pain flashed across her bruised face. "Are you feeling any better?" he asked.

"A little." She did not open her eyes. "Mostly I feel better because Lily Carolina has been treated." Her voice had faded to a whisper.

Conor leaned over the bed and placed a hand on her cheek, relieved that there was still no indication of a fever. "Just rest now," he said quietly. "For tonight anyway, you're safe and warm and dry. Sleep."

She nodded against the pillow. "I'm safe thanks to you. But remember: you cannot sleep with me. It wouldn't be seemly." Her voice trailed off, then she added in a whisper, "Good night, Conor."

Conor smiled. "Good night." For a moment, he watched the section of the quilt that rose and fell in time with Susannah's breathing; then he turned to the bureau.

The water in the pitcher was warm, he discovered with pleasure. Dr. Kennedy must have filled it when she readied the room. He splashed water into the basin and washed his face, hands, arms and torso. In the mirror, his eyes fell on the scar covering the front of his left shoulder. Against his will, his weary mind again filled with the images of the military hospital, of the sickness, hopelessness and death that had surrounded him during the long, pain-filled months of recovery. Resolutely pushing away the memories the scar evoked, he stretched his arm and winced. The ever-present ache always became more pronounced in damp or cold weather, and tonight was no exception.

He glanced at Susannah self-consciously, then, convinced she was asleep, stepped out of his wet pants and reached for the robe. After gathering his clothes, he silently left the room and padded down the stairs on bare feet. He grabbed his rifle from where it rested against the wall behind the door and headed toward the kitchen, breathing in the aroma of freshly brewed coffee with keen appreciation.

From her chair at the table, Alexandra nodded in silent greeting when he entered. She rose to fill another cup with the steaming brew. Conor saw that drying clothes were draped over the backs of the chairs. He added his pants and shirt to the collection, then sat down, leaning his rifle against the table.

"I appreciate the use of the robe, Doctor. And thank you for the coffee. I can't tell you how good it smells."

"It tastes good, too," the doctor said brusquely. She hesitated for a minute, then opened a cupboard and pulled out a bottle and two glasses. She returned to her chair, placing the bottle between them. Conor pulled the cork and poured a small amount of the whiskey into each glass. She pushed one glass toward him and picked up the other, lifting it in a silent toast before she took a sip. Conor returned the gesture and took a healthy swallow. The fiery liquid burned a welcome path to his stomach. He set the glass down. "Did Lily Carolina need the whiskey and warm milk?"

"No, she hasn't awakened. I think she's as exhausted as her parents are." Dr. Kennedy arched an eyebrow at him and sipped her own whiskey.

Conor reached for his cup. "I'm glad she's resting well." He sampled the coffee. It was excellent, as he had known it would be. He sat back in his chair and waited, resigned to the inevitable questions.

"Where do you live?" Dr. Kennedy began.

"Nowhere right now. We're looking for a place to settle." That much at least was true, Conor thought wryly. He swallowed more of the coffee. The doctor stared at him. He continued. "We were camped up one of the valleys, over by the river. Susannah had gone into town for a few supplies. On the way home she was accosted, and like I told you, she went down the mountain and into the river to escape them. Lily Carolina fell trying to hide from them. And that is the truth, ma'am," he finished harshly.

Dr. Kennedy sighed and lowered her eyes. "I'm sure it is, Mr. O'Rourke. I'm just real touchy about men beating on women; I don't hold with it at all." She drained her glass.

"I don't hold with it either, ma'am," Conor said, his voice low and dangerous. He stared off into space. "I wish to God I'd been there. But I'll find who did it."

The deadly determination Dr. Kennedy read on his face gave her pause. She suspected that Conor O'Rourke was not a man to underestimate. Without a doubt, those men would regret the day they attacked his wife. She got up and brought the coffeepot from the stove. "Do you know who it was?" she asked as she refilled his cup.

Conor took up his rifle and examined it. "We haven't been in the area long enough to know many folks around here," he answered evasively. He hated lying, even for a good reason, but he didn't dare mention the Bannings until he knew where the doctor's loyalties lay. "But I'll find them." He pulled a rag from his saddlebag and wiped the rifle barrel.

"I'm sure you will." The doctor returned the pot to the stove and moved to the cupboard. She took something from inside, snatched a match from the box on the wall, and opened the back door. After watching the rain for a minute, she stepped onto the porch and out of Conor's sight.

Conor dried his rifle, then finished his whiskey and coffee. Still she did not return. He took his glass and cup to the sink and peered through the window into the black night. Unable to see anything, he went to the door. In addition to the clean smell of the still-falling rain, a trace of tobacco smoke reached his nose. He leaned around the edge of the door frame and made out the doctor's thin form leaning against the wall. A small red glow not far from her face cast her features into eerie relief. A puff of smoke floated in the air.

"Come on out," she invited. "There's paper and tobacco in the cupboard, if you'd like some, matches in the box on the wall."

Conor joined her. "Thank you, but I don't smoke."

"Does it shock you that I do?"

He shook his head. "No, ma'am. It's unusual, but not shocking. My grandmother on my father's side smoked a pipe all her life, and dared anyone to tell her not to." He chuckled. "She was a character. Stood no more than four-foot-ten, but let me tell you, no one tangled with her." His voice grew soft at the memories. "She lived in the hill country of Tennessee, and had a little plot of ground where she raised her own tobacco."

Dr. Kennedy laughed. "She sounds like my kind of woman."

Conor looked at her. "Yes, Gram would have liked you, Dr. Kennedy. She'd like that you're not adverse to a little whiskey every now and again, and that you smoke."

"Every now and again," the doctor interjected.

"But she'd especially like that you're a doctor."

"Really," Dr. Kennedy dryly commented. She flicked the remains of the cigarette into a puddle near the edge of the porch. "Few people, men or women, are taken with the idea of a female doctor." She looked at Conor. "Did you stay tonight because it truly didn't matter to you, or was it because you wanted to get your family treated as soon as possible?"

"It truly didn't matter, Dr. Kennedy. I hesitated only because I was surprised. My gram was a healer, and so was my mother, so I'm used to women treating the sick and wounded. I've just never met a real female physician before."

"There aren't many of us. But my father was a doctor, and it's all I ever wanted to do. From the time I was old enough to follow him on his rounds, I did, and of course I went to medical school. I even studied in Europe for a few years. They are a little more open-minded about women in the medical profession over there." She smiled. "It was my father who taught me to smoke. I don't indulge often. Just sometimes, at night, if I've had a bad or a long day. It makes me think of my father, feel close to him."

"Do you see him often?"

"He died shortly after the war ended. He had served as a doctor for the Union, and never fully recovered from the awful carnage he witnessed."

Conor nodded. "I can understand that."

"Did you serve in the war?"

"Yes, ma'am, for the Confederacy."

"I would have guessed that from your accent." Conor was silent. "Which side we supported doesn't matter anymore," she said softly. "The war is long over, Mr. O'Rourke."

"Yes, it is, Doctor. Thank God." Conor pushed away from the wall. "I'd best get up to bed. I don't want to leave Susannah alone too long."

Dr. Kennedy did not move. "I'll be up in a minute. Call me if you need anything, or if Susannah worsens."

"I will. And thank you, Doctor. For everything. For seeing to my family, for sharing your bed with Lily Carolina, and your whiskey with me."

"You're welcome, Mr. O'Rourke. Good night." She stared into the night.

"Good night, ma'am." Conor went back inside, pausing to grab his rifle before he headed down the hall. He glanced into the parlor, and something on the floor caught his eye. Upon closer inspection, he saw that it was Lily Carolina's doll. He took it with him. When he reached the top of the stairs, he peeked into the doctor's room. Lily Carolina had not moved.

Conor quietly moved to the side of the bed. A wistful smile touched his lips as he stared down at the sleeping child. He leaned over and tucked the doll under the blanket near her shoulder, then quietly retraced his steps to the door.

"Has she awakened?" Dr. Kennedy's quiet voice came from the stairs.

"No."

"I'm sure she'll be fine, Mr. O'Rourke. I know this is hard for you. In a few days we'll set up a bed for her in your room. Now get some rest. You're done in."

"Yes, ma'am."

"Good night." The doctor closed her door.

Conor entered his own room. His eyes were drawn to the woman in the bed. Susannah had turned onto her side and faced the center of the bed, with Jesse curled at her feet. Conor leaned the rifle against the wall by the headboard within easy reach and stared down at her. Her blond braid lay across the pillow, and because of the way the shadows fell, the bruises on her face were not so obvious. To him, she was lovely. And spirited, and courageous, and loyal to her family. An aching loneliness overwhelmed him. What would it be like to have such a woman to call his own? And a child like Lily Carolina? And a dog like Jesse? The dog's sleepy eyes opened.

"I don't know how the doctor would feel about you sleeping on her nice quilt, Jess," Conor murmured. Jesse's only response was to sigh contentedly. Conor smiled. Susannah, Lily Carolina and Jesse made a family. A family. What would it be like to have a family? A family of his own. The smile fled his face, and he shook his head. What was he thinking? It was a farfetched dream.

He took the robe off and draped it over the footboard, wishing he had a nightshirt or something to wear. Ignoring Jesse's indignant look, he climbed between the sheets, then leaned over to blow out the lamp. Susannah shifted, but did not awaken. Conor hoped she wouldn't start yelling when she found him in her bed. It was too late and he was too tired to make other arrangements. He lay back on the pillow, his hands under his head, and listened to the rain on the roof. It was a comforting sound. The sound of Susannah's breathing was also comforting. He rolled onto his side to face her and drew the blankets up over his shoulder. In a matter of minutes he was asleep.

Susannah stirred. Hot, burning pain pounded in her head with an intensity that made her stomach feel sick. She raised a shaking hand to her forehead and gingerly felt the bandages. A soft moan escaped her lips, and her eyelids fluttered open. The pale light that crept past the curtains told her it was early morning. Her gaze fell on the lacy cuff of her nightdress. When had she put on her nightdress? Confused, she lowered her arm to her side and realized that she was lying on her back in a very comfortable bed. She stretched her stiff and aching body thankfully. The sheets felt soft against her toes, and it was wonderful to be warm again. Wearily she closed her eyes and turned on her side, snuggling closer to the source of warmth.

Conor was asleep, facing her. His arm instinctively went over her when she moved closer to him. He held her for a moment; then gradually the memories of the night before nudged him from his deep, exhausted sleep. He lay still for a few moments, looking at her face. With a gentle hand, he smoothed soft golden tendrils back behind her ear.

Susannah stirred again, her hand coming up to rest against his chest. His bare chest. Her eyes flew open.

"Mr. O'Rourke!" she gasped as she pushed away from him.

His hand instantly covered her mouth. "Shh. Whisper, Miss Duncan. Dr. Kennedy may still be asleep."

Susannah blinked in confusion. She stared into his blue eyes, struggling to make sense of the images and memories that raced through her mind. God, how her head hurt! His hand fell away from her mouth.

"Where are we?" she asked weakly.

"We're in the home of Dr. Alexandra Kennedy. I brought you here last night. Do you remember any of it?"

Susannah closed her eyes, her face twisted with pain. "Yes, I think so." The effort to remember seemed to make her head hurt worse. Then the memories rushed in with sickening clarity. Her father was dead, Lily Carolina was hurt, and so was she, as if her aching head would let her forget that. Her eyes flew open again. "You told her we were married!"

Conor reached for her hand and lifted it. "She came to that conclusion on her own." The morning light shone on the gold band.

Susannah snatched her hand away. "You should have corrected her."

"Miss Duncan, you told me the Bannings are well-known and very powerful in this town."

"Yes, they are, and you're changing the subject."

Conor spoke with careful patience. "As I explained to you last night, I did not correct her because I don't know yet if she is sympathetic to the Bannings, and I didn't want to divulge your name." He raised an eyebrow. "You were awake. You could have corrected her yourself."

Susannah paused. He had a point. Still, she was reluctant to concede to him. "I told you we could not share a bed," she whispered heatedly.

"I was too tired to come up with another arrangement last night." Conor suddenly remembered he was naked under the sheets and eased away from her, thankful that Jesse was nestled between them farther down. He pulled the blankets up higher on his chest.

Susannah turned on her back and stared at the ceiling, uncomfortably aware of the man lying next to her. Surely she should be upset that he had shared the bed, especially after she had told him not to. But somehow she could not be angry with him. She could not seem to get past the terrible ache in her head and her worry over her sister. "How is Lily Carolina?" she asked.

"This morning, I don't know. But the doctor again assured me before I came to bed that there's no reason to worry. We'll check on her as soon as the doctor awakens."

Susannah pressed her palms to her temples. "How long are we to play this little charade of being a family?"

"I don't know. As long as we have to, I guess, providing no one accidentally lets the cat out of the bag." Conor inched up to a sitting position against the tall headboard, careful to keep the blankets tucked around his hips.

"It'll be difficult for Lily Carolina," Susannah cautioned. "She is a guileless child."

"I know. I told her we were playing a game, but it might be hard for her to remember, especially if she doesn't feel well. We'll just have to ride it as long as we can. Maybe I'll learn something about Dr. Kennedy today and we can tell her the truth."

Susannah looked at him. His eyes were closed as he rested his head against the wooden headboard. She owed so much to him! Without knowing them, asking nothing in return, he had taken her and Lily Carolina under his wing, had protected them, fed them, brought them to safety, with no regard for his own plans, or physical comfort. Her heart softened in sympathy. His fatigue was evident on his drawn features, and his cheeks were covered with a day's growth of beard.

She could not help but notice that his weariness did not detract from his good looks. Her gaze left his face and wandered over the expanse of his bare chest. She unconsciously caught her bottom lip between her teeth at the sudden, absurd idea of running her fingers through the fine brown hair that covered his chest. Her eyes followed the pattern of hair as it narrowed and disappeared beneath the blanket. Was the rest of his body as naked as his chest? Surprised and appalled at her train of thought, Susannah forced her attention to his scars. In addition to the one on his left shoulder, another angled across the ribs on his right side. She was about to ask him what happened when he spoke.

"As soon as I have a bite to eat, I'll return to the cave and see to your mares. I'll bring more clothes and supplies back with me. Dr. Kennedy's house is on the edge of town, and I think you and your sister will be safe here as long as we keep you out of sight. You need time to heal." He paused and looked at her. "I'm curious; did you hit your head on a rock?"

She touched the back of her head. "Here I did." Her hand moved to her forehead. "Here, Kyle Banning hit me with his gun."

"He *pistol-whipped* you? The bastard!" Conor's voice steadily rose. "That must have happened before I got out my telescope. If I had seen him do that—"

"You said we have to whisper, Mr. O'Rourke."

Conor clenched his teeth. "I want to meet Kyle Banning one day," he muttered as his fingers picked at the quilt that covered his legs.

"You won't like him."

"I don't expect I will," Conor agreed. He glanced at the robe draped over the footboard. "If you'll close your eyes for a moment, I'll get out of bed."

Susannah blushed and squeezed her eyes shut. So he *was* naked! The mattress shifted as his weight left the bed. She heard the rustle of the robe as it was pulled off the wooden footboard.

"Please don't try to get up yourself, Miss Duncan. I'll bring you something to eat and drink, and I'm sure the doctor will check on you when she arises. She was up awful late last night, so I don't know when that will be." There was a pause. "You can open your eyes now."

Susannah watched as he lifted his gunbelt from the headboard and moved toward the door. "Thank you, Mr. O'Rourke," she said softly. "Thank you for everything."

Conor nodded nonchalantly. "Come on, dog," he said to Jesse. With apparent reluctance, Jesse jumped off the bed and followed Conor out the door.

Susannah sighed and snuggled farther under the covers. She owed a great deal to Conor O'Rourke. Thank God he was Alina's cousin. That in itself assured her that she could trust him, at least a little. Surely he would help her for a while longer, until she and Lily Carolina healed. Her eyes drifted closed.

She would rest for just a while, and perhaps this afternoon she would feel strong enough to go to the marshal. She would tell him of the attack against her, and of her father's death. The Bannings would be arrested, and she and Lily Carolina would be safe. After she saw the Banning brothers hung, she would ask Conor to take her to Wyoming Territory. Satisfied with her plan, she allowed sleep to claim her.

Conor let Jesse out the back door, then built up the fire in the stove. He dressed quickly, strapping his gunbelt around his hips. A search of the cupboards turned up a burlap sack of coffee beans. It took only a few minutes to grind the beans and have a pot brewing. He was slicing thick pieces of bread from a loaf he had discovered in the bread box when he heard a noise behind him. He dropped the knife and whirled, his pistol suddenly in his hand.

Dr. Kennedy stood just inside the door, her eyes wide at the sight of his gun.

"My apologies, ma'am," Conor said sheepishly as he returned his pistol to its holster as fast as he had drawn it.

"You're very quick with that gun, Mr. O'Rourke," the doctor commented as she moved into the room. She was dressed as she had been last night; the blue brocade wrapper covered her night-dress, and her braid hung down her back. "Are you just fast on the draw, or can you also hit what you aim for?"

Conor shrugged and returned his attention to the bread. "I usually hit what I aim for."

"I'm sure you do." She sniffed appreciatively. "The coffee smells good."

"It'll taste good, too," Conor remarked, in a deliberate mimic of her words the night before.

Dr. Kennedy smiled. "I think I'm going to like you, Mr. O'Rourke," she said as she filled a cup. "Would you like some coffee?"

"Yes, thank you. I hope you don't mind that I helped myself to your bread. I'll bring some food with me when I return later today."

"There's butter in that crock against the wall, and a jar of marmalade on the shelf above. Make yourself at home." The doctor turned to the table with a cup in each hand. "Has your wife awakened?"

Conor nodded. "Yes, ma'am." He set a plate of sliced bread on the table.

"How is she?" Dr. Kennedy settled into a chair and pushed a cup toward him.

Conor brought the butter and marmalade, along with a knife,

and sat down. "Her head hurts something fierce, but she seems all right other than that. She remembers most of what happened."

The doctor nodded. "Did she have a fever?"

Conor thought for a moment, remembering the feel of Susannah's skin when he had pushed her hair back from her face. "I didn't specifically check for that, but she didn't seem too warm when I touched her," he answered. He slathered butter on a piece of bread.

"And her breathing? Was it normal? Raspy? Shallow?"

"Normal." Marmalade followed the butter, and he took a bite of the bread. It tasted wonderful.

"Good." The doctor sipped her coffee. "I'll go check on her in a minute."

"Both Susannah and I are anxious to know how Lily Carolina is."

"She's fine. She awakened about an hour ago and asked for some water, but now she's sleeping again. I'll take her in to your wife when she wakes up." She eyed him curiously. "Where are you going?"

"I was forced to leave our draft horses up at our camp last night," Conor explained. "I need to see to them. I should be back by late afternoon." He drained his cup and stood. "I appreciate you looking out for Susannah and Lily Carolina while I'm gone, Doctor. We can't thank you enough. I don't know what we would have done." He fished in his vest pocket and laid a few silver dollars on the table. "This is a start toward what we owe you."

Dr. Kennedy nodded. "Thank you, Mr. O'Rourke. It's kind of nice to have the company."

Jesse barked at the door. Conor set his cup in the sink, then let the dog in. He looked at the doctor. "Do you have something to feed him?"

"I do. I'll take care of him," she replied with a smile.

"Thank you." Conor headed toward the door. "As soon as I've said goodbye to Susannah, I'll be on my way."

"Are you going to look for those men?" Dr. Kennedy asked casually.

Her question caught him off guard. He paused. "What men, ma'am?"

"Those men who beat your wife."

"Uh, no, ma'am, not now. Like I said, I don't know who they were. And I'd hate to run into them alone. I'd be outnumbered. I'll see you later." Conor made his escape down the hall, feeling very uncomfortable. He wished he could tell the doctor the whole truth, but he did not yet dare.

"Somehow I don't think you'd have much trouble, Conor O'Rourke, even if you were outnumbered," the doctor murmured into her cup. "And I know you're lying to me about something. I wonder if you don't know who did it." She sighed and reached for the coffeepot.

Conor took the stairs two at a time. He let himself into the dim bedroom and sat on the edge of the bed. Susannah had dozed off.

"Miss Duncan," he whispered, then realized how that would sound to the doctor if she ever overheard him. "Susannah." He gently shook her shoulder. Her eyes drifted open. "I'm leaving now," he said. "Dr. Kennedy will check on you in a few minutes. She'll bring you something to eat. And Lily Carolina is fine. She's sleeping, and when she awakens, the doctor will bring her to see you."

"Good." A sudden fear gripped Susannah. She grabbed Conor's hand. "You are coming back, aren't you, Mr. O'Rourke?"

"Of course I'm coming back," he reassured her with a smile. "And you should call me 'Conor.' Remember, we're supposed to be married." He patted her hand.

Susannah relaxed against the pillow. "Very well, Conor. That is a nice name," she murmured as her eyes closed again.

"Susannah, listen to me for a minute longer, please." He rubbed the back of her hand until her eyes opened again. "When Dr. Kennedy brings Lily Carolina to visit you, if you get a chance, remind your sister of the game we're playing, that we're pretending to be a family and the doctor mustn't guess."

Susannah nodded. "I'll try," she whispered.

"Good." Without thinking, he brushed her cheek with the fingers of his free hand. He realized what he was doing and jerked his hand away from her soft skin. "I'll be back later this afternoon. You just rest."

"I will, Conor," she sighed. Her eyes closed again.

Conor laid her hand on the quilt and stood as he reached for his rifle. His eyes fell on the bandage wrapped around her head and the bruise that marred her jaw. Contrary to what he had said to Dr. Kennedy, he fervently hoped he ran into Kyle Banning and the men who had hurt Susannah. He silently let himself out of the room.

A few hours later, Alexandra Kennedy climbed the stairs with a tray balanced on one hand, holding her skirts up with the other. She had checked on Susannah soon after Conor left, but she had been sound asleep. By now, her patient should be good and hungry.

The doctor set the tray on the bureau and pulled the curtains back from the window. She perched on the edge of the bed, laying a cool hand on Susannah's forehead. The skin felt normal. She gently shook her patient's shoulder.

"Mrs. O'Rourke."

Susannah stirred, a frown creasing her forehead.

"Mrs. O'Rourke, you need to wake up for a while. I'm sure you're hungry, and your daughter wants to visit you."

Susannah forced her eyes open. The soft light that streamed

through the window seemed bright. She squinted up at the doctor. "Hello, Dr. Kennedy."

"Since you'll be staying here for a while, why don't you and your husband call me Alexandra? I'm proud of being a doctor, but sometimes the title sounds stuffy. Besides, I have a feeling we are going to be friends." The doctor's smile was warm and genuine.

Susannah smiled back, surprised at the tears that suddenly filled her eyes. It had been a long time since she had had a woman friend. "Only if you call me Susannah," she answered.

"Agreed," Alexandra said. "Now, can you sit up?"

Susannah nodded. With the doctor's assistance, she moved to a sitting position, the pillows cushioning her back. "How is Lily Carolina?" she asked. "When can I see her?"

"She's doing fine, and you can see her after you've eaten," Alexandra said firmly as she settled the tray on Susannah's lap.

Susannah obeyed with no argument. The delicate fragrance of the steaming tea made her mouth water, and never had plain toast looked so tempting. It seemed to her that the food disappeared very quickly.

Alexandra removed the tray and took the cup from Susannah's hand. "I'll give you the rest of the tea in a minute. I want to examine you." With gentle hands, Alexandra inspected the bruises on Susannah's face and neck, felt the bumps on her head, and listened to her lungs and heart with the stethoscope. She nodded in satisfaction. "Still no sign of pneumonia."

"Good," Susannah sighed. "I've been lucky."

Alexandra arched an eyebrow at the last word. She handed Susannah the teacup. "There is something I must ask you," she said.

Susannah eyed her new friend nervously over the rim of the cup. "What is it?"

"Your husband told me he didn't know who did this to you."

"He wasn't there."

"Do you know?"

Susannah dropped her eyes. "No."

Alexandra stood up and put her hands on her hips. "I think you do know, Susannah," she said quietly. "I don't know why you and your husband feel you have to lie to me, but I don't like it." She snatched up the cup and walked over to place it on the tray on the bureau, her lips pressed in an angry line.

Racked with guilt, Susannah twisted her hands in her lap. She was desperate to change the subject. "May I see Lily Carolina?"

Alexandra paused at the door, the tray in her hands. "I'll bring her up in a few minutes. She's resting downstairs in the parlor. After breakfast I gave her a bath and made her promise to stay close to the fire until her hair dries."

An intense longing to see her little sister filled Susannah. She felt so alone! "Thank you, Doctor." And a bath! How she wanted a bath! She did not dare ask the doctor for anything right now though.

"There's a chamber pot under the bed. You'll need to use that until you're strong enough to walk across the yard." Alexandra left the room without another word.

Susannah stared guiltily at the doorway, then closed her eyes as a dizzying wave of pain and fatigue washed over her. She realized she was not well enough to go to the marshal this afternoon; maybe Conor would go when he returned, and bring the marshal to the doctor's house. She had to tell him about her father!

"Oh, Papa," she whispered. "What are we going to do without you? I miss you so much." A single tear squeezed from each eye, and Susannah angrily brushed them away. There was no time to cry, no matter how her head pounded and her body ached, no matter how wounded her heart was. She had to be strong now, and heal. Lily Carolina needed her. Her mouth tightened into a determined line.

The sound of her sister's young voice came up the stairs. Susannah wiped her eyes again as the door opened.

Alexandra guided Lily Carolina to the bed and lifted her to sit next to Susannah. Jesse bounded into the room and jumped onto the bed, his tail wagging furiously.

"Do you mind the dog on the bed?" Susannah asked anxiously as she tried to dodge Jesse's enthusiastic tongue.

"No. I'll come for the child in a while." Alexandra backed out of the room.

"Thank you," Susannah called as the door closed. Alexandra did not answer.

Susannah hugged Lily Carolina to her breast, careful of her little splinted arm. "It's so good to see you!" she cried. "And you, too, Jesse." She scratched the dog's ears with one hand until the animal lay down in a contented curl at her side. "How do you feel, Lily Carolina?"

"I'm tired, and my hand hurts, but not as much as last night."

"Good. It will get better fast."

Lily Carolina clung to her. "Are you going to be all right, Susannah?"

"Yes, I'm going to be fine. I'm just sore."

Lily Carolina pushed back and touched Susannah's face with a gentle, seeking hand. She stopped when she found the bandage wrapped around Susannah's head. "Oh, does this hurt?" Her little face was filled with sympathy.

"Not too much," Susannah lied. She took Lily Carolina's hand in her own. "Have you been a good girl for Dr. Kennedy?" She stroked the child's soft, clean curls.

Lily Carolina nodded. "I promise I have, Susannah. And Amy has been good, too. Where is Mr. O'Rourke?" She clapped a hand over her mouth. "I'm supposed to call him 'Papa,' " she whispered.

Susannah smiled. "I know, honey. He told me about the game we are playing. I'm supposed to call him 'Conor.' He went to get Minnie and Muffin. Do you remember that we had to leave them at the cave last night?" At Lily Carolina's nod, she continued. "He'll be back later this afternoon."

"Will he bring Minnie and Muffin here?"

"I think so," Susannah answered. "Are you remembering to call Mr. O'Rourke 'Papa' when you talk to Dr. Kennedy?"

"Yes." Lily Carolina hesitated. "But, Susannah, do you think Papa minds that I call Mr. O'Rourke 'Papa'? Mr. O'Rourke said he didn't think so, but I don't want Papa to feel bad."

"No, I think for now Papa wants you to call Mr. O'Rourke 'Papa.' It's only for a little while, and it's only a game."

"All right." Reassured, Lily Carolina snuggled against her sister again. "I miss Papa," she said sadly.

Susannah rested her cheek on the child's head, blinking away the maddening tears that threatened again. "So do I, honey," she whispered. Her body tensed with a rush of fury.

Kyle Banning had taken Lily Carolina's father from her. Thomas would not be there to teach her to dance, as he had taught Susannah. He would not be there to watch his youngest daughter grow to be a woman, to give her away at her wedding, to play with his grandchildren. And for that, Susannah vowed, Kyle Banning would pay dearly, as would his brother Fletcher.

"What's the matter?" Lily Carolina patted Susannah's arm.

Susannah had forgotten about Lily Carolina's uncanny ability to sense when something was wrong. "Nothing, honey. I'm just tired. Let's rest for a while." She forced her body to relax, but her mind would not.

Six

Later that night, Conor sat on the edge of Alexandra's bed, involved in the enjoyable task of tucking Lily Carolina in for the night. They had already visited Susannah, who was resting after having eaten supper. Now Conor examined Lily Carolina's injured arm, gladdened by the knowledge that she was feeling better.

"The swelling has gone down, and your fingers aren't cold anymore," he reported. The child wiggled her fingers, then giggled when he kissed them. "All right, Poppet, it's time for you and Amy to go to sleep." Conor lightly poked Lily Carolina's nose, then pulled the blankets up to her chin.

Lily Carolina's face wore a puzzled expression. "Why did you call me a puppet?"

"I called you 'Poppet,' which means dear, or precious," Conor explained with a laugh.

"Oh." She smiled. "I like that." Her hand patted the blankets. "Where *is* Amy?"

Conor joined in the search, to no avail. "She's not here. Do you remember where you left her?"

Lily Carolina's brow wrinkled in a way Conor absurdly found adorable. "I think I left her in the kitchen."

"I'll go get her right now."

"Wait." The child sat up. "Papa always reads to me before I go to sleep."

Conor shook his head, forgetting that she could not see him.

"It's too late. Dr. Kennedy said you must sleep now. I promise I'll read to you tomorrow, though."

Lily Carolina was very quiet.

"What is it?" Conor asked gently, touching the child's cheek with his finger. She looked so sad.

"Papa always holds me while he reads to me."

Conor hesitated for only a moment. "Well, it's never too late for that," he declared, and pulled her onto his lap. She nestled against him. Conor hugged her close, his hand stroking her soft hair. He determined to hold her for as long as she wanted him to, no matter how late it got.

After several minutes, she whispered, "I miss Papa."

Conor's heart grabbed. "I know, honey."

She was quiet for a few minutes more, then Conor realized her hand was traveling over his arm.

"May I see you?" Her hand paused. "Papa told me I always have to ask first," she explained.

Puzzled, Conor nodded, then remembered she couldn't see his nod. "Yes," he answered.

Lily Carolina's little hand moved up his arm and across his chest. "You're big," she whispered. Her fingers wandered along his neck to his face. "Your cheeks aren't as scratchy as they were last night."

Conor smiled. "That's because I shaved." Now he understood how she was "seeing" him. He closed his eyes as her hand continued its journey. She paused on his upper lip.

"You don't have a mustache," she marveled. "Papa does." Her fingers touched on his closed eyelids, as light as a butterfly. "What color are your eyes?"

"Blue," he answered, surprised at her question. "Do you know what color blue is?"

Lily Carolina nodded. "Like the sky. Papa taught me my colors before I got sick, when I was little."

"When you were little," Conor repeated with a smile.

"Yes." Her hand moved to his hair. "Now your hair is dry. What color is it?"

Conor opened his eyes. "Brown."

"It's longer than my papa's, but it's not as long as mine," she pronounced solemnly.

"Shall I grow my hair as long as yours?" He smiled and tickled her ribs.

Lily Carolina giggled again and squirmed against him. "No, 'cause then you'll look like a *girl!*"

Conor laughed out loud at that. His arm tightened around the child.

Lily Carolina returned her hand to his cheek, holding very still, suddenly very serious. "Are you handsome?" she asked.

"I don't know," he answered with a shrug. He watched Lily Carolina's beautiful face and felt another unwelcome surge of tenderness.

The little girl's hand fell to her lap. She absentmindedly stroked her bandaged arm. "I'll ask Susannah tomorrow," she said. "She'll know. She said our papa is handsome."

"And she's right." After a moment he asked, "Are you ready to sleep now?"

"Yes, sir."

Conor returned her to the sheets and tucked the blankets around her as she settled back against the pillows. "I'll be right back with Amy," he said, and left the room. When he returned a few minutes later, he found Jesse curled up on the end of the bed at Lily Carolina's feet. He eyed the dog doubtfully. Jesse looked up at him without raising his head, the whites of his brown eyes showing, and wagged the last few inches of his tail one time.

"I don't know if Dr. Kennedy is going to want Jesse sleeping on her bed, Lily Carolina."

"She will," the child drowsily assured him. "Jesse will keep her warm."

Conor snuggled the doll at Lily Carolina's side. "Just don't argue with the doctor if she wants Jesse to sleep on the floor. It's the doctor's house, and we must respect her wishes."

"Yes, sir." Lily Carolina hugged the doll.

"Good night, Poppet." Conor hesitated, then placed a kiss on her forehead.

"Wait." Her searching hand found and grabbed the front of his shirt, pulling him toward her. She felt for his face, raised her head, and kissed him. Her lips hit his cheek near his mouth. "Good night," she whispered, and nestled into the pillow. Her eyes closed.

Conor blinked in surprise, swallowing around a sudden lump in his throat. He straightened and patted Jesse's head before he turned to go.

Alexandra leaned against the doorjamb, her arms folded across her chest. Conor wondered how long she had been there.

"Just say the word if you don't want the dog on the bed." He waved at Jesse.

Alexandra shook her head with a sad smile. "Thank you for asking. I don't mind the dog. I used to have one, but she died last winter. She always slept on my bed. I still miss her." She started down the stairs. "I put on a fresh pot of coffee."

"I'll be right there." Conor looked into the room he shared with Susannah. She was lying on the bed, her eyes closed. He quietly backed away from the door. Coffee sounded good, and so did a little more of Alexandra's whiskey. It had been another long day.

In the bedroom, the lamp was turned low, the curtains closed against the darkness outside. Although Susannah was exhausted, sleep eluded her. She shifted, trying in vain to find a comfortable position for her sore body, tempted to negotiate the stairs alone and join Conor and Alexandra in the kitchen. With a sigh, she decided she was too tired for that. Her mind replayed the events of the evening.

Conor had returned just after nightfall. She had been relieved to hear the sound of his voice, for she had not been entirely certain he would come back.

He had climbed the stairs a few minutes later, coming into the room with Lily Carolina on one arm. A happy smile covered the child's face. Susannah had smiled herself at the sight of them, and had completely forgotten to ask him about speaking to the marshal.

Conor O'Rourke looked so good to her! He had shaved sometime during the day, and wore a clean flannel shirt. From the shine of his long hair, she could tell he had washed it.

He explained that he had stabled Minnie and Muffin in the nearby town of Downieville, seven miles down the Denver and Georgetown road. He did not want to risk the chance that someone would recognize the mares as belonging to the Duncans. Although he had been forced to leave some of the supplies at the cave, he had returned with more clothes and food.

Later he brought her supper, and Alexandra checked on her one more time. She had pleaded with the doctor to be allowed to bathe, and Alexandra promised that with Conor's help, they would arrange that tomorrow. She could hardly wait.

Now footsteps sounded on the stairs. Susannah settled on her side and closed her eyes. The hinges on the bedroom door twisted with a soft sighing sound; then the latch clicked into place. Conor had come to bed. They had made no other sleeping arrangements for him. Her pulse quickened at the thought of him lying next to her again. She did not know whether to let him know she was awake or not.

Conor moved quietly around the room. Susannah opened her eyes a crack and watched him take off his gunbelt and hang it on the corner of the headboard. He unbuttoned his shirt and, with a yawn, stretched his arms over his head. She silently delighted in the view of his chest. He shrugged out of the shirt, then sat on the bed and pulled off his boots and socks. Her breath caught in her throat as she watched the muscles play across the smooth, broad expanse of his back. When he stood up, she squeezed her eyes shut, thinking he would take his pants off next.

But he moved to the bureau instead. Water splashed in the basin. After a few minutes, she heard him move closer to the bed again. Now, she could tell, he did remove his pants. She kept her eyes tightly closed. He pulled back the blankets and settled on the bed next to her.

"You can open your eyes," he whispered.

Susannah felt the hot color flood her cheeks. She cautiously opened her eyes. Conor was sitting up against the headboard, the blankets pulled to his waist, a humorous twinkle in his eyes.

"I'm having trouble falling asleep," she said defensively.

Conor nodded. "I'm sure you're uncomfortable."

Unable to stop herself, she blurted out, "How did you know I was awake?"

"Most people don't sleep like this." He scrunched up his nose and tightly squeezed his eyes closed.

Susannah struggled to prevent it, but a giggle popped out of her mouth. "No, I guess they don't," she admitted.

Conor opened his eyes and smiled at her. Once again, her breath seemed to stick in her throat. That smile lit up his handsome face, erasing the signs of worry and fatigue. He had never before smiled at her like that. Of course, there had not been much to smile about in the few days since he had pulled her from the river. Her own lips curved in shy response.

After a moment, he asked, "Would you rather I slept on the floor?"

Susannah was surprised at his question, and at her emotional response to it, for she definitely did not want him to sleep on the floor. She stared at him, taking in the fatigue on his face, at a loss for words. Finally she shook her head.

"I don't mind, Susannah. You're right that it's not proper for us to share a bed."

She found her tongue. "And you need a good night's sleep, which you won't get on the floor. If you promise to behave yourself, I'll not tell anyone we shared this bed."

Conor smiled. "Thank you. I shall behave as a perfect gentleman." He angled his body more toward her and laid a gentle hand on her bandage. "How does your head feel?"

"It's better," she hedged.

"But it still hurts terribly, doesn't it?" His hand moved over her head in a soothing caress, taking care when he found a sensitive bump, his fingers smoothing her tousled hair.

Susannah lay still; her heart pounded in pleasure. His touch was deeply comforting. She sighed. Now she did not feel so alone.

"Alexandra knows we're lying to her, Conor."

His hand stilled for a moment, then continued its soothing movement. "She doesn't believe we're married?"

"No, it isn't that, although one of the three of us is bound to make a mistake that will tell her that's also a lie. She thinks we know who did this to me." Her eyes drifted closed.

"What did you tell her?"

"Nothing, but she's upset. She has been so good to us. I hate lying to her."

"So do I, Susannah. Tomorrow I'll scout around town and try to learn who supports the Bannings. As soon as we know we can trust Alexandra, we'll tell her the truth."

Susannah looked up at him with a frown. "Aren't you just going to go to the marshal?"

"Not yet."

"Conor, why not?" Susannah pulled away from his hand and sat up. "We have to go to the marshal and tell him what happened. He'll arrest the Bannings, and it won't matter if Alexandra is on their side or not."

"It may not be that simple." Conor held his hand up when she would have spoken again. He had learned from painful experience that powerful men often controlled the law in their area. Until he knew more about the politics in Georgetown, he did not dare go to the law. "I won't argue about this, Susannah. I need time to scout around."

Susannah dropped back onto the pillow, troubled and bewildered. "I'm too tired to argue. But I don't understand why you won't just go to the marshal. I would have gone myself if I had felt stronger today." She draped her arm over her forehead.

"Do you know the marshal personally?"

"No," she admitted.

"Do you know anything about him?"

"No."

Conor touched her elbow. "Then give me a day or two. Let me see what I can find out. You just concentrate on getting well."

Susannah dropped her arm and looked at him.

"Please trust me." His voice was low and soft.

"I have to trust you, Conor," she answered wearily. She was quiet for a minute, deep in thought. "If you won't talk to the marshal, talk to Lucas McCleave. I don't know why I didn't think of him sooner."

Conor's eyes widened. *Lucas McCleave?* "Who?" he asked casually.

"Lucas McCleave. He's an attorney and businessman, one of the few people Uncle Walter trusted. I think he's an honest man, Conor." She yawned. "Uncle Walter said he used to be a Texas Ranger. He's widowed now, and lives with his son. His office is in the Barton House." Susannah's voice had dropped off. She nestled into the pillow and sighed.

Conor leaned his head against the headboard. So Lucas McCleave had ended up in Georgetown. Conor knew of the famous Ranger captain from his own days in Texas, and wondered if McCleave had heard of him. They had never met, but McCleave was legendary as a fearless fighter and a stubbornly honest man. He could be just the one to help them, if he hadn't gone bad.

Conor focused on Susannah. Her even breathing told him she had fallen asleep. The edges of the bruises on her face were beginning to fade from purple to a greenish-yellow. She was slowly mending.

And then what? he asked himself. What would they do? The Bannings had to pay for what they had done, but how? Perhaps it was best to take the Duncan sisters far from here and help them start a new life. That was what he had promised their father he would do. Once he was certain they were going to be all right, he could come back and settle matters with the Bannings, with or without the help of Lucas McCleave and the law.

He realized that although the sisters needed him now, they no longer would when things were settled. The lovely and spirited Susannah would have her pick of potential husbands, and she would settle down somewhere far from here and raise Lily Carolina, along with children of her own.

Susannah married to another man, bearing another man's child. Lily Carolina treating another man with the same affection and trust she had shown him. Conor's mouth tightened. The familiar, aching loneliness he had known most of his life settled into his belly with a new ferocity. He stroked Susannah's hair one last time and pulled his hand away. She and Lily Carolina had come into his life only three days ago, and yet, as much as he tried to resist it, he felt a deep bond with each of them. He cared very much what happened to them, and that frightened him. And it frightened him even more that he was so uncomfortable with the idea of not being included in their future.

He leaned over and turned the lamp wick down until the flame was extinguished, then settled under the blankets. Susannah shifted in her sleep. He lay awake for a long time, comforted by her nearness. For a while at least, he was not alone.

Early the next morning, Conor stepped off Alexandra's front porch and started up the street. A thin mist floated over Georgetown, carrying with it the scent of fireplace and cookstove smoke. Somewhere a dog barked, and another answered, the sounds echoing off the mineral-laden mountains that towered above the town. Georgetown was nestled in a small, vee-shaped valley that widened on the north end. Griffith Mountain to the east, Leavenworth Mountain to the south, and Republican and Democrat Mountains to the west made for late sunrises and early sunsets. He could only imagine what winters would be like here.

Conor found the Barton House on the corner of Burrell and Taos streets with no trouble and climbed the stairs to the second floor. He stopped in front of a door with the words "Lucas McCleave, Esq., Real Estate, Mineral Land Agent and Mining Attorney" etched in the frosted glass. He knocked.

"Come in," a gruff voice ordered.

Conor entered the office, removing his hat as he closed the door.

The man seated at a battered oak desk got to his feet. "Can I help you?"

"You can if you're Lucas McCleave," Conor replied, noting that the man was of average height and wiry build, and he wore a gunbelt.

"I am. Have a seat." He waved at the two chairs facing the desk.

As Conor crossed the room, he surveyed the surprisingly sparse furnishings: two chin-high file cabinets in one corner, a small table in another that held a half-full whiskey bottle, a water pitcher and three mismatched glasses, the oak desk, and the two ladderback chairs, one of which he dropped into. The wooden floor was clean, but bare of rugs, and the two large maps—one of Georgetown, the other of the mines that crisscrossed the surrounding mountains—that were nailed to the plain board wall gave the room its only decoration. Even the window coverings were simple wooden shutters. The sole concession to luxury was the tall-backed tufted leather chair into which Lucas McCleave settled himself.

Conor eyed the retired Ranger with curiosity. Judging from the liberal amount of gray in his thick, dark hair and full beard, Lucas McCleave looked to be in his late forties. He was dressed as unpretentiously as his office was furnished, in an understated but well-tailored black suit. Conor had the feeling McCleave's piercing gray eyes did not miss much.

"Who are you and what can I do for you?" Lucas McCleave also did not beat around the bush.

"My name is Conor O'Rourke. Susannah Duncan sent me."

Lucas's eyes narrowed. "Is everything all right with the Duncans?"

"No, it isn't. Susannah said that her uncle trusted you, and she hopes she can, too. She thinks you're the only one she can turn to."

"Besides yourself, of course," Lucas observed. "Your name is familiar to me. Have we met before?"

Conor set his hat on the empty chair. "No, we haven't." He met the other man's eyes squarely. "Can Susannah trust you? With her life, if necessary?"

Lucas sat up straight. "Yes, Mr. O'Rourke, she can. Now, since she trusts you, and she trusts me, let's rely on her judgment and work together. What's this all about?"

"Both Walter and Thomas Duncan are dead," Conor said quietly.

"What?" Lucas leaned forward on his desk. "When? How?" His eyes narrowed again. "Did the Bannings have a hand in this?"

"I don't know about Walter. Thomas said only that his brother died last winter, so I don't think foul play was involved. But Thomas was beaten to death by Kyle Banning a few days ago."

"Damn." The mild tone of his voice was a strange contrast to the vehemence with which Lucas slammed an open palm down on his desk. "And where is Susannah?"

"Safe for now. She was hurt, too."

"Why haven't I heard about this?" Lucas demanded.

"The Bannings certainly aren't going to tell anyone they killed Thomas, and I hope they think Susannah is dead as well, at least for now. As long as they think she's dead, they won't be looking for her." Conor did not take his eyes from Lucas's face. He felt very uncomfortable giving out the information without knowing the man better. As he well knew, even a Ranger could go bad.

Lucas leaned back in his chair, scowling, his features tightened with suspicion. "How did you come to know so much about this, O'Rourke?"

"I pulled Susannah out of the river after she escaped from Kyle Banning, and took her to my camp. I went to check on her father and found him dying. He entrusted Susannah and, uh, his horses, to my care." Conor was thankful he had caught himself before he mentioned Lily Carolina's name. "When I returned the next day, Thomas was dead. I buried him next to his brother and brought Susannah down the mountain."

"Have you gone to the law?"

Conor shook his head. "And I won't until I understand the lay of the land. I've learned the hard way that a man as powerful as Banning usually has some influence over the local law, and I can't risk Susannah's safety." He glowered at Lucas. "I'm talking to you in confidence, McCleave. I don't want you going to the law right now, either."

"You raise a good point. I think Marshal Mason is a good man, but I also know he's real tight with Banning, as well as with Hamill and Bement and a few other influential men in this town. We'll wait awhile. I want to see Susannah."

Conor met his gaze. "No. Not yet." He ignored the fact that Lucas had pressed his lips into a thin, angry line and continued. "What's going on between the Bannings and the Duncans? I gather Banning wants the Duncan land, but I need to know more."

Lucas stared at him for a long moment. When he spoke, his voice was brusque. "Fletcher Banning is a very ambitious and ruthless man. He's convinced that a thick vein of silver runs from his property on Blue Mountain into the Duncan claim, and he may be right. He tried to buy Walter Duncan out last summer, but the old man refused to sell. So, taking advantage of our somewhat vague mining laws, Banning filed a lawsuit against Duncan over mineral rights."

Conor frowned. "On what grounds? Didn't Duncan have clear title to his claim?"

"Oh, the title is clear," Lucas assured him. "Walter Duncan came out here with the first rush of gold seekers in 1859, and he filed the claim back then. Of course, at that time, the Indians still had legal title to the land, so all claims were of doubtful legality. But he was very careful to update his claim when Colorado became a territory two years later."

"Then on what grounds could Banning file a lawsuit?" Conor repeated.

Lucas shrugged. "Like I said, some of our mining laws are vague. Mining is still a relatively new industry in this country, at least in terms of precious metals. What Banning has done is unethical and immoral, but unfortunately, completely legal. He doesn't need legitimate grounds. And until the lawsuit is settled, the Duncan mine can't be worked."

"But what does Banning hope to gain?"

"What usually happens in these cases is that the defendant will either offer the plaintiff a settlement, or will give up and sell the mineral rights, if not the entire claim, to the plaintiff. It depends on how much money either party has. If the defendant has a lot and the plaintiff doesn't, the plaintiff will usually accept a settlement. If the plaintiff is wealthy and the defendant isn't, as in the case with the Bannings and Walter Duncan, the defendant is eventually forced to sell because he has no money to offer for a settlement, nor does he have the funds to get involved in a lengthy court battle."

"Does this happen often?" Conor asked in amazement.

"Often enough," Lucas admitted. "I'm working on a territorial bill to get the law changed, because many of these lawsuits have no legitimate basis, like the Banning case. It's a real problem, especially when a large mine is shut down pending the settlement of a lawsuit. A lot of people are thrown out of work. And no matter how the case is resolved, it's usually at great cost to the often innocent defendant."

Conor shook his head in disgust. "What will happen to the mine now that Walter and Thomas are dead?"

"Susannah is probably the heir. She'll inherit."

"She is the heir; Thomas told me before he died. Will she also inherit the lawsuit?"

Lucas stroked his beard thoughtfully. "I don't think so. Banning filed it against Walter Duncan, not against a company. Of course, there's nothing to stop him from filing another lawsuit against the estate when he learns Walter is dead."

"Well, what can we do? Susannah is all alone now, and she needs help."

"I want to talk to her myself."

Conor leveled his gaze on Lucas. "For now, you'll have to talk to me. I won't tell you where she is, McCleave. I won't jeopardize her safety."

Lucas jumped up from his chair, making an obvious effort to control his anger. "You offend me, O'Rourke."

"I don't mean to." Conor got to his feet. "I don't know you, and until I do, you'll have to trust me. I give you my word she is safe. What are we going to do to help her?"

"Unless Susannah comes forward to claim her inheritance, the property will be auctioned off. So we need to get the title transferred to her name as soon as possible. I'd bet that Banning will file a lawsuit against her as soon as we do, though, and she probably has no more financial means to fight him than Walter did."

Conor shook his head. "She doesn't."

"Let me check into the matter, quietly, mind you. I'll go to the County Recorder's Office and see what I can find."

"Don't say anything about the Duncans to anyone."

Lucas glared at him. "I won't, O'Rourke," he snapped. "How do you know the Duncans?"

Conor reached for his hat. "You could call it an old family connection. Susannah and my cousin are close friends. I was in the area and looked her up."

"And you just happened to be there when Susannah needed help." Lucas crossed his arms over his chest.

Conor did not like the tone of Lucas's voice, nor his aggressive stance. "That's right. I just happened to be there." His straight-forward gaze carried a challenge of its own.

Lucas did not back down. "Walter Duncan was an eccentric old character, but he was a good man. He didn't deserve the trouble Fletcher Banning visited upon him. Thomas was also a good man, and I'm determined that his death will not go un-punished. For now, I'll do as you ask, but let me caution you, O'Rourke." He leaned forward and placed his palms on the desk, then rested his weight on his braced arms. "I care a great deal about what happens to Susannah. God help you if I ever find out you've hurt her, or betrayed her interests. I'll be on you like fleas on a dog."

Conor stiffened and clapped his hat on his head. "I could say the same to you, McCleave. And I do." He moved toward the door.

"How will I find you?"

"I'll be around. I'll check with you in a day or two."

"Give my best to Susannah."

Conor nodded and left.

Lucas McCleave stared at the closed door for a long, frustrated minute, then sank back into his chair.

Ben Hollister let himself into Fletcher Banning's office at his boss's gruff invitation.

"Well?" Fletcher demanded.

Ben settled into a chair in front of the desk. "I tore that place apart, Mr. Banning. There was no trace of the claim deed."

"Damn!" Fletcher stared into space over Ben's head and stroked his mustache. After a moment, his eyes focused on Ben. "I assume our friend Thomas is no longer with us."

"I don't think he is."

"What do you mean, you don't think he is? His body wasn't there?"

"No, sir, but there was a new grave next to the old one. I'd guess it was his, but I don't know who buried him."

"This isn't good, Ben." Fletcher leaned back in his chair. "You're telling me someone else has been there. Who? What if Thomas was able to talk before he died?"

Ben shrugged. "Like I said, I don't know." He hesitated. "But I have an idea."

"Go on."

"Most of the bedding, clothes and supplies were gone. The furniture was there, some household goods, dishes and such, and the wagon, but not the horses. The place had been neatly cleaned out, not ransacked."

"What are you getting at?"

"I just wonder whether Miss Duncan really died in the river."

Fletcher stared at him, concern wrinkling his brow. "Do you think it's possible she survived? Could she have made her way back to the claim, buried her father herself, and taken what she could? Or perhaps Thomas survived and it is Susannah's grave you saw?"

Ben shook his head. "Even if Thomas survived, he couldn't have gone to the river to search for his daughter, or bring her home, or dig that grave. He was bad hurt, Mr. Banning, bad hurt. I don't think he could have survived the night. As for Miss Duncan, she was hurt, too, when she went into the water. Kyle was rough with her, and so was the mountain. But she's a tough little gal. Maybe she did make it." He paused. "And maybe she had help."

"What makes you say that?"

"Just a hunch, I guess. There were no tracks that I could make out, but we've had a lot of rain, so that's not surprising. No matter how tough she is, I think it would have been damn near impossible for her to dig a grave and pull her pa to it all alone, especially if she was hurt herself."

"I don't like what you're saying, Ben. Susannah's untimely reappearance could complicate the situation, and I don't like the idea that we may be dealing with another, unknown person. I need to know who I'm up against."

"I don't know anything for certain, Mr. Banning."

Fletcher stood up and pulled a gold watch from his vest pocket. He observed the time, then snapped the piece shut. "For now, I think we'd better assume you're right. Alert the men to keep their eyes and ears open for any word of the Duncans. You check around town, discreetly, of course."

"Yes, sir." Ben stood up.

"Did you burn the cabin?"

"Yes, sir," Ben repeated. "If the deed was hidden somewhere that I couldn't find, it's ashes now."

"Good." Fletcher moved from behind the desk and walked with Ben to the door. "I'm going to town myself this afternoon for a meeting with Mr. Jackson, our illustrious assessor. Kyle went in earlier to make sure the county recorder doesn't have any information on the Duncan mine that we don't want known." He looked at Ben, his nose wrinkled in distaste. "Get cleaned up before you go into town, Ben. You smell like smoke."

Seven

Before he returned to Dr. Kennedy's house, Conor stopped by the Metropolitan Stable and rented a single-horse farm wagon, complete with horse, then continued on to the St. Clair Saw Mill and bought a supply of lumber. He left the wagon out by the doctor's small stable and came in the back door as Alexandra carried a plate to the sink. Lily Carolina sat at the table, carefully guiding a spoon to her mouth, and Jesse slurped with enthusiasm from a bowl on the floor.

"Hello, Conor," Alexandra said cheerfully. "What's all that?" She pointed out the window at the lumber-laden wagon.

"I couldn't help but notice that some of the boards in the stable need to be replaced," Conor explained. "The fence could use some work, as well. Since we'll be here for a few days while Susannah and Lily Carolina recover, I thought I'd help out with some of the chores."

Alexandra was surprised. "Why, thank you, Conor. I'd appreciate the help. I took over this property last fall, and did what I could to ensure that my mare and I would survive the winter, but I know there's more to be done. What do I owe you for the lumber?"

"Absolutely nothing, and I won't hear another word about it," Conor said firmly. "We owe you for your services." He held up his hand. "Not a word," he warned. "It's the least we can do."

Alexandra gave in. "Very well. I accept your kindness, with

thanks." She waved at the stove. "We saved you some soup. Are you hungry?"

"Yes, ma'am, I am," he acknowledged. "Hello, Lily Carolina."

"Hello, *Papa.*" Lily Carolina emphasized the last word.

Alexandra handed Conor a clean bowl. "Susannah just went back upstairs."

Conor frowned. "You let her out of bed?"

"She's doing fine, Conor. She was desperate to take a bath, and she ate with us. She was feeling a little tired, so she went back to bed."

"I thought we had agreed that I would bring her downstairs for her bath."

Alexandra arched an eyebrow at him. "Conor, if I felt there was any danger, I would not have let her come down." Her tone was mildly reproving.

"I'm sorry, Alexandra." Conor turned to the sink. "I meant no offense," he said as he pumped water over his hands.

"I know. You're worried about her." Alexandra gave him an understanding smile. "But she can't stay in bed forever."

"I helped her, too," Lily Carolina informed him.

Conor dried his hands, then touched the child's golden head. "Well, that makes all the difference," he teased. "How does your arm feel today?"

"Better. But Amy's arm doesn't feel so good. Dr. 'Xandra said she'll look at it after dinner. Amy might need a splint, too." Lily Carolina's tone was very solemn.

"Well, she'll be in good hands with Dr. Alexandra," Conor assured her.

"Why don't you go check on Susannah before you eat?" Alexandra suggested. "Put your mind at ease."

Conor nodded. "I'll do that." He dropped a kiss on Lily Carolina's head. "I'll be back in a few minutes."

He ran quietly up the stairs and tapped on the bedroom door.

At Susannah's call, he entered, closing the door behind him. The curtains at both windows had been opened, and soft sunlight filled the room.

Susannah sat on the edge of the bed, wearing Alexandra's blue wrapper over her nightdress. The bandage was gone from her head, and her hair was wet and falling down her back.

"I'm surprised you're up," he said. "How do you feel?"

She smiled weakly. "Better, now that I've had a bath."

"I wish you had waited until I returned so I could have carried you down the stairs," he admonished as he came close to examine the wound on her head. The gash had scabbed over and appeared to be healing well. He wondered if they'd be able to untie the hair knots that served as stitches without cutting off the strands of long hair. He hoped so.

"Alexandra helped me, Conor. I really am feeling better."

Conor sat next to her. "Why didn't Alexandra bandage your head again?"

"She will when my hair dries." A note of exasperation had crept into Susannah's voice. "Will you stop worrying?"

"I think you got up too soon."

Susannah shook her head in protest. "I have to start moving around, Conor. Besides, I desperately needed a bath." She untied the wrapper.

Conor helped her get her arms out of the wrapper. "We could have sponged you off up here." He stood up and watched as she scooted between the sheets.

"I wanted to wash my hair, and Alexandra has better things to do than wait on me hand and foot," she argued. She settled back against the pillows and pulled the blankets up to her chest.

"I could have washed your hair, and I could have sponged you if Alexandra was too busy." Conor threw the wrapper over the footboard.

Susannah's eyes flashed. "I think not, Mr. O'Rourke! We are

pretending to be married. I would not have allowed you to perform such intimate duties."

Conor planted his hands on his hips and glared down at her. "And why not, *Mrs. O'Rourke?* I've already seen most of your lovely body, and what I haven't seen, I felt that first day in the cave when I dried you off." He ignored Susannah's outraged gasp. "I've worked hard to keep you alive, and I don't want you to break your fool neck by falling down the stairs if one of those dizzy spells hits."

"A *gentleman* would never mention that he has seen a lady in a . . . a state of undress!" Susannah retorted. She crossed her arms over her chest in righteous indignation.

Conor unceremoniously pushed her legs over to make room for him to sit. "I've never claimed to be a gentleman. I only promised to behave like one while sharing this bed with you." He held up his hand when she opened her mouth to speak. "Please, Susannah, not now. We have business to discuss. I went to see Lucas McCleave, as you suggested. I hope we can trust him."

Susannah relaxed against the pillows. Conor was right; this was not the time to argue. Whether she liked it or not, she had to depend on the infuriating man. For now, he was all that stood between her and the Bannings. "I really think we can," she said quietly. "I've only met him once, when I came to town with Uncle Walter last fall, but I immediately liked him. And Uncle Walter was certainly no fool. He was a good judge of character, and he trusted him. Lucas was outraged by that lawsuit and was representing my uncle at no charge. I believe he is a kind, decent man, as well as one not easily intimidated. What does he think we should do?"

"He thinks *you* should do nothing but get better," Conor said firmly. "Meanwhile, McCleave will check the records at the County Recorder's Office. He said we have to get the title transferred to your name or the property will be put up for auction.

But he and I are concerned that if you come forward now, Banning will just file another lawsuit against you, and you'll be in the same position your uncle was." He hesitated. "How do you feel about selling the property, and putting an end to this?"

"There will be no end, Conor, until the Bannings pay for what they did to my father," Susannah said harshly. "And I hope you are not suggesting I sell to them. I'll die before I let the Bannings have that mine."

"Of course I don't mean sell to them. Sell to someone else. Then you'll be out of it. You surely didn't plan to work the claim yourself."

Susannah plucked at the quilt. "No. I don't want it. It has caused nothing but misery and death for my family."

He watched her sympathetically. Her face still seemed pale, with the exception of the bruised areas. Her drying hair lay on her shoulders and down over her breasts. To his surprise, his stomach tightened with a sudden rush of desire. Bruises and all, she was beautiful to him. Disturbed by the direction his thoughts had taken, he forced himself to focus on her bruised forehead as she spoke.

"Did you tell Lucas how my father died?"

"Yes."

"And?" she prodded. "What did he say? My father's death is a completely separate issue from the mine. Is Lucas going to the marshal?"

"Not right away."

Susannah sat up straight. "Why not?"

"Because we want to keep you safe, Susannah."

"What does that have to do with my father's death? Conor, I don't want to wait. Kyle Banning must pay for what he's done."

Conor nodded. "And he will. But not yet. Give McCleave time to find out what's going on. Men like Banning have their fingers in all kinds of pies, sometimes even legal ones."

Susannah stared at him. "Are you telling me the marshal is in league with the Bannings?"

"No. I'm telling you we don't know what is the best thing to do yet. We need more information. Your safety is our primary concern. You must stay here and get well."

"I will not just hide in this room, Conor. I want to involve the law, have the Bannings arrested. I want to tell Alexandra the truth." Worry and doubt clouded her features. "I don't understand why you won't do as I ask. I thought I could trust you."

Conor sighed. "And you can. Susannah, I'm just being cautious. Perhaps too much so, but that's better than not being cautious enough. Kyle Banning has already killed once, and Fletcher Banning wanted to see you. Who knows what he had in mind?"

"They will be brought to justice, Conor." Susannah's eyes flashed with determination and hate. "I'll make sure of it, if I have to do it myself."

"You won't have to. The law will take care of the Bannings, in time." Conor was concerned by the rage he saw on her face, and in her clenched fists, the tension with which she held her slender body. He deliberately changed the subject. "Have you given any thought to what you and Lily Carolina will do when this is all over, where you'll go?"

"Yes, but I haven't decided anything. And I won't until my problems with the Bannings are settled." She leaned her head back and closed her eyes. "I'm very tired, Conor. Maybe I did try to do too much too soon. I'd like to rest, if you don't mind."

Conor frowned at her sudden and obvious dismissal. "I'll be working on the fence for the rest of the afternoon. Call me if you need anything." He moved to the door and glanced back at her. "I think I'll go into town after supper tonight, maybe visit one or two of the saloons, see if I can learn anything."

"Do whatever you want," was her cool response.

Conor shook his head in frustration and stepped out into the hall, closing the door behind him.

Susannah opened her eyes and stared at the door. What was wrong with her? Why did Conor O'Rourke's concern bother her? She thought over the last few days. He had been nothing but kind to both her and Lily Carolina, and he had become fast friends with Alexandra. He was a charming man, an honorable man. Why did she find him so irritating?

"Because he tells me what to do," she snapped out loud to the empty room, folding her arms across her chest. She repeated his words like a litany. " 'You can't come with me to see to your father, Miss Duncan.' 'Don't follow me, Miss Duncan.' 'You shouldn't be out of bed.' 'I could have sponged you.' " She ground her teeth. "As if I'd let you wash me, Mr. O'Rourke." Even as she spoke the words, a picture formed in her mind of Conor's hands moving over her, his long, graceful fingers touching her in places no one had ever touched. Now the idea of him washing her was achingly appealing. Susannah pressed her palms to her suddenly hot cheeks.

She was fantasizing about a cowboy with no home, no goals, no future, who owned nothing more than what he could carry on his horse. On *one* horse. *A drifter,* for heaven's sake! Her grandmother would be appalled.

At that thought, Susannah sat up straighter. "Since when do I care what Grandmother thinks?" she demanded of herself. Her angry, unhappy grandmother had hated Thomas, had thrown the gentle, loving man out of her house the day they had buried Violette. Susannah's hands clenched into fists at the memory of her grandmother's hate-twisted face.

Just as Helene Robinson had never approved of her daughter's choice of a husband, she would never approve of a man like Conor O'Rourke. Not that Susannah cared; she doubted she would ever see her grandmother again. But she did wonder if she was following in her mother's footsteps. Her attraction to Conor could not be denied.

"There's a lot more to a man than his pedigree and his possessions, Grandmother," Susannah said to the image in her mind. "That will not sway me."

What would? And sway her from what? She had known the man for four days! He had made no declarations. "He only saved my life," she whispered. And her sister's. He had eased her father's final hours and buried him. She trusted him. She didn't always agree with him, but she did trust him. And she felt safe with him.

The sound of Alexandra and Lily Carolina coming up the stairs reached her ears. Susannah slid down under the blankets and closed her eyes, feigning sleep in the event they peeked in on her. She was in no mood to talk to anyone. She heard Jesse sniff at the door, but other than that, she was not disturbed. Except by the vision of Conor O'Rourke's handsome face.

Raucous piano music could be heard coming from the Silver Star long before Conor reached the saloon. He paused in the doorway. The Friday night crowd consisted mostly of miners evidently not concerned with the fact that tomorrow was a working day. Conor made his way toward the long bar on his left, his gaze traveling the smoky room. A red-haired woman in a bright yellow dress led a man up the stairs that climbed the opposite wall, her painted lips curved in a calculating smile. A makeshift stage had been built along the back wall. The flimsy structure shook with the enthusiastic efforts of three female dancers to keep time with the piano music. Only one was successful, a pretty dark-haired woman in a purple satin dress. She caught Conor's eye and smiled. Conor nodded to her, then moved up to the bar.

"Brandy, if you have it," he said to the waiting bartender.

"Sure do, mister. You want the good stuff or the not-so-good stuff?" The man wiped a glass out with his towel and set it in front of Conor.

"How bad's the not-so-good stuff?"

"Bad."

"In that case, I'll have the good stuff. And pour one for yourself."

"Why, thank you, sir. Don't mind if I do." The man set another glass next to the first one, then pulled a bottle from under the bar and filled them both. "That'll be one dollar."

Conor raised an eyebrow as he fished coins from his vest pocket. "At that price, this better be the good stuff."

"Oh, it is," the man unabashedly assured him. He lifted his glass, grinning beneath a flamboyant, well-waxed mustache. "To your health, sir."

Conor raised his glass. "And yours." He sipped the brandy, grateful to find that it was indeed the good stuff.

The bartender squinted at him. "Say, aren't you the fella that was in here a few days ago asking for directions to the Duncan mine?" The piano music abruptly ended, the noise replaced by cheering and applause.

Conor nodded, silently cursing the bartender's memory.

"Did you ever find the place?"

"No, I haven't headed out that way yet. Had some business to tend to in Denver." Conor drained his glass.

"Now what's this about Denver?" a breathless, feminine voice asked at the same time a small hand touched Conor's forearm. Conor looked down to find the dark-haired dancer at his side, her generous bosom heaving from the exertions of her performance. A fringe of jet beads decorated the low neckline of her dress and swayed in time with her breathing, as did the black feather that ornamented her hair. "What does Denver have that we don't have right here in Georgetown?" she purred.

Conor pulled his gaze from the interesting movement of the beads to the woman's pretty face.

"This here's Polly. She's one of my dancers," the bartender explained helpfully.

"Refill my glass and get Polly whatever she's drinking," Conor instructed. Maybe the pert little dancer with the big brown eyes could give him some information. He set his money on the bar and turned to Polly just as a lean man wearing double holsters grabbed her arm.

"What do you think you're doing?" the man demanded in a nasal, rasping voice.

"My job, as you well know," Polly retorted, jerking her arm free. She stared at him. "My God, Kyle, what happened to you? And what's wrong with your voice?" A merry grin lit up her face. "Did you wrestle a bear? Whatever or whoever you tangled with, you lost." She did not seem to notice the murderous expression in the man's eyes.

"You want your usual, Mr. Banning?" the bartender asked nervously, placing a full bottle within easy reach of Banning's hand.

Conor leaned against the bar, hostilely surveying the man. So this was Kyle Banning. Black half-moons colored the skin under Kyle's eyes next to his swollen nose. Conor was filled with admiration for Susannah; she had held her own. But surely she had not caused the bruises on Kyle's neck that his neckerchief could not hide. How had that happened?

Kyle glared at him. "Is there a problem, mister?"

"There will be if you don't allow the lady to finish her drink with me in peace." Conor's quiet tone carried a clear warning.

Kyle's lips tightened. One hand drifted down to rest on the butt of one of his two pistols.

"Kyle, honey, why don't you take the bottle and go on upstairs?" Polly asked hurriedly. She thrust the full bottle into Kyle's free hand. "It would be rude if I didn't spend a few minutes with this gentleman after he bought my drink. I promise I'll be right up."

Kyle hesitated, locking eyes with Conor.

"Please, Kyle," Polly begged. "You know this is my job. I'll get in trouble if you make a scene. I won't be long." She pushed him toward the stairs.

"Don't push me, you little whore." Kyle knocked her against the bar with his elbow, then walked away, speaking over his shoulder. "If you're not up in five minutes, I'm coming down, and I won't be in a good mood."

Conor steadied Polly and moved to follow Kyle. Polly jumped in front of him, her small hands braced against his chest. "Please don't," she whispered. Her eyes were huge with fear and pleading. "He'll kill you."

"No, ma'am, he won't," Conor grimly assured her. He looked around the crowded room, then up at Kyle, who had just topped the stairs. "But this is not the time or the place to settle my differences with that man."

From the landing, Kyle glowered threateningly down at Conor before he disappeared from view.

Conor forced his tense features to relax. "Let's finish our drinks."

Polly grinned, her relief evident. She snatched up her glass and clinked it against his. "Thanks for the brandy." She took a sip, her beautiful eyes twinkling impishly at him over the rim.

Conor could not resist smiling at her. There was something very appealing about the plucky dancer. "Just say the word if you don't want to go up there, Polly. I'd be happy to explain to Kyle Banning that you changed your mind."

Polly lowered her glass with a quick, nervous glance at the bartender, who had moved to the far end of the bar. "No, thanks. Kyle's one of my regulars." She shrugged. "He gets a little rough sometimes, but he's not too bad. And he doesn't come in often." She looked up. "What's your name?"

"Conor."

"Well, Conor," Polly drained her glass, then continued, "you can be one of my regulars, too." She set the glass on the bar and turned to him, placing a hand on each of his cheeks. "Anytime." She stood on tiptoes and planted an enthusiastic kiss on his mouth.

Caught by surprise, Conor's hands automatically settled on Polly's trim waist. "Anytime except now," he corrected, speaking against her lips.

Polly pulled away from him with a nod. "I'd better go," she said, her voice heavy with regret. "You come and see me, Conor." She took a step backward. "Thanks again for the drink, and for being willing to stand up for me."

"You're welcome, Polly." Conor lifted his glass to her in a salute.

She wiggled her fingers at him, then whirled and ran lightly up the stairs.

Conor emptied his glass and headed toward the door. He didn't dare ask the bartender any questions about the Bannings, and he didn't want to be around when Kyle Banning came back downstairs. He'd stop by in the next day or two and see Polly. Although she was Kyle Banning's lover, she did not appear to have deep-seated feelings of loyalty for the man. She would probably be willing to shed some light on the situation in town. Conor stepped out into the street. It was still early. Perhaps he'd have better luck at the Treasury Saloon.

An hour later, Kyle Banning came down the stairs and made his way to the bar, pushing a man out of his way. He motioned the bartender over with a terse jerk of his head.

"Yes, sir, Mr. Banning?" The unfortunate man furiously polished an already clean glass.

"Who was that son of a bitch?" Kyle demanded. He did not have to explain who he meant.

"I don't know, sir."

Kyle leaned over the bar and caught the man by the front of the shirt, pulling him forward. The glass fell from the bartender's hand and broke on the floor. "I said, who is he?" Other patrons moved away.

"H-he never gave his name, Mr. B-Banning. Only seen him a couple of times."

Kyle shook the man. "What do you know of him?"

"N-nothing, I swear, except that he came in a few days ago, asking for directions to the Duncan place. Haven't seen him since, until tonight."

Kyle's hold tightened on the man's shirt. "What did you tell him about the Duncans?"

"Only how to get there, n-nothing else." The bartender's eyes were wide with fear. "But tonight he said he hadn't been there yet; said he'd had business in D-Denver the last few days. That's all, Mr. Banning, I swear."

Kyle released the man with a shove that sent him stumbling against the back counter and stalked out the door.

Conor quietly let himself in Alexandra's back door, grateful that the lamp still burned on the kitchen table. The tall case clock in the parlor chimed one, the sound echoing in the silent house. He took off his hat with a weary sigh. Instinct had warned him against asking the bartender at the Treasury Saloon about the Bannings, and the bartender at the Depot Saloon had been of no help. With the exception of meeting Kyle Banning and Polly, the night had been a bust.

At the memory of the pretty dancer, Conor smiled. He poured himself a cup of lukewarm coffee and sank into a chair. Polly's image danced before him in the glass chimney of the lamp.

Conor saw again the attractive woman in the black-trimmed purple dress, the feather waving from the arrangement of her dark
hair, her warm brown eyes expressing her frank interest in him.
Polly was an engaging woman. A week ago, he would have taken
her up on her offer to become one of her customers. But somehow, in the course of the last few days, he'd lost his taste for the
casual relationships women like Polly offered. He longed for
something more.

In his mind, dark hair turned golden. Brown eyes turned
green. The fancy dress became a simple white nightdress. His
stomach tightened. Conor groaned and leaned his face into his
hands. As the days passed, as Susannah's bruises faded and her
wounds healed, he was finding it more and more difficult to see
her as a convalescing patient who needed his help rather than
as a lovely woman he longed to claim for his own.

Sharing a bed with her was proving to be a torturous arrangement. The memories of her beautiful body in the wet, clinging
undergarments haunted him. His fingers itched to travel over
her curves again, as they had when he dried her off that day in
the cave, a day that seemed so long ago, although it had not even
been a week. Surely he had known her longer than four days!

With a grimace, he forced down one more swallow of the old
coffee, then stood and emptied his cup in the sink. He blew out
the lamp and made his way down the hall. A tormenting picture
filled his mind as he climbed the stairs. He saw Susannah, imagined her waiting under the sheets for him, her magnificent hair
falling down around her, a welcoming smile on her lips, her
splendid eyes shining up at him as she pulled back the blankets
in invitation. And he cursed himself for a fool.

His hand curled around the doorknob. He shook his head in
self-ridiculing frustration, then slipped into the room and closed
the door without a sound. His gaze went to the bed.

She had left the lamp on. The soft light caressed the golden
perfection of her hair and kissed the pale skin of her beautiful

face. She lay on her side, facing the middle of the bed, and him. Her rosy lips were slightly parted, one hand flung out where he would soon lie.

Conor unbuttoned his shirt and took it off, his eyes never leaving her. The shirt fell unnoticed to the floor. His hands automatically unbuckled his gunbelt, just as his feet automatically moved him to the side of the bed. He hung his gunbelt over the headboard, then sank to a sitting position on the mattress. His shoulders slumped and he closed his eyes against the now familiar pain in his stomach, the raw longing that threatened to engulf him, the uncomfortable tightness in his groin. She stirred.

He looked over his shoulder at her. She rolled onto her back. Her even breathing continued. Without thinking, he turned and leaned down to place his lips on hers. His eyes closed as he focused all his attention on the feel of those soft lips against his. She sighed, and her mouth moved in response. Conor moaned, softly. He increased the pressure of his mouth, his lips parting, his tongue tasting her sweetness. His heart pounding, he pulled away and watched her eyes drift open. He lifted one shaking hand to brush a soft golden curl away from her cheek.

She smiled up at him, sleepily. "Conor." She breathed his name.

"I should not have done that," he whispered. "I'm sorry."

"No," she sighed. "It's all right." The smile did not leave her lips as her eyes closed again. "Come to bed." She pulled her hand to her side. Conor stretched out on top of the blankets. Susannah moved closer to him and rested her bandaged forehead against the side of his shoulder. Her even breathing told him she slept again.

He lay still for a long time, staring at the pattern of lamplight on the ceiling. The delicate scent of lavender assailed his senses, as did her light breath against the bare skin of his shoulder. He was painfully aware of her body, although the blankets separated them.

His thoughts raced. She had not protested his kiss. She had snuggled against him. But did she even know what she was doing? Had she fully awakened? She always slept so hard, almost as if she were drugged, and Alexandra had assured him that was normal with a head injury. Would Susannah remember his kiss in the morning? And if she did, would she be angry, or would she be glad for it? He had promised he would behave as a gentleman, and he had broken that promise. A gentleman would not take advantage of a sleeping woman, an injured woman. A gentleman would not share a bed, however justifiable the reason or honorable his intentions, with a decent, innocent woman who was not his wife.

With a muffled curse, he eased himself off the bed and blew out the lamp. He grabbed his pillow from the bed and his bedroll from the corner and settled on the floor. Still, although away from her lavender-scented warmth, it was not easy for him to sleep.

Susannah awakened in the early morning, feeling that something was vaguely wrong. Her gaze fell on the empty side of the bed. Even the pillow was gone. She sat up, suddenly fearful. Had Conor finally left them? As the thought came to her, a logical part of her mind responded with the knowledge that he would not have taken a pillow that belonged to Alexandra. Her breath came out in a sigh of relief when she saw him on the floor. She stared at his still form for a moment, then fell back on her pillow, her brows pulled together in a troubled frown. Why was he sleeping on the floor?

A memory tugged at her mind. Her fingers strayed to her lips. Had he kissed her last night? She closed her eyes in confusion. *Blast this headache!* The constant pain made it so difficult to concentrate, to remember! But she had an image of him leaning over her, his handsome face softly lit by the glow of the lamp, the look in his blue eyes one of tender longing. She felt again his lips on hers, gentle and caressing. Surely she had not dreamed it!

Her eyes flew open and found him again. What on earth was wrong with her? Her father was lying in his grave, his murder unavenged. Lily Carolina had a broken wrist, and she herself was recovering from serious injuries. She was now alone in the world, responsible for the safety, support and raising of her sister. She had no home, no family she could turn to, no work experience, and very little money. How were she and Lily Carolina to live? Her life was in a shambles, a potentially dangerous shambles, thanks to the Banning brothers, and all she could think about was Conor O'Rourke's kiss!

Susannah buried her face in her hands as the enormity of her situation truly hit her for the first time. What was she going to do? It had been easy to stay in this bed the last few days and let Conor worry about everything. But her problems were not his responsibility.

Conor had asked her to give him time, to give Lucas McCleave time. Very well. They had two, at the most, three days. If, at the end of that time, the situation had not been resolved, she would take matters into her own hands. She would be sufficiently recovered by then to fully shoulder the responsibility of her own life, and that of her sister.

She heard Conor stir. Her hands fell to her sides and she raised up on one elbow. "Good morning," she said.

"Good morning," he answered gruffly. He covered his eyes with his forearm.

Susannah hesitated, then asked, "Why did you sleep on the floor?"

Conor threw back the blanket. Susannah held her breath, then saw that he wore his pants. That was all he wore. He scrambled to his feet. "Because we had an agreement, and I broke it." His tone was harsh.

Susannah watched in bewilderment as he snatched up the bed-roll and pillow. "But all you did was kiss me."

"So you do remember." Conor advanced on the bed and tossed his pillow to its usual place. "Yes, Miss Duncan, all I did was kiss you. But no gentleman would have taken advantage of you like that, as injured as you are. From now on, I'll sleep on the floor. Alexandra will probably be moving Lily Carolina in here in a day or two anyway. You'll be safe from me." He flung the bedroll into the corner and stalked from the room.

Susannah lay back down, nagged by an irritating sense of disappointment. Now it was she who stared at the ceiling for a long time.

Eight

Late Sunday morning, Conor came in the back door, straw and dirt clinging to his clothes. He took off his hat and wiped his sweat-covered forehead. It had taken all day yesterday and most of this morning, but the repairs to the stable were finally finished. He checked the water reservoirs on the warm stove and was happy to see they were full.

The sound of voices drifted down the hall. He followed them and stopped at the opened doors of the parlor to see Susannah and Lily Carolina on the sofa, Jesse curled up on the rug at their feet. Susannah was reading from an open book on her lap. As Conor listened to her melodious voice, he realized she was reading from the Bible.

Conor leaned against the door frame and let himself enjoy the picture before him. Lily Carolina wore a plum-colored dress covered with a white, lace-trimmed apron. Her golden curls had been brushed to a shining softness and adorned with a ribbon that matched the color of her dress. Her right arm was cradled protectively in her lap, Amy snuggled at her side. She listened to Susannah with sincere intensity.

Conor closed his eyes at a sudden, severe rush of affection for the child. He had made certain to spend time with her over the past two days, to reinforce the story of being Lily Carolina's father, he had told himself. Taking care with her injured arm, he had guided her hands and patiently explained each step of sawing boards to size and nailing them in place. He had allowed her to help brush the horses. And each night he held her on his lap and read to her before he put her to bed. The little girl was stealing his heart, and not only was he helpless to prevent it, but he knew he'd never get back the part of himself that Lily Carolina had so innocently taken.

He opened his eyes, and his gaze fell on Susannah.

Alexandra had removed her bandage that morning. Her long hair was arranged in a becoming style, piled high on the back of her head. The hair ties were hardly noticeable, and almost all traces of bruising were gone. She wore a sprigged calico dress of dark green, its very simplicity highlighting her beauty.

As if she sensed his presence, Susannah paused in her reading and looked up at him. "Hello, Conor." A smile lit her face.

Conor nodded. "Hello." He could not help but notice that the color of her dress made Susannah's eyes a beautiful shade of green.

"Hello, Papa," Lily Carolina piped up. "Are you finished in the stable?"

"Yes, I am."

"Susannah is reading to me and Jesse and Amy. Do you want to sit with us?"

"Thank you, honey, but until I take a bath and get into some clean clothes, you won't want me sitting next to you. I'll join you later." He looked at Susannah. "Is Alexandra back from church?"

"Not yet, but I expect her soon."

Was there a softness in her expression? Conor wondered. The smile had not left her lips, nor had her eyes left his face. He nodded again to Susannah and turned to the stairs. Lord, he did need a bath!

A few minutes later, Conor was immersed in the large, high-backed tub, his clean clothes waiting on a hook by the door. His aching muscles welcomed the warmth of the water, and he closed his eyes with a sigh. He absentmindedly massaged his throbbing shoulder as he thought over the last two days. He had worked hard and, not surprisingly, slept little, for the floor did not offer a comfortable bed. He had spoken again with Lucas McCleave, and had finally agreed to let him meet with Susannah. Hopefully McCleave would bring some news when he came tomorrow.

With a frustrated groan, Conor slid down in the water until his head was covered. He sat up a moment later and lathered his hair. The sooner the Duncan sisters were settled, the better. He had to get on with his own life, for there would be no room for him in their lives, no matter how much he was beginning to care for them.

He was out of the tub and toweling his hair, dressed only in his pants, when he heard a strange voice in the kitchen. Instantly cautious, he dropped the towel and snatched his pistol from the shelf. In one quick movement, he opened the door and stepped through, his gun aimed.

"Oh, my!" A short, rotund gray-haired woman carrying a covered pot came to an abrupt halt not three feet from him. A very tall, very thin, white-haired man bumped into her from behind.

"Forgive me, precious," the man murmured.

Conor stared at the couple, as they stared at him. He lowered his gun, feeling unclothed and very foolish.

"Perhaps Alexandra has a beau, Horatio." The woman tilted her head back and perused Conor through the spectacles clinging to the end of her nose. "And a handsome one at that, although perhaps a bit underdressed for Sunday dinner."

"Uh, excuse me, please." Conor managed a smile, then ducked back into the bathing room, thankful to close the door. He returned the pistol to the holster and grabbed his shirt from the hook. That was the second time he had pulled a gun unnecessarily in Alexandra's house. He shook his head as he struggled into his boots. Who were those people? Did they know the Duncans? Had they seen Susannah and Lily Carolina? He strapped his gunbelt on, ran his fingers through his wet hair, and opened the door.

The kitchen was full of people. Susannah stood by the door, her eyes shining with ill-concealed amusement. Lily Carolina was at her side, holding the doll, and Jesse sat in front of her.

Alexandra turned to him with a smile. "There you are, Conor. I'd like to introduce you to some very dear friends of mine. This is Horatio and Minerva Potter. Horatio, Minerva, this is Conor O'Rourke, Susannah's husband."

"We've already met, in a way," Minerva tittered. "You must think me silly, Mr. O'Rourke, to have suggested you might be one of Alexandra's beaux."

Alexandra stopped in the process of pulling a hatpin from her hat. "You thought he was my beau?"

"Well, he came out of the bathing room wearing nothing more than his britches . . ."

"And holding a gun, dearest," Horatio interjected.

". . . and holding a gun, and he seemed to be quite comfortable in your house, so I assumed he was your beau, ready to do battle for you." Minerva opened the door of the oven, shoved the covered pot inside, then slammed the door shut again. The huge bouquet of silk flowers that decorated her outlandish hat waved drunkenly with her movements.

"You mean you *hoped* he was my beau," Alexandra said dryly as she removed her hat.

"Well, that was before I knew he had such a lovely wife and daughter. You'll have to find another man, Alexandra dear." Minerva bustled to the cupboard and took down a stack of plates.

Alexandra rolled her eyes. "Excuse me for a minute," she said, and left the room, hat in hand. Conor motioned to Susannah with his head. She nodded, then guided Lily Carolina to a chair.

"You and Jesse wait here," she said. "I'll be right back."

"We'll keep an eye on that lovely child, Mrs. O'Rourke. You don't worry about her at all." Minerva settled an apron around her thick waist and backed up to Horatio. He obligingly tied the strings for her. "Go on, now." Minerva shooed them out the door. "Horatio, dear, take this hat of mine. I can't cook wearing a hat." Her voice followed them down the hall.

Conor led Susannah to the parlor and closed the doors. "Do you know those people?" he asked in a tense whisper.

Susannah shook her head. "Not until today. Aren't they funny?" She was unable to suppress a smile.

"They could be dangerous," Conor snapped.

"For heaven's sake, Conor." Susannah put her hands on her hips. "You can't be serious. They are a sweet old couple who have come to have Sunday dinner with Alexandra. There's no danger in that."

Conor ran his hands through his damp hair. "I don't like it. I wanted to keep you hidden. Now, in addition to Alexandra, the Potters know of you, as does Lucas McCleave, and God only knows if any of Alexandra's other patients have seen you. The more people who know of you, the greater the chance someone will say or do something that will lead the Bannings here."

"Conor, you are carrying this too far." Susannah spoke in an angry whisper. "You can come and go as you please, but I can't. I am sick unto death of being cooped up in this house, and I welcome the company. Besides, you can't very well tell Alexandra she can't have visitors in her own home, can you? Not unless you're prepared to tell her the whole truth."

"It's dangerous to have them here," Conor repeated stubbornly.

"Perhaps it is," Susannah said as she moved to the parlor doors. "But the damage, if there is any, has been done. There's nothing we can do, except enjoy what promises to be a very entertaining dinner." She opened both doors simultaneously and swept out, meeting Alexandra in the hall. With a sigh of exasperation, Conor followed.

A little while later, when all were gathered around the table, Minerva bowed her head.

"Bless this food, Lord, that it may nourish our bodies as Your Word nourishes our souls. And please send Alexandra a nice man to care for and love, so that me and my Horatio can quit worrying about her. Amen."

Susannah pressed her napkin to her lips, determined to keep from laughing. She could tell by Conor's shaking shoulders that he was also struggling.

"For crying out loud, Minerva." Alexandra glared at her friend. "There's no need to bend the Lord's ear with such foolishness. There are far more serious problems in the world than my marital status."

"Or lack thereof," Minerva commented, not bothered in the least by Alexandra's scolding. "Horatio, dear, pass that ham, if you would." Her gaze fell on Susannah. "Alexandra tells us you were accosted by ruffians, my dear. How terrifying that must have been for you."

Susannah glanced at Conor, then accepted a bowl of potatoes from Alexandra. "Yes, it was. I was lucky to escape."

Minerva shook her head. "Imagine. Attacked on a public road like that. Now all travelers to and from Denver should be wary."

"It was on the river road, not the Denver road," Susannah corrected. She put a small amount of potatoes on Lily Carolina's plate, then passed the bowl to Conor.

"The river road?" Minerva eyed her over the rim of her spectacles. "Land sakes, honey, what were you doing way up on that mountain? There's nothing up there, except old Walter Duncan's mine."

"We were camped up there," Conor smoothly interjected. "Being new to the area, we didn't know any better."

Horatio nodded in understanding. "It is easy to get lost in these mountains, that's for sure."

Susannah looked up to find Alexandra's suspicious eyes on her, then watched as the doctor's gaze shifted to Conor.

"You don't strike me as the kind of man who would get lost, Conor O'Rourke, and I don't believe for one minute that you were," Alexandra stated flatly.

Conor looked down at his plate. An uncomfortable silence settled over the table.

After a moment, Alexandra cleared her throat. "Lily Carolina, what do you think of that ham? Is it as good as what you used to have in South Carolina?"

"Yes, ma'am, Dr. 'Xandra. It's very good."

Minerva and Horatio valiantly joined the effort to fill the silence.

Susannah met Conor's troubled gaze over the table. He was right. Having dinner with the Potters had proved to be a bad idea. Alexandra was more suspicious than ever. Susannah's shoulders sagged as she picked up her fork, although she was no longer interested in eating. How much longer would the lies have to continue?

The next morning, Susannah awakened early and, as had become her custom, lay quietly, deep in thought. The sound of Conor's even breathing reminded her of his presence, and she tried to ignore the confusing and irritating sense of loneliness she felt at being alone in the bed. She missed the feel of his body beside her. His presence was warm, reassuring. She glanced at the man sleeping on the floor and sighed.

It had been a week now since Conor had brought her here. That cold, rainy night seemed like a lifetime ago. Her bruises and scrapes had healed, and Dr. Kennedy had cut the hair ties from her scalp the night before. Thankfully, Susannah's long hair could be arranged to cover most of the area, and her hair would soon grow in. Although her head still ached constantly, the pain had dulled, and the dizzy spells had ended. She was mending fast. It was time to get on with her life, just as she had planned.

Conor stirred. She watched as he rolled over onto his back.

"Good morning," she said softly.

"Good morning, yourself."

She was struck anew by the beauty of his eyes. In the early morning light, they seemed to shine, highlighted by his hair and the dark stubble that covered his cheeks and chin. He wore his pants at night now, but, as was his habit, no shirt. The light touched his chest, showing off the expanse of muscles, turning the soft covering of dark hair to gold. Susannah turned away for a moment, disturbed by the sudden, painful longing that washed over her. She resisted the fascination she felt for the man.

"I'd like to visit my father's grave today," she said, more harshly than she intended.

Conor rose up on one elbow. "I don't know that you're ready to ride."

"I'll be the judge of that, Mr. O'Rourke. I cannot lie around here for the rest of my life. If you'll not take me, I'll go myself."

Conor frowned. *Mr. O'Rourke?* What was wrong with her this morning? "We can't go today. It's too light already; someone is bound to see you. Besides, Lucas McCleave is coming by this afternoon."

Susannah crossed her arms over her chest in frustration. She had forgotten that Lucas was coming. And she grudgingly admitted that Conor was right about the danger of traveling in daylight. Why was she so irritated with him for being right? "Then we'll go tomorrow, before first light."

"Yes, ma'am."

Now it was Susannah who frowned. Conor's tone had turned decidedly cool. But could she blame him? She sighed and looked at him.

"I apologize, Conor. You've been very patient with me

throughout this whole ordeal, and I've no right to talk to you in such a manner."

So it was back to "Conor" again. Conor shook his head in bewilderment. *Women!* He got to his feet, pulling the blanket with him. "That's all right," he said as he snatched his pillow from the floor. He tossed it to the bed and folded the blanket. "I'll wash up downstairs." He grabbed his gunbelt and his boots, a clean shirt and a pair of socks, and was gone.

Susannah stared at the closed door, biting her lip in guilty remorse. She pressed her hands to her temples. What was wrong with her? Why did she feel so out of sorts? Yes, her head hurt, but that was nothing new. It was more than pain.

A light knock came at the door, followed by the sound of Lily Carolina's voice. "May I come in?"

Susannah sat up against the headboard. "Of course, honey," she called with forced cheerfulness. The door opened to reveal Lily Carolina standing in her nightdress, barefoot, her long hair pulled into a sleep-tousled braid. Jesse rushed by the child to jump on the bed. His greeting to Susannah was boisterous and wet. She scratched his ears, then pushed him away with a laugh. "Lie down, you big oaf!" Jesse obeyed, happily curling up at her side.

Susannah watched her sister cautiously cross the distance from the door. She fought the urge to jump out from under the blankets and lead Lily Carolina to the bed. Her father's words echoed in her head. *Let her do it herself. She must learn not to be afraid.* Thomas had been so good with Lily Carolina, knowing instinctively what the little girl was capable of. He had never spoiled her, nor had he pushed her too hard. The realization that in addition to providing for her sister financially, she was also now responsible for Lily Carolina's well-being, education and upbringing filled Susannah with a crushing feeling of fear and self-doubt. Could she do it?

"Only a few more steps," she encouraged. Lily Carolina

reached the bed and climbed up. Susannah pulled the child into her lap. "How are you this morning, sweetie?"

"I'm fine." Lily Carolina's voice was muffled against Susannah's chest.

Susannah adjusted Lily Carolina's nightdress to cover her legs. "Your feet are cold," she said as she tugged on one small toe. Lily Carolina giggled. Susannah pulled the blankets over her sister's legs and held her close.

"I think I made a mistake, Susannah," Lily Carolina said in a mournful tone.

"I'm sure it can't be too bad," Susannah soothed. "Tell me about it."

"I called Mr. Conor 'Mr. Conor' instead of 'Papa' in front of the doctor. Does that mean the game is over?"

Susannah laid her cheek against her sister's head. "No, it isn't over yet. That wasn't a serious mistake. Many little girls call their papas 'Mister.' "

"Will Mr. Conor be mad at me?"

"Did you feel that he was mad at you?"

Lily Carolina thought for a moment. "No. He hugged me."

"Then I'm sure he won't be mad at you. He likes you very much."

"I like him very much, too. Susannah, is he handsome? I asked him, but he didn't know."

Susannah's eyes widened in surprise at her sister's question. "Yes," she answered softly. Conor's image filled her mind. "He's very handsome."

"As handsome as our papa?"

"He looks different than our papa, but yes, he's just as handsome."

"I thought so." Lily Carolina was quiet for a minute, then spoke in a sad tone. "I wish our papa was here. Will we ever be with him again?"

Tears filled Susannah's eyes. "Not for a long time, honey. I wish he was here, too. With all my heart." Her arms tightened around her sister. How would she support and raise this child on her own? As Susannah held Lily Carolina's warm little body, she realized why she felt out of sorts this morning. She was afraid of what the future held for them. In truth, she was terrified.

"Dr. Kennedy isn't here. She had a call and doesn't expect to return before supper," Conor explained over his shoulder as he led Lucas McCleave into the parlor. For the first time, he noticed that Lucas favored his right leg when he walked. "Susannah is upstairs. She'll be down in a few minutes."

"Good. I was hoping for an opportunity to speak to you alone."

Conor turned to find Lucas's stern eyes boring into him. "Say what's on your mind, McCleave."

"Your name was familiar to me, but I couldn't place it. I wired Texas."

"I figured it was only a matter of time." Conor indicated a chair as he sank onto the sofa. "I recognized your name the instant Susannah mentioned you. I'm glad to have finally met you. You were a legend."

"Only because I retired, and I only did that because I caught one bullet too many." He slapped his right leg as he cocked an eyebrow at Conor. "You were a legend yourself."

Conor shrugged. "It was all a long time ago."

"Why didn't you tell me who you were that first day in the office?"

"I knew of you, but I didn't know you. There's a difference. No offense, but even the best of us can go bad. My main concern was for Susannah's safety, so I figured the less you knew about both of us, the better. I feel different now, obviously, or you wouldn't be here." Conor met the older man's eyes. "I'd like to tell you that I'm honored to know you, Mr. McCleave."

Lucas leaned back in the chair with a satisfied nod. "I can say the same thing, Mr. O'Rourke."

Conor flashed a wry smile. "Then let's dispense with the 'misters.' "

"Fair enough." Lucas studied him, stroking his beard. "You had a lot of promise, Conor. You were a good Ranger, could have been great. I was sorry to hear it when you quit, and I never did understand why."

Conor shifted, wishing Susannah would come downstairs. "I had my reasons."

"I'm sure you did. I often wondered if it had anything to do with Everhart."

Conor remained silent. What the hell was Susannah doing?

Lucas continued. "I rode with him for a while, before you joined the Rangers. Dick Everhart was a good man, but he was a loose cannon, especially after his sister and her family were murdered. He went a little crazy, and I always wondered if that didn't help get him killed." When Conor did not comment, he added, "Maybe someday you'll tell me what really happened that day at Diablo Canyon."

"I doubt it," Conor said dryly.

Lucas shrugged. "Suit yourself. Like you said, it was a long time ago." He paused. "Did you know Ben Hollister works for Banning?"

That got Conor's attention. "Hollister?"

"Like you said, men can change."

"Still, I can't believe Hollister would work for Banning."

"Are you talking about Ben Hollister?" Susannah asked from the door.

Both men came to their feet.

"Yes," Lucas answered.

"He works for Fletcher," Susannah affirmed as she came into the room. "He was there that day on the mountain. He kept Kyle from shooting me." She held out her hand to Lucas. "It's good to see you again, Lucas."

Lucas took her offered hand. "And you, Susannah, although I regret it's under such strange and unhappy circumstances. My condolences on the loss of your father and your uncle." His fingers tightened on hers for a moment, then he released her. She settled onto the sofa, and the men took their seats.

"Thank you." Susannah blinked teary eyes. She wondered if the mention of her father would always make her feel like crying. "It's good to have a sympathetic friend." She glanced at Conor. "We have felt very alone in this matter. Thank you for coming."

"I would have come sooner, but Conor was very protective of you. He wouldn't tell me where you were." He sent a reproving look to Conor, who raised an eyebrow, but did not say anything.

"We meant no offense," Susannah assured him. "The situation is very delicate, and perhaps even dangerous."

Lucas absentmindedly stroked his beard. "I know. We must decide what to do, and quickly. Conor has probably told you that I could find nothing on your uncle's claim at the County Recorder's Office. I've waited to visit the territorial assessor because I saw Fletcher Banning going into his office last week, and I don't want to arouse suspicion by expressing interest in your uncle's mine. But I'll go tomorrow and see what I can find out. It's imperative that we get the mine title transferred to your name as soon as possible."

He looked at her, his gray eyes sharp and serious. "You must decide what to do with the property. I know Conor has spoken to you about selling it quickly, before Banning can file a claim against you. And there is the matter of your father's death. Justice must be served."

Susannah looked down at her hands, tightly clasped in her lap. "I know," she said quietly.

"How is your sister?" Lucas's voice was calm.

Susannah's head snapped up. She stared at Lucas, then turned accusing eyes to Conor. He held up his hands.

"I swear, I didn't tell him, Susannah." Conor was obviously as shocked as she was.

"No, he didn't," Lucas said. "Walter told me about the child the last time I saw him. He explained why he and Thomas had decided to keep her presence a secret, but he wanted someone outside the family to know should anything happen."

"Why didn't you ask me about her when I first came to see you?" Conor demanded.

"Because I wasn't sure *you* knew about her, Conor, and if you didn't, I wasn't going to be the one to tell you. I didn't trust you at first any more than you trusted me. Your story about finding Susannah was simply too convenient."

Susannah gently interrupted. "Obviously Uncle Walter trusted you a great deal, Lucas, if he told you about Lily Carolina. My sister is fine."

"Where is she? Is there anything I can do for her?"

"She's here with us, posing as our daughter. I'll bring her down later and introduce her." Susannah leaned forward. "Do you know anything at all about Dr. Kennedy? We hate this lie we're living, especially after she's been so good to us, but we are afraid to tell her the truth."

Lucas shook his head. "I've heard of her, but never met her. She's been in Georgetown for not quite a year, and tends to keep to herself."

"Then we must wait to tell her," Conor said firmly. He turned his attention to Lucas. "We all agree that the first thing to do is to get the mine title transferred. If Susannah then sells the mine, the Bannings should pose no further threat to her. When that is done, our next step will be to inform the law how Thomas Duncan died."

Lucas watched him thoughtfully. "You're the one who will

be in danger then, Conor. If I understand correctly, you are the only witness."

"Oh, Conor, it isn't right that you should be endangered because you helped me," Susannah cried.

"I can take care of myself," Conor assured her.

"We have another problem, one that I hadn't thought of before now." Lucas continued to stroke his beard.

Susannah stared at Lucas with bleak and weary eyes. What more could there be?

"You are the *only* witness," Lucas repeated. "It'll be your word against Kyle Banning's, and you can bet Banning will have a dozen witnesses who'll give him an alibi." He shook his head. "And you can't actually place Banning at the scene. You know only what Thomas Duncan told you."

"Doesn't a deathbed statement carry some weight in court?" demanded Conor.

"It does. But the court will need more information. They will probably insist on verifying the cause of death, which will mean digging up the grave."

"No," Susannah moaned. Conor looked at her. Her face was deathly pale.

"No offense, Conor, but it comes down to this; as far as the good people of Georgetown are concerned, you are an unknown drifter. You can change that image if you choose to, but if not, it will be a drifter's word against that of a man from a powerful and respected family, even though Kyle himself is not highly regarded. They could even twist it around that you killed Thomas Duncan."

"No!" Susannah cried. *"I* sent Conor to check on my father and told him how to get there. And Lily Carolina was there, too. Although she didn't see anything, she may have heard something." Her eyes widened as another thought came to mind. "My God. She was there when Kyle was."

The three exchanged startled looks.

"No one must learn that," insisted Conor. He tried to ignore the sudden pounding of his heart. Surely the Bannings would not hurt a little girl.

Susannah sank back against the sofa. "Kyle Banning murdered my father. He cannot get away with it." Her hands clenched into fists.

"He's already gotten away with one murder," Lucas said.

Both Conor and Susannah looked at him.

"Two years ago, shortly before I arrived here from Texas, tensions were escalating between the Bannings and the owners of the Eagle, a big mine on the south side of Blue Mountain. Banning filed one of his famous lawsuits against them over a lode he claimed was connected to his land. But the owners wouldn't settle. One day Kyle got into a fist fight with Max Treadwell, a part-owner of the Eagle. Max was trouncing him good, and when Kyle realized he was going to lose, he pulled his gun and shot Max in cold blood, right there on Alpine Street, in front of a hundred witnesses."

Susannah gasped.

"And no one did anything?" Conor demanded.

Lucas shrugged. "Kyle managed to get out of town, and the acting sheriff at the time was nowhere to be found. When he finally did surface a few days later, no one was willing to speak up because a band of Banning's men had terrorized the town. Kyle disappeared for over a year. The matter was dropped, and now is mostly forgotten."

Conor rested his elbows on his knees and leaned forward. "You're right, Lucas. We must be very careful."

Susannah was silent for several troubled moments. "Wait a minute." She looked from one man to the other, hope shining in her eyes. "I'm a witness against Kyle, too. I met him and his men on the road coming from my uncle's claim. Kyle told me he had seen my father and that he had . . . oh, what were his words?" She hesitated, pressing one hand to her aching temple.

"He said that Papa had not been nice to him, so he taught him some manners," she finished triumphantly.

Conor and Lucas exchanged glances. Neither man spoke.

Susannah watched them in confusion. "What?" she cried.

"Then you'll still be in danger, Susannah, no matter what you do with the mine," Conor gently explained.

"I don't care! The Bannings must pay for what they've done to my family!"

"What will become of Lily Carolina if anything happens to you?" argued Conor. "You're not alone in this."

Susannah fell silent. Despair washed over her. "Then what are we to do?" she finally whispered.

Lucas stood up. "For now, let's worry about getting the title transferred. Do you have anything to prove your relationship to Walter Duncan?"

Susannah frowned. "The Duncan family Bible, and a lot of family papers; marriage and death certificates, old letters, things like that. They were in the trunk." She looked at Conor questioningly.

"The trunk is still at the cave," he answered.

"We'll get it tomorrow," Susannah said firmly.

"Tomorrow?" asked Lucas.

"We're going to the claim. I want to see my father's grave."

Lucas raised a doubtful eyebrow. "I must urge you to use great caution, Susannah. Don't let anyone see you. Although I haven't heard of anyone asking about you, Banning's men have been all over town lately."

"We'll be careful," Conor assured him. He rose and moved to the door. "I'll get Lily Carolina." He disappeared into the hall.

Susannah stood up. "Thank you for coming, Lucas. I don't know what we'd have done without you. This has been an ordeal."

"I think you have Conor to thank much more than me, Susannah." He took her hand. "He's a courageous young man, and very devoted to you. How do you know him?"

"His cousin is a dear friend of mine," explained Susannah. "His story of finding me in the river is the truth."

"I know that now. You're very fortunate it was he that found you."

"Yes, I am," Susannah murmured. She frowned. She knew she was lucky. Had she ever told Conor that? Had she ever properly thanked him for all he had done?

She heard him coming down the stairs, heard him talking to her sister. He entered the room with Lily Carolina in his arms. Susannah realized in that instant that a powerful bond had developed between the man and the little girl. It was evident in how Conor looked at Lily Carolina, in how the child responded to him. A sadness washed over Susannah. He would leave them one day soon, when everything was settled. How would that affect her sister? How would it affect her?

"This is Lily Carolina, Lucas," said Conor. "Lily Carolina, say hello to Mr. Lucas."

"Hello, Mr. Lucas." Lily Carolina held out her hand.

Lucas noticed that the child did not look at him, nor was her hand held in his direction. "Hello, Lily Carolina," he said, and reached for her hand.

"Oh, you're over there," the child said with a giggle, and adjusted the position of her hand just as Lucas took it. Her head moved also, but it seemed she looked past him.

Lucas's eyes widened in startled comprehension.

"I guess Uncle Walter didn't tell you everything," Susannah commented gently.

"No." Lucas looked at the beautiful child. "No, he didn't. So much makes sense now."

"Did you meet Jesse?" Lily Carolina asked.

"Jesse?"

"Our dog," Susannah explained with a smile. She pointed to the large black dog at Conor's side.

"Hello, Jesse," Lucas said agreeably. He turned back to the little girl. "Yes, Miss Lily Carolina, I did meet Jesse. And now I must be on my way."

"Goodbye, Mr. Lucas." Lily Carolina shook his hand and released him. At that moment, the front door opened to admit Alexandra. She stopped in surprise at the sight of the group in her parlor.

"Hello, Alexandra," said Conor. "I'd like to introduce you to Mr. Lucas McCleave. Lucas, this is Dr. Kennedy."

Lucas held out his hand, which Alexandra accepted. "Nice to meet you, Doctor. I've heard a lot about you. You've been a great help to my friends."

Alexandra's blue eyes were alight with interest. "And I've heard of you, Mr. McCleave, though not from your . . . friends. I was not aware the O'Rourkes knew anyone in Georgetown." She glanced meaningfully at Susannah, then looked back at Lucas. "I'm pleased to meet you."

"Well, I was just leaving." Lucas accepted the hat Susannah held out to him. "Conor, Susannah, I'll be in touch. If you need anything, please don't hesitate to contact me. And goodbye to you, Lily Carolina." He gallantly kissed the back of the child's hand. "It was a pleasure to meet you."

Lily Carolina giggled. "You have a mustache, just like my papa! It tickles!"

The smile froze on Conor's face. He, Susannah, and Lucas exchanged worried glances.

Alexandra removed her hat and placed it over a curved arm of the coat tree. "Whatever are you talking about, child? Your papa doesn't have a mustache."

"Not Mr. Conor. My *real* papa," Lily Carolina explained innocently.

Alexandra stiffened. Her gaze settled on the three subdued

adults, one person at a time. "And where is your real papa, Lily Carolina?" she asked gently, the kindness in her voice a sharp contrast to the fierce expression on her face.

"He's with . . . my . . . mama." Lily Carolina's voice dropped. "Uh, oh," she said woefully. "Now the game is over, isn't it, Susannah?"

Susannah sighed. "Yes, honey, now the game is over."

"I'm sorry," the child whispered.

"It's all right, Lily Carolina," Conor soothed. "We were all getting tired of playing anyway."

"Lily Carolina, have you had your nap yet?" Alexandra asked.

"No, Dr. 'Xandra."

"Then come with me this minute. You, too, Jesse. You can keep this child company." She took the little girl from Conor's arms and started up the stairs, barking orders back over her shoulder. "The rest of you wait for me in the kitchen. Conor, put on a pot of coffee, and you'd better make it strong. By the time I'm finished with the lot of you, you'll be needing it."

Conor, Susannah and Lucas sat at the kitchen table, each silently nursing a cup of coffee, as Alexandra's approaching heels beat an angry pattern on the hall floor.

"Mr. O'Rourke." Alexandra's cold voice dripped over him, all the way from the hall door. "I'll start with you."

He hated being called "Mr. O'Rourke." It seemed he was always in trouble when people used that formality. Conor raised his eyes to her. "Yes, ma'am."

The doctor's arms were crossed over her chest, her lips pressed in a forbidding line, her eyes flashing fire. Conor inwardly groaned. Alexandra could hold her own with Minerva Potter any day. He was sure of it.

"You told me that neither of you were in trouble with the law."

"Yes, ma'am, and that's true."

She jerked her head in Lucas's direction. "Then why do you need the services of an attorney?"

"Because of another legal matter. But it's not a criminal matter."

Alexandra advanced into the room and stood across the table from him, her hands gripping the back of a chair. "Lily Carolina tells me that Susannah is her sister, and that you are not her father. Are you and Susannah married?" Her angry words seemed to echo in the small room.

Conor straightened his shoulders. "No, ma'am."

"You have been sleeping in the same bed with a woman not your wife in my house?"

Conor glanced at Susannah's red face, then at Lucas's suspicious one. "I've been sleeping on the floor, Alexandra. Ask Susannah." Given the doctor's mood, and Lucas's, Conor decided there was no reason to mention the first two nights he *had* shared Susannah's bed.

"He sleeps on the floor," Susannah interjected quietly. "He's been nothing less than a gentleman."

"You will tell me what is going on, Mr. O'Rourke, and you will tell me everything." Alexandra jerked the chair back and plopped into it. "Then it will be your turn, young lady, and finally yours, Mr. McCleave." She settled her gaze on Conor.

Conor leaned his elbows on the table. "I apologize for this, Alexandra. Susannah and I hated lying to you, but we felt it was necessary."

"Why, for God's sake?"

"Because of who we're up against."

"And who is that?" When he did not answer, Alexandra's eyes narrowed. "I said you will tell me *everything,* Mr. O'Rourke."

Conor stared at her. The memory of her many kindnesses to all of them over the past week flashed in his mind. No matter what Alexandra Kennedy thought of the Bannings, she deserved to know the truth. "What are your feelings toward the Banning brothers, Alexandra?"

Alexandra leaned against the back of her chair. "Of course," she breathed. "I should have known those two were behind this." She was quiet for a moment, then pierced Conor with her sharp gaze. "Who are you?"

"I didn't lie about my name, ma'am."

She looked at Susannah. "And you?"

"I am Thomas Duncan's eldest daughter."

"And Walter Duncan's niece. This is beginning to make sense now." Alexandra swept from her chair to pace the rug in front of the stove. "I *knew* you were in some kind of trouble." She glanced at Susannah. "I didn't know there were two Duncan daughters."

"You never answered my question," Conor pointed out. "Are you for the Bannings or against them?"

Alexandra whirled to face him. "I despise the Bannings, Conor. Fletcher is a ruthless man, determined to build an empire at any cost. He and his lawsuits! He has no care for the effect they have on the innocent; the miners who are thrown out of work, the families those miners can no longer support, the old, eccentric men like Walter Duncan who only want to mine their little claims in peace."

Conor watched in amazement as Alexandra advanced on him, her hands at her hips.

"And that Kyle!" she continued. "He's a bloodthirsty gunslinger who likes to beat up on women. He—" Alexandra stopped, her eyes widening in sudden comprehension as she stared at Susannah. "He did it, didn't he? He beat you."

Susannah nodded. "Yes, but what we told you about me going down the mountain into the river to escape Kyle Banning was the truth. We didn't lie about everything."

Alexandra slid into her chair, her gaze traveling from Conor to Susannah. "And you didn't tell me because you didn't know if I was sympathetic to the Bannings or not."

"Powerful men have a lot of allies, ma'am."

"Well, I'm not one of them," Alexandra snapped. "Where are Thomas and Walter, and how exactly do you fit into this picture, Mr. McCleave?"

"Thomas and Walter are dead," Lucas explained. "Walter of natural causes, Thomas by Kyle Banning's hand. I am working with Susannah and Conor to settle Walter's estate."

Alexandra's expression changed to one of shock and sorrow. She was about to say something when a knock sounded at the front door. "I'll be right back." She jumped up from the chair and was gone, closing the kitchen door behind her.

Susannah leaned back in her chair, staring thoughtfully at her mother's wedding band. She slipped it off her finger. The ring now belonged in the leather bag with the rest of her jewels. She sighed with relief. "I'm glad the truth is out, Conor."

He nodded. "So am I." He turned to Lucas. "I think we can trust her."

Lucas pulled a watch from his vest pocket. "I agree."

Alexandra stuck her head around the edge of the door. "It's the Potters," she said in a loud whisper. "Minerva is having another attack of the vapors." She rolled her eyes. "Swears it's from eating that ham yesterday. More likely her corset is too tight again. It's nothing serious, although she thinks it is. I'll be with her for a while." She looked at Lucas. "I'd like to know the rest of the story, and I'd like to help as much as I can. Will you join us for supper? We can talk more then."

Lucas snapped his watch closed as he stood up. "I'd be delighted."

A smile brightened Alexandra's attractive face. "Seven o'clock?"

"I'll be here." Lucas returned her smile.

Alexandra disappeared.

"I think I'll leave by the back way," Lucas said as he settled his hat on his head. "Minerva Potter is a sweet old woman, but she's insatiably curious. There's no need to get her wondering why I'm here." He moved toward the back door.

Conor rose. "She'll assume you're one of Alexandra's beaux," he said with a grin.

Lucas looked at him in surprise, then grew thoughtful. "I don't think I'd mind. Until tonight, then."

Nine

Only a hint of light touched the dark eastern sky when Conor and Susannah rode away from Alexandra's house the next morning. Charlie and Alexandra's gray mare were both anxious to run, and the riders had their hands full with the excited horses. They encountered no one on the way out of town, and by the time the sun had risen over the mountains, they had traveled over half the distance to her uncle's cabin.

Susannah pulled the mare to a halt at the dip in the road where she had rested her team the day Kyle Banning found her. Once again she looked out over the lovely valley.

"I used to dream of raising horses here," she said softly.

Conor followed her gaze. "It's a beautiful place, no question." He paused. "A little high for horses, though, at least all year around."

Susannah smiled. "I wondered about that. You wouldn't believe the amount of snow that falls up here. We were virtually snowbound on Uncle Walter's mountain. It's fortunate we all got along well together." She stared down the mountainside at the river far below. Conor waited, watching her face. Her eyes were hidden by the shadow of the felt hat she wore.

"It's a long way down there," Susannah observed soberly. "It's hard to believe I did it."

"I heard your scream, and saw you from across the valley, with my telescope." Conor pointed to a clearing that was visible on the side of the opposite mountain, then crossed his forearms over the saddle horn and leaned forward. "I was too far away to help you. You can't imagine how I felt."

Susannah turned to him. "But you did help me. You saved my life, Conor. I've often wondered why you got involved. You didn't know who I was. Why did you care?"

Conor shrugged. "I would have tried to help anyone." He straightened and took up the slack in the reins.

Susannah urged the gray mare next to Charlie and placed a gloved hand on Conor's arm. She looked into his eyes. "Thank you," she said quietly. "From the bottom of my heart, thank you. I haven't always shown it, but I appreciate what you've done more than I can say. If not for you, I surely would be dead, and I shudder to think what would have happened to Lily Carolina." Her fingers tightened on his arm as her lips curved in a shy smile.

Conor shifted uncomfortably in the saddle and covered her hand with one of his. His heart pounded in his chest, all because she had smiled at him! "You're welcome, Susannah. I'm glad I was there." She was so close. He fought the urge to kiss her smiling lips, and reluctantly released her hand. Without another word, they headed up the road.

They turned off the river road at the cutoff to Walter Duncan's claim. "Tell me how you and your family ended up out here," Conor invited.

Susannah shrugged. "There's not much to tell, really. After my mother died last summer, there was nothing to keep us in Charleston. We came out here a few months later. Papa's only kin was his older brother, Walter, whom he hadn't seen since Walter left for the gold fields of California in 1849." She shook her head. "Uncle Walter sure had the fever. He traveled around the West, following any rumor of a new gold find. Through the years, he stayed in touch with Papa. Getting a letter from Uncle Walter was always an event when I was growing up." Susannah smiled at the memories. "Then he found this place and, for some reason, loved it enough to stay, even though that old mine never gave him his glory hole."

"If he was older than Thomas, he had to be getting up there in years. Maybe it was just time to settle down. From what your father and Lucas McCleave have told me, Walter was contented with his life here."

Susannah glanced at him, surprised and pleased at his perception. "I think he was," she agreed. "He was an old dear. I'm glad I got the chance to know him, at least for a little while."

"How did he die?"

"Old age, I guess. He just didn't wake up one morning. It was in late February, the twenty-seventh, to be exact. Papa took it hard. We had to wrap Uncle Walter up and leave him in his beloved mine until the snow melted and the ground thawed enough to dig a grave." Susannah resolutely kept her eyes on the track they followed. "It's still hard to believe they're both gone." Her voice had dropped to a whisper.

Conor studied her profile under the hat. A tear coursed down her cheek. He urged his horse closer and caught the tear with his finger. "I'm sorry," he said softly. His hand did not leave her skin.

She leaned into his hand, and after a minute, straightened.

Conor twisted in the saddle and looked back the way they had come, then searched the area around them. He found nothing out of the ordinary, but something tickled his senses. Something was not right. He pulled Charlie to a halt.

"What is it?" Susannah asked.

"I'm not sure." Conor closed his eyes and listened, then breathed deeply of the morning air. His eyes flew open. "Smoke. Can you smell it?"

"Now that you mention it, yes, but just barely. Do you think it's someone's camp fire?"

"I don't know. I smell the smoke, but I don't see any."

They both searched the surrounding mountains, finding no visible signs of a fire.

"Let's go on." Conor pulled his rifle from the case and nudged Charlie forward. Susannah and the gray followed close behind.

After a few tense moments, Susannah gasped. "Conor, the cabin is gone!"

Conor's eyes riveted on the location where the cabin should have been. He saw nothing but trees.

The smell of smoke became more pronounced the farther they went. Finally they topped a small rise, and were able to see the blackened remains of the cabin.

Susannah slumped in the saddle as a feeling of devastation rushed through her. Even her home was gone, such as it had been. Although she had not intended to live there again, it hurt to see the total destruction. "The graves," she said wearily. "I must make certain they haven't been disturbed."

Conor led the way to the claim. The wagon still stood next to the small corral, looking forlorn and lost. He stepped down from the saddle and helped Susannah off her horse. She walked slowly toward the two graves as Conor tied the mare to the corral fence. He took off his hat and waited by the wagon, watching her. She stopped at the foot of her father's grave and stood straight and tall, holding her slim body with determined dignity. Her hands, protected by stylish riding gloves that seemed out of place, were tightly clasped in front of her. Conor was filled with concern and admiration for her. She was beautiful to him.

Susannah was not aware of his scrutiny. Relief washed over her when she saw that the two simple crosses had not been disturbed, nor had the piles of rocks. *Oh, Papa.* Her eyes closed against the crushing pain that circled her heart. She sank to her knees and sat back on her heels, lifting her face to the sky.

A tall aspen stood guard over the final resting place of the Duncan brothers. The morning breeze whispered through the young green leaves and coaxed the boughs of the neighboring pines to dance. A strand of golden hair brushed Susannah's cheek. A tear forced its way between the long lashes of one eye, then the other. Her lips trembled. Her brow wrinkled as another tear fell. She bowed her head and wrapped her arms around herself. The abyss opened and she stepped in. For the first time since her father's death, she allowed herself to cry.

Conor stepped forward as Susannah folded up. He twisted his hat in his hands for a long, undecided minute. Her body shook with the force of the sobs that tore through her. Finally, he could stand it no longer.

He tossed his hat in the wagon bed and strode to her side. With gentle strength, he picked her up and carried her a short distance, then settled himself on the ground against the trunk of a tree with her on his lap. He removed her hat and guided her head to rest against his shoulder. She plucked at the lapel of his duster and cried harder. He took off his gloves and with one hand stroked her hair, rocking her in the instinctive, age-old attempt to offer comfort.

Susannah cried until she could cry no more. Her sobs gradually quieted and she took a deep, shaky breath. Conor offered her his handkerchief. After removing her gloves, she wiped her eyes and nose. An occasional shudder ran through her as she relaxed against him. Her eyes fluttered closed and she slept.

Although his arm was beginning to ache and his legs had fallen asleep, Conor did not move. He breathed in the scent of lavender that emanated from Susannah's golden hair and continued his gentle stroking.

A half an hour later, Susannah awakened. She leaned back so she could see his face. He smiled down at her.

"Hello," he whispered.

"Hello." There was no answering smile.

Conor brushed back her hair. "Do you feel better?" He noticed that except for her red-rimmed eyelids, her face was very pale. After a long pause, she answered.

"I feel empty." Susannah's voice was flat, devoid of emotion.

"I expect that's natural." Conor shifted one leg into a slightly more comfortable position. "We'll stay here as long as you like, since we can't go back to Georgetown until after dark."

Susannah nodded against his shoulder. She focused on the cross over her father's grave. "You never told me exactly how my father died, except that he was in pain. Did Kyle shoot him?" she asked dully.

Conor's arm tightened around her. "No."

When he did not say more, she said, "Please tell me, Conor. I need to know."

Conor looked out over her head and sighed, wishing he did not have to speak his next words. "Banning beat your father, Susannah."

Susannah inhaled sharply. Tears filled her eyes again. "Poor Papa," she whispered. She remembered the pain she had endured from her own ordeal and knew her father's had been much worse. Her gentle, loving father had died in agony at the hands of a sadistic killer. Her knuckles whitened as her fingers squeezed the crumpled handkerchief she still held. She pictured Kyle Banning hitting her father again and again, smiling with the same sinister glee that had covered his cruel face when he had assaulted her.

She blinked away the tears; the time for crying was past. The sorrow that had filled her heart was put away, and a terrible, consuming determination took its place. Kyle Banning would pay, as would Fletcher. She did not know when, or how, but they would pay. They would pay with their lives.

Conor's quiet voice pulled her away from her grim thoughts. "I wonder if lightning hit the cabin."

"Banning did it."

Conor raised a doubtful eyebrow. "Perhaps." He could think of no reason why Banning would burn the cabin, but felt it was best not to say so. Suddenly his head snapped up, his eyes narrowed and searching. He scooted Susannah off his lap and got to his feet.

"What is it?" she whispered.

"I heard something." He shrugged out of his duster and tossed it toward her. She caught the garment and gathered it close. He shook one tingling leg, then the other, his eyes intent upon the trees behind the ruined cabin.

A twig snapped.

Conor's pistol was instantly in his hand, cocked and ready, pointed in the direction from which the sound had come. Susannah watched him in amazement.

It became evident that someone or something was coming toward them through the trees. Then silence. The mare nickered. Charlie shook his head in response, and both horses turned to look at the trees, their ears up. Conor knew that if it was a cougar or a bear, the horses would be much more nervous. He backed closer to Susannah. His shoulders slumped in relief when a doe daintily stepped around a full pine. She stared at them with large, innocent eyes, then wheeled about and bounded gracefully away.

Conor unconsciously twirled the pistol on his finger and replaced the weapon in its holster. He turned to Susannah and found her looking up at him in wonder, the depths of her eyes shining green in the dappled sunlight. His brow furrowed in confusion. "What?"

"I've never seen anyone pull a gun so fast." She struggled to her feet, still clutching his duster. "My God, Conor, I couldn't see your hand move."

Conor shrugged.

Susannah stepped closer to him. "I'll bet you're faster than Kyle Banning."

"So what?" He marched over to Charlie's side and threw the stirrup up over the saddle. He did not like the direction this conversation was taking.

Susannah came up behind him and watched as he tightened

the cinch. "We'll have a hard time proving Kyle killed my father if we accuse him. Chances are the law will do nothing. If we don't do something, Conor, the Banning brothers will get away with murder."

Conor pulled the stirrup back into place. He leaned on the saddle for a moment, then turned to face Susannah, crossing his arms over his chest. "Why don't you just tell me outright what you're suggesting?" His voice was low and dangerous.

Susannah did not seem to notice. "I want you to kill the Bannings." Her eyes were bright with eager desperation.

Conor could only stare at her. Disappointment and pain slammed into his stomach as if she had hit him there. "Is that what you think of me?" he demanded. "That because I'm fast with a gun, I am also a cold-blooded killer?"

"No!" Susannah let the duster slip to the ground and placed a hand on his arm. "The Bannings are responsible for my father's death, and the law is not going to do anything about it. They deserve to die!"

Conor pulled away from her touch and retrieved his duster. As he tied it behind the saddle, his words came out like bullets. "I would kill to defend you, but I will not kill *for* you."

Susannah whirled away, twisting the handkerchief. Her mind raced as her eyes roamed over the blackened ruins of the cabin. The stone chimney stood steadfast against the sky, a lonely sentinel, reminding her again of all the Bannings had taken from her family. There had to be some way to convince Conor to help her! She glanced back over her shoulder. By the set of his jaw, she knew he'd not change his mind about killing the Bannings. She bit her lip. Her eyes widened as the answer came to her.

"Then you'll teach me to shoot as well as you can, and I'll do it myself. It's not really your battle, anyway."

Conor turned to her, incredulous. "Did I hear you correctly?"

"It's the perfect solution, Conor." Susannah stepped closer to him.

"No."

"Conor, you must." She clutched his arm.

"Absolutely not, Susannah. Get this ridiculous notion out of your head. The law will take care of the Bannings." He pulled away from her again and moved around Charlie to the mare.

"No, the law won't. You heard Lucas yesterday. Fletcher Banning is too powerful. He's prominent in territorial politics, and I've heard he even has friends in Washington. He can buy anyone. He'll ensure that Kyle has a solid alibi for the day of my father's death." As she spoke the words, she knew in her heart they were true. Kyle Banning would never be convicted of killing her father in a court of law. Her determination flared to new heights. "Please, Conor, I beg you. I know a little about guns, but not enough. Teach me to shoot like you can. I'll pay you for your time."

"I don't want your money." He ground the words out without looking at her. "And it took years of practice for me to get as fast as I am. You won't learn in a few days." He checked the cinch.

Susannah had not thought of that. Of course it had taken him years. How fast could she get in a week? Faster than she was now, that was for sure. He simply had to teach her. She tried a different approach. "I should know how to shoot anyway, so I can protect myself and Lily Carolina."

Now Conor whipped his head around to glare at her. "It's about time you remembered your sister. You won't be able to practice shooting in Alexandra's kitchen, so who is to care for Lily Carolina while you're off somewhere learning to be a gun hand? Suppose you fail and they kill you instead? And what if you actually succeed? Who will care for her when you are hung for murder?"

Susannah shrank from the fury and disgust in his eyes. "It won't be murder," she said defensively. "It will be justice."

"You're talking about murder, Susannah, no matter how jus-

tified you think it is. You'll be no better than the Bannings." He
took a step toward her. "Let go of it. The Bannings should be
punished for what they have done, but not like this. Your father
would not want you to do this."

Susannah's bottom lip trembled at the mention of her father.
She turned away from Conor and walked to her father's grave.
After a few minutes she sank to the ground, deep in thought,
her skirts swirled around her. Conor waited by the corral for a
while, then came to her side. "We should go on to the cave."

She did not appear to have heard him. "I apologize if I insulted
you," Susannah said formally. She did not look up at him. "But
your refusal to help me does not change anything."

Conor's brow furrowed. Her voice sounded very strange.
"What do you mean?"

"You won't help me, Mr. O'Rourke. I'll find someone who
will."

"Susannah . . ." Conor rolled his eyes.

"I mean it, sir! I will go to Denver and hire a teacher." Susannah scrambled to her feet, her lovely face void of all expression
except for the burning resolve in her eyes.

A chill ran down Conor's back. She was deadly serious.

When he made no reply, Susannah stepped onto the pile of
rocks at her feet. She stared at Conor until he met her eyes.

"I cannot go on pretending nothing has happened. There will
be no peace for me until the Bannings are brought to justice."
She raised a fist to the sky, and her clear voice rang out over
the homestead. "I swear on my father's grave that his death will
be avenged. I swear the Bannings will pay for what they have
done to my family, so help me God." Her arm fell to her side.
She did not look away from him as she stepped off the rocks.
"With or without your help, Conor O'Rourke."

The expression on her face frightened him. He had never seen
her like this, and somehow he knew it was not an act. "I'll teach
you to shoot."

"And what is your price?"

Conor turned away. "There will be no charge, Susannah." He stalked to the wagon and retrieved his hat.

"I'll pay you fifty dollars." She walked to the tree where her own hat waited.

"I said there will be no charge." Conor clapped his hat on his head.

"And I said I'll pay you fifty dollars. I will accept no other terms." She smoothed her tangled hair with one hand, then put on her hat and tightened the string under her chin.

"Yes, *ma'am!*"

Susannah picked up her gloves from the ground and pulled them on, smoothing the soft leather over fingers that trembled.

Conor untied the mare and led the animal from the fence. Susannah joined him and handed him his gloves. She did not look at him as she accepted the reins and allowed him to help her into the saddle. When she was settled, he snatched up Charlie's reins.

"What are your plans now, Mr. O'Rourke?"

He gritted his teeth. He hated it when she called him "Mr. O'Rourke"! "We'll go to the cave, *Miss Duncan,* and see if there is anything you want to take back to Alexandra's." He vaulted into the saddle.

"I won't be returning to Alexandra's house today."

With exaggerated patience, Conor leaned on the saddle horn and pushed his hat back on his head. "Then why don't you just save us both a lot of time and tell me what your plans are?"

Susannah urged the mare to Charlie's side. "We'll go to the cave, where you will leave me. Since you can safely travel in daylight, you will take Alexandra's mare back to town, as well as anything else we decide to send. When you return, bring Lily Carolina with you. My sister is my responsibility, and I'll care for her." She kicked the mare's sides and coaxed her to a walk.

Conor positioned his hat in its proper place. He could do nothing but follow. Susannah continued the cold recitation of her plans.

"You know where Uncle Walter's gold bag is, in the bureau drawer. Purchase a gun for me, as well as ammunition and anything else you think we might need. I will trust your judgment."

"Thank you *so* much!" Conor drew alongside of her.

Susannah ignored his comment. She sat rigidly in the saddle, unmindful or uncaring that because of riding astride, her skirts were hitched up to her knees, revealing shapely calves in dark stockings. "I'll expect you and my sister back at the cave sometime tonight, and we will begin my training tomorrow at first light."

"Yes, ma'am," Conor snapped. "Is that all?"

"For now, Mr. O'Rourke, yes, it is. I would like to ask you a question, though."

"Oh, by all means, miss." Conor waved his arm in a sarcastic gesture.

"Why did you stay with my sister and me once you got us to the safety of Dr. Kennedy's house?" She still would not look at him.

Her question surprised Conor. He decided to tell the truth, or at least part of it. "Because I promised your father I would see you safely through this, Miss Duncan. I gave my word to protect you from the Bannings and to see you and Lily Carolina settled, and I will, if it kills me."

Susannah's heart lurched. Why did his answer cause her pain? "Then you're here only because of a promise," she said quietly, bitterly.

Conor watched her. His promise was not the only reason he had stayed, but he did not dare tell her that. Not now. He said nothing. Her next words surprised him even more.

"I release you from your vow, Mr. O'Rourke. While I understand my father's fears for us, my sister and I do not need you, not any longer. When my training is finished, you'll be free to leave. Until then, I will pay you for your time."

With a curse, Conor leaned over and caught her reins, forcing both horses to a halt. "Listen to me very carefully, Miss Duncan." His eyes bored into hers, his fury making them a glorious blue. "I gave my word to your father, and only he can release me from it. Since he can't, and probably wouldn't if he could, you're stuck with me, whether you like it or not. I will do as you wish tonight, but starting tomorrow, you will do as *I* say. You've hired me to train you to shoot, and by God, I will."

Susannah tugged her reins from his grasp. "Agreed, Mr. O'Rourke. Shall we go?" When Conor did not stop her, she kicked the mare to a lope and rode away from him.

Conor stared after her, desolation sweeping over him. He felt that something beautiful and full of hope had been destroyed beyond repair. Where had the sweet woman he had come to know and care for during the long days of her recovery gone? The hard-hearted woman who had taken her place was a stranger to him, a stranger he wasn't sure he liked. With a weary sigh, he adjusted his hat against the late morning sun and allowed Charlie his head. The stallion jumped to a gallop and gladly chased after the mare.

Ten

Conor let himself in Alexandra's back door, then crossed the kitchen and shifted Susannah's trunk from his shoulder to the floor in the corner by the bathing room. Jesse barked as he raced down the hall from the parlor. The big dog skidded to a stop at Conor's side, his tail wagging furiously. Joyous whimpers came from his throat as he licked Conor's hand.

"Hello, Jess." Conor dropped to one knee, genuinely happy to see the dog. He had become attached to all of Susannah's family. *Too bad she doesn't like me as much as Jesse does,* he thought sadly.

"You're back early." Alexandra's worried voice preceded her into the kitchen. "Susannah shouldn't be out during the day." She paused. "Where is she?"

Conor straightened. "At the cave. She wouldn't come back." He took off his hat and ran a hand over his hair. "Where's Lily Carolina?"

"Down for her nap, unless that fool dog woke her up with his infernal barking." Her words did not disguise her affection for Jesse. Alexandra studied Conor's face, finding worry, fatigue, and most disturbing, sadness. "Let's talk, Conor. Sit yourself down." She took the whiskey bottle and a glass from the cupboard as Conor obeyed her.

"It's like something inside Susannah snapped when she saw her father's grave, Alexandra. I don't know what to do." He gratefully accepted the glass she pushed toward him. "She said the law would never bring Kyle Banning to justice for her father's murder." Conor glanced up. "She's right." His gaze dropped back to the table.

Alexandra waited.

"She asked me to kill the Bannings."

"Oh, Conor, no." Alexandra laid a hand on his arm.

"That's what I told her. So she insisted I teach her to shoot. Said it was her fight."

"She's just overwrought."

"No, it's more than that." Conor twisted the untasted glass in his hands. "She threatened to go to Denver if I didn't teach her. Find someone there who would." He raised tormented eyes to Alexandra's face. "She meant it."

"What did you tell her?"

"I agreed to teach her." He shrugged. "What else could I do? At least this way I can keep an eye on her." He finally sipped from his glass, then continued. "I know how she feels. If the Bannings had killed my father, I swear, I'd see them brought to justice, even if I had to kill them myself. Nothing would stop me. Susannah is at that point."

Alexandra sighed. "I suppose I would feel the same. But what about her sister? Lily Carolina needs her."

"She wants me to bring her with me when I go back. She said Lily Carolina is her responsibility."

"Go back where?"

"The cave. She wants to stay up there for a week or so."

"Conor, you can't take that child into the wilderness. She has a broken wrist, for heaven's sake! And it wouldn't be good for her to be there when Susannah is so upset. I won't allow it."

Conor flashed her a weary, grateful grin. "I agree. Will you keep her?"

"As if I'd let anyone else take care of her. You know I'll keep her."

A knock sounded at the front door. "I'll be right back," Alexandra said. She disappeared down the hall. A moment later she cried, "Conor! Come quickly!"

Conor hurried down the hall to find Alexandra struggling to support a blood-covered woman in a torn dress. He caught the woman up into his arms and carried her into the examination room, where he laid her on the table. "My God," he whispered at the sight of her battered face. "Polly."

Alexandra washed her hands. "Do you know her?"

He nodded. "Her name is Polly. She's a dancer at the Silver Star Saloon."

Polly's eyes opened. She focused on Conor's face and tightly held his hand. "Hello, handsome," she whispered. "You didn't come back to see me."

"No, not yet." He smiled and brushed her hair back from her forehead. "What happened, Polly? Now it looks like you're the one who tangled with a bear."

"Not a bear. A bastard." Her hold on his hand tightened, and her face twisted with pain.

Conor met Alexandra's gaze, then looked back down at Polly. "It was Banning, wasn't it?"

"The son of a bitch," Polly spat. "I told him I wouldn't be with him if he hit me. I won't allow any of them to hit me. Kyle Banning won't touch me again."

Alexandra laid a wet cloth on Polly's head. "Shh. You rest now. It's going to hurt some when I clean you up."

"Where is he?" Conor's voice was cold and deadly, his rage barely controlled.

Polly shook her head. "Gone. Back to his brother's place." She squeezed his hand again. "Stay out of it, Conor. He'll kill you. He's killed before."

"I told you: he won't kill me." He patted her shoulder and eased his hand from her grip. "He has to be stopped, though. He seems to delight in beating on women and old men."

"And shooting unarmed men in cold blood." Alexandra's

voice was tight and sharp. "Conor, put the kettle on in the kitchen, will you? We can't worry about Kyle Banning now."

Conor clenched his fists and left the room. Alexandra was right. He needed to get back to Susannah. Kyle Banning's day would come.

When Alexandra had Polly cleaned and bandaged, and dressed in a borrowed nightdress, Conor carried her up to the room he had shared with Susannah.

"I can't stay here," Polly protested weakly as he laid her on the sheets.

"You can and you will," Alexandra ordered from the door. "You need nursing for a day or two, and rest, and you won't get either at the Silver Star."

"But my job . . ."

"You'll stay here," Conor said firmly. "For as long as Dr. Kennedy tells you to. I'll stop in at the saloon and explain that you'll be taking a few days off."

Polly reached for his hand. "Will you be here?"

"No. I'll be away for a few days, maybe a week." He smiled at her. "But I'll check on you when I get back."

Polly's brow furrowed. "Be careful. He was asking about you, Conor. He's crazy to know who you are, and where you are. He even roughed up the bartender." Her eyes fluttered closed.

"Just sleep now, Polly." Conor took some clothes from the drawers of the bureau and left the room, following Alexandra downstairs. The doctor marched into the examination room and began to clean things up. Conor watched from the door as she slammed drawers closed and threw bloodied instruments into the basin. He dodged a soiled towel she threw in the direction of the door.

"What is it?" he asked gently.

"I told you I don't hold with men hitting women. It makes me insane." Alexandra began to pace the room. "Banning did this to another woman last winter, a woman who worked over at the Treasury. He almost killed her, Conor. She was just seventeen, and her face will wear the scar he gave her for the rest of her life. But no one cares if a man beats a whore." She paused. "Any more than they care if a man beats his wife," she finished almost under her breath.

Conor set the clothing he carried on the side table in the hall and stepped into the room. "Tell me about it, Alexandra. Why is this so personal for you?" His voice was soft with understanding and compassion.

Alexandra stopped her frenzied pacing and stared at him, startled. "You are very perceptive, Conor O'Rourke," she said tightly. Her shoulders sagged and she twisted her hands together. "It was my younger sister. Her name was Deborah. She married a man who took her to Boston to live, far away from her family and friends. I later learned the violence had started soon after that."

She resumed her pacing. "One day I received a wire that my sister had fallen down the stairs and was dying of internal injuries. I got there just in time to say goodbye. She was only nineteen." She faced Conor, her eyes filled with tears. "She told me what had actually happened, said it had been going on for months. She begged his family for help, but he was a prominent and respected man, and no one believed her. I would have, if only she had confided in me. She said I was too far away. That was the worst of it, Conor. I would have gone to her if I had known, no matter how far it was."

Conor put his arms around her and held her close. "I'm so sorry."

Alexandra sniffed against his shirt. "He broke not only her body, but her spirit as well. I'll never forget the absolute hopelessness in her eyes. She welcomed death."

"What happened to the bastard?"

"You know me." Alexandra shrugged. "I get pretty pigheaded sometimes. I pressed charges, caused a big stink, even though he came from a powerful old Boston family. The coward committed suicide rather than face a trial. And I mysteriously lost my license to practice medicine in the state of New York, and no other state along the eastern seaboard would grant me a license. That's how I ended up out here."

"No wonder you thought I hurt Susannah."

Alexandra sniffed again. "I was so wrong about you. I still feel bad about that." She pushed away from him, suddenly businesslike. "You'd best get going. You need to get back to Susannah before dark." She wiped her eyes with a corner of her apron.

"I want to see Lily Carolina first."

Alexandra nodded. "Wake her up. She's had plenty of sleep." She looked at him, saw the concern on his face. "Go on with you. I'll be fine."

Conor took the stairs two at a time. He eased the door to Alexandra's bedroom open.

"Who's there?" Lily Carolina asked from her prone position on the bed.

"It's Conor, honey." He moved to the side of the bed.

Lily Carolina sat up. "Is Susannah with you?"

"No, but Jesse is."

The dog jumped up on the bed and greeted Lily Carolina with a lick on the cheek. The child giggled as Jesse curled up at her side.

"Where's Susannah?"

"Do you remember the cave we stayed in last week?"

"Yes. It was smoky and cold."

"That's where Susannah is. She and I are going to stay there for a few days." Conor took Lily Carolina's hand in his.

The little girl's brow wrinkled with worry. "Can I go, too?"

Conor's heart lurched. "No, Poppet, you have to stay with Dr. Alexandra and Jesse. They need you here."

"But I want to go with you." Her bottom lip trembled. "Please?"

"Ah, honey." Now Conor felt that his heart was being torn in two. He pulled the child onto his lap and held her close, one hand stroking her soft curls. "I wish you could, but your arm needs to heal."

"This stupid old arm!" Lily Carolina slapped the bandage. "I hate it!" She started to cry. "Please, Mr. Conor, t-take me with you. What if S-Susannah forgets me? What if you never come b-back?"

Conor tightened his hold on her. "I promise that won't happen," he fiercely vowed. "Susannah and I both love you very much. We could never forget you, and your sister would never leave you." His words did not surprise him. He loved this child with all his heart. The fact that one day he would have to leave her caused a terrible ache to settle in his gut.

Her sobs eased. "But you're leaving now," she said, her young voice filled with sadness. "Mama left, and so did Papa, and they didn't come back."

"They didn't want to leave, Lily Carolina, and if they could come back, they would. Susannah and I don't want to leave, either, but we have to, for a little while. I swear to you, we'll come back."

"Promise?"

"I promise." He kissed her forehead. "You like Dr. Alexandra, don't you?"

"Oh, yes. Amy likes her, too, 'cause she fixed her arm, and Jesse likes her, too. He told me so."

"Well, let's go find her then." He reached for the doll that rested on the pillow and smiled to see a neat little splint on the doll's left arm. "Here's Amy. You carry her and I'll carry you."

Lily Carolina clutched the doll, and he stood up with the child in his arms. "Dr. Alexandra has a patient now, Lily Carolina." He moved to the door. Jesse jumped off the bed and followed.

"What's a patient?"

"A sick person who comes to see the doctor. A real nice lady named Polly got hurt, and she'll be staying here for a few days, in Susannah's room. So you must remember to be very quiet, because Polly needs to rest." As he reached the bottom of the stairs, the front door flew open to reveal Minerva and Horatio Potter.

"Well, Mr. O'Rourke! How nice to see you again. Horatio, dear, take my shawl. I want to say hello to Lily Carolina." Minerva Potter bustled through the doorway, her formidable bosom leading the way, her shawl held out behind her.

"Yes, precious." Horatio accepted the shawl. "Hello, Mr. O'Rourke."

Conor nodded a greeting and set Lily Carolina on her feet. She daintily curtsied to the Potters.

"My goodness, child," cried Minerva as she pulled a long pin from her unusual hat. "Your curtsy is pretty enough for Queen Victoria over in England. Horatio, dear, take my hat."

She flung her arm out, causing the large, strange-looking bird that decorated the hat to bob up and down. Her hapless husband accepted the monstrosity and carefully placed it on the side table.

"Poor Horatio has a touch of the gout," she explained cheerfully. "Alexandra can always fix him up, so we decided to come right away." She took Lily Carolina's hand. "Come, child. I'll bet we can find Dr. Alexandra in the kitchen."

Lily Carolina hesitated. "Mr. Conor, when are you leaving?"

Neither of the Potters seemed to take notice of what Lily Carolina called him.

"Later this afternoon, honey. I need to get some supplies. I'll come back and say goodbye." He bent down and kissed Lily Carolina's cheek. "I promise."

"All right," she said, squeezing her doll. She allowed Minerva to lead her down the hall. "Come with me, Jesse." The little girl's sad voice trailed back to Conor. "I need you." She disappeared into the kitchen, followed by Jesse and Horatio.

Conor stared after her, suddenly filled with anger toward

Susannah. "You need your sister, too, honey," he muttered. "And she's not here for you."

Susannah paced back and forth in front of the cave. The sun had gone down behind the mountains over an hour ago, and there was a definite chill in the air. Where was Conor? Surely he should have been back by now.

She stared across the little clearing in the direction from which he would come, straining to hear any sound. Only the wind spoke to her, whispering through the trees. It would be dark soon. She shivered and hugged herself.

He wouldn't have left her for good. Not like this, with very little food and no horse. He wouldn't. He was bringing Lily Carolina, and probably Jesse as well. Perhaps that had slowed him down. Perhaps he had trouble finding the supplies they needed. Perhaps he ran into Kyle Banning again. She stomped her foot in frustration. How she hated depending on him!

She stormed back into the cave and began laying a fire. Conor O'Rourke would get a piece of her mind when he arrived. Just see if he didn't!

A small voice nagged Susannah, scolding her, telling her she wasn't being fair. What did she expect of the man? He had already done more than anyone could have asked of a stranger. And he had done it cheerfully, setting aside his own plans. She shut off that voice, just as she shut off the memory of Conor's words, words that had haunted her all day. *Your father would not want you to do this.*

She heard the sound of an approaching horse and ran to the mouth of the cave. Conor stepped down from the saddle.

"Where is Lily Carolina?" Susannah demanded.

"With Alexandra." Conor untied a bundle from behind the saddle and carried it into the cave.

Susannah followed him, her hands on her hips. "I told you to bring her."

"Alexandra said no."

"And you accepted that? It's not Alexandra's place to say anything! Lily Carolina is my sister, and my responsibility!"

Conor returned to Charlie's side and loosened the cinch. "Then perhaps you'd better start making responsible decisions concerning her." He pulled the saddle off.

"What is that supposed to mean?"

"In case you've forgotten, Lily Carolina has a broken wrist. As her physician, Alexandra would not allow me to bring the child into the wilderness, as she called it. I agree with her. Perhaps you should put your sister's welfare before your own needs. She was heartbroken to be left there without you."

Susannah crossed her arms over her chest, resolutely refusing to acknowledge a growing feeling of guilt. "That's why I wanted you to bring her."

Conor dropped the saddle and advanced on Susannah, his hands on his hips. "So she can stay in this cold, smoky cave with us? So she can listen to the sounds of gunshots all day while her revenge-driven sister learns to kill? So she can be frightened by the change in you? You would wish that for her?"

Susannah turned away from the fury in his eyes. "What I wish for my sister is none of your business." Her voice was harsh and forbidding. "What took you so long?"

"I had supplies to buy, remember? And I stopped by Lucas McCleave's office to let him know we'd be gone for a few days, and I stopped by the bank, and I stopped by the Silver Star Saloon." He pulled Charlie's saddle blanket off. "Is there anything else you'd like to know?"

"No." Susannah tended the fire while Conor brushed Charlie down. Neither of them spoke again until Conor pulled a sizzling rabbit carcass off the spit over an hour later. It was now com-

pletely dark. The fire burned warm and high, touching the walls
of the cave with golden light.

Conor drew the knife from his boot and sawed a leg off the
rabbit. He handed it to Susannah.

"Thank you," she said quietly. She held the meat, her hands
resting in her lap.

"You're welcome." He cut the other leg for himself, then set
it aside with a sigh.

"I hate arguing with you, Susannah." He looked at her over
the dancing flames.

Surprised by his words, she met his eyes. "I hate it, too," she
admitted.

"You didn't ask why I went to the saloon."

"I suppose you went to talk to that dancer, but it's none of
my business."

"Polly came to Alexandra's house while I was there. Kyle
Banning had beaten her."

Susannah's eyes widened in horror. "Oh, no. That poor
woman. Will she be all right?"

"I think so. She's staying with Alexandra. I went by the saloon
to let them know she'd be gone for a few days."

"She's staying in . . . our . . . room?"

"Yes."

Susannah nibbled at her rabbit, the same way an irritating
jealousy nibbled at her. Why did the thought of another woman
sleeping in the bed she had shared with Conor bother her so
much? Suddenly she was not very hungry.

"I want you to learn to protect yourself, Susannah."

Her head snapped up in surprise.

Conor continued. "I'm not always going to be around, and
I'll feel better knowing you can defend yourself against men like
Kyle Banning. I don't want anyone to hurt you again the way
he did, the way he hurt Polly."

Susannah watched him, watched the firelight play on his hair, for he would not look at her. How soon would he leave? How much did the dancer mean to him?

"Just know one thing." His voice had hardened, and now he lifted his head. His blue eyes burned into her. "I understand why you want to kill the Bannings; truly I do. But I can't condone it, because I know what it will do to you." He plunged the knife into the sand next to his foot.

There was a strange look in his eyes. Susannah waited silently for him to go on.

"When you kill someone, a part of you dies, too, Susannah. Even when you kill in self-defense, even when you kill someone who truly needs killing, like Kyle Banning does. A part of you always dies." His gaze dropped to the flames, and his voice dropped to a whisper. "Always."

Susannah stared at him, fascinated, fearful. The sincerity, the pain, the remembered horror she saw in his eyes drew her, transfixed her, touched her. She wanted to tear those memories from him, whatever they were, so they could never torment him again.

The uncomfortable silence lasted for a few minutes longer; then Conor shook his head. "Eat. Get some rest. We start at first light. And I'm warning you, Susannah Duncan." He again raised his eyes to her. They were cold, hard. She could find no sign of warmth in those blue depths. A shiver raced through her. She did not really know this man after all.

"You hired me to do a job, and I'm going to do it. This will not be a stroll in the park. I'll tolerate no whining, no excuses. At the first complaint, the deal's off."

She stiffened. "There will be no whining, Mr. O'Rourke."

They did not speak again, and soon after, both were rolled in their blankets, on opposite sides of the fire.

"Let's go, Susannah. Time to get up." Conor nudged her foot. Susannah struggled to awaken from deep, troubled dreams.

After trying futilely to sleep for hours, it seemed she had dropped off only minutes ago. She poked her nose out from under the blanket. It was cold, although Conor had built up the fire. Very little daylight showed at the mouth of the cave. As she sat up, she caught the welcome aroma of fresh coffee.

Conor cut thick slices of side pork into a frying pan. "After we eat, we'll start your first lesson. Your new gun is there in that package beside you."

Susannah drew the wrapped bundle into her lap and opened it. A leather holster held a walnut-handled pistol. She gingerly pulled the weapon free. "Is it loaded?"

"No," came his curt reply. Conor stabbed at a sizzling piece of pork and flipped it over. "It's a Colt Single Action Army revolver, also known as the Peacemaker, .45 caliber, seven-and-a-half-inch barrel. The model just came out this year and already has a good reputation. I think we'll find it's a nice little weapon. If not, we'll trade it in when we go back to town. Today you'll learn how to load and clean it."

Feeling strangely disturbed, Susannah returned the gun to its holster and set the package aside. "I'll be right back," she said, and left the cave.

The early morning chill quickly penetrated her wrinkled dress. Susannah breathed deeply, her breath coming out in a cloud. Frost-kissed grasses crunched under her feet. She fell to her knees at the little creek that wound its way down the mountain and cupped her hands in the cold water. The shock of the icy liquid hitting her face was oddly welcome.

"What are you doing?" she asked herself mournfully as she sat back on her heels. Water dripped off her chin and jaw. Did she really want to do this? Did she truly intend to kill the Bannings?

Images and sounds warred in her mind. Her gentle father's beloved smiling face. Conor's words: *Your father would not want you to do this*. Kyle Banning's twisted, sneering face, his fists hitting her father, again and again. Trusting, innocent Lily Carolina, who no longer had a father.

She buried her face in her hands. The Bannings had to be punished, and she desperately wanted to be the one to administer their punishment. But could she go through with it? Could she actually kill them? She sighed and shook her head. That decision did not have to be made today. Under any circumstances, she needed to know how to defend herself and her sister. As he had said, Conor would not always be there.

Her hands dropped to rest in her lap, and Susannah raised sad eyes to the gradually lightening sky. She found the thought of Conor leaving frightening. How had she come to trust him so completely in such a short period of time?

He hollered to her from the cave, his voice brusque. "Breakfast!"

Susannah released her hair from its untidy braid and combed the long tresses with her fingers. She slowly walked back toward the cave, rebraiding her hair, determined to see this through. A curious, aching loneliness settled over her.

Ben Hollister weaved his way between the tables in the almost deserted dining room of Sulphuret's Oyster House and Restaurant. Fletcher Banning sat alone at a table against the wall, enjoying a feast of raw oysters and champagne. As Ben approached, Fletcher noisily slurped an oyster from its shell, then wiped his fingers on the napkin tucked into his collar. He reached for his glass and indicated that Ben should sit in the opposite chair.

"I hope you have news for me." Fletcher's hard eyes bored into him.

"No, sir, I don't. There's been no sign of Susannah Duncan, and I can't learn anything about that man Kyle met at the Silver Star. No one knows him. I tried to find the dancer who was talking to him, just to see if she could tell me anything, but Kyle got to her first. As usual, he got rough with her. She took some time off to recover, and no one at the saloon knows where she is." There was no disguising the disgust in Ben's tone.

Fletcher drummed his fingers on the table. "Forget the whore, Ben. Something's going on. I can feel it. We have to find that man. I must know who he is and why he wanted directions to the Duncan mine." He rocked his chair against the wall, turning the stem of his glass with one hand. "You said a man and a woman had been at the claim since the last rainfall."

Ben nodded. "That's my guess, from the tracks."

"It was a good idea to go by there yesterday to check," Fletcher said approvingly. He slurped the last oyster.

Ben raised his eyebrows at the unexpected praise, but said nothing.

Fletcher washed the oyster down with another swallow of champagne and motioned to the waiter. Both Ben and Fletcher remained quiet while the man refilled Fletcher's glass from the bottle in the standing ice bucket and cleared the plate. When the man was out of earshot, Fletcher continued.

"I'd bet the visitors were Susannah and the stranger from the bar. We must find them, Ben. If Susannah is alive, she will either marry me and settle the issue of the mine once and for all, or I'll see to it that she disappears again. Permanently this time."

"And what of the man, whoever he is?"

"That is exactly the point! I have to know *who he is.*" Fletcher slammed his palm down on the table so hard that the stemmed glass rocked, spilling champagne. "I don't like playing with a wild card in the deck."

"Kyle's the only one who can identify him, Boss, other than that bartender over at the Silver Star. It's hard to find someone when I don't know his face."

"But you will find him, won't you?"

"Suppose I do? What then?"

"Kyle can take care of him. He has a grudge to settle with him anyway. It's time my brother started earning his keep."

Ben looked down at the hat he held in his hands. "I did learn one thing, Boss. That mining attorney, Lucas McCleave, stopped by the assessor's office this morning, looking for the file on the Duncan claim. He knows it's gone."

Fletcher waved the comment away with a derisive snort. "Lucas McCleave worked with Walter from the day I filed that lawsuit and he wasn't able to accomplish a goddamned thing. He sure as hell can't do anything with Walter dead." He emptied his glass and returned it to the table, emitting a loud belch.

"I wouldn't underestimate the man, Mr. Banning," Ben cautioned. "He's one tough old Ranger, and he's no fool."

"He's a gimp-legged old man, Ben. I can squash him like a bug, anytime I choose to." Fletcher jerked the napkin from his collar and fastidiously patted his mustache. "Now get out of here. I want some answers and I want them soon. As long as there is the possibility that Susannah is alive and could turn up at any time, I have to lay low on the mine, and I'm not happy about that."

Ben rose and put on his hat. "I'll do my best, Mr. Banning."

"You'll do it, period." Fletcher's tone was harsh as he pushed up out of his chair. "Find them, Ben."

Ben stared unflinchingly at Fletcher. "I'll do my best," he repeated. He retraced his steps between the tables.

Fletcher watched his foreman leave. "You've never let me down, Ben Hollister," he said softly to himself. "Don't start now."

"Well, Mr. McCleave!" Minerva Potter's exuberant voice echoed throughout Alexandra's house. "You come right on in here." As if she were afraid Lucas would disobey her, she grabbed the sleeve of his coat and pulled him through the door. "Are you here to call on Alexandra?"

Lucas managed a smile. "Yes, Mrs. Potter, I am. Is she about?"

Minerva jerked a thumb over her shoulder in the direction of the closed door to the examination room. "She's in with my Horatio. He's feeling somewhat under the weather, and at his age, we don't dare take chances." She snatched his hat from his hand as she pushed Lucas toward the parlor. "You wait in here with Lily Carolina while I make us some tea." She set the hat on the side table and marched down the hall to the kitchen.

Lucas entered the parlor and found Lily Carolina sitting cross-legged on the floor next to Jesse, her doll in her lap, an unusual-looking book spread out in front of her.

"Hello, Lily Carolina."

"Hello, Mr. Lucas," the child answered. "I'm reading Amy a story."

Lucas crouched down next to her and patted Jesse's head. "So you are." He saw that the book had rows of tiny raised bumps, with words printed below. "How did you learn to read at such a young age?"

"My papa was a school teacher," she explained. "He taught me my letters and numbers before I got sick. Then he taught me Braille." Her fingers moved over one row of the dots.

"Your papa was quite a man, wasn't he?"

"Yes, sir." Lily Carolina's voice took on a sad quality.

"How's your arm?" Lucas straightened and settled on the edge of the sofa.

"Better. And so is Amy's." She held up the doll so Lucas could see the tiny splint. "But not better enough so we could go with Susannah and Mr. Conor. Me and Amy and Jesse had to stay here 'cause Dr. 'Xandra needs us."

"I certainly do," Alexandra said from the door.

Lucas rose. "Hello, Dr. Kennedy." He smiled at her, taking

in the simple white blouse she wore, the dark blue skirt, the neat apron tied at her narrow waist. Her rich auburn hair was arranged at the back of her head, and her blue eyes sparkled. She seemed happy to see him, which made him happy. He finally managed to nod at Horatio Potter, who stood at her elbow. "Hello, Mr. Potter. I hope you're feeling better."

"Yes, sir, Mr. McCleave." The old man's head bobbed up and down. "Alexandra always knows what to do. She's a *fine* doctor."

"Get out of my way, you two, so I can set this tray down." Minerva's dictatorial voice boomed from around the corner. Alexandra and Horatio obediently moved, and Minerva sailed into the parlor bearing a tea tray. "Horatio, my dear, you and Lily Carolina will join me in the kitchen, so Alexandra and Mr. McCleave can have a nice little chat." She winked conspiratorially at Alexandra, who realized by the quivering smile on Lucas McCleave's lips that he had seen the wink.

"Yes, dearest." Horatio started down the hall.

"Come along, child." Minerva took Lily Carolina's hand. "I'll bet I can find something sweet in the kitchen for you to have with your milk."

"Yes, ma'am, Mrs. 'Nerva."

Minerva laughed. "Why don't you call me 'Aunt Minnie,' child? That's easier to say than 'Mrs. Minerva.' " She guided Lily Carolina toward the door.

"But our horse's name is Minnie!" Lily Carolina said with a giggle.

"Well, is she a nice horse?" They reached the door and turned into the hall. Minerva sent Alexandra another exaggerated wink.

"Very nice," Lily Carolina assured her.

"Then I guess it's all right if we have the same name." Minerva's voice trailed down the hall and was finally muffled by the closing of the kitchen door.

Alexandra smiled at Lucas. "I hope Minerva didn't embarrass you, Mr. McCleave. She certainly did me."

"Not at all, Dr. Kennedy. How is Mr. Potter?" He waited until Alexandra was seated on the sofa, then settled next to her.

Alexandra's voice dropped to a whisper. "As healthy as a horse, just as Minerva is, although you'd never believe it, to hear them talk."

Lucas laughed. "They care for you, Doctor, and this way they can keep an eye on you."

"I suppose so." Alexandra reached for the teapot. "I just wish they wouldn't be so obvious about some things."

"Conor stopped by yesterday and told me you have another patient. How is she doing?"

"She's in bad shape, but she should pull through." Alexandra spoke through tightened lips as she handed Lucas a filled cup. "I tell you, I'd like to take a board to that damned Kyle Banning and give him a taste of his own medicine." Her cheeks suddenly turned red. She pressed her fingers to her mouth, then dropped her hands to her lap. "Please forgive my profanity, Mr. McCleave."

Lucas set his cup on the table and took Alexandra's hand in his. "There's no need to apologize, Dr. Kennedy. The word fits the man exactly. I find your forthrightness refreshing."

Surprised, Alexandra looked up to see him smiling. Her own lips curved in response. "Thank you," she said softly.

Lucas had trouble looking away from Alexandra's blue eyes. He reluctantly released her hand and reached for his cup. "I've come with some bad news, I'm afraid."

"What is it?"

"I went to the assessor's office this morning. He has no record of the Duncan claim. No paperwork of any kind. No file, no deed, nothing. He was at a loss to explain what had happened. I fear Mr. Jackson is in the employ of Fletcher Banning."

"Oh, no." Alexandra leaned against the back of the sofa. "What do we do now?"

"I need to get word to Conor and Susannah. We have to go

to the territorial assessor in Denver, and pray that Banning doesn't get there first."

"Surely Banning doesn't have that much influence in Denver," Alexandra protested.

Lucas shrugged and returned his cup to the table. "I don't know if he does or not. We can't take the risk. Do you know where Conor and Susannah are?"

Alexandra shook her head. "I don't. I just know they're camped in a cave somewhere. We could search for them, I guess."

"It would be a waste of time, because Conor O'Rourke is too smart. He has no way of knowing that we're looking for them, so he'd dodge anyone in the area in an attempt to protect Susannah. We'd never find them." He stroked his beard, deep in thought.

Alexandra silently watched him, her gaze wandering over his face. Lucas McCleave was an attractive man, with his neatly trimmed beard and intelligent gray eyes. She liked that his dark hair had turned gray. She liked the way he dressed, the way he carried himself. He exuded a calm confidence that she found appealing and reassuring. Lucas was a contented man, secure with who he was and his place in the world.

Yet there was an edge about him, an undercurrent of danger. Instinctively Alexandra knew he was not a man to cross. He was a fighter, and she respected that in him, because it matched the fighter in her. She focused on his hand, still moving over his chin, and wondered if the neatly combed beard was as soft as it looked. Suddenly she realized what she was thinking and turned away, her cheeks again feeling hot. Then something Lucas had said sunk in. *Conor O'Rourke is too smart.* Desperate to get her mind on a more comfortable track, she said, "It sounds like you know Conor well."

"I know of him." At her puzzled expression, he continued. "I think you know I was with the Texas Rangers for many years."

Alexandra nodded.

"After the war, Conor was, too, although I had already retired by the time he joined. We never worked together, in fact, never met until he came into my office last week. He had an excellent reputation, courageous, trustworthy, dependable. He went on a mission with a couple of other Rangers about four years back, to capture a band of renegades who had been terrorizing the small towns along the Brazos River. There was a battle, and out of all the outlaws and Rangers, Conor was the only one who survived. He was touted as a hero. But then he quit, and went to work punching cattle."

Alexandra stared at him. "He just quit? Did he ever give a reason?"

Lucas shook his head. "Not that I know of. He worked for some of the big ranchers in Texas. King, Chisum, Goodnight. In fact, he told me he's supposed to be meeting Goodnight here in Colorado, to help set up some new cattle operation down around Pueblo. Now he's just a cowboy who tries real hard to mind his own business, although I've heard he's fast with a gun. Real fast. And he's not afraid to use his talent when necessary."

"I've seen him draw," Alexandra admitted. Lucas raised his eyebrows. "I startled him in the kitchen the first morning he was here," she explained. "It was like that gun just appeared in his hand. I never saw him move." She was quiet for a moment. "Actually, I'm glad to know this. If anyone can take care of Susannah, he can. Kyle Banning has nothing on him."

Lucas stood up. "Did Conor indicate how long they'd be gone?"

"For perhaps a week." Alexandra reluctantly rose also; she did not want Lucas to leave. "He needs time to dissuade Susannah from seeking revenge against the Bannings, time to let her work out some of her rage."

Lucas stroked his beard again. "I don't dare wait until they return. I think I'll send a man to Denver."

They moved to the entryway and Alexandra handed him his hat. "Thank you, Mr. McCleave, for all your help."

"You're welcome, Dr. Kennedy." He took the hat as his gaze lingered on Alexandra's face. "I invite you to call me 'Lucas.' "

With a pleased smile, Alexandra nodded. "Only if you'll call me 'Alexandra.' "

His face lit up with a broad grin. "Agreed, Alexandra. I'll stop by in a few days, sooner if I have any news. Good day to you."

"Good day, Lucas," Alexandra said softly, and closed the door behind him. She stood in the entryway, her hands at her cheeks. For heaven's sake! Here she was, thirty-eight years old, and that man had her feeling as giddy as a school girl! She smiled again.

Eleven

Susannah shifted on the hard ground, trying to get comfortable. She was exhausted, but sleep eluded her. The fire had burned down to a glowing bed of coals, and a creeping chill invaded the cave. She could just make out Conor's form on the other side of the fire circle. A deep sadness filled her.

He had become a stranger, a man she did not know. A coldly efficient man, distant almost to the point of rudeness. Today, again and again, he had made her load the pistol, then unload it, load it, then unload it. She had taken the weapon apart numerous times, cleaned the parts, recited their names as she reassembled the pieces. Again and again and again. He had not allowed her to shoot the gun; that phase of her training would begin in the morning.

She rolled onto her back and stared up into the shadows, suddenly overwhelmed by grief. In the last year she had lost almost everything and everyone important to her. Her mother. Her home and friends in South Carolina. Her uncle. Now her father. Even the little cabin; her new home, such as it had been. A tear rolled from the corner of each eye and trailed down into her hair. All she had left was Lily Carolina.

Susannah grieved for her orphaned sister, for the hardships the child would face growing up in a world she could not see. She grieved for her own lost innocence, for now her life had been touched by violence. Touched and irrevocably changed.

She had lost Conor, as well. Gone was the easy friendship

they had enjoyed, the budding attraction she was sure he felt for her, as she felt for him. And she had only herself to blame. There was no denying that she had driven him away. She brushed impatiently at the tickling tear in her hair and turned her back to the circle of glowing coals, and to him. Morning would dawn soon, and she needed to sleep.

Conor listened to Susannah's restless movements, unable to sleep himself. He knew his curt manner hurt her today; he had seen it in her eyes. But what was he to do? He had to protect himself against her. In one short week, she had made him feel things he had never felt for a woman, made him dream of things that could not be. Yet she had never indicated a personal interest in him. She and Lily Carolina would go their own way when their situation was settled, with no room in their lives for a man born under a wandering star. He, too, turned his back to the coals, pulling the blanket up over his shoulder.

"Put this in your ears." Conor handed her a wad of soft, white cotton, keeping some for himself. He twisted a small amount and put it in one ear. "If you don't use it, your ears will be ringing by the time we finish," he explained at her puzzled expression. "A few shots wouldn't matter, but we'll be practicing for hours."

Susannah obediently followed his example, then waited as Conor checked his weapon. They were in a picturesque clearing about a quarter of a mile from the cave. Tall pine trees and newly leaved aspen danced together around the perimeter of the flower-strewn meadow while the silent mountain peaks looked on. In the beauty of the soft morning light it was difficult to remember the very serious reason for their presence here. But the weight of her weapon reminded her.

Her new gunbelt was strapped around her hips, the gun-laden holster hanging heavy against her thigh. Susannah pushed a strand of hair back under her hat. In addition to her nervousness, she felt a thrill of excitement. These lessons were interesting. And they offered her an odd comfort. She was learning from Conor, emulating him. In a strange way, it made her feel closer to him.

"There are different ways to hold a pistol, depending on the situation you're in and the time you have." His voice sounded muffled to her. "I'm going to start you with holding the gun in two hands, like this." He positioned himself with his legs slightly apart and his arms held out straight, chest high. His right hand held the grip while his left cupped the butt of the pistol. He pulled the hammer and squeezed the trigger. One of several pinecones he had positioned on a boulder about fifty feet away disappeared. "But I want you to sit down." He pointed to the ground.

Susannah followed his instructions, arranging her skirts around her legs.

"No." Conor dropped to the ground beside her. "Raise your knees, and cross your ankles, like this. That's right. Now get the gun."

She again arranged her skirts, then pulled the loaded weapon from the holster. It felt heavy to her.

"Rest your elbows on your knees," Conor continued. "Hold the gun like I showed you, cock it, aim, and squeeze the trigger, don't pull it. No, put your left hand under the butt, here." He leaned over and positioned her hand. "That's right. Now aim at one of the pinecones."

Susannah eased the hammer back, then adjusted her aim, sighting down the barrel. She focused on a pinecone and slowly moved her forefinger. Suddenly the gun jumped. So did Susannah. A strange whining sound echoed through the clearing as the bullet ricocheted off the boulder. The number of intact pinecones had not lessened.

She shrugged away her disappointment. "At least I hit the rock."

"It's a big rock," Conor observed dryly.

Susannah arched an eyebrow at him, but did not comment.

"Try again. This time, relax and take a deep breath before you fire."

"All right, but why are you having me sit?"

"Believe me, Susannah, by the end of the day, you'll be thankful you had something to brace your elbows on. That gun will feel like it weighs fifty pounds. Now try again."

It took only a few hours for the pistol to become surprisingly heavy. Susannah's arms ached from the strain of her efforts and the shock of the kick every time she fired. Conor showed her how to lie on her belly and fire. That offered some relief for her arms for a little while, but only that. When the clouds rolled in early in the afternoon, he pulled the cotton from his ears and announced she had practiced enough for one day. Susannah gratefully removed the cotton from her own ears, feeling that she had just endured the longest morning of her life. But she did not utter one word of complaint as they trudged back to the cave.

"I'm going to work with you on the rifle, as well," Conor said as he threw wood on the fire. "Again, depending on the circumstances, a rifle is sometimes better than a pistol."

"Your cousin is great with a rifle," Susannah commented as she wearily sank onto her blankets. She massaged her upper arms.

"Alina is a marksman. She's the best rifle shot I know."

"Better than you?" Susannah teased.

Conor kept his gaze on the struggling flames. "Better than me. With a rifle, that is. Last summer she saved an innocent man from being hung by shooting the hanging rope, at night. It was the greatest shot I've ever seen." There was no mistaking the pride in his voice.

Susannah shook her head in wonder. "I'm not surprised. Did she tell you about the shooting match she entered a few years ago when we were in school in England?"

Conor looked up at her. "No."

"She dressed like a man and entered as Andrew Gallagher. She won, too." Susannah smiled at the memory.

"I find it hard to believe Alina could pass for a man," Conor said firmly, thinking of his beautiful, curvaceous cousin.

"We said she was a boy, actually, a plump boy, with padding around her stomach to disguise certain female features. Those men sure were upset when she bested them all. It was a great deal of fun." Her smile turned wistful as she gazed into the fire. "It was also a long time ago. A lifetime ago."

Conor straightened. "I'll get some fresh water, and I want to check on Charlie. I won't be long."

Susannah absentmindedly nodded, not taking her weary eyes from the flames. When Conor returned, she was asleep.

The next few days passed in an obsessive haze for Susannah. Conor pushed her relentlessly, hour after hour, and she eagerly absorbed all he said. He not only taught her to shoot, he taught her to pay attention to her surroundings, to watch, to wait, to listen, to hide. He coached her with the pistol and instructed her on the use of the rifle. She worked hard and without complaint, determined to ignore the painful bruise on her right shoulder from the rifle kick, the constant ache in her arms, the blisters on her right hand.

Susannah enjoyed more success ignoring the small pains that plagued her body than she did the irritating thrill of excitement that rushed through her whenever Conor touched her to position her hands, her arms, her stance. Once he had stood very close behind her, his arms coming around her to turn her hips, to correct her grip on the rifle. One strong hand had rested on her shoulder while the other had reached in front of her to adjust the angle of the rifle barrel. His rough, unshaven cheek had touched hers; his sensual mouth had been only a kiss away. She had found it very difficult to concentrate on what he was saying. She learned that the excitement he unknowingly roused in her was not easy to ignore.

By the third day, Susannah was firing from a standing position, and beginning to hit some of the pinecones. She found a pair of her father's pants in the last bundle of clothes they had left in the cave and took to wearing them so she could tie the holster to her leg. Then she began to practice her draw.

One evening Conor sipped on his coffee and watched her. She stood in the back of the cave, the gunbelt buckled over her father's pants, which were way too big for her, as was the flannel work shirt she wore. Over and over, she whipped the pistol from the holster, aimed at the stone wall, then returned the weapon to its place. The end of her long golden braid danced around her hips at her movements. He found her obsession troubling and sad, but he had to admire her tenacity. Not once had she complained about anything. And she was improving.

"You're wasting your time trying to speed up your draw, Susannah. In order to be really fast, you need your holster tied down, which you can't do unless you wear pants. And you can't wear pants anywhere but out here."

Susannah returned the gun to the holster again and came over to sit on her blanket. "I know," she sighed. "But I enjoy practicing, even though it would take me years to get as good as you are."

Conor raised an eyebrow. Was there a note of admiration in her voice? He grabbed the coffeepot and leaned forward to refill her cup, then his. "Accuracy is much more important than speed. Never forget that. Take the time you need to be sure you hit what you're aiming for."

"That's fine for a shooting match, Conor, but what if you don't have the time to take? What if you're attacked?"

He shrugged. "In that case, you just do the best you can, and hope your instincts don't let you down."

"Hopefully it will never come to that," she said soberly. She stared into her cup, then sipped the steaming brew.

"Hopefully it won't," Conor agreed. He changed the subject. "Tell me why your father decided to bring you and your sister out west."

Susannah folded her legs Indian style and rested her elbows on her knees, holding the cup with both hands. She stared at him across the flames. "Why do you want to know?"

"I'm just curious. This place, and this way of life, is a long way from Charleston society. I wonder what made your father, and you, leave all that."

Susannah dropped her gaze to the fire. "When my mother was sixteen, my grandparents hired a tutor for her. He was many years older than she was. They scandalized my grandparents, and all of Charleston society, by falling in love. When my grandparents would not condone the match, they eloped. I was born a year later." She took another sip of coffee.

"Did your grandparents ever bless the union?" Conor asked.

"Oh, no." Susannah shook her head emphatically. "When I was young, we lived in Richmond. Papa found a job as a school master, and although our lives were simple, we were happy. Then my grandfather died, and soon after, the war began." A new sadness seemed to settle over her. "I was ten at the time. Mama didn't want her mother to be alone, so we returned to Charleston to live with Grandmother. Lily Carolina was born when I was seventeen." Susannah smiled. "What a surprise she was!"

"I can imagine, after all those years."

"But Mama never fully recovered from my sister's birth, and my grandmother never forgave my father for that. She also never forgave my parents for being happy together, in spite of her best efforts to the contrary. The day we buried my mother, my grandmother sent Papa and Lily Carolina from the house."

Conor choked on his coffee. "Why the child?" he demanded.

"Although it was a fever that killed her, my grandmother felt Lily Carolina was partly to blame for my mother's death, since her birth had weakened Mama's constitution. Grandmother also considered Lily Carolina an embarrassment after she lost her sight, and threatened to put her in an institution."

The image of Lily Carolina's sweet face filled Conor's mind, and a fierce anger rushed through him. "Your grandmother must be a miserable person," he stated harshly. "What about you? Did she want you to leave, too?"

"Oh, I was welcome to stay," Susannah assured him, her tone bitter. "If I denounced my father's name, and allowed Grandmother to pick a 'suitable' mate for me. Of course I refused, so I was disowned as well. Uncle Walter was our only kin, besides her. We had little money and no place else to go, so we came here." She took another sip of coffee, avoiding his eyes. The liquid finally worked its way around the sudden lump in her throat.

"What's wrong?" Conor asked softly.

Susannah twisted the cup in her hands. "Papa came out here so full of hope, and for a while, it looked like things would work out for us. But then Uncle Walter died, and now—" she swallowed—"now, everything is gone." She bowed her head.

Conor reached out in sympathy and touched her shoulder.

Susannah jerked away from his hand and wiped at her eyes with her sleeve. "I think I'll sleep now," she snapped, determined not to cry in front of him. She set the cup down and turned away, lying back on the blankets.

His lips pressed in a tight line, Conor threw the remains of his coffee against the wall. She even resisted his touch now. The last few days had been torturous for him. He'd been so close to her, touching her, guiding her, as he taught her the intricacies of target shooting, how to hold the pistol, the rifle, how to aim, how to stand. And she tormented him with her nearness, her beauty, her eagerness to learn, her damned lavender scent! They had spent every minute of several days and nights together, separated only by the invisible, insurmountable wall that had sprung up between them.

The cool politeness with which they now treated each other grated on his nerves and stretched his patience to its limit. As much as he hated arguing, he'd rather have an honest, healthy argument than tiptoe around each other like they had been doing. He sighed. The day after tomorrow would make it a week since they had left Georgetown. The day after tomorrow, it would be time to go back.

Late the next afternoon, Conor approached the cave with an armload of firewood. He looked up at the dark, rumbling sky, wondering how soon the clouds would drop the rain they held. It had been a long day, and he could tell Susannah was growing anxious to return to her sister. One more day, he thought. One more day.

He quietly stepped into the cave and stopped in his tracks, mesmerized by the scene in front of him.

Susannah sat cross-legged on her blankets, the light of the fire bathing her in gold. She had taken off her father's baggy clothes and now wore her chemise and petticoats. Her folded dress waited at her side.

Her head was thrown back, her eyes closed, her glorious hair, freed from its confining braid, brushing the blanket behind her. She ran a wet cloth down her neck and over the top swells of her breasts. While Conor watched in silent torment, the small piece of material first traveled the length of one shapely arm, then the other. How he longed to be guiding that cloth himself! Or, better yet, guiding his lips along the same path. Although a branch dug into his arm, he held perfectly still, unwilling to let her know he was there, unable to tear his eyes away.

She pulled the chemise strap from her right shoulder; then her beautiful face twisted in a grimace of pain when she touched the cloth to her skin. The spell was broken. Conor dropped the wood and was at her side in a moment.

"Conor, please!" She crossed her arms, covering her breasts and her shoulders. "I'm not dressed!"

"Hush." He gently pulled her hands down and was appalled to see that the front of her right shoulder was covered with a dark bruise. He knew instantly what had caused it. "The kick of the rifle," he whispered, his voice heavy with agonized guilt. "This is why you pulled away from me last night, isn't it? It hurt when I touched you."

She nodded.

"Why didn't you say something?"

"I didn't want to complain." She tried to free her hands from his, but he would not release her. "The bruise will heal, Conor. I was afraid that if I told you, you'd make me quit, and I need to learn all I can from you. I must be able to defend myself and my sister." Her voice had taken on a desperate note.

Conor settled into a sitting position next to her right knee, facing her. "You've learned enough to do that now. What have you decided about the Bannings?" He turned her palms up and examined them. Her left hand was fine, but blisters had raised on her right thumb and palm. He silently cursed himself for an insensitive brute.

"I don't know," she said wearily. "I don't know anything anymore. I only know that I want to see Lily Carolina." She paused. "And I know how to load, shoot and clean a pistol and a rifle, thanks to you," she added with a smile.

Conor raised his gaze from her hands and stared at her.

She blinked. "What is it?" she whispered.

"I'm so sorry." His voice was soft with remorse and concern. "I shouldn't have pushed you that hard."

"Conor, really, it's all right." Susannah could not look away from his eyes, his beautiful blue eyes, shimmering in the fire-light. His thumbs caressed her palms; then he leaned forward and kissed her bruised shoulder. She caught her breath, over-whelmed at the tender gesture. His lips touched her again and again, lightly, gently. She leaned her head against his and closed her eyes, no longer caring that she was dressed only in her un-derclothes. Her heart thundered beneath her breast, so loudly she was sure he could hear it.

He guided her right hand to his waist and released it as his lips moved from her shoulder to her neck. His free hand trailed up and down her arm, causing her to shiver in delight. She moved her fingers over his ribs. Her breathing quickened. She tilted her head away from him now, giving him access to her throat. He greedily accepted her unspoken invitation, allowing his lips to wander. He released her other hand, and his arms closed around her.

Susannah turned her face, blindly seeking his mouth as her hands explored his back. His lips fastened on hers and he moaned deep in his throat.

At the sound, a floodgate of emotion opened inside her. She gave herself up to his kiss, helpless against the fire that raced through her veins. Her hands feverishly roamed over his pow-erful shoulders, his muscled chest, his flat, hard stomach. She was sorry he wore a shirt.

Conor pulled his mouth away, breathing hard, holding her face between his hands. She opened her eyes and was stunned to read on his face a passion that matched hers, a longing as deep as her own. She could not bear it.

"Oh, Conor." His name came out in a whisper. She leaned her forehead against his and caressed his forearms. One of his hands stroked her hair, then tangled in the long tresses, gently tugging her head back, and she lifted her mouth for his kiss. His lips settled on hers once more, tantalizing, teasing, nibbling. His tongue sought entry to her mouth and she allowed it, shifting closer to him. How could his kiss be gentle and demanding at the same time? How could she be on fire and shivering at the same time?

Ever so slowly, Conor's determined hand traveled from her cheek to her neck, and from there down over her collarbone to her chest, and still lower, until it rested firmly, possessively, on her breast. Susannah gasped against his lips as her eyes flew open.

"I can feel your heart," he whispered.

"I-I'm sure you can." She pressed her hand to the identical place on his chest, thrilled to feel the hammering of his heart. She snuggled closer to him, planting little kisses down his throat as far as she could before her lips met his shir.

Conor closed his eyes and rested his cheek against the top of her head. The sweet scent of lavender reached him, tormented him. His hand moved over her breast, and he was elated to feel her nipple harden against his palm, to hear her soft gasp of pleasure. Her response sent a fresh wave of exquisite agony to his stomach, and lower. He groaned.

"Susannah. Woman, we have to stop this." He pulled his hand from her breast and helped her sit up straight. "I'm not behaving as a gentleman yet again." She stared at him, her wet lips trembling, her eyes huge and soft with some emotion he could not name. Longing, perhaps? Disappointment? He willed his breathing to return to normal. "We'll go back tonight, as soon as it gets dark."

She opened her mouth, but he placed a finger against her lips before she could say anything. He tried to ignore her warm, irregular breath on his finger.

"No argument. Your shoulder needs to heal, and we both need some rest."

She kissed his finger.

Conor suddenly had trouble remembering his train of thought. "Besides, uh, we should . . . see if Lucas has learned anything."

He moved his finger from her lips to her cheek and regained his composure. "And I don't know about you, but I miss your little sister like the dickens."

At the mention of her sister, Susannah dropped her gaze and nodded. "So do I." The thought struck her that at least Conor had been enough of a gentleman to stop. She, on the other hand, had not behaved as a lady. How could she, with his mouth on her, his hands on her? To her dismay, desire flared again, just at her thoughts, and refused to die a quick death. A blush heated her face. She self-consciously pushed a long strand of hair back over her shoulder, now very much aware that she was not dressed.

Conor reached across her lap and grabbed her folded dress. "You'd better put this on," he said hoarsely as he pressed it into her hands. "Please. And braid your hair." He met her eyes, and his lips curved in a tender smile. "We'll fix something to eat, then head out." He looked to the mouth of the cave. "I'm surprised it hasn't rained yet. Maybe it'll blow over."

"I hope so," Susannah murmured, relieved to be speaking on more neutral topics. "I could do without another trip down this mountain in the rain." She hesitated. "Conor, we have only one horse."

"I know. We'll take it slow, and Charlie will be all right."

Two hours later, Susannah stood outside the cave, staring at its yawning mouth. The light was almost completely gone from the sky. The cave had been emptied and swept clean, except for the ring of stones around the fire circle and a stack of dry wood. A strange melancholy washed over her. The cave represented a haven to her, a haven that would always be associated with Conor.

"Susannah."

She turned to him. He waited in the saddle, his hand held out to her. She took it and he pulled her up behind him. She looked at the cave one last time, then wrapped her arms around his waist and rested her cheek against his back. He nudged Charlie forward, and her hold on him tightened.

Jesse started barking joyously the moment they set foot on the back porch of Alexandra's house late that night. By the time they got into the kitchen and took off their coats, Alexandra had come from the parlor, and Polly, obviously just awakened, was being dragged down the hall by a jubilant Lily Carolina.

"Susannah! Susannah!" the child cried when she reached the kitchen, her hands out in front of her. Susannah dropped to her knees as Polly guided Lily Carolina to her. She hugged her little sister, her eyes filling with tears.

"Where's Mr. Conor?" Lily Carolina demanded.

Conor crouched down at Susannah's side and touched Lily Carolina's shoulder. "I'm right here, Poppet."

Lily Carolina felt for him, then threw her arms around his neck and hugged him fiercely. "You came back," she exulted.

"Just like I promised." Conor's voice was suspiciously husky. He stood up, taking Lily Carolina with him. Alexandra and Susannah embraced, and Conor turned to Polly.

Most of the bruising on her face had faded, and the cut on her bottom lip had scabbed over. Her long dark hair flowed around her shoulders. She smiled at him, happily, shyly, and shifted her bare feet. Like Lily Carolina, she wore only a nightdress.

"You look a lot better, Polly," he said. "How do you feel?"

"Fine." She moved closer to him. "Doc Alex took good care of me."

"I knew she would." Conor turned to Susannah and noticed a strange, wary expression on her face. "Susannah, this is Polly, the woman I told you about. Polly, this is Susannah."

"My sister," Lily Carolina volunteered proudly.

"How do you do?" Susannah said, her tone as stiff as her back. Polly was a lot prettier than she had imagined.

Polly nodded in Susannah's direction, then grabbed Conor's free hand. "Come to the parlor and talk to me." She pulled him toward the door.

"Not until that child is put back in bed," Alexandra said firmly. "Conor, you and Susannah take her upstairs, and that dog, too. They both still sleep with me. I'll make some coffee, and we'll all meet in the parlor in a few minutes." She fixed her eyes on Polly. "And you won't be up much later yourself, missy. You need your rest."

Polly rolled her eyes. "She acts like she's my mother," she said to Conor in an exaggerated whisper.

"You'd just better not say I'm old enough to be your mother, although I probably am," Alexandra retorted. "Now off with the lot of you. Do as I say." She shooed them out the door.

"I'll wait here," Polly said when they reached the door of the parlor. She flashed a smile at Conor, glanced thoughtfully at Susannah, then turned into the room.

Susannah followed Conor up the stairs, more disturbed by Polly's presence than she had expected. Polly obviously thought very highly of Conor, and he seemed to like her, as well.

Jesse jumped on the bed as Conor settled the child between the sheets. The dog curled up with a contented sigh, and Susannah sat at her sister's side. She took Lily Carolina's right hand in hers and lightly stroked the length of the splint. "How is your wrist?"

"It doesn't hurt anymore. Neither does Amy's." She searched with her other hand. Susannah found the doll and nestled it against Lily Carolina's side.

"Were you a good girl for Dr. Alexandra?"

"I was, Susannah. And for Aunt Minnie, and Mr. Lucas."

"So Mr. Lucas was here," Conor commented.

"He comes to see Dr. 'Xandra. He ate supper with us." She tried to stifle a yawn. "So did Joseph. He's real nice."

"Who is Joseph?" Conor asked.

"Lucas's son," Susannah answered as she pulled the blankets up to Lily Carolina's chin. "You need to get to sleep, little sister," she said, her voice soft with love. "We'll talk tomorrow, and you can tell us everything you did while we were gone."

"All right," Lily Carolina said sleepily.

Conor bent down and kissed the child's forehead. "Good night, Poppet."

Susannah's heart lurched. It was as if they were a family, she and Conor and Lily Carolina. She watched as he pushed the hair back from Lily Carolina's face and settled her braid on the pillow. His long fingers had touched her like that, touched her face and her hair . . . and other places. Her stomach leapt in excitement at the memory. Did Conor want a family? It occurred to her that she did not know what he wanted, from her, from life. She made a mental note to ask him the next time they were alone.

"Good night, sweetheart," Susannah whispered, and kissed her sister's cheek.

"G'night." Lily Carolina closed her eyes. "I'm glad you're home."

Conor and Susannah quietly left the room.

"Is 'Aunt Minnie' Minerva Potter?" Susannah asked in a low tone as Conor pulled the bedroom door closed.

He nodded. "She told Lily Carolina to call her that."

"What do you think of Lucas coming to see Alexandra?" Susannah continued as they started down the stairs. "Do you think it was all business?"

"I don't know," Conor whispered with a wink. "I hope not."

Susannah smiled. "I hope not, too."

Alexandra was waiting in the parlor with Polly, the coffeepot and four cups on the low table.

"It's late, so let's get down to business," she said briskly. "How are you two?" She grabbed the pot and filled the cups.

"Fine," Susannah answered, too quickly. She accepted a cup and bent over it. Alexandra glanced at Conor, who shrugged, then spoke.

"We had no trouble." He looked at Polly. "I want to ask you about Kyle Banning."

Polly snorted. "That jackass. Ask me whatever you want, Conor O'Rourke." Her smile was smug. "Dr. Alex told me your full name, and I know who you are. No wonder you're not scared of Kyle. I'd love to see you kill the bastard."

Susannah stared at Conor, puzzled. The look on his face was guarded, almost defensive. "I don't understand," she said. "Who are you?"

"The hero of the battle at Diablo Canyon, that's who," Polly interjected proudly. "And he's fast enough to take Kyle Banning; I just know it."

A hero? Diablo Canyon? Polly's words seemed to slam into Susannah's brain.

"That's enough, Polly," Alexandra snapped. "Sometimes you talk too much, girl."

Polly flounced back against the sofa, her arms over her chest. "Well, it's the truth."

"Truth or not, Conor's story is Conor's business, and you'd best not be talking around town about him." Alexandra glared at her a moment longer, then looked apologetically at Conor. He was staring at the floor.

Susannah set her cup on the table and clasped her hands in her lap. Conor's story? What were they talking about? How did Polly know so much about Conor? She glanced at him, then quickly away.

"Do you know anything about the Bannings' plans for the Duncan mine?" Conor asked Polly. His voice was strained and tired.

"Only that Fletcher intends to own it, no matter what it takes. He wants to own all of Blue Mountain." Polly curled her feet under her and fussed with the hem of her nightdress. "Kyle thinks his brother will be a big shot in Washington some day, and then he will be, too. Can you imagine?" She shook her head derisively. "I don't know much else, Conor. Kyle tends to talk mostly about himself and how great he is." Her pretty face sobered and her eyes took on a bleak, bitter look. "About the only thing he's great at is hurting people."

"Especially women and old men," Alexandra added venomously.

Conor sighed and rested his elbows on his knees. "Thank you, Polly."

She brightened. "For what? I didn't do anything."

"Every little piece of information is helpful," Alexandra said. "Now get on up to bed. You need your rest and we need to have a private discussion."

"Oh, all right." Polly pouted. "If I've learned anything in the last week, Alex, it's that arguing with you is a waste of time." She marched to the doorway, her hair swaying against her back, then whirled and looked at Conor. "I'll see *you* tomorrow." She winked at him, then ran lightly up the stairs, holding the hem of her nightdress high above her knees.

Conor uneasily watched Susannah's bowed head. She did not move. He turned to Alexandra. "So you've seen Lucas?"

"Yes. He went to the assessor's office. There is no file for the Duncan mine. It's as if Walter Duncan didn't exist."

Susannah raised her head. "What does Lucas suggest we do now?"

"He took the liberty of sending a man to Denver, a trusted man, mind you, to the territorial assessor. He should be back any day now. Lucas will come by the minute he has word."

"Then there's nothing more we can do tonight." Susannah stood up, and Conor jumped to his feet. "I'm very tired, Alexandra," Susannah said. "I'm going to bed." She turned to the door.

"You'll have to bunk with Polly," Alexandra commented as she gathered the cups. "Conor, you'll sleep down here, on the floor, I'm afraid. You're too tall for the sofa."

Susannah hesitated only a moment, then continued out the door and up the stairs without a backward glance.

"Susannah." Conor moved to follow her, but Alexandra put a hand on his arm.

"Let her go. She's too tired tonight, Conor. Talk to her tomorrow."

Conor looked at her. "How does Polly know about Diablo Canyon?"

"She lived in Texas for a while. She said it was real big news when it happened, down there, anyway."

"You don't seem too surprised."

"I already knew. Bring the pot, will you?" She left the room, cups in hand.

Conor grabbed the coffeepot and followed. "I suppose Lucas told you?"

She nodded.

"Well, why don't we just take out an ad in the *Daily Miner?*" Conor asked sarcastically as he set the pot on the stove.

"We haven't told anyone else, Conor, and we won't. Your past is your business. Don't worry about it." She pumped water over the cups in the sink. "These can wait until morning," she said, almost under her breath. She turned to him. "Now get that troubled look off your handsome face and go get some sleep." She pushed him toward the hall.

Susannah trudged up the stairs. She dreaded the idea of sharing a room with Polly, but there was no other choice. Maybe she would sleep on the floor, as Conor had done when they had shared this room. *Conor.* Did she really know the man at all? It seemed that Polly knew more about him than she did. Her stomach twisted with a pain that she tried to ignore as she knocked lightly on the bedroom door.

"Come in," called Polly, her voice curiously hopeful.

Susannah entered the room and closed the door.

"Oh, it's you." Polly's face showed her disappointment. She sat on the edge of the bed, a brush in her hand.

"Alexandra said we have to share this room," Susannah said woodenly. She moved to the bureau and opened a drawer.

"And I'll bet you'd rather be sharing it with Conor, wouldn't you?" Polly demanded. "Well, if it's any consolation, I'd rather be sharing it with him, too."

Susannah did not answer. She pulled a clean nightdress from the drawer and set it on the bureau, then struggled to reach the buttons down the back of her dress, blinking at the tears that had formed in her eyes.

Polly watched Susannah for a minute, then sighed. "Let me help with that," she said as she got off the bed. She set the brush down and pushed Susannah's hands out of the way. After a few moments of silence, Polly spoke again. "I sure do like your little sister. What a doll she is. Lily C. makes me want to have kids of my own." She undid the last button and stepped away.

Susannah looked over her shoulder, finding nothing but wistful sincerity in the dancer's expression. Her heart softened at the sight of the fading bruises. She turned to face Polly. "You know, there's no reason we can't get along."

Polly grinned. "You're right, Susie. You're so pretty and proper, I was afraid you'd be snotty, too. But you're not, and I'm glad. You and I actually have a lot in common. We both like Conor O'Rourke, and that damned Kyle Banning has beaten both of us, although Kyle didn't kill my pa. I was damn sorry to hear about your pa."

"Thank you. I guess we do have a lot in common, don't we?"

Susannah pulled the dress from her shoulders and down over
her hips. "From what Conor told me, though, Kyle hurt you
worse than he hurt me. How are you feeling?"

Polly plopped back on the bed. "A lot better, but I wish my
head would quit hurting." She looked up at Susannah. "Damn,
girl, did Kyle do that to your shoulder?"

Susannah glanced at the ugly bruise, pushing away the memory of Conor's lips there. "No, the rifle stock did. Conor taught
me to shoot both a pistol and a rifle. I practiced too much, I
guess."

"That's what you've been doing? Learning to shoot?" Polly
asked skeptically.

Susannah turned her back and opened the buttons down the
front of her chemise. "Yes."

"And that's *all?*"

"Yes." Susannah quickly slipped the chemise off and the
nightdress on.

Polly fell back on her pillow, giggling. "You're crazy, girl.
You had that man up there in the mountains, all to yourself, and
you're telling me all you did was shoot guns?"

"Yes," Susannah repeated through gritted teeth. She pushed
her petticoats down over her hips and settled the nightdress in
place.

Polly suddenly sat up straight. "You're telling the truth, aren't
you?"

Susannah did not answer. She pulled the ribbon from the end
of her braid and worked the plaits out.

"But I thought you liked Conor. And from what Alex tells
me, he likes you."

Susannah saw Polly's perplexed expression in the reflection
of the mirror. "I do like him," she said softly.

Comprehension dawned on Polly's face. "Oh. But you're a
good girl." She shook her head. "Morals can get in the way,
can't they? Sometimes it's better to have a . . . shall we say, more

relaxed code of honor. Then you can do what you want." Her mouth curved in a lascivious grin. "I know what I would have done if that had been me up on that mountain with Conor O'Rourke. We'd both be smiling now, I can guarantee that." She gleefully hugged herself.

Hot color flooded Susannah's face. "I'm sure you would be," she said tightly. She ran the brush through her hair with long, forceful strokes.

"Ah, don't get all snippy with me, Susie. I was just funnin' with you. It's against my religion to go after another woman's man." Polly patted the bed. "Come here and let me braid your hair. Come on."

Susannah could not resist the woman's engaging smile. She handed Polly the ribbon and settled on the edge of the bed. After a minute of silence, she worked up the courage to ask, "How do you know so much about Conor?"

"I first heard of him a few years ago, when I was working in San Antonio. Where have you been, girl? He's *famous,* a real hero."

"I've been back east. Charleston, to be exact."

"Well, maybe you wouldn't have heard about him there," Polly allowed. Her fingers flew through Susannah's hair. "I could tell you weren't from around here. You talk funny."

Susannah smiled. "Polly, no one is from around here, except maybe the Indians."

"That's true," Polly conceded with a giggle. "I'm from Ohio, myself, by way of New Orleans and Texas." She tied the ribbon at the end of Susannah's braid and sat back.

Susannah shifted to face her. "Tell me what you know of him."

Polly shrugged. "Not much other than what I heard. I know he fought in the war, for the Confederacy, and he was a Texas Ranger, and I heard he's real fast with his gun."

Evidently there was a lot about Conor Susannah didn't know.

She wondered if the scars on his body were from the war or from a Ranger gun battle.

Polly was silent for a minute; then she covered Susannah's hands with one of her own. "What's the matter, Susie?"

Susannah shook her head. "I feel like I don't know anything about him at all. He never told me any of this. He let me think he was just a drifter, maybe even a gunman, because he's so fast with that pistol."

"He's no gunman," Polly assured her. "At least not that I've heard." She looked searchingly at Susannah. "Did you ever ask Conor about his past?"

Susannah shook her head.

"Maybe that's why he never told you any of that stuff. He doesn't strike me as the kind to brag on himself. Not like that damned Kyle Banning, who you can't shut up." Polly's features hardened. "I sure do wish he'd mouth off to the wrong man some day. As far as I'm concerned, both him and his brother need killing."

"I asked Conor to kill them," Susannah admitted. "But he refused."

Polly shook her head. "He won't do it like that. But if they push him hard enough, we both might get our wish." She patted Susannah's hands once again, then scooted over to the other side of the bed. "I will tell you one thing, Susie. I won't crowd your territory, but if you decide you don't want Conor O'Rourke, you let me know, because I'll take him as he is."

Susannah could only stare at her in surprise.

"Come on, girl, let's get some sleep. I'm bushed, and you look like hell, no offense."

With a smile, Susannah reached for the lamp. The room was plunged into darkness. "Good night, Polly."

"G'night, Susie."

Susannah settled under the sheets, vividly aware that this had been Conor's side of the bed. Her head rested on the pillow he had used. Her fingers tightened on the blanket that had covered him.

Conor was a hero. Why hadn't he told her? Why hadn't she asked him about his life? Would he have told her? Most of all, why was she so surprised?

Images of him floated in her mind. Conor caring for her father, burying him. Conor holding Lily Carolina, reading to her, tucking her into bed. She saw him as he played with Jesse, and worked on Alexandra's stable. He had tended her injuries, stroked her aching head, kissed her shoulder, her mouth, her neck, caressed her. Conor.

Pain knotted her belly again. Who was he? Soldier, cowboy, doctor, lawman, hero? Lover? Perhaps he was all of them, she mused. And if that were true, could she accept all that he was, all that he had been?

Oh, Conor.

Twelve

"Why didn't you tell me?" Susannah looked up at Conor from the sofa. He leaned one hand against the fireplace mantel and jabbed at the coals with the heavy iron poker. Sounds from the kitchen filtered down the hall and into the room. Alexandra would soon be calling them to breakfast.

"Tell you what, Susannah? That I survived a terrible battle in Texas? That I survived the war? So did a lot of other people." He put the poker in its stand and turned to face her.

"Polly said you're a hero."

"No, I'm not." The ferocity in his voice stunned her. "I used to be a soldier. I used to be a Ranger. Now I'm a ranch hand. Period." He leaned back against the mantel and hooked his thumbs in his belt. His eyes seemed to burn into her.

Susannah dropped her gaze and twisted her hands in her lap. "I just wish you had told me."

"What difference would it have made?" he asked. When she did not answer, he advanced on her and leaned over her. "What difference? Why are you so upset, Susannah?"

She looked up at him. He was so close. His jaw was clenched in anger; his eyes seemed to shoot sparks. "I don't know," she answered honestly.

Conor stared at her a moment longer, then straightened. "It won't matter for much longer. As soon as this situation with the Bannings is handled, I'll be gone."

"Breakfast!" Alexandra hollered down the hall.

Conor left the room without another word. Susannah stared into the fire, deeply troubled. *I'll be gone.* She took no comfort from his words.

Lucas McCleave arrived shortly after ten o'clock that morning, and Alexandra ushered him into the parlor. She and Susannah sat on the sofa, while Conor again stood near the fireplace. Lucas took a chair and spoke.

"Neville Thorpe returned late last night from Denver. There is no record of Walter's claim in the territorial assessor's files. Neville's brother works in the assessor's office; he'd have found the records if they were there."

Susannah's heart sank.

"Banning's power reaches that far?" Alexandra demanded.

"Evidently it does," Lucas answered. "But I'm surprised he moved so fast."

Susannah glanced at Conor, then turned to Lucas. "What will we do now? If we can't prove Uncle Walter legally owned the mine, the title can't be transferred to me."

Lucas stroked his beard. "Have you gone through all your family papers? There is nothing that would indicate ownership of the mine?"

"Nothing." Susannah shook her head. "I've searched through everything."

Conor pushed away from the mantel. "Your father told me Walter left some of his papers with a friend in Denver. I think it would be worth a trip down there to see what I can find."

Hope flared in Susannah's heart. "Of course. Before we came last fall, Uncle Walter was all alone. It makes sense that he would leave important papers where he felt they would be out of Banning's reach. Did he give you the friend's name?"

"A woman named Fannie Hodges."

"I've heard of her," Lucas said, with an apologetic glance at

Susannah. "She runs a classy sporting house on Holladay Street, called The Gates of Heaven."

The thought of her old Uncle Walter visiting a sporting house brought heat to Susannah's cheeks.

"Well, I guess everyone gets lonely," Alexandra said matter-of-factly.

"When do we leave?" Susannah asked Conor.

"We don't. I do."

"I'm going, too." Susannah stood up. "This is my problem, Conor. I insist you let me help solve it."

"It's too dangerous." Conor's firm tone invited no argument. "Banning was able to arrange the disappearance of the claim records in the territorial office, Susannah. There's a good chance he has people watching for you in Denver, hoping you'll go there looking for the claim deed. Besides, you can't travel during the day. You must stay here, and stay hidden."

"I will not!" Susannah clenched her fists at her sides. "I want this situation resolved, and I can't help if I'm in hiding. I *will* go to Denver with you."

Lucas stood up. "Susannah, I agree with Conor. It's too dangerous."

"You're outvoted, Susannah. I agree with Conor and Lucas." Alexandra spoke from her seat. "We must assume Banning has men looking for you. It won't do any good if you're captured or killed."

Susannah stepped away from them all, shaking her head with anger and disbelief. She glared at Conor. He fearlessly met her gaze. She looked at Alexandra, then Lucas. They were not going to change their minds.

"Since you all are deciding my life, may I ask what you propose to do with me?" she asked sarcastically. "Lock me in the bedroom upstairs?"

Alexandra patted the sofa. "Sit down, Susannah. We understand your frustration, but you must believe we have only your best interests at heart."

Susannah remained where she was. "I was willing to hide upstairs while I was recovering, Alexandra. I am no longer willing. I'll go mad, feeling that I'm doing nothing to avenge my father's murder. Besides, how safe is it here? Your patients go in and out of this house all day long. Sooner or later, someone will see me."

The other three looked at each other. "She has a point," Alexandra admitted. "I was caught with Lily Carolina one day last week. An injured miner barged in without knocking. I had no time to hide the child. I explained that she was the daughter of a dear friend in Denver, visiting for a while."

"Well, the next person who barges in just may know me," Susannah snapped. "If I can't stay here and I can't go to Denver, what will you do with me?"

"Susannah, we aren't doing anything with you," Lucas assured her. "You make it sound as if we are imprisoning you."

"But you are!" Susannah cried as she faced him, her hands at her hips. "From the day Conor pulled me from the river, everyone has been telling me what to do and where to go, first him, then you and Alexandra. But we're talking about *my* life, *my* little sister, *my* murdered father. The decisions should be mine."

"You may be willing to risk your life," Conor said flatly. "But we are *not* willing to let you."

"You need help, Susannah," Alexandra put in. "You can't take on the Bannings alone. We all care about you and Lily Carolina and want to help. Please let us."

"I have no choice, do I?" Susannah asked bitterly.

"Not with me, you don't," Conor snapped. "I made a promise to your father, and nothing will keep me from fulfilling it, not even you." He turned to Lucas. "Where is the safest place for her while I'm in Denver?"

Susannah clenched her teeth. "I'm going upstairs. When you've made your decision, do come and inform me." She spun around and marched from the room, her heels sounding a furious staccato as she climbed the stairs.

She reached the landing, relieved to hear a murmur of voices from Alexandra's room. Hopefully Polly was with Lily Carolina. As upset as she was, Susannah needed to be alone. Her wish was granted; the bedroom was empty. She closed the door and leaned against it.

They were right. Everything they said was right. Without proof of her uncle's ownership of the mine, she had no weapon, nothing to use against the Bannings. She could not come forward yet. "But I shall go mad," she said again, this time in a whisper. Tears of frustration burned her eyes as she paced the small room. "There must be something I can do." Wild visions filled her mind, of riding to Fletcher Banning's mansion and calling him out, of using her hard-learned skills with a pistol to shoot both him and his brother. She pressed her palms to her temples. As inviting as the idea was, she also knew it for the lunacy it suggested. "I must be losing my mind already," she muttered. She whirled at the sound of a knock on the door.

"I'm coming in," Alexandra warned, her voice muffled. She entered and closed the door behind her, a black garment draped over one arm.

Susannah crossed her arms and waited.

"You're going to stay at the Barton House while Conor is gone," Alexandra said.

"A hotel? Alexandra, what will I do all day in a hotel room?"

Alexandra shrugged. "Read, I guess, and write letters. Get some rest. It'll be boring, and I'm sorry for that, but there isn't much choice." She laid the black garment on the bed. "Lucas's office is on the second floor, so he won't be far away, at least during the day. We will bring you your meals, and I'll try to sneak Lily Carolina in to visit you." She held out her hands in a gesture of helplessness. "We don't know what else to do."

"How soon do I have to go?"

"Now. Conor wants to see you settled, then he'll be on his way."

Susannah was not concerned with Conor's wishes, but she refrained from saying so. "Since I can't be seen in Georgetown, how do you propose to smuggle me into the hotel?"

Alexandra waved at the garment on the bed. "I wore this when my father died. You'll pretend to be a distraught woman who has just suffered a death in the family. I have a hat with a heavy veil that goes with the dress. No one will recognize you."

"How long will Conor be gone?"

"I would guess at least three days, maybe longer. The railroad comes no farther than Floyd Hill. He'll have to ride there—about fifteen miles—and catch the train."

"I don't want to leave Lily Carolina again so soon, Alexandra. Can she come with me?"

Alexandra gave her a sympathetic look, then shook her head. "It's not a good idea. I don't want her away from me in the event anything happens with her arm, and it wouldn't be fair to coop her up in a small room for so long. Surely you can see that."

Susannah's shoulders slumped in resignation. "You're right," she admitted.

"I know how difficult this is for you, Susannah, but Conor, Lucas and I feel it's for the best," Alexandra said kindly. "We are dealing with killers, and our main goal is to keep you alive. The mine is not worth your life, my dear. Nor is vengeance against the Bannings. Now let me help you into this dress."

Susannah dutifully turned her back. A short time later, she stood in front of the bureau, staring at her reflection in the mirror. Alexandra's costly, fashionable dress was tight in the waist, tight in the ribs, tight in the bosom, and the skirt was too long, but it would do if she didn't breathe too deeply. The veil that fell from the wide hat brim to below her shoulders was so thick that no hint of her features or her hair color showed through. A big black shawl was the final touch. Alexandra was right; no one would recognize her.

"Will you be gone long, Susannah?" Lily Carolina had come into the room and now sat on the bed, her lovely little face showing her sadness.

Susannah moved to sit beside her sister, mindful of her bustle. She took Lily Carolina's hand in her own. "Only for a few days, honey, and I wouldn't be leaving at all if it weren't so important."

"But you just got home."

"I know." She gathered Lily Carolina into her arms. "I wish I didn't have to leave." The child clung to her. Susannah looked up to see Conor standing in the open doorway.

"We have to go," he said soberly.

Susannah pushed the veil out of the way and planted a kiss on Lily Carolina's cheek. "I'll see you soon," she promised.

"All right. Mr. Conor, will you be back soon, too?"

"I will, honey." Conor dropped to one knee beside the bed. He touched Lily Carolina's shoulder. "I'll be back before you know it."

The child felt for him, then put her arms around his neck and hugged him tightly. Susannah could see that Lily Carolina's splint dug into Conor's skin, but he did not complain. He kissed her cheek and scooped her into his arms as he stood. "I'll miss you, Poppet," he said.

Susannah was startled at the emotion in his voice. She let the veil drop into place and watched as Conor carried Lily Carolina out of the room. Conor O'Rourke loved Lily Carolina, and the child returned his feelings. Susannah stood up and reached for her carpetbag, feeling troubled and sad.

* * *

A half an hour later, Conor escorted a furious Susannah into a nicely appointed suite on the third floor of the Barton House. She waited until he closed the door, then turned on him.

"How dare you tell the clerk I'm your wife?" She tore the veiled hat from her head, mindless of the strands of hair that pulled free. "And that our baby died? How dare you?"

Conor shrugged as he set her carpetbag on the high, four-poster bed. "I had to tell him something. If the staff believes you're in the depths of a terrible grief, they'll leave you alone. Aside from Alexandra and Lucas, no one must see you, Susannah."

Susannah marched across the room and set the hat on the mirrored mahogany bureau. "I am so sick of the lies, of sneaking around," she said through clenched teeth to her reflection in the mirror. She whirled to face Conor. "It ends when you return, Conor O'Rourke. One way or the other, the lies end. I'll hide no longer."

"Agreed. I hate the lying, too." He pushed his hat back on his head. "I wish it wasn't necessary in order to keep you safe." He looked at her for a long moment, struck by her beauty. The black dress highlighted the narrowness of her waist, the paleness of her skin, the gold in her hair. A sad loneliness washed over him. He missed her, the Susannah he knew was there under this harsh, angry, frightened facade. Chances were she would never show that side of herself to him again. "I'll stop at the stable in Downieville and check on the mares. Is there anything you want me to bring you from Denver?"

"Just the deed to my uncle's mine," she coldly replied.

His mouth tightened. "Yes, ma'am." He pulled his hat into its proper position and turned toward the door.

Susannah was suddenly filled with shame. "Conor, wait."

He paused, his hand on the doorknob, and turned to her. The expression on his handsome face was impassive, guarded.

She took a hesitant step forward, then closed the distance

between them, the silk skirt rustling as she walked. "Please be careful."

The wary look in his eyes softened. "I always am." He stared at her, then reached out to touch her cheek. "Keep the door locked."

She could not help smiling. "You're doing it again."

His fingers moved to tuck a strand behind her ear. "What?"

"Telling me what to do."

His lips curved in a tentative smile just before they brushed her mouth. "I know," he whispered. "Be sure you do as I say." Then he was gone.

Susannah turned the key in the lock. "You *infuriating* man," she muttered. Then she closed her eyes and leaned her forehead against the door, her hand on the knob that was still warm from his touch. "Please come back safely," she whispered.

Early the next evening, Conor stepped out of the Denver Post Office and settled his hat on his head. He heard the sound of the clerk locking the door behind him. The sun had sunk below the magnificent mountain range to the west, and the air had taken on a coolness.

Conor looked up and down the street, his brows drawn together in a troubled frown. According to the postmaster, two days earlier a boy had claimed the letter from Wyoming Territory that had been waiting for him for over a week. Who could the boy be, and why would he have told the postmaster he was Conor's son? Of what interest would a letter from his cousin Alina be to anyone but him? All of Conor's finely honed instincts were on edge. He lifted his face, as if he could get a scent of the danger he felt, then set off in the direction of Holladay Street.

A thin boy watched as the man walked away. With one hand, the boy pushed a pair of spectacles farther up on the bridge of his nose while the other patted the pocket of the worn, too-small coat he wore. A grim smile covered his pale face at the feel of the crumpled letter. He pulled his collar up and his hat brim down, then shouldered an old single-shot breechloader rifle and followed the tall man.

"So you're Conor O'Rourke." Fannie Hodges slammed a glass on the table in front of Conor and poured a generous amount of amber-colored liquid into it. She refilled her own glass, then stuffed the cork back in the bottle and settled her ample figure into the chair opposite him. They sat at a tea table in the privacy of Fannie's opulent office. She raised her glass. "To Texas."

Conor raised an eyebrow. Had everyone in Colorado Territory come from Texas? "To Texas." He touched her glass with his and took a sip of what proved to be fine cognac. He briefly closed his eyes in appreciation of the choice liquor as it made its way to his empty stomach, then focused on his hostess. "How do you know of me?"

"Hell, honey, most people from Texas have heard your name." Fannie chuckled, an action that set her breasts to jiggling above the low neckline of her lime-green satin dress, a dress that was barely able to restrain the large mounds. "What brings you to Colorado Territory?"

"If you spent time in Texas, you know who Charles Goodnight is," Conor ventured.

"I sure as hell do," Fannie boomed.

Conor hid a grin by taking another swallow of cognac. Although he figured Fannie to be past her fortieth birthday, the woman's luxuriant black hair showed no sign of gray, and the thick tresses were artfully arranged in a becoming style. The color of her hair set off the peaches-and-cream quality of her once-superior complexion, a complexion that was beginning to show the effects of years of alcohol consumption and the inhalation of tobacco smoke.

"Goodnight's planning to start up a new cattle operation down by Pueblo. I've hired on to work for him, as soon as I finish a little business in Georgetown."

Fannie's glass paused for an instant before it found its way to her painted lips. Suddenly guarded, she sipped the cognac, then set her glass on the table. Her brown eyes bored into Conor. "I was beginning to like you, Conor O'Rourke, so I sure as hell hope you're not going to tell me you've been working for that damned Fletcher Banning."

Conor returned her stare, a little smile tugging at his mouth. He had always found saloon women refreshingly honest. "No, ma'am. I've never met the man, although I had a run-in with his brother."

Fannie snorted. "That pissant. Kyle Banning ain't worth the effort it would take to spit on him. He's a braggart and a fool, and fancies himself a gunfighter. He also likes to hurt women."

Conor's jaw tightened. "I know."

She grabbed her glass again. "If you're not for the Bannings, you're against them."

"Yes, ma'am."

Fannie visibly relaxed. "All right, Conor O'Rourke. Tell me what I can do for you."

Conor sighed and leaned back in the tall wing-backed chair, twisting a long, narrow cigar between his thumb and fingers. He and Fannie had been served a fine supper, one of the best he had eaten in years, by her French chef himself. They had shared several congenial hours over the meal. Now, she was across the room, bent down as she searched through her safe for Walter Duncan's papers, and he was enjoying the superior cigar and more of the imported cognac.

His eyes wandered around her office, examining the rich furniture and the interesting decorations. Fannie was a woman of exuberant tastes, as was demonstrated by the wildly patterned red and black carpet, complemented by floor-length, red velvet tasseled curtains at the windows. In case there was any question, her profession was announced by the very detailed painting of a nude man and woman entwined in an intriguing position that hung on the wall behind her desk. Fannie Hodges was evidently very proud of her establishment, as well as very successful in her business dealings.

"I still find it hard to believe old Walt's gone," Fannie said, her voice muffled in the reaches of the safe. "He'd come down just a few times a year, maybe three at the most. Once when the snows melted enough to let him off his mountain, and once in the fall before the snows came again, and sometimes he'd come down in the summer. I wondered if something had happened when he didn't come this spring."

A few pieces of paper fluttered up into the air. With a curse, Fannie grabbed for them, then added them to the growing pile on the floor at her feet. She flashed Conor a sheepish grin. "His papers are in here, Conor. I swear they are." She glanced down at her bosom. "Lord have mercy, the dam is about to overflow."

Conor's gaze innocently followed Fannie's. His eyes widened and he choked on a swallow of cognac.

"When I bend over, it strains this poor old dress something terrible," Fannie explained without a trace of self-consciousness as she rearranged herself within the confines of the endangered neckline. "There." She nodded with satisfaction and returned to her task.

Conor struggled mightily not to laugh. In desperation, he swallowed more of the cognac and only succeeded in making himself cough again.

Fannie lifted her head out of the safe and looked over her shoulder at him. "You need me to pound on your back?"

He held up a hand and shook his head. The coughing eased.

"I guess you'll live," Fannie decided, and poked her head back into the safe as Conor wiped his streaming eyes.

"He sure was a cute old coot, old Walt was," Fannie continued. "He always stopped off at the barber's first, for a bath, and to get his beard trimmed. He'd show up with his hat in his hand, his hair all slicked back, smelling like the barber had spilled the whole bottle of cologne on him. He always brought me something, too. Some little gew-gaw he bought with his hard-earned gold. He was so damned proud of his gold mine."

She straightened, triumphantly holding up a flat packet tied with a string. "Here it is!" She lifted her skirts over the pile of papers on the floor, then again adjusted her neckline as she crossed the room to her chair. "I never looked in it, so I don't know what's there." She handed Conor the packet, and her voice took on a sad, wistful note. "Walter always treated me like I was a lady. I'm gonna miss him."

"To the Duncan brothers," Conor said around his cigar as he raised his glass.

"To the Duncan brothers," Fannie repeated. She emptied her glass, then fell silent and watched Conor pull the string off the packet and spread the papers out over the table.

He picked one up. "This is a marriage certificate, from California."

"Now, I didn't know he was married," Fannie exclaimed. "Of course, a lot of our customers are."

Conor pulled the cigar from his mouth and set it in the ash bowl. He turned the certificate sideways. "Something's handwritten here. 'Lucinda and infant son died in childbed, November 12, 1854.' " Now he knew who the mine had been named for.

"Damn," Fannie muttered. "That's too damn bad. Poor Walter. He never spoke of her."

Conor stared at the paper. The stark words, written in a shaky hand, some of them smudged by long-dried water drops, tore at his heart. How sad that the physical expression of the love Walter and Lucinda shared had led to her death. What a cruel twist of fate. He was surprised at the compassion and grief he felt for Walter Duncan, a man he hadn't even known. Remembering the smile he had seen on Thomas Duncan's death-stilled face, he was comforted by the hope that Lucinda and her son had been waiting for Walter on the day he left this world.

Suddenly, Conor thought of Susannah. How would he feel if she died? His stomach knotted at the terrifying thought.

He shook his head and set the certificate aside, then picked up another yellowed piece of paper, eager to focus his mind on the concerns of the living. He stared at the paper in his hand. "This is the original claim made in 1859, Fannie," Conor said excitedly. He grabbed another paper and perused it. "This is the claim filed in 1861, when Colorado became a legal territory. And this"—he waved yet a third paper—"is the deed the assessor gave him. Everything's here; surveyor's reports, records of tax payments, receipts for ore samples, everything. This is exactly what we needed." He jumped up from the chair and lunged over to kiss Fannie's cheek.

"Well, if I'da known you were gonna kiss me, I'da found them papers a long time ago," Fannie declared, a pleased grin lighting up her face.

Conor organized the papers and wrapped the packet up neatly, tying the string around it once more. "We can defeat Banning now, at least as far as the mine is concerned."

"What are you going to do about Kyle Banning killing Thomas Duncan?" Fannie asked. "It don't seem right that he should just get away with it, though he did get away with killing that Max Treadwell a few years back."

"There's no statute of limitations on murder, Fannie. We may not be able to get Banning convicted of Thomas Duncan's murder, but plenty of people saw him kill Treadwell. An attorney in

Georgetown is looking into that now. If he can find enough witnesses willing to talk, he's going to ask the federal marshal and the U.S. attorney to file charges."

"That could prove difficult," Fannie said doubtfully. "If I remember correctly, no charges were brought against him in the first place because Fletcher Banning's henchmen terrorized the town. There's no saying they won't do it again." She eyed Conor thoughtfully. "But then, you weren't there two years ago."

"No, I wasn't, and neither was Lucas McCleave."

"I heard that old Ranger ended up in Georgetown. Is he the attorney you're talking about?" At Conor's nod, she continued. "He wasn't a man to mess with."

"He still isn't," Conor assured her.

"Well, I'd say the Banning brothers have a fight on their hands, Conor O'Rourke, and my money's on you."

"Thank you, Fannie." Conor stuffed the packet in his shirt pocket as he stood up. "And thank you again for the fine meal. I have to get an early start tomorrow, so I'll get on over to the hotel."

Fannie fell into step with him as he headed toward the door. "You're welcome to stay here if you like." She glanced at him from the corner of her eye. "I'd even offer you your pick of the girls, on the house, except for the tone of your voice and the look on your face when you talk about the elder of Walter's nieces—now, what's her name?"

"Susannah," Conor said softly.

Fannie nodded with a wise smile. "Even from the way you say her name, I'd guess that none of my girls would interest you."

"You're too smart for me, Fannie Hodges." He winked at her. "But thanks for the offer. A month ago, I would have gladly taken you up on it." He opened the door.

"She must be one hell of a woman," Fannie commented as

she guided Conor through the dimly lit parlor toward the front door.

"She is."

A low murmur of voices, both male and female, flowed around them, joining the strains of a violin that came from a corner. A lone musician sawed on his instrument, his eyes closed in concentration as he struggled with the difficult piece. Conor had to admit the man played fairly well.

He glanced at each person he passed, still unable to shake the feeling of impending danger. No one seemed to be paying him any attention. Well-dressed men and women sat together on sofas and loveseats scattered throughout the room, sipping wine and champagne served by a young woman in a maid's cap and apron. The difference between Fannie's establishment and the Silver Star Saloon in Georgetown was striking.

"What is it?" Fannie asked in a whisper.

Conor shook his head. "I don't know. Just a bad feeling."

Fannie's gaze traveled over the room. "For what it's worth, I know all these men, Conor."

He shrugged and took his hat from the hook it rested on. "I can't put my finger on it, but I've learned the hard way not to ignore these feelings."

"You're carrying something important now, something Fletcher Banning would probably kill for, so you be real careful, and get yourself back here if you run into any trouble." She jerked her thumb over her shoulder in the direction of a huge man who stood silently against the far wall. "We don't call my bouncer 'Ox' for nothing. He ain't too bright, but he's real strong, and a hell of a fighter. And I'm not bad with a shotgun myself."

"Thank you, Fannie," he said, genuinely touched by her concern. He kissed her cheek again and settled his hat on his head. "I'll remember that. Good night now."

Fannie opened the door for him. "Good night yourself, Conor O'Rourke. I'm pleased as hell to finally meet you."

"And I, you." He touched the brim of his hat and stepped out onto the porch. After a moment, Fannie closed the door.

Conor looked up and down Holladay Street, letting his eyes adjust to the dark. It was Thursday night, and late. With the exception of two obviously drunken men who appeared to be holding each other up as they rounded a corner a block away, everything was quiet. He closed his eyes, listening, sniffing the air. The feeling of uneasiness grew stronger.

With his hand resting on the butt of his pistol, he set off in the direction of his hotel. He had not gone twenty feet when a shot rang out. Conor hit the ground in a roll, his pistol in his hand, straining to see in the dim light. A strange glow and muffled swearing came from behind two wooden boxes stacked against the side wall of a dark building, but no other shots followed.

Puzzled, Conor got to his feet and silently approached the boxes, his pistol cocked and ready. The glow disappeared, and another whispered curse sounded. He heard a match being struck, and the glow appeared again. Conor leaned over the top box, and his mouth fell open in astonishment.

A boy crouched on the ground, holding a lighted match between his lips as he struggled to load an old breechloader rifle. The flare of the match reflected off the spectacles that had slipped down his nose.

Conor eased the hammer back into place and spun the pistol into the holster. In one swift move, he reached over the box, grabbed the boy's collar and hauled him to his feet. The match fell from the startled boy's lips, and he yelped when it hit his hand and went out. The rifle dropped to the ground.

"What the hell are you doing?" Conor thundered as he pulled the boy away from the rifle.

"Let me go!" The boy swung over his head at Conor's imprisoning hand.

"I don't think so, boy," Conor growled. He snatched up the

rifle and strode into the street, dragging the boy with him, back to Fannie's place.

"Let me go!" the boy shouted again as he twisted and kicked to get away.

"Shut up!" Conor snapped. He gave the boy a shake.

Ox opened the door and Conor thrust the boy into the big man's hands.

"Take him to Miss Fannie's office, Ox, and you'd be well advised to put your hand over his mouth."

Ox did as he was instructed, and Conor followed them into the house. Fannie came running to him.

"Conor, tell me that wasn't a shot we heard. We couldn't be sure."

"It was."

"And it was that boy who shot at you? Whatever for?"

"I don't know, Fannie," Conor said through clenched teeth. "Let's go ask him."

The boy sat in one of the wing-backed chairs in Fannie's office, his arms crossed over his chest, his expression defiant and unrepentant. Ox stood guard over him.

Conor advanced on him. "I want to know why you shot at me, boy," he said harshly. "You could have killed me."

"I wish I had!" the boy snarled.

Conor was taken aback by the rage and hatred that twisted the boy's face. "Who are you?" he demanded.

"I won't tell you."

"Search him, Ox," Conor coldly ordered.

"No! You can't! Leave me alone!" The boy struggled in vain as Ox pulled him from the chair and none-too-gently patted him down and emptied his pockets.

"That's all," Ox announced. He plopped the boy back down in the chair.

Fannie and Conor examined the small pile. A handful of bullets, an old pocket knife, less than a dollar in various coins, and a crumpled letter.

Conor recognized his cousin's handwriting. He snatched up the letter and put it in his pocket. So this was the boy who had taken the letter, who had claimed to be his son. Conor searched the boy's face for some familiar feature. Something, some memory, tickled the back of his mind, then was gone. Although he had always been very careful, could the boy be his son? he wondered. Even as he thought the words, he dismissed the idea. The thin and gangly boy looked to be eleven or twelve; if so, he would have been born around 1861, when Conor was just seventeen and fighting for the Confederacy. It wasn't possible; the boy could not be his son.

"You stole my mail, boy, claiming to be my son. Why?"

The boy pushed his spectacles back into place and crossed his arms over his chest.

"Let me try," Fannie whispered. At Conor's nod, she settled into the chair across from the boy and smiled broadly. "What's your name, honey?"

"I won't tell you," the boy snapped.

Ox immediately cuffed his ear. "You say 'ma'am' when you're talkin' to a lady," he admonished. "Didn't your ma teach you no manners?"

The boy pressed a hand to his red ear and glared up at Ox. "I won't tell you, *ma'am.*" Ox nodded in stern approval.

Fannie leaned back in her chair with a sigh. "I don't think the kid is gonna talk."

"Stealing mail is a federal offense, and attempted murder is pretty serious, too," Conor said. "Ox, you'd better go get the sheriff. Maybe he can get some answers out of him." Conor saw the flicker of fear in the boy's eyes.

Deputy George Wentworth had no better luck. For over an hour the deputy interrogated him, and the boy said nothing. Gradually the boy's anger faded to weariness, but his stubbornness did not abate. The deputy finally motioned Conor and Fannie out into the corridor.

"I agree with you, Miss Fannie. I don't think the kid's going to talk. What do you want to do with him?"

"You have to ask Conor, George. He's the one the kid shot at."

"Do you want to press charges, Mr. O'Rourke?"

Conor sighed and leaned against the wall. "He's just a kid, Deputy. And I don't have time to get involved with this. What do you suggest we do?"

George scratched his head. "Kid or no, he shot at you, and if the light had been better, maybe you'd be dead. I think I'll let him sit in a cell by himself for a few days, see if that won't persuade him to talk."

"Sounds good to me." Conor straightened and held out his hand. "I appreciate your help, Deputy."

"George, do you have any food over there?" Fannie asked. "The kid looks like he hasn't been eating too regularly, and a bath wouldn't hurt him, either."

"It's late, Miss Fannie. There's no food at the jail."

"Will you leave him with me for a bit, let me feed him and get him cleaned up? I'll have Ox bring him over later."

"I don't see why not."

Conor pulled a roll of bank notes from his vest pocket and peeled off a few. He handed them to George. "See the kid has some decent clothes when you let him go, and money enough for a train ticket back to wherever he came from."

Suddenly suspicious, George accepted the notes. "You're sure you don't know the kid?"

"I don't know him," Conor said wearily. "But he's in trouble, and I don't think he has anyone to turn to. Good night again, Fannie." And he was gone.

Conor lay on the bed in his hotel room, propped up against the pillows. He smoothed the wrinkled paper against his chest and read the letter, dated May twentieth, for the third time.

Dearest Conor. Beau and I have wonderful news. I was safely delivered of a healthy daughter on May 19. We named her Elizabeth Brianna, after Aunt Elizabeth and my mother. She is so sweet and beautiful! I cannot describe the true depth of the love we feel for her.

Pike is his usual dear, querulous self. He would not want me to tell you this, but I fear he is quite smitten by the baby.

I will write more when I feel stronger. Although we all miss you dreadfully, we hope your job with Mr. Goodnight is going well. Did you have a chance to look in on Susannah and her father?

Remember, you promised to visit after the baby was born. She is born, but I shall not pester you. Come when you can.

I remain, affectionately, your cousin, Alina.

Conor let the paper fall to his chest, and locked his hands behind his head. So Alina was a mother, Beau a father. He felt a strange mixture of elation and longing, elation for them, longing for himself. He wanted to see them, to hold their beautiful daughter. He ached for a family, for a daughter of his own. Lily Carolina's face came to his mind. It did not surprise him to realize he loved her like a daughter.

And Susannah—he thought of her beauty, her courage, her strength, her loyalty. He knew he loved her, too. From the moment he watched her stand up to Kyle Banning on the mountain, he had loved her.

But did she care for him? She had softened toward him, just a little, right before he left. He remembered the night in Alexandra's house, when she had smiled at him and patted the bed in sleepy invitation. She had not pulled away from his kiss that night. Nor had she yesterday, he realized. Was it possible that she could grow to love him? That she would let his past stay in the past?

And what if she did love him? he asked himself. What then? What could he offer Susannah and Lily Carolina, other than the labor of his hands and the love in his heart? Over the years he had saved enough money to buy a small spread. And he still had the option of accepting Alina and Beau's proposal of equal partnership in their ranch.

He could not offer Susannah and Lily Carolina the kind of life they had known with their grandmother, but then neither of them had ever indicated that they missed their old life. Maybe a simple life with him, raising horses and children, would be good enough. Besides, Susannah would probably like living near Alina.

Just before he left her, Alina had told him that she hoped he found whatever he was looking for. The thought occurred to him that he had. And he was not going to let Susannah slip away. Nothing would take her from him, Conor vowed. He would fight for her, for his dream of a life with her, for their future. He would fight the Bannings, fight her doubts about him, fight the world if he had to. She was his, as surely as he was hers.

Thirteen

In the suite on the third floor of the Barton House, Susannah also lay on a bed, propped against the pillows. Never had a day passed so slowly. She glanced at the locked door, then at the pistol on the table next to the bed, and shook her head. She'd much rather meet her enemies head on, face-to-face, and settle things. The hiding and lying had pushed her to the breaking point.

She sighed and slid down on the bed until she could curl on her side. Alexandra had told her when she brought supper that she expected Conor back the next night, unless there was trouble with the weather or the train. Where was he now? Had he found Fannie Hodges? Susannah frowned. Conor was a handsome, healthy man, with, she blushed to remember, a healthy appreciation for women. Would Fannie offer him more than Uncle Walter's papers?

She'd better not. And if she does, he'd better not accept. Susannah sat up, startled at her own thoughts. Why would she care if Conor chose to be with another woman? She jumped off the bed and paced the floor. But she did care. She wrapped her arms around herself as a picture of Conor filled her thoughts. She cared a great deal. Why? It was a question whose answer she was reluctant to explore, but then, she had nothing better to do.

What did Conor mean to her? Were her feelings for him based on need? Had she come to depend on his strength and protection so completely that she misinterpreted need for affection? He had saved her life, and that of her sister. Perhaps her feelings for him were based on gratitude?

Perhaps my feelings are based on love.

On love? Was it possible? Susannah didn't know. She had never been in love. And if it was love, what then? Did he love her? She came with a ready-made family. Was he ready to settle down, take on the responsibilities of a family? If not, there wasn't much hope of a future for them.

Susannah pressed her hands to her temples, realizing that her head had begun to ache. She was too tired to wrestle with such emotional questions tonight. Besides, she thought wryly, she didn't know the answers anyway. She pushed the thought of Conor O'Rourke from her mind, refused to acknowledge that she missed him, and went to bed.

Early the next morning she awakened from a troubled sleep, feeling tired and irritated. Only the faintest suggestion of light showed at the curtained window.

"I cannot bear another minute in this room," she whispered fervently as she threw back the covers. It took time, but eventually she managed to close most of the hooks down the back of Alexandra's dress. The hooks between her shoulder blades she simply could not reach. She draped the black shawl around her shoulders and positioned the hat and veil over her head, then slipped out the door, careful to lock it behind her.

She encountered no one until she reached the lobby, and the sleepy-eyed desk clerk did not seem to notice her. She crept out onto the porch and pulled the door closed behind her with a sigh of relief.

The sun had not yet topped Griffith Mountain to the east, and a thin, low-lying mist floated down the valley. Susannah breathed deeply of the cool, early morning air, thankful to be outside. Surely a short walk would pose no risk. No one would recognize her, dressed as she was. She pulled the shawl tighter around her shoulders and set off down the street.

* * *

"I can't believe you took such a risk!" Alexandra turned from the table, where she had placed Susannah's breakfast tray, and planted her fists on her hips.

Susannah rolled her eyes as she turned the key in the lock, then faced her friend. "For heaven's sake, Alexandra, calm down. As you can see, I'm fine. There was no danger." She moved farther into the room, struggling with the dress hooks. "I couldn't stand being cooped up any longer. Will you please help me?" She presented her back to Alexandra.

"Susannah, you can't just brush this off." Alexandra made short work of the hooks.

"But I learned some valuable information," Susannah argued. "William Hamill is going to have a big party right here in the hotel, in honor of the Volunteer Fire Department. Uncle Walter told me Fletcher Banning hates Mr. Hamill. He is insanely jealous of him, and wants to take his place, both in Georgetown society and territorial politics." She stepped out of the black dress and laid it on the unmade bed.

Alexandra folded her arms across her chest. "So?"

Susannah took her green dress from the chair and pulled it over her head. "Anyone who is anyone will be at that party, Alexandra, including the Bannings."

"So?" Alexandra repeated, her tone no warmer than it had been.

"Well, I don't know." Susannah fought with the hooks at the back of her own dress. "I just thought it might be useful information."

With an exasperated sigh, Alexandra grabbed Susannah's shoulders and turned her around. She closed the hooks with nimble fingers. "That information is of doubtful value, since I'm sure Lucas already knows it. And it most certainly was not worth the risk you took. What were you thinking of, going out alone like that?"

"I needed some fresh air," Susannah said soberly. "What possible harm could come to me, especially so early in the morning? There were very few people about." She sat down in one of the two chairs at the little table.

Alexandra took the other chair. "You have no idea what a tragically striking picture you make dressed all in black. There are three thousand people in this town, Susannah. Perhaps you didn't see many of them, but I would bet that many saw you, and those who did will remember you. You drew attention to yourself, and that is dangerous."

Susannah watched Alexandra pour two cups of fresh coffee and decided against mentioning that she had run into Ben Hollister, literally, outside Guanella's Bakery. He had come out the door just as she was passing, and collided with her. She had not spoken, had only nodded at his apology and hurried away, but she had definitely drawn his attention. The encounter had frightened her. Maybe her little walk had not been such a good idea.

"What's done is done, Alexandra. Conor will be back tonight, and hopefully we'll be able to start some kind of legal action against the Bannings tomorrow."

"Hopefully we will," Alexandra agreed. "Please just stay in this room until Conor comes for you."

Susannah only nodded before she sipped her coffee.

But Conor did not come back that night. Susannah paced the floor, growing more worried as the hours passed. She finally fell into an exhausted sleep just as the first cock crowed.

A few hours later, Polly brought her breakfast. "Alexandra had a patient come first thing this morning, so she asked me to bring your food." She set the basket she carried on the table and turned to look at Susannah, her hands at her hips. "You don't look too good, girl."

"He should have been back by now, Polly." Susannah paced the floor. "Alexandra said he'd be back last night."

"He would have been back by last night only if he took the train," Polly pointed out. "Denver is forty-five miles from here, Susie. On horseback, it's a two-day trip down and a two-day trip back, because it's too dangerous to travel at night in these mountains. Maybe he decided to ride the whole way. I bet he'll get back tonight." She plopped down on the edge of the bed, her large brown eyes sparkling mischievously. "I think you're sweet on the man."

"I am not," Susannah retorted. "I just don't want him to get hurt. He's done a lot for my sister and me."

"He's done a *hell* of a lot," Polly amended. "Just like he's done for me." She twirled one of her long curls on her finger.

"What do you mean?" Susannah pushed her untidy braid back over her shoulder as she sank wearily into a chair. She still wore her nightdress. Her bare toes dug into the carpet under her feet.

"I went to the Silver Star yesterday to see about starting back to work, and Mike—he's the bartender, you know—he told me that Conor had paid for my time through tomorrow."

Susannah stared at her, puzzled. "What does that mean, 'paid for your time'?"

"I guess when he stopped by the Queen to tell them I was hurt, old man Whitney—he's the owner—told him I couldn't be gone, that I'd lose my job. Conor told Whitney right to his face that it wasn't much of a job, but that it would be my choice to come back or quit, when I was feeling better. He slapped a bunch of money down on the bar and said my time was paid for, and that I'd be back in ten days." She shook her head, her full lips curved in a soft smile. "I don't know any other man that would have done that for a woman he hardly knows."

Susannah looked down at her clasped hands resting in her

lap. A strange pride filled her. "No, not too many men would have done that." Idly she wondered where he had gotten the money; she knew he had not taken it from the gold bag. She suspected that he had purchased their supplies with his own money as well, for the gold bag was as full as it had ever been. It occurred to her that she had not paid him the fifty dollars for teaching her to shoot.

Polly eyed her. "I think I could fall in love with a man like that."

Susannah looked up.

"And I just might if someone around here doesn't wake up," Polly continued nonchalantly.

Susannah ignored Polly's comment. She crossed her arms over her chest and chewed on her bottom lip, drawing her brows together in a worried frown. "Do you think he's late getting back because he stayed with Fannie Hodges?" she blurted out.

Polly's eyes widened. "Is that what's troubling you, girl?" She jumped off the bed and dragged the other chair from beside the table to set it in front of Susannah. "That man didn't do anything with Fannie Hodges," she said firmly as she sat down.

"How do you know?" Susannah's voice sounded small and forlorn, even to her own ears.

"Because I know people, Susie, especially men. And Conor ain't the wandering type. That's why I never seriously asked him to go with me. He'd have turned me down flat." Her sigh was heavy with disappointment. "He would have been nice about it, but he would have turned me down."

Susannah felt the heat rise in her face. She couldn't believe she was discussing the possibility of Conor "going" with other women, but she forced herself to continue. "How do you know for sure, Polly? You're so pretty, and lively, and funny, and I know he likes you. Are you sure he would have turned you down?"

"I'm sure," Polly said firmly. "In my business you develop a sense about these things. I can't explain it, but I always know when a man is interested in *that,* without him ever saying a word. And Conor isn't, not with me. He likes me, all right, but he loves you."

"Wh-what?" The word came out in a strangled whisper.

Polly sat up straight, her hands at her hips. "What's the matter with you, girl? I swear, you are more blind than your little sister. *She* knows Conor loves her; she told me so. And anyone who can see how he looks at you would know he loves you, too. That man is willing to die for you."

The dancer's words pounded into her brain. *He loves you.* Susannah closed her eyes against the powerful rush of elation and hope that filled her. "I don't want him to die for me," she whispered.

"He won't," Polly said cheerfully. "The Bannings won't get him. He's too smart, and he's too fast. You watch and see. He'll be back soon, and this whole mess will be settled for good."

Susannah reached for Polly. "Thank you," she said softly.

Polly squeezed her hands. "Now don't go getting all sweet on me, Susie," she warned, her voice warm with affection. "I should be mad at you for taking the man I want, but I just can't be." She released Susannah and stood up. "I brought enough food for both of us, so let's eat." She put her chair back in its proper place and pulled the napkin off the basket.

"Will you go back to the Silver Star?" Susannah accepted the napkin Polly held out to her.

With a nod of her dark head, Polly unscrewed the lid off a jar and poured steaming coffee. "I'll move back to my old room at the saloon tomorrow, at least for a while. It's not a great place to work, but I've been in worse, let me tell you."

"But what do you want out of life, Polly? I can tell you're educated by how you speak. Isn't there something else you could do? It seems to me there's not much future in your, ah, line of work."

Polly found no judgment in Susannah's expression. Instead, there was curiosity, and concern. "I want to dance, Susie. That's all I've ever wanted to do. I love to dance, and I'm good at it. The rest comes with the job." Her voice grew soft. "Someday I'd like to work in a real nice place, though, just as a dancer. Or maybe own the place myself. Dance all night and sleep all day. Take lovers when *I* want to. That's what I'd really like."

Susannah could only stare. "But you said you wanted children. Don't you want to settle down, marry?"

"Me?" Polly laughed. "No, not me. I said Lily C. makes me want to have kids, but it's a feeling that comes and goes. What kind of a mama would I make? I'd get bored silly being all settled down. Besides, you already got the best man, probably in the whole world." She took a sip of coffee, her eyes twinkling over the rim. "But I'm warning you, girl. You've got to go after what you want in life, and if you don't make up your mind about Conor O'Rourke, and soon, I'll consider him fair game. I guarantee, I'll give you a run for your money."

"I'm sure you would, Polly." Susannah smiled. "I'm sure you would."

"But this telegram says he left Denver the day before yesterday. Where could he be?" Susannah paced in front of the bureau, her freshly washed, drying hair falling free down her back and swaying with her movements. It was late the next afternoon, and Conor had not returned.

Lucas glanced at Alexandra. Fannie Hodges' answer to his telegram had not eased their fears. Conor was overdue.

"Perhaps there was trouble on the trail," Alexandra suggested. "Maybe he had to detour around a rock slide or something. Those things happen, you know."

"Maybe the Bannings happened," Susannah said bitterly.

Lucas held up a hand. "We can't jump to conclusions, Susannah. Conor's a man who can take care of himself. There could be any number of reasons for his delay, and I'm sure his reason is a good one. But if he's not back by tomorrow night, we'll go find him."

"I think we should begin the search now. And I'm going."

"Absolutely not." Lucas's tone was firm. "Conor would want you to wait here, and I insist that you do. We must give him time. Remember, it took Neville five days to go to Denver, do what he had to do, and get back, and he had no real trouble except that the train was late."

Susannah knew Lucas was only being sensible, but she did not want to be sensible. If the Bannings had Conor, she would never see him alive again. She looked from Alexandra to Lucas. Their expressions were a curious mixture of worry, concern and determination.

"Very well," Susannah snapped. "We'll wait until tomorrow."

Alexandra's eyes narrowed with suspicion. "You're sure?"

"What else can I do?" Susannah placed her hands on her hips. "I can't very well go look for him myself, and you won't help me until tomorrow. So we'll wait until tomorrow."

Lucas put a comforting arm around her shoulders. "I know you're worried about him, but like I said, Conor can take care of himself. I'm sure there is a simple explanation. He could still come in tonight. There's at least another hour of daylight left."

Susannah relaxed. "You're right," she admitted. "I'm being silly. I warned you I'd go mad locked up in this room."

Alexandra stood up and smoothed her skirt, obviously relieved. "I'm glad that's settled. We're going to have an early supper with the Potters. Minerva is at my house cooking right now—"

"And I'm sure Lily Carolina and Jesse are helping," Susannah gently interjected. Although she had seen her sister earlier that day, the words brought a powerful feeling of loneliness.

"I'm sure she is," Alexandra continued. She moved to the

door. "If you don't mind waiting, I'll send your supper with Lucas later. I promise we won't keep him."

"I don't mind waiting, Alexandra. I'm not hungry now anyway." Susannah gave her friend a quick hug. She stepped back and noticed the concern on Alexandra's face. "I'm fine," she said with a reassuring smile. "Really. You both go on now."

"Trust Conor, Susannah," Lucas said. "He's a smart man, and tough. He'll be back."

Susannah managed a smile. "I'm sure you're right. I'll see you later." She waved them down the hall, then closed the door and turned the key.

"You have until dark, Conor O'Rourke," she whispered fiercely against the wood. "If you're not here by then, I'm going to search for you. You could be dead by tomorrow night."

He did not return by dark. Susannah waited until Lucas brought her supper, treating him with calm politeness, pleading fatigue when he offered to stay and play backgammon with her, begging him silently to leave. The minute he did, she pulled her father's clothes from her carpetbag. She tore more than one hook from her dress in her haste to remove it.

Dressed again, Susannah picked up her holster and eased the gun out. She pulled the hammer back halfway and spun the barrel, making sure all the chambers were loaded. The action reminded her of Conor, and a wave of longing washed over her. She remembered the days in the mountains, his gentle patience as he taught her how to defend herself. He had stood close behind her, guiding the rifle to its proper position, guiding her aim, and, she now realized, guiding her heart into his hands. His teaching had been a gift to her, a gift that would perhaps one day save her life, or that of her sister.

She owed so much to him. But she now knew her feelings for

Conor were much more than need, or gratitude, or affection. She loved him. And she wanted the opportunity to tell him that.

Susannah returned the pistol to the holster, then strapped the gunbelt around her hips and tied the string at her thigh. The weight of the gun was comforting, and filled her with confidence. She shrugged into her father's coat and pulled her wide-brimmed hat down low over her pinned-up hair, tightening the string under her chin. She stared at herself in the mirror. In the baggy clothes, and in the dark, she would easily pass for a boy, or a small man.

Thoughtfully, she caught her bottom lip between her teeth. Polly had been right about the danger of traveling in the mountains at night. Without a horse, it would be useless to search far. However, the Bannings lived within walking distance, only three miles out of town.

The thought of Conor in the clutches of the Bannings made her blood run cold. In her mind she saw Kyle hitting him again and again, breaking his beautiful body the way her father's body had been broken, and a sick feeling settled in the pit of her stomach. Her mouth tightened in fierce determination. If the Bannings had Conor, she would free him. They would not take Conor from her, as they had her father.

Susannah moved purposefully toward the door. It would be a long walk, but even in the dark, she would be able to follow the road. And there would be a half-moon later. She would search the Banning property for any evidence that Conor was being held prisoner. If she found none, she would have no choice but to return to the hotel and wait for daylight.

Georgetown was quiet that Sunday night. Susannah easily slipped out of town, headed down the road that if followed far enough, would lead to Denver. She made good time, her concern for Conor lending speed to her booted feet. Grateful that she had encountered no one, she finally reached the cutoff to the Banning property, heralded by an ornate arch made of brick and wrought iron. The main house was farther up a narrow private road.

After several minutes, Susannah rounded a bend in the rough dirt road and stopped short, amazed at the distant sight of Fletcher Banning's home. The mansion sat on a rise, towering above the barn, the bunkhouse, and other outbuildings. Light poured from every window. A dog barked, once, twice, then no more. Horses moved around in the corral ahead to her left, one whinnying a welcome to her. A large carriage house rose dark and silent on the right.

Her breath came fast and her heart pounded, whether from the haste of her journey or from fear, she could not tell. How would she learn if Conor was held here, other than by searching each building as best she could? She pulled the collar of her father's coat up around her neck and looked up at the sky. A few thin clouds skittered across the face of the rising moon, and the tops of the pines whispered together. The beauty of the evening provided a strange contrast to the desperate circumstances of her presence on the land of Fletcher Banning.

Susannah circled the corral and came to one end of the huge barn. The doors were barred, but she was able to lift the board with little noise. She slipped inside.

The barn was warm, and smelled pleasantly of animals and hay. It was also completely dark. Susannah could not make out so much as the outline of the stalls she knew had to be there. But even if she had known where to find a lantern, she would not have dared to light it. A low nicker came from the right, and she heard the sound of an animal crunching hay or oats. Aside from the movements and sounds of the animals, she could hear nothing.

"Conor," she called in a loud whisper. There was no answer, save another nicker. She backed out of the building and carefully replaced the board in the brackets. The bunkhouse was farther up the rise. Perhaps she would learn more there.

A dog barked. Susannah immediately fell to the ground and jerked her pistol from her holster. There was no doubt what made her heart pound now. When the dog remained quiet, she inched forward, slowly, until she reached the back of the long, low building. She scurried around one end and settled under an opened window, straining to hear what the men inside were saying.

Someone complained about the stew, and someone else told a ribald story that elicited a round of raucous laughter and brought heat to Susannah's cheeks. She adjusted her hat, determined to wait and listen for a while longer. Although she stayed there for perhaps a half an hour, she heard nothing that indicated a prisoner had been taken, nor was there any reference to her, or to any member of her family.

From where she sat, she could see the big house clearly. What would be gained from going any closer? If she were smart, she would leave now, and wait until daylight to look for Conor. This was foolishness. Yet she did not leave. She wanted to look in the windows of that mansion, to see where Fletcher Banning had wanted her to live, to make certain there was no evidence that Conor was here. There was no cover between her position and the house. She had no choice but to sprint across the open ground, and she did, with a prayer on her lips.

The dog barked again, more fiercely, and kept barking. Susannah reached the relative safety of a bush next to the house, near a window. She crouched down and pressed into the shadows.

A man came out onto the porch of the bunkhouse. After a few minutes the dog quieted and the man stepped back inside. Susannah released the breath she had not realized she was holding. She inched up the wall until she could peek in the window. The room, an elegant, almost opulent parlor, was empty.

She eased back down to her hands and knees and crawled to the next window. A lace curtain hung out over the sill, fluttering in the breeze. Voices came from within, of men and at least one woman. Susannah cautiously raised her head and looked over the sill into a well-lit dining room.

Fletcher Banning sat at the head of a long table, dressed in fashionable evening wear, sipping from a glass of wine. Kyle Banning sat at the other end, and a woman was seated with her back to Susannah. The woman turned her head and invited Kyle to shut his mouth, and Susannah recognized her as Victoria, Fletcher and Kyle's younger sister.

Suddenly the dog barked again and a horse cantered into the yard. Susannah dropped to the ground and lay flat, her heart in her throat. She peered from under the brim of her hat and watched as a man pulled up in front of the bunkhouse and stepped down from the saddle, tossing the reins to a man who had come out on the porch. The rider crossed the yard and entered the house. A minute later, Susannah heard a door open, and a new voice floated through the window.

"Mr. Banning."

"Victoria, leave us."

A chair scraped across the floor; a door closed.

Fletcher Banning spoke again. "This time I hope you have something to report, Ben."

Susannah sat up against the wall and turned one ear toward the window. She had to hear this conversation!

"Not much, sir. There's been no sign of Susannah Duncan anywhere, including the Territorial Office in Denver."

Susannah's eyes widened. Conor had been right to keep her from going to Denver. She held her breath as Ben continued.

"Lucas McCleave seems to be minding his own business, and the man Kyle had a run-in with at the Silver Star, the one asking for directions to the Duncan mine, well, no one has seen him in days."

Susannah sagged against the wall in relief, surprised to feel tears form in her eyes. The Bannings did not have Conor. They did not even know who he was.

"He probably learned who he was messing with and decided to leave town," Kyle snarled in a strangely hoarse voice.

Susannah's lip curled in derision.

"Time will tell, little brother." Fletcher's tone held a contemptuous note. "Do you think it's safe to press for an auction of the Duncan mine, Ben?"

"I thought you were just going to transfer the title to your name," Kyle interjected.

"I was," Fletcher snapped, his irritation evident in his tone. "But I decided that's too dangerous. People would wonder how I knew the Duncans were dead. I'll still get the mine; Jackson will be able to guarantee the outcome of an auction. Now shut up and let me talk to Ben."

"I reckon you can press for the auction, Boss, but it could get sticky. It would be best if someone not associated with you brought up the fact that Walt Duncan hasn't been seen for a while."

"Arrange it," Fletcher ordered.

"Yes, sir." A pause. "You do know, sir, that Jackson, or someone, will have to go up to the mine and make an official report that the claim has been abandoned."

"Make sure Jackson does it. Tell him to report that the Duncan brothers died in a fire."

Susannah clapped a hand over her mouth to keep from crying out in fury. Her other hand tightened convulsively on the pistol grip.

"What about Miss Duncan, Mr. Banning? The normal procedure would be to advertise for her whereabouts in the newspaper."

"We don't have time for that! Walter Duncan did us a favor by dying, and thanks to Kyle, the problem of Thomas Duncan has been solved as well."

A cold rage grew in Susannah, crushing any remnants of fear. She eased the hammer back in one smooth motion.

"As I told you before, if Susannah shows up, she will either marry me or she will die. There will be no advertisement placed, Ben."

"And if that man comes back, he's mine," Kyle rasped.

"I have a feeling he will, Kyle," Fletcher said harshly. "I don't believe in coincidences, nor do I believe that man just went away. He has something to do with the Duncans, and when he shows up, I'll expect you to kill him."

The rage turned to fury. Susannah thought of all the pain the Banning brothers had brought to the people she cared about: Uncle Walter, her father, Polly, herself. Now they threatened Conor's life. They threatened her life. And if they knew about Lily Carolina, Susannah was certain they would threaten her sister's life as well.

No more. They would threaten no more. They would kill no more.

An eerie, determined calm came over her. She positioned herself on one knee. The curtain still fluttered out the window, offering some cover. She rested the tip of the gun barrel on the sill and sighted on the middle of Fletcher Banning's forehead. He was talking, but she no longer heard his words. The dog barked.

Conor's voice sounded in her head. *Take the time to hit what you're aiming for. Take a deep breath, then hold it. Squeeze the trigger, don't pull it.* She took a breath, and held it. Her finger tightened on the trigger.

Your father would not want you to do this. Susannah blinked. *What about your sister?* Susannah released her breath. Her eyes filled with tears as her finger relaxed.

She could not do it. She slumped against the wall, allowing her gun arm to drop to her knee. A tear slid down her cheek. She was a coward.

Sounds gradually penetrated her thoughts. The dog still barked, and the horses milled about nervously in the corral.

"Go see what that damn dog is barking at, Ben."

"I found cougar tracks out past the corral the other day, Boss. It could be that."

"Well, whatever it is, shut the dog up, even if you have to take him inside."

"Yes, sir. Good night, Mr. Banning."

She had to get out of there. Susannah brushed her hand across her cheek and eased the hammer back in place. She decided against retracing her steps. The farther away from the bunkhouse she stayed, the better. She slipped around the back of the house and to the opposite side. Two outbuildings waited just at the edge of the light that shone from the windows. If she could get behind them, she could work her way back into the trees and then on down the road. It was her best chance. It was probably her only chance.

Susannah darted across the yard and pressed against the side of the closest building. From the scent, she guessed it was the smokehouse. *If you think you're being followed, wait and listen.* She waited and listened. When she heard nothing out of the ordinary, she crept around the back of the building, then to the next one. Again she waited. She returned the pistol to its holster. The blackness of the trees called to her, urged her to come. She stepped forward . . . and was grabbed around the shoulders from behind. It felt as if her heart stopped.

"What do we have here?"

Susannah recognized Ben Hollister's voice.

He shook her. "Answer me, boy!" He started pulling her toward the yard.

The bones in a man's foot are easy to break. Without another thought, Susannah stomped on Ben's foot at the same time she stabbed her elbow into his gut. He grunted and loosened his hold just enough for her to twist away. She raced for the cover of the trees. Not until she reached their welcoming darkness did she look back.

Ben was not far behind her, and he was limping. *A pheasant gets killed when it leaves its hiding place.* Susannah ducked under the low branches of a pine and crouched against the rough trunk. Once again she eased the pistol out. She waited, her free hand pressed to her mouth, trying to stop the sound of her breathing. Ben approached, then stopped. Susannah squeezed her eyes shut. Ben Hollister had been kind to her that day on the mountain, had kept Kyle from killing her. She did not want to shoot him.

"Shit, I can't see anything out here," Ben muttered. "Better go let the dog loose." He backed away.

Susannah peered through the branches, watched until she saw Ben limp into the light surrounding the house before she allowed herself to breathe. The cool air felt blessed as it soothed her burning lungs. She crawled out from under the branches, knocking her hat off. It hung down her back, the string taut against her throat. She managed to stand, and with a shaking hand put the pistol back in the holster.

Then Susannah ran, as if the devil himself were after her.

Fourteen

Susannah almost dropped the key in her struggle to unlock the hotel room door. Finally she succeeded and slipped into the dark room. She sank to the floor and rested against the solid strength of the wooden door. Her breath came in heaving gasps.

That had been too close.

A myriad of emotions churned within her: relief, fear, disappointment. Relief that the Bannings did not have Conor, relief that she was safe, fear for Conor's continued absence, disappointment that she had not been able to kill the Bannings.

Gradually her breathing slowed, and she pulled her hat string off over her head. She got to her feet, surprised that her legs were shaking, and lit the lamp on the bureau. With trembling hands, she poured water from the crystal pitcher into a glass and drank it down, then looked in the mirror. The reflection of her face startled her. Her hair was disheveled, her eyes huge and haunted, her cheeks red from her exertion. "You are lucky to be alive," she whispered to herself. "The Bannings would have killed you." She stared into her own eyes. "And you would not have died a virgin."

She braced her palms on the bureau and leaned her weight on her arms. Her head fell forward. The images of what Kyle Banning would have done to her made her shiver. "I can't think about that," she said firmly, and crossed the room to the washstand. She poured cool water into the basin, then stripped out of her father's clothes and washed herself thoroughly.

The clean nightdress felt warm and comforting as it settled over her body. Susannah pulled the pins from her hair and ran her brush through the long locks, over and over. Lavender scent floated around her. The normal, familiar actions helped chase the last vestiges of terror from her mind.

She turned the lamp down low, then moved to the window. The same night breeze that had drawn Fletcher Banning's lace curtains out his window now caused her own curtains to wave, although her window was opened only a few inches. She pushed the curtains back and sat on the floor, letting the cool air fan the heat from her face.

She had almost killed a man. Thinking back over it, she found the remembered force of her rage frightening; yet at the same time she knew it was justified. Fletcher Banning deserved to die, Kyle even more so. She searched her soul and found no trace of guilt, except for the nagging feeling that she had let her father down by not pulling that trigger.

Your father would not want you to do this. As had happened each time Conor's words sounded in her head, she knew he was right. Her gentle father would not want her to kill. He would want justice, but not at the cost of his daughter's life, or Conor's. Nothing was worth Conor's life. Nothing.

"Oh, Conor," Susannah moaned. She leaned her head against the sill. "Please come back so I can tell you how much I love you."

Some time later, she awakened. She lay on the floor by the window, now completely chilled. Her stiff legs complained when she stood. She closed the window, pulling the curtains together. At the bureau, she again looked in the mirror. Her eyes looked more normal, although sleepy. She ran the brush through her hair one last time, then took the lamp to the bedside table and placed it next to her gun.

How late was it? She yawned as she pulled back the bedclothes. She'd sleep until first light; then, with or without Lucas's help, she was going out again to search for Conor.

She heard a sound outside her door and froze. There was a soft knock. She reached for the gun.

"Susannah."

Her heart started pounding in wild joy. She hurried to the door, then paused with her hand on the key. What if her mind was playing tricks on her?

The knock sounded again. "Susannah, it's Conor."

There was no mistaking his voice. With a glad cry, she turned the key and flung the door open.

He stood there, tall and handsome, his hat in one hand, his rifle in the other. "I'm back," he said.

"I'm glad." She raised an eyebrow. "Your hair is wet."

"I, uh, stopped off at the bathhouse."

"I didn't know the bathhouse was open this late."

"It's not, usually." As he watched, an enchanting smile lit up her face. Her eyes were very green, and it seemed to Conor that they were shining. Her beauty took his breath away. She was dressed simply, in a white cotton nightdress, her glorious golden hair down around her shoulders, a few strands curling over her breasts. He had never seen a more beautiful sight.

"Are you going to come in?" Susannah asked quietly.

He nodded and stepped into the room, leaning his rifle against the wall. The lamp spread its warm, welcoming light over the bed, the inviting bed, with the blankets pulled back. Suddenly he felt awkward and shy. He watched as Susannah locked the door. "Your uncle's papers, they—"

"I don't care about my uncle's papers." Susannah took his hat from his hand and tossed it toward the chairs. Conor watched in surprised silence as the hat hit the edge of one seat and fell to the floor. He looked back at Susannah when she moved against him and put her arms around his neck.

"I prayed for the chance to tell you I love you," she whispered, her lips so close that he could feel her breath on his mouth. "I thank God I got it." She kissed him tenderly. "I love you, Conor O'Rourke." Her arms tightened on him.

A deep joy surged through Conor as he wrapped his arms around her and crushed her to his chest. He knew he loved her, and had hoped she would grow to love him. He had dreamed of their life together. But not even the sweetest and wildest of those dreams had prepared him for the effect her words would have on him. Suddenly his empty life had meaning. Purpose. Love. He felt blessed, truly and deeply blessed. "Susannah." One hand moved to cradle the back of her head. "My sweet woman. I love you more than life itself."

She pulled back from him, just enough to place a hand on each side of his face, and stared into his eyes. *"Nothing* is worth your life; not revenge, not the mine, not anything. You'll not die for me, Conor. I want you to live for me. I won't have it any other way."

Conor smiled. "Yes, ma'am." He brushed a golden curl back from her forehead. "But only if you kiss me."

Her lips parted and her eyes closed, very slowly, as she moved her mouth to his. Her fingers wandered through his damp hair; she pressed the soft fullness of her breasts against his chest.

Conor groaned. His mouth responded to her sweet, seeking one. Her little tongue pushed between his lips, and he granted her access. His hands roamed up and down her back, from neck to hip. The realization that she wore nothing under the thin night-dress caused a shudder of fierce desire to run through his body. He pulled his mouth from hers and nuzzled the side of her neck. One hand pressed the small of her back, holding her against him, while the other caressed her arm. "We'd best be careful, sweetheart." His voice was husky, his breathing harsh. "I don't want us doing anything you aren't ready for."

Susannah rested her head against his shoulder. Her breathing seemed fast to him. "I'm ready, Conor. For anything you'll give me." Her breathing was definitely fast.

"Susannah?" he whispered hopefully, wonderingly. Had he understood her meaning?

She planted a kiss on his cheek. "We'd best get to bed." He looked down at her, found her honest, intent gaze on him. "But tonight you're not sleeping on the floor, Conor O'Rourke, and you're not wearing these pants, either." She tugged at his belt, then wrapped her arms tightly around him and lifted her mouth to his in sweet invitation.

The wave of love and desire that roared through him took his breath away. His feelings were communicated in his kiss, his fierce, passionate kiss. She moaned and sagged against him. He swept her into his arms and carried her to the bed, laying her on the sheets. His eyes did not leave her as he stood back and took off his vest, allowing it to fall to the floor, then removed his gunbelt and hung it over the corner of the headboard. He sat on the edge of the bed, next to her hip.

A smile curved her lips. He could not resist the beckoning in her love-soft eyes. Their mouths touched, moved, opened.

He leaned his weight on her, and she put her arms around him. He smelled clean, and masculine.

"Love me, Conor," she whispered. "Make me yours."

He pushed away from her and sat up, one hand caressing her cheek. "You are already mine, Susannah."

She sighed with happiness. "You're right." Without taking her eyes from his, she opened the buttons of his shirt, one by one. He needed no further encouragement. In a matter of moments, he stood before her, tall and proud, hiding nothing.

Susannah could not breathe. The soft lamplight washed over his body, touching him with gold. He was beautiful. Absolutely beautiful. Although she had never before seen a naked man, she knew that Conor was magnificent. Magnificent and fascinating. She met his eyes. From the expression in those hot, blue depths, she also knew he read her thoughts, understood her desire. Her nightdress suddenly felt very confining. She sat up and undid the buttons down the front with trembling fingers.

Conor stepped forward to help her pull the garment off over her head, then stood back again. Susannah bowed her head, overcome with shyness, grateful that her hair covered her breasts. She felt his hand on her hair, pulling its length back behind her shoulders.

"Don't hide yourself from me, Susannah," he said huskily. "I love all of you, want all of you, accept all of you. Let me see all of you."

She slowly sank back on the pillows and stared up at him as his eyes roamed her body. It was as if his gaze burned wherever it touched, branding her. All sense of shyness disappeared. Her breath came quickly. Her breasts tingled, her nipples hardened, a hot flame started in her belly and spread, lower and lower. The force of the wonderful, unexpected sensations startled her. He hadn't even touched her yet.

Now his breath seemed to come faster. Susannah's eyes widened at the sight of his body's physical response to her. She had done that to him. She bit her bottom lip, delighting in the sense of feminine power she felt. She held her hand out. "Conor." She breathed his name. "Come to me."

A shudder ran the length of his body as their hands touched. He joined her on the bed, lying beside her, propped on one elbow, his hand on her stomach. One of his legs covered one of hers, his unfamiliar hardness pressed against her hip.

"I think I've waited all of my life for you, Susannah Duncan." He kissed her again, with reverence, as his hand moved over her.

Even against his mouth, Susannah gasped when his fingers caressed the swell of her breast. A low moan escaped her when his gentle fingers touched the hardened, sensitive peak.

"My woman," he whispered, a note of wonder in his voice.

"My lovely woman." His mouth moved to her neck, kissing, nibbling, licking, then moved down, burning a trail to her breast.

She cried out when his tongue touched her, and again when his lips fastened on her. Filled with sweet aching, she ran her fingers through his long hair, holding his head against her. His hand moved lower to stroke her thigh. Gradually his fingers wandered to the inside of her leg, then higher, and higher. She shifted her hips, instinctively raising them, and tossed her head back and forth. His fingers were upon her, parting the curls, exploring gently, relentlessly.

"You are so soft," he murmured against her breast. "So warm, and wet." He moved between her legs and rested there.

Her hands moved over him feverishly, captivated by the feel of his skin, in some places smooth, in others, hair-roughened. She delighted in the strength of his muscles, the power that emanated from him.

"Are you ready for me?" he asked in a strange, pleading tone.

"Oh, yes." She opened up to him, her body and her heart, and he pressed into her, slowly. His heart pounded against her breast. He stopped moving, suddenly held very still.

"What is it?" she whispered fearfully. She stared up at him.

"I don't want to hurt you." He kissed her nose, then her cheek. "God, I don't want to hurt you."

Susannah moved her hands down his back to his flanks and held him, urging him on. "Please, Conor, don't wait."

He groaned and covered her mouth with his, and in one swift thrust buried himself in her.

She gasped. The pain was sharp, but faded quickly. Again he did not move. She held him tightly, savoring the indescribable feel of him inside her.

"Are you all right?" he asked, his voice heavy with emotion.

"Yes. Oh . . . yes." She shifted her hips and tightened herself around him.

"Susannah." He moaned her name and began to move against her, with gentle slowness at first, then faster, and faster.

She moved with him, instinctively, reveling in his power. She knew he was leading her to ecstasy, and when she found it, her eyes opened in surprise and wonder, and she cried his name.

"Conor!"

Tears of joy filled her eyes, her heart pounded, her body quivered. His ragged breathing matched hers, as did his racing heart. Still he moved within her. Finally, with a shuddering groan, he drove deeper yet, and stopped, panting.

She clung to him, thrilled to feel his seed pump into her. Love for him overwhelmed her, and in that moment, she gave him her soul.

Susannah sat up against the headboard, the blankets reaching only to her waist. They had left the lamp burning, and now she watched him sleep. An overpowering tenderness filled her. She reached out to touch his hair. It had dried, and felt soft. His long eyelashes lay on his cheek, and his breathing was deep and even.

A sense of awe filled her. This man had given himself to her, in every way. He had protected her, defended her, nursed her, taught her, claimed her, loved her. He was hers, as surely as she was his. A deep and abiding joy settled into her heart.

His arm moved across her thighs. "What are you thinking?"

She smiled and snuggled down next to him. "Only about how much I love you, how much you've given me."

He brushed her love-tangled hair back from her face, then stroked the bare skin of her shoulder. "What have I given you?"

"Everything," she whispered. "Conor, you saved my life tonight."

His brows drew together in confusion. "Because you were dying to have me?" he teased.

"Conceited man!" she exclaimed with a smile that quickly faded. "No, you really saved my life. Well, your lessons did."

His hand paused for a moment. "What happened?" All traces of humor had fled his face.

"I went to the Banning estate, looking for you."

The wondrous mood between them shattered. "You did *what?*" Conor pushed up to a sitting position and stared down at her.

Susannah sat up as well, pulling the sheet over her breasts. His anger did not surprise her. She met his gaze fearlessly. "When you didn't come back last night, I was afraid something terrible had happened. Lucas wanted to wait until morning to look for you, but I couldn't. I was tortured by the idea that the Bannings had captured you."

"So you went out to their place to find me." He ran his hands through his hair in angry frustration. "My God, Susannah, do you know what would have happened if they had caught you?"

"Ben Hollister did catch me, but I was able to get away, thanks to you. It was almost as if you were there coaching me, Conor. I could hear your voice."

He stared at her. "I knew you'd be worried. That's why I came in tonight, even so late." Anger flashed in his eyes again. "I decided against taking the train because I think Banning had it watched. Then, yesterday, Charlie threw a shoe; that's what held me up. You should have trusted me, Susannah, trusted that I had a good reason for the delay. You should never have gone up there. Now they know you're alive."

She placed a gentle hand on his chest. "No, they don't. I understand why you're angry, Conor, but please let me explain." Her eyes were huge and pleading. He did not respond, and her hand fell back to her lap.

"I do trust you. Completely. But I also know the Bannings. The thought of you in their hands . . ." She shook her head. "I swear I did not act rashly tonight. I wore my father's clothes, and was very careful. In fact, when Ben caught me, he thought I was a boy. I got away from him, Conor. But before that, I listened outside Fletcher's window. They had people waiting for me in Denver; you were right about that. And I learned they didn't have you, that they don't even know who you are. I can't describe the relief I felt when I heard that. It was worth it."

"Not to me, it wasn't," Conor said harshly.

She inched closer to him and covered his hand with hers. "Please try to understand, Conor." When he looked at her, she continued. "I've been forced to hide for weeks, first to heal, then to buy time. They killed my father, for God's sake! How was I to know they hadn't killed you as well? I couldn't wait any longer. Surely you, of all people, can understand that. I had to do something to help." He said nothing, but the expression on his face softened.

"Thank you for teaching me to take care of myself, Conor. Your lessons are the reason I was here when you returned, alive and able to love you."

He looked into her eyes, saw the honesty and love there. With a groan, he pulled her into his arms. "I found your uncle's papers. Among them was his marriage certificate. Did you know he had married?"

Susannah pulled back to stare at him. "No. He never mentioned it."

"He married a woman named Lucinda Talbot in 1852, out in California. There was a note written on the certificate that she and their infant son died in childbed two years later."

"Oh, Conor, how sad. He wouldn't tell us who he had named the mine after. I don't think even my father knew."

Conor caressed her arm. "It made me think of how I would feel if anything ever happened to you. I don't know what I'd do if I lost you," he said, his voice harsh with anguish.

"You won't," she promised. He leaned back against the headboard, and she rested her head on his shoulder. The sheet fell to her waist. "But we must be very careful, Conor. Fletcher Banning knows you are connected to me. He wants you dead."

"How could he know that?" Conor's hand stroked her hair.

"He said something about you asking for directions to the mine."

"That damned bartender," he muttered.

"What?"

"Nothing, sweetheart. What else did you hear?"

"He said that if I reappear, I will either marry him, or he'll kill me. I'm sure he wouldn't hesitate to kill Lily Carolina as well. We must all be very careful." She felt his jaw tighten against her forehead.

"They won't touch a hair on Lily Carolina's head, nor will they hurt you," Conor vowed.

Susannah moved her fingers through the fine hair on his chest. "There's something else."

"Tell me." Conor kissed her forehead, enjoying the feel of her roaming hand, of her soft breast pressing against him.

"I almost killed Fletcher."

His eyes widened, but he remained quiet.

Her troubled voice continued. "I had him in my sights, and I couldn't pull the trigger. This whole thing could have been ended tonight. On some level, I feel like a coward."

"But it wouldn't have ended, Susannah. Even if you had killed him, chances are you would have died, too." He sighed and tightened his hold on her. "My brave woman. You risked your life for me tonight, and had the courage to walk away from a chance to avenge your father's death. I'm proud of you." He kissed her forehead again.

She pushed away from him and looked into his eyes. "Really?"

"Really." He lifted her chin. "But you must never do anything like that again. At least not by yourself."

"All right." She smiled shyly at him. "You're not angry any longer?"

He shook his head and reached for her. She happily settled back in his arms, her hand resuming its travels. Her fingers paused when she touched his scarred shoulder.

"What happened to you?" she asked gently.

His jaw tightened. "I was shot, just at the end of the war."

Her hand moved over the ravaged skin in a soothing caress. "It looks like it was a terrible wound, Conor. I hate to think how you suffered."

He shrugged. "I lived."

Susannah hesitated, concerned by the strange tone of his voice. "Do you want to tell me about it?" she asked quietly.

Conor trapped her hand with his.

"You don't have to," she hastened to add. "It doesn't matter, Conor. Your past made you who you are, and I love who you are. I don't have to know what happened. If you want to leave the past in the past, it's all right with me."

He met her eyes, his own filled with emotion. "Right now, all I want to tell you is how much I love you. Better yet, I want to show you." He slid down under the blankets, taking her with him.

She looked at him in pleased surprise. "Again?"

He tenderly touched her cheek. "If you're not too sore."

A blush warmed her face as she caught his meaning. "No," she said softly. "I'm fine."

"Good," he growled, his voice low and sensual. He pounced on her, nibbling at her neck, while one hand stroked her breast. She giggled and squirmed as shivers raced down her body. He soon had her breathless again.

She felt him rising against her leg, and reached down with a curious hand. He gasped when she touched him. "It's my turn to explore," she whispered.

"Very well, Miss Duncan." He rolled onto his back and stared into her eyes. "Explore."

Susannah smiled slowly, with great anticipation. She pulled the blankets back and, much to Conor's pleasure, explored.

Fifteen

"Are you sure this is going to close?" Conor asked doubtfully. He was attempting to connect the hooks of the black dress between Susannah's shoulder blades. "Alexandra is . . . smaller than you."

"Alexandra got it closed," Susannah gasped. "I'll hold my breath."

The hooks met and held. Conor looked over her shoulder and frowned at her in the mirror. "It's awful tight, Susannah." He put his arms around her from behind and covered her flattened breasts with his hands. "I don't want this dress to hurt you."

She leaned back against him, enjoying the feel of his hands on her. "It won't hurt me permanently," she assured him. "But I may need doctoring when I take the dress off."

Conor nuzzled her ear. "Just call me Dr. O'Rourke."

Susannah rubbed her hands up and down the outsides of his thighs. "Well, Doctor, we'd best go see Lucas. The sooner we do, the sooner I can take off this dress."

"All right." Conor reluctantly released her. He retrieved his gunbelt from the headboard and strapped it on.

She took up the black hat and placed it over her pinned-up hair, then turned to him. "Kiss me," she ordered.

He looked surprised, but he obeyed.

"That will have to hold us for a while," she said mournfully, and pulled the heavy veil into place.

Conor laughed and tucked her hand in the crook of his arm.

"You are a lustful woman, Susannah Duncan." He led her toward the door.

"If I am, you have only yourself to blame, Conor O'Rourke," she retorted.

He laughed again, and escorted her out the door. They descended to the second floor and Lucas's office. At Conor's knock, Lucas let them in, then closed the door. He and Conor shook hands.

"I had coffee with Alexandra this morning, and she told me you stopped by her house late last night." Lucas waved at the two chairs in front of his desk and moved to his own chair. "I'm thankful you've returned safely. We were worried about you."

Susannah lifted the veil from her face and draped it back over the hat.

"He found the papers, Lucas." She watched with eager anticipation as Conor handed Lucas the tied packet.

Lucas spread the papers out on the desk. "Yes," he murmured as he stroked his beard. "This is everything we need." He pulled a paper from a drawer, then unscrewed the cap to his inkwell. He dipped the pen and wrote rapidly, the only sound in the room the scratching of his pen. At last he finished and turned the paper to them.

"This is the transfer of title, Susannah. You need to sign on this line here." He pointed with the pen before giving her the writing instrument.

She dipped the pen and signed her name in a graceful hand.

Lucas picked up the paper and waved it gently to dry the ink. "Congratulations, Susannah. You are now the proud owner of the Lucky Lucy mine."

Susannah leaned back in her chair. "Lucas, I'll sell you the mine for one dollar."

Lucas gaped at her. It took him a minute to find his tongue. "I don't understand."

"I am perfectly serious, Lucas. That mine has brought nothing but misery and death to my family. I don't want it. One dollar and it's yours, on two conditions: that you keep up my father's and my uncle's graves, and that you never sell it to Fletcher Banning, at any time, for any price."

"I would never consider selling to Banning, Susannah."

"I meant no offense. I just want to be certain that we both understand the terms."

"If you buy the mine, you'll be taking on Banning," Conor warned. "He'll probably come after you like he did Walter Duncan."

Lucas leaned back in his chair and made a tent of his fingers. "I'll be waiting." His gray eyes flashed with steely resolve.

Susannah looked at Conor. He winked at her and reached for her hand, a gesture Lucas did not miss.

"I'll buy the mine from you, Susannah, and I'll accept your conditions." Lucas rested his forearms on the desk. "I'll sleep better knowing you're out of it, and I think Banning will think twice before tangling with me. If he does, you can be sure he'll regret it. But I insist on paying you fair market value for the property."

"One dollar." Susannah raised her chin. "Not a penny more, not a penny less."

Lucas smiled. "Very well. One dollar it is, but only if you agree to accept fifty percent of any profit I make."

Susannah stubbornly shook her head. "No."

"Susannah, you have the support of your sister to consider."

"Lily Carolina's support will not be a problem," Conor interjected.

Lucas eyed him thoughtfully, then turned to Susannah. "Then put it in trust for her. God forbid anything should ever happen to you"— he glanced at Conor again, then corrected himself— "to either one of you, but, as you well know, there are no guarantees in life."

"There are also no guarantees that anything will come of that mine, Lucas," Susannah said. "And I don't think anything will. I think I'm selling you a worthless piece of land. But you raise a good point." She looked at Conor for a long minute, then back to Lucas. "Fifteen percent to Lily Carolina, fifteen percent to me, fifteen percent to Conor, fifty-five percent to you. That's my final offer."

"Just a minute," Conor protested. "Give my share to Lily Carolina. I've no right to it, nor do I want it."

"Conor." Susannah squeezed his hand. "If not for you, I'd be dead, and my sister most likely would be, too. I feel very strongly about this. Please honor my wishes."

Conor read the determination in her eyes; he knew her well enough to know she would not back down. Perhaps he could sign his share over to Lily Carolina at a later date. He nodded reluctantly. "Very well, Susannah."

"Thank you," she said softly. "We are not to be considered active partners, Lucas. All business decisions pertaining to the property are solely yours to make, all percentages paid on net profit only."

"Agreed." Lucas stood up. "I'll get Neville Thorpe. He's the man I sent to Denver to look for the deed. Besides being a notary public, he's totally trustworthy. He can act as witness on the bill of sale." He moved toward the door. "I'll be back shortly." The door closed behind him.

Susannah relaxed against the back of the chair with a sigh. "It'll be over soon, Conor."

Conor played with her fingers. "That it will." He raised his eyes to her face. "You look tired."

She managed a weary smile. "That's because someone kept me up too late last night."

Conor planted a quick kiss on her cheek. "It will never happen again," he said solemnly.

Her smile widened. "I don't believe you, Mr. O'Rourke." She leaned forward and kissed him full on the mouth, just as the door opened. Conor jumped up, his gun in his hand, and spun to face the door, kicking his chair aside. Susannah's heart pounded in sudden fear when she saw Lucas whip his pistol from its holster in automatic reflex. The bespectacled man behind Lucas held up his hands and stood back from the doorway.

Conor and Lucas stared at each other over their leveled guns.

"You *are* fast," Lucas commented dryly as he slid his weapon back into its holster.

"So are you," Conor replied. "I'm impressed." He spun the pistol home. "But an old Ranger like you should know better than to come up behind an old Ranger like me with no warning." He bent down and set the chair upright.

"I won't do it again," Lucas assured him. "Of course, if I were you, I wouldn't make a habit of drawing on me in my own office, either. I tend to get a little territorial."

"Fair enough," Conor said with a rueful grin.

Susannah's racing heart resumed its normal pace.

"Neville was on his way to see me, so I didn't have to go far to find him," Lucas said as he closed the door. "Neville, this is Susannah Duncan and Conor O'Rourke."

Neville Thorpe, a thin, conservatively dressed man of average height, exuded a comforting calmness. He wore his dark hair parted down the middle and slicked back, and his mustache was neatly trimmed. He bobbed his head in Susannah's direction and extended his hand to Conor. "Pleased to meet you both." When Conor released his hand, Neville adjusted his spectacles and turned to Susannah. His magnified eyes displayed a genuine compassion.

"My condolences on your recent losses, Miss Duncan. I sure was sorry to hear about Walter and your father. Fine men, both of them."

"Thank you, Mr. Thorpe." Susannah smiled at him. She stood up and walked over to the window as the men gathered around the desk.

"This is a straight-forward bill of sale, Neville, with a fifty-five/fifteen/fifteen/fifteen split on . . ." Their voices faded into the background as Susannah stared up at the mountains.

It was over. A sadness gripped her as she remembered the dreams of the Duncan brothers, dreams that had come to naught. What unfulfilled dreams would be buried with her one day? *None,* she fiercely vowed. She'd grab her dreams by their tails and hogtie them if she had to. And a lot of her dreams centered on the man who stepped up behind her and placed gentle hands on her shoulders.

"It's not too late to change your mind if you're having second thoughts," he said quietly.

She shook her head. "No. It's for the best."

Conor lightly squeezed her shoulders, then released her. She turned to the desk, where Lucas and Neville waited.

"Are you sure about this, Susannah?" Lucas waited for her answer, his eyes soft with affection.

"Absolutely. Where do I sign?"

"These are drawn up according to the terms we agreed upon. Read through them, then sign here, and here, and sign here for Lily Carolina, and Conor will sign here."

She accepted the pen from Lucas and did as he instructed, then handed the pen to Conor. He signed, and Neville gathered the documents.

"Neville is going to take the documents to Denver and personally see that they are properly filed with the territorial assessor," Lucas explained.

"Thank you, Mr. Thorpe." Susannah held her hand out to him. Neville accepted it. "Please be careful, sir. We are dealing with ruthless men."

"I will, Miss Duncan. Don't you and Mr. O'Rourke worry about a thing." He nodded to Conor, then to Lucas. "I'll wire as soon as it's done."

"Thank you, Neville. Watch your back."

"I always do." Neville closed the door behind him.

"He's a quiet and unassuming man, but as sharp as a tack," Lucas commented. "Men like the Bannings always underestimate men like Neville."

Susannah sank into her chair. "I just don't want him getting hurt."

"I'm sure he'll be fine, Susannah." Lucas sat down. "The first thing I'm going to do is have the deputy U.S. mineral surveyor do a thorough survey of that claim. I'm very curious to see if there really is any silver."

"Uncle Walter didn't think so. I hope you won't be wasting your money."

"Either way, it won't be a waste. If there is no silver, I should be able to persuade Banning that there's no reason to continue with the lawsuit."

"Good luck," Conor said.

Susannah fixed her gaze on Lucas. "How much longer do I have to stay in hiding?"

"I've been thinking about that. Can you last until the day after tomorrow?"

She looked at Conor and shrugged. "I guess. What do you have in mind?"

"Neville can't get to Floyd Hill in time to catch the train today, so he won't get to Denver until tomorrow, late in the afternoon. He may not be able to get the papers filed until Wednesday."

"What's so special about Wednesday?" Conor asked.

Lucas smiled at Susannah. "Alexandra told me you know all about William Hamill's party Wednesday night."

"I don't know *all* about it," Susannah protested, with a guilty glance at Conor. He wouldn't be pleased with her little walk the other morning, any more than he had been with her excursion to the Banning estate. "I'll tell you later," she said at his questioning look.

"By then we should have word from Neville," said Lucas. "I

think the party will be the perfect occasion to let the Bannings know you are still alive. You'll be safely surrounded by Georgetown society. The story can be told, and the Bannings won't be able to do anything about it."

Conor nodded his approval. "It's a good idea. If everyone in town knows what happened, the Bannings won't dare make any move against Susannah. By then you'll own the mine anyway."

"I like it, too," Susannah said. "But won't we need invitations?"

"William Hamill is a good friend of mine," Lucas said. "With your permission, I'll take him into our confidence. He won't want to miss an opportunity to put Fletcher Banning in his place. I'm sure you both will be welcome." He stood up. "In fact, I'll call on him now."

Susannah rose and they moved toward the door.

"Let's make an evening of it," Lucas suggested. "I've invited Alexandra to accompany me. We can all go together."

"It sounds wonderful!" Susannah exclaimed.

Lucas hesitated with his hand on the door. "The party is to be held here at the Barton House, in the ballroom. You'll both need proper formal attire," he warned.

"I have a dress," Susannah assured him. She looked at Conor.

"It won't be a problem," he said with a smile. "It's been a while since I've been duded up, but I can manage."

Susannah turned to Lucas. "Thank you," she said softly, and impulsively hugged him.

Lucas hugged her back. "I'm glad you felt you could trust me."

"We'd have been in trouble without you, that's for certain," Conor added. He held out his hand, which Lucas accepted.

"And Susannah would have been in trouble without you, Conor. She's right about you saving her life."

Conor shifted his feet, obviously uncomfortable. "Let's cut

the mutual admiration society stuff and get going. This woman hasn't had breakfast yet, and I don't want her wasting away."

Lucas and Susannah both laughed.

"I don't know, Conor," Susannah said as she lowered the veil into place. "This dress might fit me a little easier if I skip a few meals."

Conor took her elbow and guided her out the door. "You won't need to be wearing the dress much longer," he said.

Susannah blushed, wondering if he intended the double meaning in his statement. She was grateful the veil hid her face.

"Where will you be staying until Wednesday, Conor?" Lucas asked as he locked the office door.

"With Susannah," Conor answered calmly. "Will that present a problem?"

Now Susannah was very thankful for the veil.

Lucas faced Conor. "Not as long as you do right by her, and I already know I don't have to worry about that. I'll have the desk clerk send a breakfast tray up. Good day to you both." He put his hat on, touched the brim and nodded at Susannah, then set off down the hall.

Back in the suite, Susannah breathed a sigh of relief as Conor released the hooks. "Thank you," she murmured. She pulled the dress forward off her shoulders and stepped out of it, then held it up in front of her, suddenly gripped by a strange shyness. She had shared her body with this man in the most intimate of ways, and yet she felt self-conscious undressing in front of him.

"Don't hide from me, Susannah." Conor pulled the dress from her grasp and tossed it on a chair, then took her hand and led her to the bed. He sat on the edge of the mattress and positioned her so that she stood between his knees. His eyes were at the level of her breasts, his brows drawn together in a frown. "I told you the dress was too tight," he said. He ran a fingertip over the red marks the garment had pressed into her skin just above her chemise.

"It doesn't hurt, Conor." She placed her hands on his shoulders. "The marks will fade very soon."

He pulled her closer and touched his lips to her skin. "Just in case, I'd better kiss them." He nuzzled her soft fullness, breathing in her lovely scent.

Susannah shivered when his mouth pushed the neckline of the chemise lower.

"Why don't . . . you wear . . . a corset?" he asked between kisses.

"I used to, before we came west." She took his face in her hands and forced his head up so he would look at her, knowing that if she did not stop his tormenting lips, she would push him back on the bed and crawl on top of him. The thought brought a very intriguing image to her mind. She shook her head, shocked at herself. One night with this man and she was turning into a wanton! "They're very uncomfortable, you know. Corsets, I mean. Once I left South Carolina, they didn't seem necessary, and certainly not up at my uncle's cabin." She lifted his chin. "Do you want me to wear one?"

"God, no!" Conor said with a laugh. "I want to feel my woman when I touch her, not whalebone. I was just curious, because I know Alina doesn't wear one, either."

"Alina doesn't *own* one," Susannah corrected. "Which created quite a stir when we were in England, let me tell you. The headmistress of the school was scandalized. But Alina said her father forbade her to wear one because he felt they were dangerous to a woman's health. She happily obeyed. I was jealous."

Conor opened the top button of her chemise. "Well, as far as I'm concerned, you can throw yours away." He freed the next button and kissed the soft swell of pale skin he was gradually exposing.

Susannah worked her fingers through his hair and closed her eyes, concentrating on the pleasurable sensations his mouth brought her. Conor knew the secrets of her body better than she did herself. She'd had no idea she had so many sensitive areas that would leap to aching life at his touch.

They both started at the sound of a knock on the door.

"Breakfast," called a rough voice from the hall.

Conor motioned Susannah to the corner behind the door, where she scurried, closing the buttons he had undone. He pulled his pistol and cracked the door, then opened it wider to accept the tray from a waiter.

"Add it to the room bill," Conor instructed.

"Mr. McCleave took care of your meal, sir. I hope your wife is feeling better. Good day to you both."

Conor nodded and closed the door. He slid his pistol back into the holster and carried the tray to the table. "Are you hungry?" he asked with a smile.

She nodded eagerly as she settled in one of the chairs. "Starved."

He sat opposite her and pulled the napkin from the tray, revealing two steaming cups of coffee and two plates piled high with bacon, ham, fried potatoes and biscuits. Susannah's mouth watered; then she remembered that she wore only her underclothes.

"Oh, my," she gasped as she jumped up. "I apologize, Conor. I shouldn't come to the table dressed like this."

"Stay as you are," he said, laughing, and reached out a hand to her. "Please."

She touched his fingers. "But you're fully clothed. It doesn't seem proper."

"It's perfectly proper in the privacy of our own room," he said firmly. "And I like you that way. Please sit down."

With a smile, she sank back into her seat and grabbed a biscuit.

They were quiet for a while, enjoying the food, the coffee, the easy comfort of each other's company. Finally, Susannah leaned back in the chair and tucked her feet under her, holding her cup in two hands. She stared down into the cup, her brows drawn in a troubled frown.

He watched her, delighting in the way her long eyelashes seemed to brush her cheeks. Soft tendrils of golden hair had escaped from her simple bun and curled at the sides of her lovely face and along her neck. He reached across the table and brushed her forehead with his fingertips. "What's making you frown?"

She looked up at him, the full force of her beautiful eyes hitting him like a blow.

"I hope Lucas didn't embarrass you when he questioned where you were staying," she said.

"No, I wasn't embarrassed, but I think you were."

She shrugged. "A little. By him bringing it up, I mean. I've no regrets about anything we've done. I want you to know that."

Conor smiled. "I know that," he said softly.

"Lucas is very protective of me. I don't want you to feel pressured by him, or by anyone else, in any decisions you make concerning the future. It's no one's business but ours."

"Come here." Conor pushed back in his chair and held out his hand. When she did not move, he motioned with his fingers. She set the cup down and came to his side. He took her hand and pulled her into his lap, wrapping his arms around her.

"No one makes me do anything I don't want to, Susannah. Not your father, not Lucas, not even you." He nuzzled her neck. "I'm here because I want to be, and I'll stay because I want to stay. I hope the same is true for you."

Susannah curled an arm around his neck. "It is," she whispered.

"Good." Conor stood up, lifting her in his arms. "Now to bed with you."

She grinned. "All right."

He laughed as he set her on the bed. "No, ma'am. As you pointed out, I kept you up all night, and you need to get some sleep. I'm going to check on Charlie, and see to a few other things, like finding something to wear to that party on Wednesday night. If I can work it out, I'll bring Lily Carolina here for lunch."

Susannah stretched on the sheets. "That would be wonderful," she said around a yawn. She pulled the pins from her hair and set them on the night table, then nestled into the pillow. "I am tired," she admitted.

Conor pulled the blanket over her and sat by her side. "You'll have a few hours of rest. Sleep well." He kissed her cheek.

She looked up at him. "I love you," she whispered.

Conor's expression softened. "And I love you, my precious woman." He kissed her again, then left the room, locking the door behind him.

Susannah smiled, a gentle, happy smile. A wondrous peace filled her heart, and a sense of well-being. Everything would be all right. Together, she and Conor would make sure of it. Her eyes drifted closed and she slept.

"There's no trace of whoever it was, Mr. Banning." Ben Hollister held his hat in his hand and watched as Fletcher Banning slammed his china coffee cup down on its saucer. The cup cracked, allowing dark liquid to seep into the saucer and overflow onto the white linen tablecloth.

"An intruder came onto my property last night, Ben, invaded my territory. I want to know who it was."

"For Christ's sake, Fletcher." A very grouchy, sleepy-eyed Kyle spoke from the other end of the table. "You've already kept us up all night combing the woods. It was probably just a goddamned kid looking for a handout. Let it rest."

An angry flush darkened Fletcher's face. "A kid who knew there was a house a mile up an unlit road?" he scoffed. "No one comes here by accident, you fool. Letting it rest could get us killed, and your suggestion that I do is just another example of your careless stupidity."

Kyle pushed back out of his chair, his eyes blazing with hatred. "Then go look for him yourself, you bastard." He stormed from the room.

Fletcher did not react to Kyle's words or departure. He looked at Ben and drummed his fingers on the table. "You're certain it was a boy, rather than a man."

"I know what you're thinking, Boss, but it couldn't have been the stranger from the saloon. Kyle said he was a tall man. This boy wasn't. Besides, he was too small and lightweight for a full-grown man."

Small and lightweight. Fletcher's fingers stilled. "Could it have been a woman?"

Ben rubbed his chin thoughtfully. "He was dressed like a boy, and fought like one. But I guess it could have been a woman." His eyes lit up. "Wait a minute. Now I know what's been bothering me ever since last night. Lavender."

"Lavender? Ben, what the hell are you talking about?"

"Our intruder smelled like lavender."

Fletcher sat up straight in his chair. "Susannah Duncan wore lavender scent." He slammed the table with his hand. "I *knew* she was alive! And we almost had her!"

"Boss, if it was her, why would she come here? And where has she been all this time?"

"Who knows where she's been? That's not important now. She might have come for vengeance. You found tracks underneath the windows." Fletcher's face drained of color. "She could have killed me last night. She had a clear shot." He waved in the direction of the window. "Why didn't she shoot?"

"Maybe it was Kyle she was after. He's the one that killed her pa and hurt her."

"She had a clear shot at him, too. Maybe you saved our lives by coming home when you did." Fletcher stared at his foreman.

"Post extra guards around the clock. No one is to get within shouting distance of this house without our knowledge."

"Yes, sir."

"My miners have followed the vein of silver as far as I dare let them go onto the Duncan property. The vein shows no sign of petering out. I must have that mine, legally. You have to find her, Ben, now more than ever, especially if she wants to kill me. Bring her in, dead or alive."

Ben raised a disapproving eyebrow. "When I bring her in, she'll be alive, Boss. You tell everyone else, including your brother, to stay out of my way." He positioned his hat on his head. "I'll find Susannah Duncan, but it might take awhile. Don't be surprised if you don't hear from me for a few days." He moved toward the door.

"Just do it, Ben."

Ben did not answer. He closed the door behind him, leaving Fletcher Banning to stare broodingly at the coffee stain on his fine linen tablecloth.

Susannah tucked a final pin into her hair to hold the freshly washed locks out of the way and leaned against the slanted back of Alexandra's tub with a deep sigh. The deliciously warm, scented water covered her to her shoulders. After days of sponge baths in the hotel, the luxury of a good soak was more than welcome. She closed her eyes and sighed again.

The past two days with Conor had been wondrous. The hotel room had become a haven, much like the cave had been, only much more comfortable, and infinitely more intimate. He had introduced her to pleasures she had never imagined, had made her body sing and her heart soar with the joy of being alive and being with him. But even more than the physical pleasure, she treasured the emotional and spiritual closeness she felt with him.

He made her feel beautiful, and cherished, and respected. He made her feel safe, and most importantly, loved.

She ran the sponge over her body, wincing when she touched the tender place between her legs. Now she was sore, she had to admit. But the soreness itself made her feel good. She shifted in the water, feeling the first stirrings of desire again, just at the memories of what he had done to her. A smile curved her lips. She moved her hands to her stomach. Had his seed taken root? Did Conor's child grow there now? The thought filled her with a deep, primal pride. One day she would bear his child. Of that she was certain.

"Susannah." Alexandra rapped on the door. "The Potters are here, and Minerva has agreed to dress your hair. You can't stay in there all night."

"All right," Susannah called regretfully. "I'll be out soon." She finished washing and stood up, reaching for the towel. Conor was at Lucas McCleave's house, preparing for the Hamills' party, and the men would come later to escort the ladies. She could tell by the lack of light at the curtained window that evening had fallen. Getting ready for a social event such as this always seemed to take longer than expected, and she wanted to look her best for Conor tonight. She would have to hurry.

An hour later, Susannah looked in the mirror over the bureau in the room she had shared with Conor and caught her breath. "Oh, Minnie. You made me beautiful." Turning from side to side, wielding a hand mirror, she stared at the arrangement of her hair. Minerva had caught most of it up at the back of her head and pinned it there, allowing long strands to fall from behind one ear. Those strands had been coaxed into ringlets with the help of a curling iron. A strand of pearls was cleverly woven throughout, to match the pearls that decorated Susannah's dress.

Minerva snorted. "Like I had anything to do with it, Susannah. You'd be beautiful bald-headed wearing a burlap sack."

Susannah kissed the bespectacled woman's plump cheek. "Thank you," she said softly.

"Ah, you're welcome, honey. It was fun. Now you get your jewelry on, and don't forget your gloves. I'm going to check on Alexandra. The men are downstairs waiting, so don't dally." Minerva left the bedroom, her heavy, ungraceful step sounding loud on the floorboards.

Susannah turned to her sister, who sat patiently on the bed. "Would you like to see my hair, Lily Carolina? Aunt Minnie made it real pretty."

"Oh, yes. I promise I'll be very careful." Lily Carolina reached out with eager hands as Susannah settled on the bed, again mindful of the bustle at her back.

"Can you feel the pearls?" Susannah asked.

"Yes." A wondering smile curved Lily Carolina's mouth as her little hands touched Susannah's hair, lightly, carefully. She patted the ringlets that fell over Susannah's shoulder, then moved her hands down over the pearled neckline of the dress, over the white lace insert on the bodice, over the dark green velvet over-skirt, over the shirred white satin underskirt trimmed with white fringe. Her little hands then returned to Susannah's face and rested on her cheeks.

"You *are* beautiful, Susannah," she said quietly.

Tears formed in Susannah's eyes. "Thank you, Lily Carolina. So are you." She pulled her sister onto her lap, mindless of the velvet, and held her close.

Lily Carolina snuggled against her. "Do you think Aunt Minnie will fix my hair when I'm a big girl?"

"I think she will. And if she's not there, I'll fix it. Someday it will be you getting ready to go to a fancy party, and you'll be wearing a fancy dress, and there will be a special man waiting downstairs for you."

"Is Mr. Conor your special man?"

Susannah smiled and kissed the top of her sister's head. "Yes, he is, Lily Carolina. He's very special. I love him very much."

"I love him, too. So does Jesse. Will he live with us forever?"

Susannah's heart lurched. Although she and Conor had spoken of many things over the past two days, they had not discussed marriage. "I hope so, honey. Now up with you. I have to finish getting ready." She lifted Lily Carolina to the floor and stood up. "I'll show you Mama's jewels. I'm going to wear some of them tonight."

She emptied the small leather bag onto the doily on top of the bureau. The emerald and pearl necklace was easy to find in the tangle of sparkling jewelry, but she had to search for the matching earrings. At last she found them and hung the earrings from her pierced earlobes, then fastened the necklace around her neck. She faced Lily Carolina and sank down on one knee.

"Come here, honey." She guided Lily Carolina to her side and placed the child's hand at her throat. "This necklace is made of pearls and emeralds. You know what pearls are. Can you tell me what color emeralds are?"

Lily Carolina fingered the necklace. "I think they're green."

"That's right. And my dress is made of green velvet and white satin, so the jewels match the dress."

The child nodded approvingly. "Don't forget your gloves," she warned.

Susannah smiled. "I won't, Poppet."

"That's what Mr. Conor calls me," Lily Carolina said with a giggle. "He said it means 'precious.' "

"Yes, it does. And you are precious." Susannah got to her feet and reached for her gloves. "You be a good girl for Aunt Minnie and Uncle Horatio." She smoothed the long white gloves over her fingers and up to her elbows.

"I will," Lily Carolina promised.

Susannah looped her fan and her reticule over her wrist and

pulled the white lace shawl from the footboard. "You're always a good girl, Lily Carolina." She kissed her sister's forehead.

"All right, ladies, let's go." Minerva's strident voice sounded from the landing. Susannah took Lily Carolina's hand and stepped through the door. She stopped when she saw Alexandra. "Oh, Alexandra," she breathed. "You look lovely."

Alexandra self-consciously smoothed the skirt of her burgundy satin dress. "It's been a long time since I've had occasion to wear this dress," she admitted. "It feels kind of strange."

"Well, the dress is stunning," Susannah said sincerely. She reached out and took Alexandra's hand. Minerva had worked her magic with Alexandra's thick auburn hair, weaving it into a fascinating swirl of rolls and curls. A small black feather, held in place with a jeweled pin, complemented the arrangement and matched the black lace accenting the dress. Alexandra had clasped a gold bracelet over the long black gloves she wore, and gold winked from her earlobes. Her blue eyes seemed to shine with a special light.

Alexandra squeezed Susannah's hand. "Thank you. You look splendid yourself."

"You two quit gabbing and get downstairs to your men," Minerva ordered. "Lily Carolina, give me your hand, child. Your sister needs to hold her skirt out of the way."

Susannah's heart pounded with excitement and anticipation as she followed Alexandra down the stairs. The sound of masculine voices grew louder. Would Conor be pleased with her appearance? And how would he look, all dressed up?

They reached the opened parlor doors, and the male voices instantly quieted. Alexandra entered first and made her way to Lucas's side. He kissed her cheek and said something to her that brought a flattering touch of pink to her cheeks. Susannah noticed that Lucas looked particularly handsome.

Then she saw Conor. She waited in the doorway, unable to take her eyes from him.

He wore a black broadcloth suit, perfectly tailored to fit his tall frame, complete with a frock coat, a dark blue brocade vest shot through with gray silk thread, and a gray stock arranged neatly at his throat. His long hair was brushed back, and his eyes were heart-breakingly blue in his tanned face.

Conor's fingers tightened on the sherry glass he held. His eyes riveted on the golden woman in the doorway; his breath stuck in his throat. He took in everything about her, from her artfully arranged hair and her shining green eyes, to the elegant gown that bared her shoulders and hugged her breasts and kissed her narrow waist, then draped gracefully to the floor. His eyes returned to her face, to her dear, beloved face, and the shy, happy smile that lit it.

He set the glass on the mantel and crossed the room, holding both hands out to her. She took them. "You are beautiful, Susannah." His voice was full of admiration and pride.

"So are you," she breathed.

He raised a teasing eyebrow. "I'm beautiful?"

"Oh, yes." Susannah tightened her fingers on his and brought one of his hands to her mouth. She watched his eyes widen as she placed a kiss on the back of his hand, saw the flare of desire in the blue depths. She made a mental note to remember to kiss his hands more often.

Conor tucked her hand in his elbow and escorted her into the parlor. Susannah noticed that Lucas seemed to be having a difficult time taking his eyes from Alexandra's radiant face. He did finally succeed in pulling his attention away from the doctor long enough to warmly greet Susannah and introduce her to the tall young man at his side.

"My son Joseph," Lucas said proudly. "Joseph, this is Susannah Duncan, Walter Duncan's niece."

Susannah guessed Joseph to be about eighteen years old, and he was as handsome as his father. She held her hand out to him, which he shyly accepted. "How nice to meet you, Joseph."

"The pleasure is mine, Miss Duncan." He released her hand and turned to Minerva and Lily Carolina, who waited in the doorway. "But there is the light of my life," he said with a smile. "It's been too long since I've seen you, Miss Lily Carolina."

Lily Carolina giggled and advanced into the room, guided by Minerva.

"I think you were here for supper just three days ago, Joseph," Alexandra said dryly.

"That's too long," Joseph repeated. He picked Lily Carolina up. "How's your wrist, darling girl?"

Lily Carolina lifted her arm to show him. "It's a lot better, Joseph, but Dr. 'Xandra said I have to wear the splint for a few more weeks."

Joseph caught her hand and kissed her fingers. "There," he announced. "Now it will get better faster." The child giggled again as he carefully set her on the sofa.

"Just so you know, Susannah," Lucas said. "I did get a wire from Neville late this afternoon. All is well. The title transfer and sale are officially filed."

"Good." Susannah was relieved at the news, but a trace of apprehension about seeing Fletcher Banning remained.

Lucas pulled out his watch. "We'd best be on our way. We're already fashionably late." He took Alexandra's hand and guided her out of the room, with Joseph right behind them.

Conor leaned down and kissed Lily Carolina's forehead. "Good night, Poppet. Mind Aunt Minnie and Uncle Horatio now."

"I will, Mr. Conor. Bye, Susannah."

Susannah also kissed her sister. "Good night, Lily Carolina. I'll tell you all about the party in the morning." She turned to Minerva. "Thank you so much for watching her for us."

Minerva waved a plump hand. "Heavens, Susannah, it's nothing. You know we love this child."

"Where is Horatio?" Conor asked.

"He's in the kitchen keeping Jesse company. I didn't want that dog jumping all over everyone when you all look so nice. Scoot now." She shooed Conor and Susannah toward the door. "The others are waiting. Have a lovely evening."

Conor grabbed Susannah's hand. "We will. Thank you, Minnie." He led her outside to the carriage where the others waited.

Susannah took a deep breath. The evening's adventure was about to begin.

Sixteen

No one spoke on the way to the Barton House. Susannah sat on the edge of the leather carriage seat in an attempt to keep from crushing her bustle. Conor held her hand, offering her comfort and a feeling of safety. Although she looked forward to the ball with anticipation, she could not forget the danger. The Bannings would be there. She knew that under their fine coats, both Conor and Lucas wore their guns.

Joseph pulled the horses to a halt outside the hotel. Light poured from every window, and the sound of the orchestra could easily be heard. Conor lifted her from the carriage. She snapped her fan open and held it over the lower half of her face, then hooked her arm through Conor's.

"Are you ready?" he asked gently. At her nod, he patted her hand where it rested on his arm. "I'm right here," he said. "The Bannings can't hurt you."

"I know." She flashed him a brave smile from behind her fan. They followed Lucas, Alexandra and Joseph up the stairs to the grand ballroom on the second floor.

Light blazed from huge chandeliers placed at spaced intervals along the high ceiling and reflected off the hanging crystals, showing a room tastefully decorated in muted shades of blue. Dark wainscoting covered the lower half of the walls while the wallpapered top half sported several lovely oil paintings. Fashionably dressed men and women wandered over the highly polished floor, talking in politely subdued tones. Elegant overstuffed

sofas and chairs were arranged in seating groups complemented
with potted palms.

Susannah was amazed. The room could have been transplanted to Charleston or Philadelphia and nothing would have
looked out of place. Who would have guessed such an assem-
blage would be gathered in a small mining town high in the
mountains of Colorado Territory?

The receiving line had already broken up, but Lucas located
William and Priscilla Hamill across the room. He led his little
party to their hosts and made the introductions.

Susannah was impressed by the stately couple. Priscilla
Hamill was a charming woman, wearing an exquisite gown of
silver watered silk, and William Hamill's quiet self-assurance
made her glad that Lucas had confided in him. They had addi-
tional allies in the Hamills.

After a few minutes of pleasant small talk, Lucas guided Alexandra onto the dance floor, Joseph wandered off seeking
young people closer to his own age, and Conor escorted Susannah to a sofa positioned next to one of the potted palms.

"Joseph is speaking to Victoria Banning," Susannah said as
she motioned with her fan. "Her brothers must be here. Do you
see them?"

"Not yet." Conor scrutinized the room. He noticed that many
people were staring at them, their curiosity evident on their
faces. Suddenly Susannah stood up next to him, her fan again
in front of her face.

"There's Fletcher," she whispered. "Over by the refreshment
table."

Conor extended his arm. "Shall we pay our respects, Miss
Duncan?"

Susannah curtsied. "By all means, Mr. O'Rourke." The gra-
ciousness of her tone belied the fierce determination in her eyes.
She took his arm.

Conor caught Lucas's attention and motioned with his head.

Lucas nodded and said something to Alexandra, then danced her toward the refreshment table.

Fletcher Banning turned with a punch cup in his hand to see a couple advancing toward him from across the room. Dancers moved out of the way, giving the couple a clear path. There was something familiar about the stylishly dressed woman, but he could not put his finger on it. Only the top half of her face showed above the lace fan she held. He did not know the man walking beside her, but he knew he did not like the man's aggressive attitude. There was a challenge in those blue eyes, a dangerous challenge.

"That's him," Kyle rasped at his shoulder. "That's the bastard from the Silver Star, the one that was asking directions to the Duncan place."

Fletcher waved his brother's comment away, like he would an irritating gnat. His eyes locked on the woman. That coolly elegant woman in the costly satin and velvet gown could not possibly be Susannah Duncan. The Susannah he knew, although educated and refined, wore simple day dresses, with her golden hair pulled back in a practical bun or braid.

But those eyes, those eyes that glittered with ill-concealed rage above the fan. He'd recognize those striking green eyes anywhere. Fletcher set the cup on the table behind him without looking.

"The bastard is mine," Kyle whispered. His hand moved to his gun.

"Not here, you fool!" Fletcher ordered in an angry whisper. He straightened his vest.

Susannah and her escort stopped a few feet in front of him. Lucas McCleave appeared at her other side, quiet and protective. After a moment, Susannah whipped her fan from her face and snapped it closed with the expert grace of a true Southern belle. Fletcher was stunned by the full force of her beauty and spirit. What a magnificent woman!

"Mr. Banning." Her voice, with its charming accent, was cold and hard. "We meet again, an event I'm certain you did not anticipate. Allow me to introduce my dear friend, Mr. Conor O'Rourke."

Fletcher did not miss the subtle message of possession in the way Conor O'Rourke kept his hand at Susannah's waist. "Mr. O'Rourke." Fletcher's jaw clenched as he stiffly inclined his head. "How nice to see you, Miss Duncan. No, I didn't know you would be here this evening."

Susannah smiled tightly. "How could you, when no doubt the last news you had of me was that your brother failed to bring me to your home, as he had been instructed?"

A slow flush colored Fletcher's face. The room grew quiet. People were beginning to stare.

Susannah continued. "Did your brother explain why I could not respond to your arrogant summons, Mr. Banning? Did he explain that he physically assaulted me, and that I was forced into the river to escape him?"

A collective gasp went up from those close enough to hear her words. The silence spread; even the orchestra quit playing.

"You fell down the mountain," Kyle rasped in his curiously hoarse voice.

Susannah turned to him. "Why, you're right, Kyle. I did fall down the mountain, after you struck me repeatedly, pistol-whipped me, shot my dog, then tried to shoot me." She smiled sweetly. "How silly of me to forget."

A low murmuring started in the room.

"And that was after you left my father mortally injured from the beating you gave him. Or are you going to tell me that he simply fell off the step?"

A man came forward from the crowd. Susannah recognized him as James Gunn, the town police judge. "Are you saying your father is dead, Miss Duncan?" he asked.

"Yes, sir, I am. Thomas Duncan is dead by that man's hand."

She nodded to Kyle. "And probably by that man's order." She inclined her head toward Fletcher. The murmuring in the room rose.

"That is a most serious accusation, Miss Duncan."

"Indeed it is, Judge," Susannah agreed. She arched an eyebrow at Fletcher. "The assault upon me was witnessed by a third party. That same witness cared for my father before he died and heard my father's deathbed statement."

Kyle flushed with anger. "I have an alibi for the day your father died. I was nowhere near your family's claim."

Susannah faced Kyle, a small smile playing about her lips. "No doubt your brother's henchmen will swear you were far away. But tell me, Kyle; how do you know what day my father died? And where?" she asked softly.

Kyle's eyes widened, and his face drained of color as quickly as it had flushed only moments before.

"I'm certain this is all a misunderstanding, one that can easily be cleared up," Fletcher interjected smoothly. "The marshal went to Denver for a meeting of the territorial legislature and isn't expected back until the day after tomorrow. Out of respect for our hosts, can't this wait until he returns? I'll gather my attorneys and we can arrange a meeting."

"Mr. Banning brings up a good point," Lucas said. "Let's not ruin the evening for William and Priscilla. This has already waited almost a month. It can wait a little longer." He fixed his steely glare on Kyle. "But don't leave town, Kyle Banning, the way you did after you killed Max Treadwell. If you do, it'll be me on your trail, not some drunken sheriff."

Kyle fumed in impotent fury. Lucas motioned to the orchestra leader, who obligingly lifted his baton. The strains of a waltz filled the room.

"There is one more thing, Mr. Banning." Susannah stared at Fletcher, unintimidated by his seething anger.

"What is it, Miss Duncan?" Fletcher snapped.

"Your unethical lawsuit against my uncle is null and void because my uncle is also dead, of natural causes. I inherited the mine, and have since sold it."

Fletcher drew in a shocked, outraged breath. *"You sold it?"*

Susannah continued. "If you wish to file another claim against the owner of the Lucky Lucy mine, you'll be dealing with Lucas McCleave. And somehow I doubt you will find him the same easy target you found my poor uncle."

Lucas simply smiled at Fletcher.

"We're leaving now," Fletcher said through tightly clenched teeth.

Conor spoke for the first time. "Stay away from Susannah." His flashing eyes bored into Fletcher, then Kyle. "If anything happens to her, if either of you touch a hair on her head, you'll answer to me. There won't be a place on this earth where you can hide."

"And Mr. O'Rourke won't be alone if he has to come after you," Lucas added.

Fletcher stared at Conor a moment longer, then stomped off. He took hold of Victoria's arm and, without a word, dragged her from Joseph's side and out of the room.

Conor pushed Susannah behind him as Kyle grabbed the lapel of his frock coat with one hand.

"I'm not impressed with you, Conor O'Rourke," Kyle snarled. "I'll take you, here and now." He reached for his gun.

There was an ominous click.

Kyle stopped in mid-action, his fingers still clenched on Conor's lapel, his free hand hovering above his gun. He blinked and looked down. Conor's pistol was cocked and pressed into his stomach.

"Take your hands off me." The lethal tone in Conor's voice sent a shiver down Susannah's back. Kyle Banning was playing with Death, and she could tell by the look in his eyes that he knew it. Kyle released Conor and stepped back.

"You're an ill-mannered bastard, Kyle," Conor said in a low, dangerous voice. "It's only out of respect for the Hamills that I don't end this right now." He pointed toward the door. "You'd better go home with your big brother."

Once again Kyle's face flushed red. "Some day I'll kill you, O'Rourke," he spat.

"No, you won't." Conor returned his pistol to its holster. "But you're welcome to try."

Kyle spun on his heel and stormed from the room.

Conor turned as William Hamill approached. "I apologize for drawing my weapon, Mr. Hamill."

"Think nothing of it, Mr. O'Rourke. You handled the situation beautifully. The Bannings have been a thorn in my side for years. I'm glad they've finally hung themselves, although I regret it was at the cost of Thomas Duncan's life." He smiled at Susannah. "Perhaps now you can enjoy the evening."

"Thank you, Mr. Hamill, for everything. I shall rest easier than I have in weeks."

He bowed and left them.

"It's really over, isn't it?" Susannah asked as Alexandra and Joseph joined them.

Conor took her hand. "Not completely, but I do think the worst is over."

"I agree," Lucas said. "Let Banning bring on his attorneys. Thanks to Kyle's little slip about your father's death and the witnesses I've found regarding the Treadwell incident, Kyle's days of freedom are coming to a close. I don't think he'll escape the hangman this time." He turned to his son. "How do you know Victoria Banning?"

"From school, Father," Joseph answered. "She's a nice girl, not at all like her brothers. I've always felt sorry for her. She seems so unhappy."

"With brothers like that, it's no wonder." Lucas reached for

Alexandra's hand. "I don't know about the rest of you, but I want to dance. Alexandra?"

"Gladly, Lucas." She kissed Susannah's cheek. "Enjoy yourself, my dear. You deserve to."

Susannah smiled and turned to Conor.

He bowed formally. "May I have this dance, Miss Duncan?"

She curtsied. "I'd be delighted, Mr. O'Rourke." She put her hand on his shoulder, felt his hand at her waist. Strength emanated from the man. Her man. Conor whirled her out onto the floor. Susannah was surprised to learn that he could waltz, and very well. There were many fascinating facets to Conor O'Rourke, she realized. It would take a lifetime to learn them all. Now, perhaps, they had a lifetime ahead of them. For the first time since she had met Conor, she felt genuine hope for the future. Hope for their future.

Later, Conor and Lucas withdrew to the smoking lounge for a few minutes.

"What do you think?" Lucas asked around his cigar.

"I think Fletcher Banning folded too easily. I don't like it." Conor held a lighted match to the end of his cigar.

"Me, either. He'll fall back and regroup. We can't count him out. You know the old saying: 'Never take your eyes off a desperate man.' I'd say Fletcher is now a desperate man."

Conor nodded as he blew out a puff of smoke. "We can't underestimate Kyle, either. He's not too bright, and he's a little crazy, and that makes him dangerous. You never know what he's going to do."

"Hamill offered to have some of his men follow the Bannings home, to make sure they aren't waiting for us tonight. I took him up on it."

"Good." Conor drew on the cigar and slowly released the smoke.

Lucas eyed his friend. "What do you want to tell the women?"

"The truth. We all need to be careful." Conor pushed the cigar into the silver sand bucket. "This isn't over yet."

"I don't think it will be over until the Banning brothers are in jail." Lucas put out his cigar, and the two men headed for the door.

"Or dead," Conor said darkly.

"Will Joseph join us at the house?" Susannah asked Conor.

"No. He said he'd go on home after he returns the carriage to the livery."

They had decided to walk back to Alexandra's house and take advantage of the lovely June night. Lucas and Alexandra walked a short distance ahead of them, holding hands, talking quietly. Conor put an arm around Susannah's shoulders. "I sure did enjoy dancing with you," he said.

Susannah's arm circled his waist. "You're not a bad dancer yourself. Where did you learn to waltz?"

"Alina taught me. She insisted that every man should know how to waltz."

"I'll be sure to thank her." She sighed contentedly, then looked up to the heavens. "I swear, the stars seem so close, I feel I could reach up and just pick them out of the sky." She raised her free hand over her head, as if to prove her point.

They stopped and Conor followed her gaze. "I've always found the night sky incredible out here in the West," he said. "So different from the East. You should see it sometime out on the trail, when there are no lights to detract from it. You feel like you're in touch with all of creation."

Susannah watched Conor's shadowed face, her heart full of love. "I think there's a poet hiding somewhere in you, Conor O'Rourke," she said softly.

He shrugged self-consciously. "I don't know about that. What

I do know is that some of Alexandra's coffee sounds real good right now. Then I want to get you out of that beautiful dress and take you to bed."

Susannah laughed. "You are a man of healthy appetites, sir."

"Yes, ma'am, I surely am, and I mean to—" Conor's words were cut short by the sound of a gunshot. He pushed Susannah around a corner and against a building, his pistol in hand, shielding her body with his own. His wild gaze searched the darkened street.

Susannah could feel his heart pounding against her breast. Her own raced with fear.

"Conor." Lucas's worried voice reached them.

"We're all right," Conor called out.

Lucas joined them. "Where did the shot come from?"

"Across the street." Conor pointed with his pistol.

"We know it isn't Banning. Who else could it be?"

"I think I know," Conor said grimly. "Thankfully he can shoot only once, then he has to reload. Where is Alexandra?"

"Just ahead, taking cover in that doorway."

"Get the women home, Lucas, then come back and help me search. They'll be safe. It's me he wants."

Susannah placed a hand on Conor's chest. "Come home with us, Conor," she begged. "Let the law handle it."

"Go with Lucas, Susannah. Please. This is something I have to take care of myself." He kissed her hard and fast. "I'll be careful. And I don't think I'll be long."

"Come on, Susannah." Lucas took her arm. "Hurry. Then I can get back and help him."

Susannah hurried. They joined Alexandra in the next block.

"Go help Conor," Susannah said to Lucas. "Alexandra and I can get home from here." Lucas hesitated. "Go," Susannah urged. "He needs you; we don't. The house is just ahead."

"Go straight there," Lucas cautioned; then he ran off.

Susannah and Alexandra hooked arms and hurried to Alexandra's house, where they explained the situation to the Potters.

Alexandra made a pot of coffee while Susannah paced the kitchen, anxious and scared. The Potters waited patiently at the table. After a few minutes, the front door opened with enough force to bang against the wall behind it. Conor's angry voice sounded down the hall, although his words could not be deciphered.

"Land sakes, I hope that didn't wake Lily Carolina," Minerva fretted. Jesse barked from the upstairs bedroom.

Conor stormed into the kitchen, dragging a struggling boy by the collar with one hand, carrying an old rifle in the other. Lucas followed right behind. Conor shoved the boy into a chair.

Minerva grabbed Horatio's arm. "Let's go check on the child," she urged, pulling him toward the door. "If the commotion didn't wake her, the dog did, and she'll be scared." She looked back at Susannah. "We'll take care of your sister. You stay with your man."

Susannah nodded her thanks and turned to Conor. She was shocked by the rage on his face. He towered over the frightened boy.

"This is the second time you've taken a shot at me, boy. But this time you could have shot a woman!" Conor waved in Susannah's direction. "You'll tell me who you are, or I'll take you out to the stable and whip it out of you. So help me, I will."

The boy pushed his spectacles up on his nose and glanced at Susannah guiltily.

"I wouldn't have shot her," he protested. "It's you I intend to kill, Conor O'Rourke!"

Susannah looked at Lucas with horrified eyes. He shrugged and held his hands out to his sides. He apparently didn't know any more than she did.

"I know that!" Conor roared. "Tell me *why!*"

"You killed my father!" the boy screamed. "You killed him, and I'm going to kill you for it!"

Conor stared at him. "What was your father's name?"

The boy remained quiet, glaring hatefully at Conor.

"His name!" Conor shouted.

"Franklin Grant!" The boy's eyes filled with tears. "Do you remember Franklin Grant?"

Conor stepped back, his eyes wide with shock. *Franklin Grant.*

"What's your name, son?" Lucas asked gently.

The boy wiped his nose with the back of his hand. "Hamilton," he said sullenly.

Conor saw Franklin Grant in the boy's face. It all came back, with staggering force.

It was a warm day, in the third week of April, 1865. The war was over. Conor O'Rourke was heading home to Tennessee, after fighting for the Confederacy for four long years. Exhausted and disheartened, he trudged down the road in southwestern Virginia, wondering why he was going to Tennessee. His folks were dead, as was his old Gram. Who knew what condition the homestead would be in? He hadn't been back in over two years.

He looked around. It truly was a beautiful spring day. The trees had leaved out, the dogwoods were in bloom, and a gentle breeze washed over him, carrying the good scent of the earth and new life. He was alive. Against tremendous odds, he had survived, had come through four years of hell with no serious wounds. He still had all his limbs, which could not be said for many of his compatriots. All in all, there was much to be grateful for.

The peace of the morning was shattered by the blast of a rifle. Conor was slammed to the ground, a hole torn in his left shoulder. His breath came hard and fast as he struggled to get his rifle in position, while his eyes frantically searched the surrounding forest for a sign of his attacker. He saw a movement among the trees, saw the blue uniform, saw the sunlight glint off the rifle barrel pointed at him. In desperation he swung his own rifle in that direction and got off one shot, then another. The blue uniform fell to the ground.

Conor slumped back onto the dirt road, wondering how bad his wound was. The fingers of his left hand obeyed his command to close into a fist, but with great reluctance. He touched his shoulder with his right hand. There was not much pain, although his hand came away covered with blood.

He heard moaning from the forest. Keeping his rifle ready, Conor crawled toward the sound. He came upon a young Union soldier, not much older than Conor himself, curled on his side, his arms wrapped around his middle. His blue uniform coat was soaked with blood.

Conor pulled the man's rifle out of reach. "Why'd you shoot?" he gasped.

The soldier's brow furrowed in confusion. "Ain't . . . you . . . a reb?"

"Yes, but the war's over."

"Over?" Relief washed over the man's features, then he grimaced. "When?"

"A week ago." Conor pulled a rag from his sack and stuffed it inside his blood-soaked shirt, against his wounded shoulder. "Where have you been, soldier?"

"Lost in these damn woods . . . for weeks. Got separated from my unit." The man moaned again.

"Let me have a look." Conor pulled the man's arm away, saw the gaping wound in the man's stomach, and knew there was nothing anyone could do. "I've killed you," he said quietly. "I'm sorry."

"Was my fault," the man panted. "Name's Franklin Grant, of Pennsylvania."

"Conor O'Rourke, of Tennessee." Conor sat at the man's side and leaned back against the trunk of a tree. His shoulder was beginning to hurt, and badly.

"Sorry for shooting you, Conor O'Rourke. All you was doing was going home. Sure hope I ain't killed you." Franklin squeezed his eyes shut. A moan escaped his lips.

"It's too early to tell," Conor said with a groan. "Maybe you did."

"If not, take my effects to my wife. Tell her what happened." Conor shook his head.

Franklin grabbed his hand. "I beg you. Don't let her go on wondering what happened to me. We have a son. He needs to know his pa didn't abandon him." His fingers tightened on Conor's hand with desperate strength; his brown eyes burned with fervent hope. "I beg you."

A wife and a son. Conor closed his own eyes in anguish. "I wish you had killed me, Grant, before I could shoot back," he whispered to the dying man.

"Conor." Susannah laid a gentle hand on his arm.

He blinked and the scene faded. His eyes focused on the boy. "You look like your father," he said quietly.

Hamilton stared at him in surprise. "You admit it?"

Conor glanced at the faces around him, read their reactions. Lucas, curious; Alexandra, compassionate; Susannah, lovingly concerned, her hand at her throat, her eyes huge in her pale face.

He wearily settled into the chair across from Hamilton. "I'd like to tell you what happened."

"I know what happened," Hamilton snapped. "You gut-shot my pa and he died."

"There's more to it than that, son."

"You killed my pa." Hamilton's voice was beginning to rise. "That's all I need to know. The Bible says, 'an eye for an eye.' "

"The Bible also says, 'Vengeance is mine, sayeth the Lord,' " Alexandra said sternly. "In my house, you'll mind your manners, and that includes being respectful toward your elders. I suggest you hear the man out."

Hamilton crossed his arms over his chest and sat back in the chair, his mouth pressed in a tight line.

"Your father was separated from his unit, Hamilton. He didn't know the war was over. He shot me, I shot back. It was self-defense. I thought your father was going to kill me. There was nothing else I could do. Didn't your mother tell you that?"

Susannah's eyes filled with tears. The anguish on Conor's face was almost more than she could bear. She longed to go to him, but instinctively knew not to.

"You lied to her," the boy snarled. "She believed you, but I don't. My pa wouldn't just shoot someone for no reason."

"He had a reason, Hamilton. He was young, and scared, and he thought I was his enemy. He made a mistake. I wish to God I had missed him, but I didn't. Killing me won't bring him back."

"No, but I'll feel better."

"No, you won't. Believe me, you'll feel a lot worse. What does your mother think about all this?"

Hamilton slumped sadly in his chair. "She died last winter." Then he glared at Conor. "But you didn't know. You kept sending money, just like you always have, and I kept it, saved it until I had enough to track you down myself."

Susannah stared at Conor. He had been sending money to Franklin Grant's widow for all those years? She glanced at Lucas, then Alexandra. They were watching Conor with the same wonder she felt.

"I still don't believe your story," Hamilton continued, his young voice ringing with anger. "And I still intend to kill you."

Conor pushed back out of his chair, his eyes riveted on the boy, his jaw clenched. He tore the stock from his neck and dropped it on the table, then peeled off his coat and tossed it to Lucas. He unbuttoned his vest, then his shirt, as he advanced on Hamilton. The boy stared up at him, his eyes behind the spectacles wide with fright.

"This is what your father's bullet did to me," Conor ground out as he jerked the shirt back off his left shoulder, exposing the terrible scar.

Susannah covered her mouth with one hand as the tears now silently coursed down her cheeks.

"I was badly hurt, Hamilton. I almost died, but I didn't. When I recovered, I found your mother and told her what happened. I did what I could to help her over the years. And now I can do no more than tell the truth." He leaned over the boy. "I am telling the truth. I have regretted your father's death from the moment it happened. You'll have to decide for yourself what to believe." He straightened and put his hands on his hips. "But I'm warning you. I'll not allow you to kill me. I have too much to live for now. If you continue pursuing me, I'll stop you somehow, even if I have to ship you to Australia. You might try to remember that the war is over." He turned on his heel and went out the back door, closing it firmly behind him.

Susannah started after him.

"Let him go," Lucas gently advised. "He's been sitting on this for years, and he probably needs some time to sort through things."

Susannah nodded. Alexandra came to her side and took her hand.

Lucas fixed his stern gaze on Hamilton. "What's to be done with you, young man? Attempted murder is a very serious offense, even if you're only . . . what? Eleven? Twelve?"

"Twelve."

"Conor O'Rourke is a good man, Hamilton. He is also my friend, and I won't stand by and let you take another shot at him. Maybe we'll have to put you in jail."

"I've been there before," Hamilton retorted, although his voice had lost some of its bravado.

"And I'll bet you didn't like it." Lucas draped Conor's coat over a chair. He looked at the two women. "I'll take him home with me tonight. Joseph and I will keep an eye on him for a day or two, even if it means locking him in the closet. Conor doesn't need to be worrying about this on top of all the nonsense with the Bannings."

"Thank you," Susannah said. She looked at Hamilton. Something in the boy's face tore at her heart. She moved to his side and placed a hand on his shoulder. "Hamilton."

He met her eyes, then quickly dropped his head. "I'm sorry if I scared you, ma'am. I wouldn't have hit you."

"I'm sure you would not have intended to, but you could have," she admonished. "It was very dangerous to shoot like that in the dark."

"Yes, ma'am."

Susannah settled into the chair next to him. "Hamilton, I want to tell you something about Conor O'Rourke, and I want you to look at me and listen to me while I'm talking to you."

Hamilton reluctantly raised his head and adjusted his spectacles. "Yes, ma'am," he muttered.

"Several weeks ago, Conor saved my life, as well as that of my little sister, who is only five years old. We would both be dead if not for him. He is a good and honorable man, and I love him very much." She took note of the rebellious expression on Hamilton's face. "I know how it hurts to lose your father," she said softly.

Now the boy looked fully at her.

"My father was murdered, while your father's death was a tragic accident. You were very young when your father died, and I was grown. But no matter when it happens, or how, it hurts when your father dies. And you want to do something to make the hurt go away. Believe me, I know how that feels, too." She paused. Hamilton's eyes had filled with tears. She reached out and laid a gentle hand on the boy's arm. "Killing Conor would

not make the hurt go away, Hamilton. All it would do is hurt
other people, like me, and my sister, and Dr. Kennedy here, and
Mr. McCleave. You are wrong about Conor. He's not a bad man."

Hamilton would not meet her eyes.

"Will you think about all I have said?" she asked.

"Yes, ma'am."

"Thank you. Perhaps now you should go with Mr. McCleave.
It's late, and we're all tired." Susannah stood up and pulled the
shawl around her exposed shoulders, suddenly feeling exhausted.

Hamilton wiped his cheeks and looked uncertainly at Lucas.
"Can I take my gun?"

"No," Lucas said firmly. "You won't be needing it at my
house. Dr. Kennedy will keep it for you."

Alexandra eyed the boy. "Have you had any supper?" she
demanded.

"No, ma'am." Hamilton stood up and shifted his feet.

"I'll feed him," Lucas said. He took Alexandra's face between
his hands. "You look absolutely lovely." He kissed her, then
stepped back. "Let's go, boy. Ladies, we'll see you soon."

"Good night, Lucas," Alexandra said with a tender smile.
Lucas and Hamilton left, and she turned to Susannah. "I see no
reason for you and Conor to return to the hotel tonight. You
don't have to hide any longer."

Susannah's brows drew together with concern. "I think it
would be best if we stayed at the hotel, Alexandra. Conor's not
going to want to sleep in the parlor, and frankly, I don't want
him to, either. We don't want to offend or upset you." She felt
the heat rise in her face, but she faced Alexandra squarely.

"Susannah, you're not telling me anything I don't already
know. I'll feel better if you both stay here, and you're welcome
to share the room, just as you did before. Your sleeping arrangements behind that closed door are your own business."

"Thank you, dear friend." Susannah caught Alexandra's hand

and gave it a squeeze. "Conor's been out there a long time. Do you think I should check on him?"

"I'd give him a little longer. He'll come in when he's ready. Come on. I'll help you out of that dress, and while you get ready for bed, I'll explain everything to the Potters. If Conor's not back by then, we'll go look for him."

Susannah nodded. "All right."

The lovely dress was folded away in the trunk, the jewels returned to the leather bag, and Susannah, wearing a nightdress, was brushing her hair out when he knocked on the door. She called for him to enter. When he did, she waited for him to speak.

"Go on with what you were doing," he said. He took off his gunbelt and hung it over the corner of the headboard.

Susannah turned back to the mirror and continued her brushing, deeply troubled. She did not know what he needed from her, or how to take the pain from his eyes.

Suddenly he was behind her, shirtless, looking over her shoulder in the mirror, his hands at her waist. He nuzzled her neck, and she dropped the brush on the bureau and turned in his arms.

"I love you," she whispered.

"I know, Susannah, and it is my salvation."

They held each other tightly; then she took his hand and led him to the bed. "Tell me about it," she invited.

Conor sighed. "You heard most of the story. We were both lying there, shot all to hell; only he was dying, and we both knew it. He begged me to find his wife and let her know what had happened to him. He didn't want his son growing up thinking he had abandoned him. I was taken to a military hospital outside Washington, and it took a long time to recover. I'm lucky I still have my arm."

"Is that where you learned so much about medicine?"

He nodded. "Once I could get out of bed, they couldn't keep me down. I helped out as much as I could. I had to do something to keep from going crazy." He smiled at her, a gentle, sad smile.

"I really do understand how difficult it was for you being cooped up these last weeks, Susannah. I just didn't know what else to do to keep you alive. I still don't know what we could have done differently."

"It's all right," she whispered. "Go on."

"This one old doctor took me under his wing. In addition to teaching me a lot, he worked with my arm, trying everything he could think of to strengthen it. It's thanks to him I have the use of the arm. Then I went to find Mrs. Grant. That was one of the hardest things I've ever done."

His fingers tightened on hers. "She had a little plot of land in Pennsylvania, was just barely hanging on, with the help of her neighbors. Hamilton was about four years old, and the cutest little kid I'd ever seen." Conor's voice softened. "Her name was Ella. She was young, and pretty, and loved Franklin Grant with all her heart. At the time, I wished he had killed me."

Susannah's eyes filled with tears as she embraced him. "I love *you* with all my heart, Conor, and I'm glad he didn't kill you. I'm so sorry. For everyone involved."

They sat in silence, holding each other. Finally Susannah straightened. "It's late. Let's try to get some sleep."

Conor nodded. Susannah scooted between the sheets while Conor shed his pants and turned the lamp off. He pulled her close. Susannah's heart ached with love and compassion for him. They did not speak again, and soon fell asleep in each other's arms.

Early the next morning, Susannah awakened to the feel of Conor's wet, caressing mouth on her breast. He had opened the buttons of her nightdress, and one of his hands found its way up under the hem of the garment. She sighed and shifted her position, giving his searching fingers easier access to the warmth they sought.

"You make me feel happy to be alive," he whispered against her skin.

"I'm glad," she moaned, closing her eyes at the intense rush of pleasure that radiated from the secret place his fingers had found. She restlessly grabbed her nightdress, pulling at it. "I want this out of the way."

"Serves you right for wearing it in the first place," Conor teased as he helped her remove the offending garment.

When nothing material was left between them, they fell silent and let their hands, lips and bodies express their feelings. Their loving was tender rather than passionate, filled with reverence. Unspoken vows were made. Along with their bodies, their hearts and souls became one.

Seventeen

"Are you leaving again?" Lily Carolina's face was puckered in a worried frown.

"We're only going for a ride, honey." Susannah spoke from her kneeling position on the floor behind her sister. She carefully brushed the tangles from Lily Carolina's soft hair. "The horses need the exercise, and so do I. I've been cooped up for too long."

"I've been cooped up too long, too," Lily Carolina announced. "I better go with you. And Jesse wants to go, too."

The dog raised his ears at the mention of his name, but did not move from his comfortable berth on Susannah's freshly made bed.

Susannah smiled. "No, sweetheart, it's too soon. Your arm isn't completely healed yet. But I promise in a few weeks we'll take you and Jesse on a ride." She gave her sister a quick hug. "We don't have to hide anymore, Lily Carolina. The bad men who hurt Papa will pay for their crimes. When all the legal stuff is finished, we'll decide where to make our new home. Give me the ribbon."

Lily Carolina obediently held out a long blue ribbon. "Won't we live in Uncle Walter's cabin?" she asked.

"No, we can't live there anymore because it burned down." Susannah tied the ribbon around a strand of Lily Carolina's hair at the side of her head and fashioned a bow from it. The tails of the bow lay among the shining golden curls that fell around the child's shoulders.

"Did our beds burn down, too?"

"Yes. It's all gone. Turn around and let me straighten your apron."

Again Lily Carolina obeyed. "Where will we live? Here with Dr. 'Xandra?"

"No, it's time for us to get settled in our own house." Susannah smoothed the ruffle that ran up one of the shoulder straps of the apron. "Maybe we'll go to Pueblo. Or maybe we'll go to Wyoming Territory for a while and visit one of my dearest friends. She just had a baby." She did not say that where they went depended a great deal upon Conor.

Lily Carolina's face lit up. "A baby? Can I play with the baby?"

"Maybe, if you're very careful," Susannah answered. "Elizabeth is still very small."

"Will Mr. Conor come with us, Susannah? I don't want to go without him."

Susannah sat back on her heels. "I don't want to go without him, either. I hope he'll come with us." Lily Carolina reached out, and Susannah gathered her sister into her arms. "We'd make a nice family, wouldn't we?"

The child nodded against her neck. "You'll be the mama, and Mr. Conor will be the papa, just like before. Only it won't be a game anymore, will it?"

"No, sweetheart, it won't be a game." Susannah fervently hoped Conor shared the dream she and Lily Carolina had for the future. "Let's go downstairs now. I'll bet Conor has the horses saddled and is waiting for me."

He was waiting. They set off from the house a few minutes later. Susannah felt gloriously free. It was wonderful to ride in the warmth of the sun, without worrying about who saw her. She watched the handsome man riding beside her, effortlessly managing his excited stallion, and her heart soared with love. What a beautiful day it was!

They rode to the cave first. Conor led the horses to the creek and hobbled the mare within easy reach of the succulent grass as well as the water. Charlie was allowed to roam.

Susannah walked around the cave, deep in thought. Conor watched her, the saddlebags containing their lunch in one hand, his blanket in the other. She met his eyes.

"So much has happened in the past month, Conor. It's hard to believe. Life with Uncle Walter and Papa on the mountain seems like years ago, and South Carolina may as well be on the moon. Nothing is left of the past."

"Nothing is," he agreed. "All things must pass. Can you accept that?"

"I have to," Susannah answered. "There's nothing else to do. I can't change anything. If I could, of course I'd change my father's death, and Uncle Walter's, and meeting Kyle Banning, but I wouldn't change meeting you."

"You had no say in that," Conor assured her. "I would have found you, no matter what. I made a promise to Alina."

Susannah came toward him. "Do you think our feelings for each other would have developed so quickly had we met under more normal circumstances?"

Conor draped the folded blanket over his shoulder. "It's hard to say. Chances are you would have seen me as little more than a saddle tramp, and if your father and uncle had been there, I wouldn't have had the opportunity to dispel that notion."

Susannah smiled as she came to a stop in front of him. "But you are a saddle tramp," she teased, then kissed him.

"You're right," he admitted with a grin, and dropped the saddlebags. He reached for her.

"What would you have thought of me?" she asked. Their arms settled around each other.

"I would have found you beautiful. But I'm sure I would not have seen you in your wet underclothes, which left nothing to my imagination, I might add, and I surely would not have been able to share your bed so quickly." He nibbled on her neck and refused to let her push away from him.

"You are ungentlemanly, sir!" she said, laughing.

"Sometimes I am." He set her back from him. "And if I don't stay away from you now, I'll become even more ungentlemanly. You are intoxicating, woman."

Susannah smiled at his words, a pleased smile, filled with a secret feminine pride. She pulled the blanket from his shoulder.

"Do you want to eat in here or out in the sunshine?" he asked.

"I'd like to stay in here for a while." She spread the blanket on the soft sand where she had slept so many times before. She pulled her gloves from her hands and removed her hat, laying them carefully next to the stone wall.

Conor knelt at the old fire circle, his back to her. "I'll build a small fire," he said. "I wouldn't mind some fresh coffee."

"All right." Susannah unbuttoned her redingote and slipped out of it, folding the garment neatly and setting it next to her hat. Her simple blouse and blue plaid skirt followed, then her petticoat and drawers, her boots and stockings.

Conor took his hat off and fanned the growing flames. "I'll get some fresh water."

"Don't be long, darling."

Something in Susannah's voice made him turn. His mouth fell open. She wore only her chemise, which reached to mid-thigh. As he watched, she pulled the pins from her hair and let the glorious mass fall in a rippling waterfall of gold. Even from where he was, hunkered down over the fire, he could catch the faint scent of lavender. Desire exploded through him, taking his breath away.

"What are you doing, Susannah?" he managed to ask.

"I have dreamed of lying with you in this cave." She settled on the blanket, staring into his eyes, bewitching him. One strap of her chemise fell off her shoulder. "Within the protection of these walls, I have eaten with you, argued with you, shared a blanket with you. I have watched you, Conor O'Rourke. And I have wanted you, I think from that first day, when I opened my eyes and looked into yours. I want you now." She held her hand out to him. "Love me in this special place." Her voice had become a husky whisper.

Conor took her hand and gladly obliged. Where their union earlier that morning had been reverent and tender, this joining was wild and hungry. He pushed her back on the blanket, she opened his shirt. He unbuckled his gunbelt, she unbuttoned his pants. He pulled up her chemise, she pushed down his pants. She raised her hips to him, he drove into her with one powerful thrust, elated to find her body ready for him. She met him eagerly, giving him all she had to give, and he took it, giving in return, until they gave each other ecstasy.

Afterward, they lay breathless in each other's arms, stunned at the force of the passion they had shared. Conor idly stroked her hair.

"You have shown me heaven, Susannah Duncan."

"As you have shown me, Conor O'Rourke." She moved her fingers through the soft hair that covered his chest. "I never dreamed love would be like this."

"Me, either," Conor admitted. "I didn't know my heart would run away, like it did. It ran right to you, and belongs to you now."

Susannah blinked, deeply moved by his words. "You *are* a poet," she whispered.

Conor smiled. "Not always." He sat up, pulling her with him. He settled her chemise around her hips and adjusted his own clothing, then took both of her hands in his. "I want to talk to you. I'd like to tell you about Diablo Canyon."

Susannah watched him closely. "I'm listening."

"I think Lucas told you the basic story. Me and two other Rangers were tracking a band of renegades. We caught up with them at their camp in Diablo Canyon, not far from Mexico. What no one else knows is that their women and children were with them." His hands tightened on hers.

"You don't have to tell me this if you don't want to," she said softly.

"I want no secrets between us, Susannah." He took a deep breath and went on. "We killed a few of the men, and the rest surrendered. That's when it got ugly. My captain was a man named Dick Everhart. His sister and her family had been wiped out by a band of renegades, so for him it was personal, even though he knew the band we had captured wasn't responsible for his sister's death. He went berserk and started shooting at everyone. Women, kids, the wounded. They were all unarmed. Roy Tate—the other Ranger—and I tried to stop him. Everhart killed Roy and shot me."

"The scar along your ribs?" she asked gently.

Conor nodded. "I had to kill him, Susannah. I let all the survivors go, and packed up the dead, Ranger and renegade alike, and took the bodies back. Suddenly I was a hero, the sole survivor of the shootout at Diablo Canyon."

"What did they say about Everhart?"

"I never told anyone what he did. His old parents were there, believing their son had died honorably. I didn't have the heart to tell them otherwise. What purpose would it have served? That's why I left the Rangers."

Susannah brushed his hair back from his forehead. "No, you couldn't stay after that. Is that when you started working for the cattlemen?"

He nodded. "Punching cows sure seemed peaceful." He raised a hand to caress her cheek. "I'm no hero, Susannah. I'm an ordinary man who tries to do the best I can in whatever situation I find myself in. That's all I am."

"That's plenty for me," Susannah assured him with a loving smile. "You're all I want."

He captured her hands again. "You have my heart, Susannah. Will you share my life? Will you marry me?"

She stared at him, her heart pounding. His blue eyes seemed to shine in the shadowed cave. She saw love there, and hope. Her fingers tightened on his hands. "Oh, yes, Conor, I will. Whatever that means, wherever you go. But I'm part of a package deal."

"I know. I'd not consider anything else." He leaned against the wall and pulled her to his side. "We'll raise Lily Carolina as our own, and I figured Jesse would insist on coming along, and those two mares probably will, too."

Susannah laughed and nestled against him. "I'm afraid you're right," she admitted. "Especially about Jesse." She paused. "I have a small dowry, Conor. Besides the bag of gold, I have the jewels my father gave me. We can sell them."

"Absolutely not. Those jewels are not for sale. They are all you have from your mother, Susannah. They're for you to wear when you get dressed up, like last night. And later, they're for Lily Carolina to wear, and perhaps one day our daughter will wear them, and then Lily Carolina's daughter, and so on."

A deep happiness filled Susannah, and her hold on him tightened.

"I have some money put away," he said. He caught up one of her golden curls and kissed it. "It's not a lot, but it's enough to get us started somewhere. We could buy a small spread, raise some horses, a few cattle. Raise Lily Carolina. And maybe raise a few children of our own."

"It sounds wonderful," Susannah said truthfully. "But what about your job with Mr. Goodnight?"

"I sent him a wire when I was in Denver, telling him I had been delayed. He wired back, saying he was encountering some financial problems and to take my time. He won't mind if I tell him I'm not coming."

Susannah leaned away from him. "Are you ready for this,

Conor? To settle down, I mean? Are you certain this is what you really want?"

He touched her cheek. "Absolutely certain."

There was no mistaking the true conviction in his voice, or in his eyes. Susannah felt that her heart might burst with happiness. "Where would you like to settle?"

"Alina and Beau have offered me full partnership in their ranch. I thought we might go up and visit them, show you the land, see how we feel about that. Even if we decide against the partnership, we may want to stay in the area. It's a truly beautiful place. I thought you might even like to get married up there."

"Oh, Conor. I was going to ask if you wanted to go to Wyoming, at least for a visit. I'm anxious to see Alina, and meet her husband and her new baby, and I'd love to get married there." Susannah looked at him shyly. "I'd like a real wedding dress, with a veil and all."

"Then you shall have one." He planted a kiss on the tip of her nose. "And now, I'm hungry."

Susannah arched a disbelieving eyebrow.

Conor laughed. "As enticing as you are, my dear, I'm afraid this time I'm hungry for food."

"Thank goodness." Susannah reached for her drawers. "I'm famished, too." She smiled at him then. "I love you, Conor. I know we'll make a good life together."

He kissed her quickly. "I know we will, too."

"When we're finished eating, can we go by the old claim? I'd like to tell Papa the news."

"Of course we can," Conor said, his handsome features soft with tenderness. "But somehow I think Thomas already knows."

Ben Hollister stepped out onto the porch of the Barton House, his eyes squinted against the glare of the late morning sun. Unaware of the events of the previous night, he had continued his search. He was getting closer; he could feel it. Susannah Duncan's lovely scent would eventually lead him to her.

He had remembered the mysterious lady in black, the one he had run into coming out of the bakery last week. She, too, had smelled of lavender, and he decided the lady in black and the intruder at the Banning estate were the same person, and that person was Susannah Duncan. It had not been difficult to learn that the lady in black had been staying at the Barton House, that she no longer was there, and that Dr. Alexandra Kennedy had called on her. He decided to pay Dr. Kennedy a visit. If nothing else, maybe she could look at his foot. It still bothered him.

He knocked on the door of the neat little house at the edge of town. A dog barked from inside. After a few minutes, Dr. Kennedy answered the door. Her eyes narrowed at the sight of him.

"What do you want, Ben Hollister?" she demanded.

Ben swept his hat from his head. "Got my foot stomped, ma'am. Thought you might be able to take a look at it for me." He pointed to the injured member.

"And I suppose Dr. Pollok was busy?"

"He wasn't there, ma'am," Ben answered smoothly, not knowing if that was true or not.

Dr. Kennedy sighed. "Come on in, then." She stepped back and allowed him to enter, closing the door behind him. "Wait in the parlor." She waved toward the open double doors. "I'm with a patient right now, but should be only a few more minutes."

Ben obeyed, moving into the parlor. He heard the door on the opposite side of the hall open and close, then heard the murmur of low voices. He could not make out the words.

The parlor was a nice room, he decided as he settled onto the comfortable sofa. A few minutes later a dog barked again. The sound came from upstairs.

"Is someone here?"

Ben looked up, startled, at the sound of a young voice at the door. A beautiful little girl stood there, clutching a doll with one hand, her other hand wrapped in a bandage. She wore a simple blue dress covered with a clean white apron, and her golden hair hung in long curls, decorated with a blue ribbon.

"I can hear you breathing," the child pointed out.

"Can you?" Ben questioned. He looked at her lovely blue eyes, eyes that did not move. "Can't you see me?"

"No, sir, I can't." Her little brow furrowed. "Do I know you?" Her voice carried a faint, delightful accent.

"I don't think so, because I don't know you. My name is Ben." Was the child Dr. Kennedy's daughter? he wondered.

She thought for a moment. "I don't know anyone named Ben, but I know your voice. Are you here to see Dr. 'Xandra?"

"Yes, I am." Ben decided the girl would not refer to Dr. Kennedy in such a manner if she were the doctor's daughter.

"Are you hurt, Mr. Ben?"

Ben could not help being charmed by the child. "Just a little. I see that you were hurt." He pointed to her arm, then closed his fingers and let his hand fall to his lap, feeling a little foolish. She could not see where he pointed.

"Yes, sir. My wrist was broken. So is Amy's." She held up her doll, showing him the tiny splint.

"So I see. Well, I know your doll's name. What is your name?"

"Lily Carolina Duncan."

The child's innocent words pounded into Ben's brain. *Duncan?*

"And my dog's name is Jesse, but he can't come downstairs when Dr. 'Xandra has patients, 'cause he barks too much."

Jesse. Ben remembered the day on the mountain, remembered Susannah Duncan's big black dog. *Jesse!* she had screamed. So, even the dog had survived that day. But who was this child? Susannah Duncan's child? A love child, perhaps? Hidden away on Walter Duncan's mountain? That would explain why no one knew of the little girl. That would explain many things about

Susannah Duncan, such as her refusal to marry Fletcher Banning. She would not have been able to explain the child. Why else would a woman turn down a rich and powerful man like Fletcher?

"Where is your mama, honey?" he asked Lily Carolina.

"In heaven, with my papa. Susannah said someday we'll see them again."

Ben was taken aback. He had not expected that answer. "Who is Susannah?" he asked cautiously.

"My sister," Lily Carolina explained with great patience. "Do you know her?"

"Yes, I do." Ben thought quickly. "Where is your sister now?"

"She and Mr. Conor went for a ride. They said the next time I can go with them."

Ben stood up and clapped his hat on his head. "You can go with them now, if you like. I'll take you."

Lily Carolina frowned. "I don't know. We'd better ask Dr. 'Xandra."

"We don't have time for that." Ben crossed the room.

Lily Carolina took a wary step backward. She held her hand out in front of her. "I can't go unless Dr. 'Xandra says it's all right," she insisted.

In one swift move, Ben put his hand over Lily Carolina's mouth and scooped her up into his arms, steeling himself against the sudden look of terror on her face. The doll fell unnoticed to the floor. He silently left the house through the front door.

A few minutes later Alexandra came from the examination room, followed by Polly. Jesse barked excitedly from the other side of Alexandra's bedroom door.

"You're almost one hundred percent recovered," Alexandra said. "Just don't get too carried away with your dancing. That one rib is still a little bruised." She spotted Lily Carolina's doll on the floor and frowned. "It's not like that child to leave her things around." She retrieved the doll.

"I'd love to say hello to the little sweetie," Polly said. "Where is she?"

"She was taking her nap, but I don't see how she can be sleeping now, with Jesse making all that noise. Go on up and check on her, Polly, while I talk to Ben Hollister."

Polly nodded and ran up the stairs. Alexandra stepped to the door of the parlor and saw at a glance that the room was empty. "That's strange," she muttered. She absent mindedly stroked the doll, then her eyes widened as a terrible suspicion came to her mind. "Oh, my God." She whirled toward the stairs as Jesse came racing down. Alexandra raised fearful eyes to Polly standing on the landing.

"She's not in your room, Alex. What's wrong? You look like you've seen a ghost." Polly started down the stairs.

"Check the other room, Polly!" Alexandra cried. She ran to the kitchen. "Lily Carolina!" The big room was empty, as was the bathing room. Alexandra yanked the back door open. "Lily Carolina!" There was no sign of the child.

Polly ran into the kitchen, followed by Jesse. "She's not upstairs. Alex, what's wrong?"

Alexandra's hands shook. "I think Ben Hollister took her, Polly."

Polly's eyes widened with shock. "Oh, no, Alex. He'll take her to Fletcher Banning."

"I know." Alexandra's voice was a despairing whisper. "Stay here and keep Jesse with you. I don't want him following me. I must tell Lucas." She hurried to the front door, then handed Polly the forlorn doll before she rushed away, without hat or gloves. Jesse pawed at the closed door and whined.

"I know how you feel, Jess." Polly clutched the doll to her breast. "If Fletcher Banning harms a hair on that child's head, I'll kill him myself."

* * *

"Do you think the mining surveyor Lucas hired has been here yet?" Susannah glanced up at the entrance to the mine from her place on the ground near her father's grave.

"Someone has been here," Conor answered. "It may have been him." Her hat hung by its string down her back, and he watched the sunlight play on her hair.

"I doubt he'll find any silver." Susannah sat back on her heels and dusted her gloved hands together. "There. What do you think?"

"I think it'll be fine." Conor smoothed the last of the soil around the base of the small bush they had transplanted from farther down the valley. The spindly plant now rested in the space between the crosses that stood guard over the graves of Walter and Thomas Duncan.

"Papa always liked roses." Susannah accepted Conor's offered hand and got to her feet. "I'm not sure he ever saw a wild rose in bloom. The flowers are so tiny and delicate compared to regular roses. They sure are pretty."

Conor leaned the shovel against the trunk of the aspen that shaded the graves and looked at her thoughtfully. "You're like that rose bush, Susannah. You're pretty, and you smell good, and you're tough when you have to be. You've been transplanted to a new and harsh environment. And just like that rose, you'll thrive." He reached out to touch her cheek, his eyes soft with love. "My mountain rose. I'm proud you're mine."

Susannah moved into his arms. "And I am, Conor. I'm yours." She lifted her mouth for his kiss. They clung together for several minutes, then strolled a short distance away, each with an arm around the other.

"I always knew my parents loved each other," she said. "But I don't think I ever understood how much, until now. I love you so deeply it almost hurts, and I think they felt that way, too."

She smiled up at him. "I also think Papa is very pleased with how things turned out."

Conor smiled. "He would approve of me as your mate?"

"Oh, yes. I think Papa would have liked you very much."

"I liked him, too, Susannah, the little I got to know him." He paused. "Would your grandmother approve of me?"

"Absolutely not," Susannah said firmly, with a laugh. "You would frighten her."

Conor raised an eyebrow. "Frighten her? Why?"

"Because she wouldn't be able to control you. She would find you dangerous."

"Well, I'm glad you don't find me dangerous."

"Oh, but I do. You proved very dangerous to my virtue, and you stole my heart." She shook her head in mock regret, trying not to smile. "You are very dangerous, Conor O'Rourke."

Conor laughed and enveloped her in a hug. "You are dangerous yourself, Miss Duncan," he said as he nuzzled her neck. Suddenly he stiffened. "Someone's coming."

They looked down the valley. The sound of an approaching horse reached their ears. Without a word, they moved back by the horses. Susannah calmly pulled the rifle from Conor's scabbard and stood beside him.

The lone rider came into view and toward them at a full gallop.

"That's Joseph McCleave," Conor said, relaxing his hold on his pistol. "Something's wrong." They hurried out to meet Joseph as he pulled his winded horse up in the yard of the burned-out cabin.

"Father sent me for you," he said breathlessly. "You must come back at once."

Conor grabbed the reins of the dancing horse. "What happened?"

Joseph looked at Susannah, his expression one of outrage and sorrow at the same time. "I hate to tell you this, Miss Duncan, but Ben Hollister took Lily Carolina. We think Banning has her now."

Susannah's eyes widened. Her heart pounded with sickening force, and her stomach knotted as the horror of Joseph's words struck her. "Oh, no." She turned to Conor, reaching for him. "We have to get her."

Conor caught her hand. "We will." His voice was harsh with fury.

She saw the tense set of his jaw, the blazing rage, and worry, in his blue eyes. She handed him the rifle.

"Go with Joseph to Alexandra's and wait for me there. Banning may have sent terms for her release." He slid the rifle into its case.

"But where are you going?" she asked.

"I'm going to scout the Banning place." He swung up into the saddle.

"Conor, let me go with you," Susannah begged. She stood beside him, placed a hand on his thigh. "I've been there. I know my way around."

Conor leaned down toward her, cupping her cheek with his gloved hand. "My brave woman. It's too dangerous, Susannah. I can move more quickly on my own."

"But I know the way! Conor, I beg you. Don't expect me to go back to Alexandra's and sit quietly waiting for word of my sister. I've already done too much waiting. Let me help."

Conor looked into her pleading eyes, shining green with unshed tears. After a long moment, he nodded. "Put your gunbelt on. And I want you to promise that you'll do as I say."

"I promise." She squeezed his thigh. "Thank you." She hurried over to the gray mare and pulled her gunbelt from the saddlebag.

"Joseph, get to Alexandra's, but don't kill your horse doing it. Let the animal rest for a bit before you start back. Tell your father that Susannah and I will be there after we scout the Banning place. Assure him that's all we're going to do. We won't do anything to endanger Lily Carolina."

"Yes, sir." Joseph slipped from the saddle.

With her gunbelt strapped securely around her hips, Susannah climbed into the saddle. "Thank you for coming," she said to Joseph.

"Yes, ma'am." Worry clouded his youthful features. "Everything will be fine, Miss Duncan. You'll see. Not even Fletcher Banning would hurt a little girl."

"He'll die if he does," Conor vowed. "Let's go."

Joseph waved after them as they cantered away. "God be with you," he whispered.

"Where the hell have you been?" demanded Fletcher Banning. "I've had men looking for you, Ben. Everything has fallen apart."

Ben Hollister watched as Fletcher paced the fine oriental rug in his office. It looked like Fletcher had slept in his shirt, if he had slept at all. His eyes were bleary and hunted. He had not shaved.

"I told you I'd be out of sight for a few days, Boss," Ben gently reminded him. "I said I'd find Susannah Duncan, but—"

"But she found herself, Ben, and presented herself to society last night at Hamill's party!" Fletcher ran his fingers through his hair. "Now the whole goddamned town knows she's alive, and that damned Lucas McCleave has started an investigation on Kyle."

"So you found Susannah Duncan."

"Yes, and she sold her uncle's mine to Lucas McCleave. You know that bastard will never sell to me, and he won't cave in, either. The bitch outsmarted me, with the help of McCleave and that damned Conor O'Rourke."

"Conor O'Rourke? That's who Kyle tangled with in the saloon that night?"

"That's him, whoever the hell he is."

"Boss, if Kyle messed with Conor O'Rourke, he's lucky to be alive."

Fletcher stared at him. "What are you talking about?"

"You know I spent some time in Texas right after the war. So did Conor O'Rourke. He and I ended up on opposite sides in a little boundary dispute between our bosses. He later joined the Rangers for a while. He's not a man to tangle with, Mr. Banning."

"Kyle will take care of Conor O'Rourke, Ben. We have to decide what to do about that damned mine!"

Ben shook his head. "I'm not one to argue, but don't count on Kyle to take care of O'Rourke. He won't be able to. But I may be able to help out with the problem of the mine."

Fletcher watched as Ben went out into the hall. The foreman returned a moment later, leading a little girl by the hand. Fletcher stared in amazement as Ben guided the child to stand before him.

"What the hell does this kid have to do with anything?" Fletcher shouted. The child flinched.

"This is Lily Carolina, Mr. Banning. Susannah Duncan's little sister."

Fletcher's eyes widened. The look on his florid face changed from one of confused irritation to fierce joy.

"You've done well, Ben. You've done very well."

"I wish we could get closer." Susannah looked down at the Banning estate from the mountainside.

"We don't dare, not with the guards Banning posted all around the perimeter of his property." Conor looked through the telescope as he spoke.

"The house is the tallest building," Susannah said. "The bunkhouse is the long building this side of it, and the barn is next to that. That's a carriage house across from the corral, and the two small buildings on the far side are the smoke house and a shed of some kind. The privy is off by itself."

"Well, at least I know the layout." Conor lowered the telescope. "There's nothing we can do for now, Susannah."

"I know." Susannah sank to the ground, fighting tears and a feeling of despair. "She's just a little girl, Conor. How could Ben Hollister take a little girl? How did he find out about her?"

Conor collapsed the telescope and hunkered down next to her, placing an arm around her shoulders. "I don't think they'll hurt her, Susannah. There'd be nothing gained by that."

"What will he want? I don't own the mine any longer."

"He wants the mine," Conor said firmly. "I'm certain of it. Banning will want to deal with Lucas."

Susannah wiped her cheeks. "We'd best get back, then, and see if there's been any word." She allowed Conor to pull her to her feet, looking at him with huge, teary eyes. "If he hurts her, Conor, I'll want to kill him."

"If he hurts her, Susannah, we'll kill Fletcher Banning together," Conor promised grimly. He led her to the horses.

The ride to Alexandra's house was quiet. Susannah thought over the last few months. So many of her perceptions and beliefs had changed. Although she had lived through the war, violence had not personally touched her until Kyle Banning had come into her life. A year ago, she would not have believed that she would ever want to kill someone. The murderous rage had abated somewhat, thanks to Conor's counsel and the fact that she had not been able to go through with it when she had the chance. But now, her fingers virtually itched to pull the Peacemaker from its holster. It was clear to her that the feud with the Bannings would not be over until they were dead. Or she was.

Conor rode easily, but the calmness of his features and his

manner was in sharp contrast to the turmoil of his thoughts. What had gone wrong? How did Ben Hollister find out about Lily Carolina? Somehow, somewhere, Conor had let down his guard. But how? Where? His gut twisted in anguish at the thought of Lily Carolina in the hands of the Bannings. Kyle Banning had brutally beaten an old man to death, and had seriously injured both Susannah and Polly. Despite what he said to Susannah, Conor could not guarantee that Kyle wouldn't use his fists on a child.

Dusk had fallen when Conor and Susannah rode into Alexandra's shadowed yard. They cared for the horses and turned them into the corral with Joseph's horse. Lucas and Alexandra waited for them on the back porch. When they got close, Alexandra held her arms out to Susannah.

"I'm so sorry," she said. Tears glittered in her eyes.

Susannah embraced her friend. "It's not your fault, Alexandra. Please don't blame yourself."

"I was in the examination room with Polly. Ben Hollister came seeking help, saying his foot had been stomped."

Susannah met Conor's eyes over Alexandra's shoulder.

"I told him to wait in the parlor," Alexandra continued. "Lily Carolina was upstairs taking her nap, and I didn't think anything of it. I don't know if Ben went looking for her, which would mean he knew about her beforehand, or if she came downstairs on her own. She wouldn't have known not to talk to him."

"I find it hard to believe Hollister knew about her," Conor said. "We were all too careful."

"I told her we didn't have to hide anymore," Susannah admitted sadly. "She probably came downstairs and introduced herself. Hello, Lucas." She held her hand out to him as she and Alexandra climbed the stairs to the porch.

He grasped her hand. "Susannah. I'm sure sorry."

"Have you heard from the Bannings?" she asked.

"Yes. They want to see you and me first thing in the morning."

"Conor thought they'd want to see you." She glanced back at him as she followed Alexandra into the kitchen, then stopped, surprised. The room was full of people.

Minerva Potter stood at the stove, stirring a large pot of beans, her eyes red-rimmed behind her spectacles. Horatio was at his wife's elbow, offering comfort if not assistance. Hamilton Grant sat at the table, as did Polly, who was peeling potatoes. Joseph stood near the sink with his arms crossed over his chest, and Neville Thorpe waited by the door leading to the hallway.

Susannah hugged Minerva. "Thank you for coming," she said softly.

Minerva patted Susannah's back. "As if I could stay at home when those Bannings have my baby," she huffed. "Horatio and I will be at your side through the bitter end of this ordeal, Susannah. You may count on us. Isn't that right, dear?"

Horatio drew himself up, his old eyes flashing with indignation. "It most certainly is, precious. We shall be here. The nerve of those Bannings, taking a child. They'll answer to Horatio Potter. Indeed they will!"

Minerva stared at her husband, a mixture of pride and awe on her plump face.

"Well said, Mr. Potter," Neville Thorpe commented. "I'm sure you speak for all of us."

Susannah held her arms out to Polly, who had risen from her chair. The two women held each other.

Conor eyed Hamilton. "And what about you?"

Hamilton pushed his spectacles up on his nose. "It ain't right, stealing a little girl. I'd like to do what I can."

"Thank you, Hamilton." Susannah smiled at him. "Thank you, all of you." She held out her hand to Conor, who took it and held it tightly.

"We both thank you," Conor said. "It means a lot to have such good friends." He looked at Lucas. "I'm going with you and Susannah tomorrow. As far as I'm concerned, Lily Carolina is my sister, as much as she is Susannah's. No one takes my kin."

"Banning instructed that she and I go alone," Lucas warned.

Susannah glanced at Conor's set jaw, at the steely resolve, and said, "We couldn't keep him away if we wanted to. And I, for one, will feel a lot better if he is with us."

Lucas nodded. "It's agreed, then. We'll leave at first light."

"Well, no one is going anywhere tonight until they've had a filling supper," Minerva announced firmly from her position at the stove. "We all need to keep our strength up. I have a hunch this is going to be a long night."

Conor pulled Susannah into his arms, silently offering comfort. Susannah clung to him, feeling his strength, needing it. Her heart ached for her sister. No doubt it would be a long night.

Eighteen

The flamboyant arch of brick and wrought iron heralded the entrance to the Banning property. The sun had just risen over the mountains to the east and kissed the silver "B" in the center of the arch with its golden light. Susannah stared up at the hated symbol from the buggy she shared with Lucas. Her jaw tightened with determination.

Lucas pulled on the reins, bringing the single-horse conveyance to a halt. "Did you say it was a mile up the road from here?" he asked Susannah.

She nodded. "I'd guess it was about that far. But remember, it was dark, and I was scared. It seemed like a hundred miles."

Conor turned Charlie around so that he faced the couple in the wagon. "From the mountainside yesterday, the road looked to be in good condition. It won't take long to get there." He looked from Susannah to Lucas. "Are you ready?"

"I'm ready," Susannah said grimly.

Lucas nodded and lightly slapped the horse with the reins. The buggy moved under the arch, and Conor followed, then urged Charlie forward until he was even with Susannah. They had gone only a short distance when four riders emerged from a dense grove of pines and lined up across the road. Again Lucas pulled the buggy to a stop. Susannah fingered her pistol, hidden in the deep pocket of her skirt.

Ben Hollister leaned over his saddle horn and stared at Conor. "You weren't invited to the party, O'Rourke."

"Lack of an invitation won't keep me from where I decide to go, Hollister. You ought to know that."

Susannah glanced up at Conor. He appeared very relaxed, but she knew he was coiled like a spring, ready to release. And although she couldn't see it, she also knew his right hand rested on his thigh, and that his pistol could be in that hand in an instant.

"Yeah, I reckon I do know that." Ben pushed his hat back on his head. "It seems like you have a personal interest in this."

"I do. You may as well have taken my sister, Hollister. That's how strong I feel about it," Conor said, speaking conversationally. "It wasn't a good idea to take the child. I'm surprised you'd do something like that."

He's chatting like we've got all day, Susannah fumed. She fidgeted on the seat.

"Stealing little girls from their homes isn't your style," Conor continued. "Or have you changed that much since you left Texas?"

Ben shrugged. "I was looking for the woman." He nodded in Susannah's direction. "I figured she was the lady in black, and Dr. Kennedy had been visiting her at the Barton House. So I decided to call on the doc. My foot was bothering me, anyway." He looked at Susannah. "You stomped me good that night you were here. You did all right for yourself." There was an unmistakable look of admiration on his weather-beaten face.

Susannah did not answer.

"Anyways, I was waiting on the doc, and the kid came in and introduced herself. I guess you could say it was a spur-of-the-moment decision to take her."

"You are despicable," Susannah said, her voice heavy with loathing. "Involving an innocent child in Fletcher Banning's murderous intrigues."

Ben shrugged again. "I ride for the man, lady. I do what's

best for him. He won't hurt the kid, as long as you do what he wants."

"Let's go find out exactly what that is," Conor suggested coldly.

The tone of his voice caused Susannah to look at him again. His jaw was tight, and his eyes flashed in a way she had come to know as dangerous.

"The boss said to make sure they was alone," one of the men pointed out to Ben.

"You're welcome to try and stop him if you want to, Shorty." Ben turned his horse's head. "But you won't live past the next minute or so if you do. Since O'Rourke has a stake in this, I'm going to let Mr. Banning deal with it." He guided his horse up the road. The other two Banning men circled around behind the buggy.

The man called Shorty stared at Conor for a moment, then shrugged and followed Ben.

Susannah breathed a sigh of relief as Lucas urged the horse on. "I'm glad they let you come," she said to Conor.

"They had no choice. Hollister knew that." Conor's voice was harsh. "Like we agreed earlier, we take no chances with Lily Carolina's life. If trouble starts, Lucas, do your best to get Susannah and the child out of there. I'll cover you."

"Conor, we're not going to leave you," Susannah protested. "We're in this together."

"I'll tolerate no argument on this, Susannah." Conor stared down at her from the saddle, his eyes boring into her. "We are at war with the Bannings, and I know all about war. You'll do as I say."

Susannah stared back at him, stunned. This was a Conor she did not know. There was a hardness about his features, in his eyes, that she had not seen before. He was a warrior, on his way to do battle, as surely as if he wore armor and carried a broad sword, like the knights she had read about in *Ivanhoe*. He gathered the reins and coaxed Charlie to a trot, moving ahead of the buggy.

"He's right, Susannah." Lucas kept his eyes on the road. "We are at war. He has experience with this sort of thing, even more than I have. You have to trust that he can take care of himself, and he has to be able to trust that we'll follow his orders. We all have a better chance of surviving if we obey him."

"He can't die, Lucas." Susannah struggled to keep the fear from her voice.

"He's a hard man to kill. Hopefully, none of us will die."

They fell into silence. Several minutes later, Lucas guided the buggy into the yard and pulled it to a stop in front of the mansion.

Conor stepped down from the saddle and let Charlie's reins hang. He lifted Susannah from the seat.

When he set her on the ground, she kept her hands on his shoulders. "I trust you, Conor, and I'll follow your orders. You won't have to worry about that."

His hands tightened at her waist. "Thank you," he whispered. He took her elbow and escorted her up the steps of Fletcher Banning's wide front porch. Lucas joined them at her other side.

The double doors opened and Kyle Banning stood in the doorway. "What the hell is he doing here?" he snarled at Ben, jerking his head in Conor's direction.

"He has a vested interest in the proceedings," Ben said calmly. "Mr. Banning will decide if he stays."

Kyle crossed his arms over his chest, refusing to move.

Ben stepped up very close to Kyle. "I said, Mr. Banning will decide. Now get out of the way."

Kyle sullenly moved back. Susannah glared at him as she passed. The weight of the gun in her pocket offered her comfort.

Ben led the way to Fletcher Banning's office. They filed into the elegant room. Fletcher sat in the chair behind his desk, his back to them, facing the large window, puffing on a cigar. Ben pointed Susannah, Conor and Lucas to the two chairs in front of the desk. They went, but remained standing. Kyle and three other hands silently lined up along the back wall.

"They're here, Mr. Banning." Ben took his hat off and waited.

Fletcher continued to smoke the cigar, ignoring them.

Susannah's jaw tightened at the insult. "We're not here to play games, Fletcher," she said sharply. "I've come for my sister, and I want her now."

Fletcher slowly turned the swivel chair around to face them. He stared at her, a malicious triumph shining in his eyes. "Ah, but it's not that simple, my dear Susannah." His gaze flicked from her to Lucas, then to Conor. He frowned. "I gave specific instructions that you and McCleave were to come alone."

"This concerns me, too, Banning," Conor said. "I'm not leaving."

Fletcher eyed him thoughtfully. "No, I don't think you will. Perhaps it's just as well. At least I know where you are. You've been a constant source of irritation, Mr. O'Rourke. I suspect things would have gone much more smoothly for me if you hadn't interfered. I won't forget that." He ended on a harsh note.

Conor hooked his thumbs in his gunbelt. "I'll make sure you don't forget. This isn't over."

Fletcher did not seem to notice the quiet menace in Conor's voice. He took another drag on the cigar, dismissing Conor's words with a wave of his hand. His eyes fell on Susannah. Smoke curled out of his mouth as he spoke. "Let's get down to business. I have something you want, you have something I want. A simple trade."

"I told you I sold the mine, Fletcher," Susannah said angrily. "But even if I hadn't, I wouldn't sell it to you."

"Not even for your sister's life?"

Susannah gaped at him. "You can't be serious. She's five years old."

Fletcher tapped the cigar on the edge of a crystal ash bowl. "Oh, I am quite serious, I assure you. Your sister's life for the deed to the mine. Surely you can persuade McCleave to give me the deed."

Susannah turned to Conor, horrified. He took her hand and held it tightly.

"You can't possibly hope to get away with kidnapping and extortion, Banning," Lucas snapped. "This nonsense has gone on long enough. Bring the child to us."

Fletcher smashed the unfortunate cigar into the ash bowl as he rose. "I have already gotten away with kidnapping, McCleave, and I guarantee this is not nonsense. If you don't sign the Duncan property over to me, the child will die."

"You won't get away with it!" Susannah cried.

"Oh, but I will, Susannah, thanks to you." Fletcher came around his desk. "No one knows you have a sister. Why did you keep her hidden? Perhaps she's not your sister at all, but your daughter, born of an indiscretion. Or perhaps you're ashamed of her because she is blind."

Hot fury roared through Susannah's veins. She stepped away from Conor and slapped Fletcher's smirking face as hard as she could. "You vile man," she spat. "We kept her hidden to protect her from you."

Fletcher's eyes widened with astonishment, which was rapidly replaced with rage. He raised his hand to strike her. Both Conor and Lucas moved forward protectively. Fletcher paused. He lowered his hand, visibly struggling to control himself. "Don't ever hit me again, Susannah." He straightened his vest. "Back to business. As I said before, no one knows you have a sister, except for a few of your friends. If the child were to disappear, you won't be able to prove she ever existed."

"For God's sake, man, you are talking about a five-year-old child." Conor's voice was low and deadly. "Not even you would go that far."

"But I will go that far, Mr. O'Rourke." Fletcher slapped the top of his desk as if to emphasize his words. "Don't underestimate the height of my ambition. I'll allow no one to stand in my way. Not Walter Duncan, not his brother, not any of you." He waved his arm at them. "And least of all, a pathetic, useless child. She is utterly expendable. If you don't agree to my terms, she will die, and I can assure you her body will never be found. No body, no crime." He held his arms out expansively. "It's as simple as that. And if you bring in the law, it *will* be as simple as that."

"You bastard." Conor clenched his fist.

Susannah could only stare at the man, horrified. She found a strange light in Fletcher Banning's eyes, one of unholy determination. In that instant, she knew he was not bluffing. He would kill Lily Carolina, as easily as he would a pesky fly. She turned to Lucas. "Please give him the mine." Her voice held a note of quiet desperation.

"I will," Lucas ground out, glaring at Fletcher. "But the deed is on file with the territorial assessor. I have to go to Denver for it."

"One week from today." Fletcher walked back around his desk. "Be here with all the necessary paperwork. The child will remain as my guest until then."

"No!" Susannah cried. "I won't leave her here!"

Fletcher's cold eyes settled on her. "When the deed is transferred, your sister will be released into your loving arms, Susannah. Not a minute before."

"Then let me stay and care for her. I beg you. She has a broken wrist. Or let her go and keep me."

"Your concern is touching, my dear, but I can't allow you to stay." Fletcher shook his head in mock regret. "You're too clever, and would no doubt cause problems. And I don't think Mr. O'Rourke would be content to wait in Georgetown if you were here. He's already proven his ability to annoy me. Keeping only the child will ensure that you all adhere to our agreement."

"Let us see her," Conor demanded. "Now. We want to be sure you haven't already killed her."

"Very well." Fletcher motioned to Ben with his head. Ben nodded and left. An uneasy silence settled over the room.

Susannah stared down at her clasped hands. How had things come to this? What could she have done differently to keep her sister safe? Grief and fear filled her, as did a smoldering rage. To use a child as a pawn!

Conor placed a comforting hand on her shoulder. She looked up at him, saw the love and resolve in his eyes, and knew he would be with her through it all. She let her own eyes reveal her love for him, and when his fingers tightened on her shoulder, she knew he had understood.

Fletcher Banning's mouth pressed into a line underneath his full mustache. He dropped into his chair and drummed his fingers on the desk.

Ben returned, followed by a sullen Victoria, who had Lily Carolina by the hand. The child's dress was wrinkled, as if she had slept in it, and her hair was uncombed. Her pale face wore a wary, fearful expression.

"Lily Carolina!" Susannah hurried across the room.

"Susannah!" Lily Carolina pulled away from Victoria and held her hands out in front of her.

Susannah fell to her knees and gathered the little girl in her arms. "Oh, honey. I'm so happy to see you. Are you all right?"

Lily Carolina clung to her. "Yes, but I want to go back to Dr. 'Xandra's. Mr. Ben made me leave without telling her. He scared me, sister."

Susannah glared reproachfully at Ben over Lily Carolina's head. He had the grace to blush. "I know, honey."

"Can we go now?" Lily Carolina begged.

Susannah closed her eyes in anguish. "Not yet. You have to stay here for a few days, until Mr. Lucas comes back from Denver with something Mr. Banning wants."

Lily Carolina's hold on Susannah tightened. "Will you stay, too?"

"I want to, Lily Carolina, but Mr. Banning won't let me stay, and it's his house."

"But Amy's not here, and neither is Jesse." Lily Carolina began to cry. "Only 'Toria is, and she's m-mean!"

Susannah felt that her heart was breaking. She held her sister close, struggling to contain her own tears.

Conor came to her side. "Lily Carolina."

"M-Mr. Conor?" Lily Carolina raised her tear-streaked face from Susannah's shoulder.

"Yes. Come here, sweetheart."

Susannah guided Lily Carolina into Conor's arms, and he picked the child up. With his free hand he helped Susannah to her feet. She turned to Victoria, wiping at a stray tear that rolled down her cheek.

"She's five years old, Victoria, and can't see. She is terrified." Susannah stared into the girl's guilty face. "Since your brother won't let me stay and take care of her, I would appreciate it if you could treat my sister with a little kindness. She doesn't deserve what's happened to her."

Victoria dropped her gaze to the floor.

"This is all real touching, but let's get on with it," Kyle said harshly.

"For once, I agree with my brother." Fletcher leaned back in his chair. "Say your farewells, Susannah, then I want you all out of here."

As Conor handed Lily Carolina to Susannah, their eyes met. Susannah was alarmed at the rage she saw in him. He spun on his heel and stormed the desk, bracing his palms on the wooden surface. His eyes bored into Fletcher's startled face.

"If the child is harmed in any way, you will die." His tone was low and deadly. He whirled to face Fletcher's men. "The same holds true for all of you. I suggest you make certain no harm comes to her." He nodded to Susannah. "We'd best go."

Fletcher jumped to his feet. "Get out!" he raged.

Susannah kissed her sister's cheek. "I'll be back soon, Lily Carolina. Be strong, and remember that we love you."

Lucas leaned over and kissed the child's other cheek. "I love you, too, honey. We'll be back for you."

"Out!" Fletcher screamed.

Susannah set Lily Carolina on the floor. Victoria reached for the child's hand.

"Take care of her." Susannah touched Victoria's arm. "Please."

Victoria nodded and led Lily Carolina from the room.

Susannah brushed her hand across her face. Conor took her arm, and they followed Lucas into the hall.

"Shame on you, Ben Hollister, for your role in this," Susannah said reproachfully as she passed him. Ben looked down at the carpeted floor.

" 'Bye, Susannah." Lily Carolina's voice carried down the stairs. " 'Bye, Mr. Conor." A door closed.

Susannah's breath caught in a sob, and she pressed a hand to her mouth. Conor held her securely against his side as they crossed the porch and descended the stairs to the yard. He helped her into the buggy, then covered her clasped hands with his.

"We'll get her back, Susannah. And I swear to you, they'll pay for what they have done."

She met his blazing eyes and nodded.

"Now, ain't that sweet," Kyle taunted from the porch.

Conor slowly turned away from Susannah and stared at Kyle. "I'll send you to hell one day, Banning."

Kyle stiffened. He glanced at the men on either side of him, saw the smirks on their faces. "Let's just settle it now, O'Rourke." He moved to the edge of the porch and pushed his coat behind the pistols at his hips.

Conor gathered Charlie's reins. "So that your brother's men can cut me down after I've killed you?" He shook his head. "No. Not here, and not now. But we'll meet later, when the child is safe."

"I said now, O'Rourke. Or are you yellow?" Kyle braced his legs apart; his hands hovered near his pistols.

Conor looked at him contemptuously. "You know better than that."

"Then prove it." Kyle flexed his fingers.

Susannah watched, holding her breath. She slipped her hand into her pocket and grasped the handle of her gun.

Conor climbed gracefully into the saddle without a word or look to Kyle. "Let's go," he said to Lucas.

Lucas picked up the reins.

"O'Rourke!" Kyle screamed hoarsely. "Don't you ride away from me!"

Conor turned Charlie's head. Lucas snapped the reins over the horse's back, and the buggy rolled forward, headed down the road away from the house. Susannah withdrew her hand from her pocket with a sigh of relief.

"O'Rourke!"

Susannah looked back through the tiny window in the canvas cover. Kyle had come down the steps into the yard. As she watched, he pulled his gun.

"Conor!" she screamed.

A gunshot sounded. Before her horrified eyes, Conor jerked forward and fell from the saddle, landing facedown in the dirt. Charlie whinnied in protest and shied away.

"Conor!" Susannah jumped from the buggy before Lucas had brought it to a complete stop. She raced to Conor's side and fell to her knees, oblivious to the armed men that suddenly surrounded them. "Oh, God, Conor." Blood soaked the leather around the hole in his vest below his left shoulder, the redness spreading quickly. She tried to roll him onto his back.

His blue eyes, clouded now with shock and pain, met hers. "Susannah," he whispered.

"I'm here, Conor," she sobbed. She grabbed his searching hand. His fingers tightened on hers for a moment, then relaxed as his eyes closed. "Conor," she cried. "Don't go."

Lucas joined her. He put a hand to Conor's neck, then glanced back over his shoulder at Kyle. "You cowardly bastard."

"What the hell is going on?" Fletcher shouted from the porch.

"Your brother shot O'Rourke in the back," Ben said, his voice heavy with revulsion.

Fletcher crossed his arms over his chest, his eyes narrowed in thought. "Is he dead?"

"If not, I'll finish him off." Kyle brandished his gun.

"He's dead," Lucas snapped.

Susannah raised anguished eyes to him. Her heart thudded painfully in her chest. "No," she whispered. Tears spilled down her cheeks.

"This doesn't change anything, McCleave," Fletcher called. "Get O'Rourke out of here."

Lucas ducked his head. "He lives," he whispered, just loud enough for Susannah to hear. "I have to get him to the buggy."

Relief and hope flashed through Susannah, leaving her weak. Lucas pulled on Conor's arm, forcing him to a sitting position. Susannah let out a grief-stricken wail to cover the sound of Conor's groan. She continued to cry, loudly, as Lucas loaded Conor over his shoulder and managed to get to his feet. He staggered to the buggy with his awkward burden, placing Conor in the conveyance as gently as he could. Susannah followed, gradually quieting her cries to sniffles. Lucas whipped his coat off and threw it over Conor's face.

"You'll have to ride Charlie," he said to Susannah as he wiped the sweat from his face with a handkerchief.

"I can," she assured him.

Kyle returned his pistol to his holster. He approached Susannah, a triumphant leer on his stubble-covered face. "Your lover's not such a big man now, is he, Susannah?"

Susannah fought the urge to fire her pistol directly from her pocket into Kyle's stomach. The thought of Conor needing medical attention as soon as possible was the only thing that kept her from doing it. Instead, her hand connected with Kyle's cheek with a resounding slap. "You murderer." Her voice was low with loathing and disgust.

Kyle snarled and backhanded her across the face, knocking her into the side of the buggy. He pulled his gun and held it on Lucas, who stopped in mid-stride. Lucas turned and helped Susannah straighten. She put a hand to her burning cheek, shaking her head in an attempt to clear it.

"Fletcher, I think we should keep Susannah with us, now that we don't have to worry about O'Rourke sneaking around here," Kyle called. He grabbed her wrist and jerked her from Lucas's grip. "She can help take care of the brat." Kyle held her tight against his body, dragging her with him as he stepped away from the buggy, keeping his gun trained on Lucas.

"As you wish, little brother." Fletcher went back into his house. The door closed behind him.

Kyle threw his head back and laughed, a harsh, ugly sound. "You heard him, McCleave. Get out of here. And make damn sure you come alone to the next meeting, or Susannah will suffer." He returned his gun to its holster and buried his hand in Susannah's pinned up hair.

"Go, Lucas," she urged. "I'll be fine. I'll take care of Lily Carolina. Please go." Her frantic eyes fell on Conor, slumped in the buggy. Kyle pulled her toward the house by her hair. "Tell Alexandra I'm counting on her," Susannah called as she stumbled up the porch stairs.

Lucas watched helplessly as Kyle dragged her into the house and slammed the door.

"You'd best get out of here, McCleave." Ben Hollister tied Charlie's reins to the back of the buggy.

Lucas climbed onto the seat and took up the reins. "You have a lot to answer for, Hollister."

Ben pushed his hat back on his head. "I reckon I do."

Lucas stared at him. Did he detect remorse in Ben's tone? He slapped the reins against the horse's back. The buggy rolled away, with Charlie obediently following.

Inside the house, Kyle pressed Susannah up against the wall in the entryway, holding her there with the length of his body. She pushed futilely at him, terrified he would feel her gun.

"Hey, Fletcher, what do you want to do with her?" He laughed at her struggles, running his hands over her breasts.

"Take her up to the Green Room, and lock her in." Fletcher's voice came from his office.

"No," Kyle protested. "I want her in my room." He pinned Susannah's neck to the wall with one hand while the other squeezed between the wall and her body, cupping one of her buttocks. He leered into her eyes as he rocked his hips against her in an obscene manner. Susannah spat into his face.

Kyle's features contorted in fury, and Susannah was certain he was going to hit her again when suddenly he was pulled from her and flung against the stairs. She pressed a hand to her aching throat.

"Keep your hands off her," Fletcher raged. "I said she goes to the Green Room!"

"Ah, Fletcher, come on," Kyle said angrily as he got to his feet, wiping his face. "What do you care what I do to her? You saw how O'Rourke looked at her, and her at him. You know he's had her. She ain't fit for marriage now. I want her."

"No!" Fletcher thundered. He turned on his brother. "You're the one that's not fit, Kyle. You're not fit for anyone but whores. None of this would have happened if you had followed my in-

structions that day you went to the Duncan mine. She would have been my wife by now if not for you."

"Never," Susannah swore to Fletcher's back. "I never would have married you."

He whirled to face her. "Yes, you would have, dear Susannah, or your family would have suffered."

"My family *has* suffered at your hand, Fletcher Banning, and I promise you will rue this day." Susannah's hands clenched into fists at her side.

To her surprise, Fletcher laughed. "Such spirit! What a pity I'll not have the chance to break you, as I had once planned." The smile fled his face as quickly as it had come. He grabbed her upper arm in a painful grip and pulled her to the stairs. "And you, Kyle, get out of here."

"I'll have her, Fletcher, one way or the other." Kyle spun on his heel and, with a vicious oath, stomped out the front door, slamming it closed with enough force to rattle the windows.

Susannah held her skirts up and struggled to keep step with Fletcher. "I want to see my sister," she insisted when they topped the stairs.

Fletcher did not answer as he drew her down the hall. He stopped before a door and threw it open, then pushed her inside. He took the key from the lock and began to close the door.

"Wait!" Susannah caught the edge of the wooden portal and pulled on it with all her strength. "I want to see my sister!"

"Later!" Fletcher snapped. "And you'd best learn to stop fighting me." He jerked on the door. Susannah released it just in time to prevent having her fingers smashed. The door slammed and the key grated in the lock. Fletcher's footsteps receded down the hall.

Susannah leaned her forehead against the door. "I have only begun to fight you, Fletcher Banning," she whispered. She stuffed her hand in her pocket and grabbed the pistol handle tightly as the picture of Conor's still body lying on the ground filled her mind. She closed her eyes, as if that would block the memory of seeing his life's blood flow from the wound in his back. It didn't. "Be with him, God," she prayed fervently. "Be with us all."

Alexandra came from the examination room, wiping her hands on a towel. Lucas followed her. They both wore blood-splattered aprons that covered them from chest to knees. She stopped in the doorway of her crowded parlor and wearily brushed her hair away from her forehead with the back of one hand. Her eyes touched on the dear, worried faces of her friends.

"He should have died, but he didn't," she said quietly. The room erupted in cautious cheers.

"How is he?" Polly urged.

"The bullet entered just below the shoulder blade. It deflected off a rib and ended up under the arm. If it had missed the rib, which it almost did, it would have hit his heart."

Minerva closed her eyes. "Praise God," she whispered.

Horatio patted his wife's shoulder. "We were all praying, Alexandra."

"Well, don't stop," Alexandra said brusquely. "Conor still faces the danger of infection. It's a serious wound." She turned to Lucas. "Thank you for your help. You make a great surgical assistant."

Lucas embraced her. "You're a great doctor, Alexandra. I'm very proud of you."

Alexandra smiled against his chest. "Thank you." She looked up at him. "When will you leave?"

"First light. The train leaves Floyd Hill at eleven-thirty, which will get me into Denver a little after two. The territorial offices should still be open, even though tomorrow is Saturday."

"Will you seek help from the marshal?"

Lucas nodded. "I'll also speak to the U.S. district attorney.

One way or another, Fletcher Banning's reign of terror is coming to an end. And his brother will pay for his crimes."

"It's about time," Polly announced as she jumped up from the sofa. "Alex, I'll start supper while you two get cleaned up."

"Thank you, Polly, but don't you have to go to work?" Alexandra asked.

Polly airily waved her hand. "I quit that lousy job." She motioned to Minerva, who was struggling to rise from the sofa. "You just rest awhile, Minnie, and keep on praying. I'm sure you're better at it than I am. Come on, Jess." She beckoned to the dog. "You can help." She left the room, with Jesse padding quietly after her.

"When will you want to move Mr. O'Rourke upstairs?" asked Neville Thorpe from his place by the window.

"Not until later," Alexandra answered. "He's sleeping well now. I don't want to disturb him."

"Then I think I'll help Miss Polly in the kitchen." He cleared his throat and weaved his way around the furniture, finally escaping down the hall.

Alexandra watched him go with a smile. "I think Mr. Thorpe was blushing, Lucas."

"I believe you're right, my dear," Lucas answered. He looked at Joseph. "Son, I'd appreciate it if you and Hamilton would feed the stock. You should have time to do that and get the buggy back to the livery before supper."

"Yes, sir." Joseph pushed away from the fireplace. "Come on, Ham."

Hamilton scrambled up from his seat on the floor. "Don't call me 'Ham,' *Joe,*" he retorted as he adjusted his spectacles.

"All right," Joseph said with a laugh. The boys passed Alexandra and Lucas and went out the front door.

"Alexandra, if you don't mind, Horatio and I will sit with Conor and do as Polly suggested." This time Minerva successfully maneuvered her ample frame up from the sofa, with the help of her husband. "I'd hate for him to awaken and find himself alone."

Alexandra nodded approvingly. "Fine, Minerva. That table he's sleeping on is narrow. See he doesn't roll right off it."

"We'll watch him good," Minerva assured her. "And we'll pray real good, too. Come along, dear." Minerva sailed imperiously across the hall.

"Yes, precious. I'm right behind you." Horatio shuffled after her, and quietly closed the door to the examination room.

"It's a good idea to have Minerva pray for Conor," Lucas commented as he untied the apron strings at his neck and waist.

"Why do you say that?" Alexandra followed his example, pulling off the stained apron.

Lucas dropped his voice to a conspiratorial whisper. "Because I don't think even God Himself would dare say no to that woman."

Alexandra covered her mouth in an attempt to smother a laugh. "I think you're right," she whispered back. Then her face sobered. "I wish there was some way we could get word to Susannah about Conor. She must be dreadfully worried."

Lucas wrapped his arms around her. "Susannah has faith in you, Alexandra. She'll trust that you did your best."

Alexandra sighed. "Oh, Lucas. Do you think she and Lily Carolina are all right?"

"Yes, dear, I do." Lucas kissed the top of her head. *They'd better be all right,* he added to himself.

Nineteen

"Susannah." Conor moaned her name as he tossed his head back and forth on the pillow.

Alexandra pressed a cool, wet cloth to his forehead. "Shh, Conor, shh," she soothed. "Just rest." Conor lay on his side, with pillows propped at his back to keep him from rolling over. She examined the bandage that covered his shoulder, held in place by strips of cloth wrapped around his chest under his arms. There was no sign of blood. He had a mild fever, but that was to be expected. Two days had passed since she treated his wound. With each passing hour, she became more confident he would live.

She laid a hand on his stubble-covered cheek, and was surprised when his eyes opened. He blinked a few times, then calmly stared at her.

"Hello," he croaked.

"Hello." She smiled. "I sure am happy to see your beautiful eyes. How do you feel?"

Conor cleared his throat. "Terrible. May I have some water, please?"

"Of course." Alexandra hurried to the bureau and filled a glass from the pitcher. She turned to see Conor struggling to push himself up on his elbow. "Conor, be careful," she admonished as she rushed to his side. "No, don't use that arm." She pushed his left arm down. "You'll have to let me help you." She guided the glass to his lips and held it while he drank deeply.

When the glass was empty, he fell back on the pillows. "Where is Susannah? I'd like to see her."

Alexandra set the glass on the bedside table. "She's not here, Conor. The Bannings kept her after Kyle shot you."

He raised off the pillow, grimacing in pain. "Those bastards," he ground out. "I'm going after her."

Alexandra pushed him back down. "You're not going anywhere, Conor O'Rourke, and I'll tie you to the bed if I have to. You've been seriously wounded."

Conor closed his eyes, trying to remember what had happened. "Kyle shot me," he stated.

"In the back, the despicable coward. He would have finished what he started if Lucas hadn't told him you were dead. Lucas got you in the buggy and brought you here."

"And they kept Susannah?"

"Yes. Lucas hated leaving her there, but he was outnumbered and outgunned, and he knew you needed prompt medical attention."

"They would have killed him if he had done anything else."

"I know. It was still hard on him, though. He did say that Susannah had wanted to stay and take care of Lily Carolina."

Conor nodded against the pillow. "So the Bannings think I'm dead," he said, almost to himself. "That's good." He focused on Alexandra again. "Can you send Lucas in?"

Alexandra shook her head. "He left for Denver yesterday morning."

Conor frowned. "What day is it?"

"It's Sunday, late in the afternoon. You've been either unconscious or sleeping since Friday, and you'll be in bed for a few more days at least. You were very lucky, my friend. The bullet deflected off a rib and lodged under your arm. That's why you have another wound here." She pointed to a spot on his bandaged chest, under his arm. "I retrieved the bullet. So far there's no sign of infection. I think you're going to live."

"Thank you," he said, with a weary smile. "For everything, Alexandra."

"You rest now." She stood up and grabbed the empty water glass. "I'll send Neville up to help you see to your bodily needs, then a little later I'll bring you some food. You'll have a few visitors, too, but I promise I won't let them tire you."

"Where's my pistol?"

"On the bureau."

"Please hang it over the headboard. I'll rest easier if you do."

Alexandra hesitated. "Very well. But you remember what I said about tying you to the bed. I will if I have to. And in case you didn't notice, you're buck naked under those blankets, so you may want to pay attention to who's around if you try to get out of bed." She buckled the gunbelt and draped it over the corner of the headboard. "I don't want you giving Minerva the vapors."

Conor's lips curved in a weak smile. "Thank you," he whispered. His eyes drifted closed.

Alexandra sighed with relief; she didn't have to worry about his getting out of bed for a while.

Susannah paced the carpet in the lavishly decorated bedroom that was now her prison. Three long days had dragged by, with interminable slowness, and the nights were worse. Fletcher refused to let Lily Carolina stay with her, claiming that Susannah would be far more likely to behave herself if the sisters were kept separated. He allowed Victoria to bring the child for a short visit twice a day, and they were never left alone.

Susannah could tell that Lily Carolina was working her guileless magic on Victoria. The girl treated the child with kindness and even affection. Lily Carolina's hair was always neatly brushed, and her dress pressed, even though it was the only dress she had to wear. Lily Carolina was more comfortable now, not as frightened.

Susannah worried constantly about Conor. Was he even alive? Her hand strayed to her pocket and stroked the pistol there. If anyone could save Conor, Alexandra could. Susannah had stormed heaven with prayers over the last few days, not knowing what else to do. There was nothing else she could do. Fletcher kept her locked in this room. Each night, he had invited her to join him for supper, and each night she adamantly refused.

Victoria brought her books. When Susannah tired of reading, she would lean over the bed and practice twirling her gun on her finger, the way she had seen Conor do it. In the beginning, the gun fell to the bed very often, and Susannah's hand and wrist tired, but she was steadily improving. She would unload the gun and reload it, wishing she had more than six bullets.

She thought again of Conor, and her heart grabbed. How she loved him! She refused to entertain the possibility that he had died. Surely she would know if he were dead, for a part of her would have died, too. As far as she could tell, all of her was still alive. She ached for the pain she knew he was in, and she ached to see him and hold him. Her hand tightened unconsciously on the gun handle.

The key scraped in the door lock. She jerked her hand from her pocket and smoothed the skirt. Just as the knob turned, she whirled and sank into a chair, knowing the bulge of the pistol would not be evident if she was sitting.

Fletcher Banning sauntered into the room, pushing the door closed behind him. He stopped by the foot of the huge canopied bed and struck an arrogant pose, hooking his thumbs in the pockets of his vest. His critical eye roamed over Susannah.

"You've grieved for your lowly lover long enough," he announced. "I'm weary of your morose demeanor and your rude refusals to join me at my table. Therefore, changes will be made. You'll join me this evening, and your mood will be pleasant."

Susannah clasped her hands in her lap and struggled to keep a rein on her temper. She lifted her chin. "On the contrary, sir. I will not join you, and you will not dictate how I shall feel."

Fletcher's nostrils flared, and his jaw tightened with anger.

"I also wonder at your audacity to accuse *me* of rudeness, when you are forcibly holding my sister and me prisoner in your home," Susannah continued. "To say nothing of the fact that you and your brother have murdered the two men I loved most in this world."

"Enough!" Fletcher roared. "I'll stand your insults no longer." He advanced on her and leaned over the chair, bracing his hands on the armrests. His face was very close to hers. She could smell tobacco, and a heavy cologne. She met his eyes defiantly.

"I sense it would be useless to threaten you," he said. "Therefore, for every act of disrespect toward me that you indulge in, your precious sister will miss one meal."

"You wouldn't," Susannah gasped.

"You keep doubting my word, Susannah. You'll learn, painfully if necessary, that I mean exactly what I say. Keep it up, and your sister won't eat, or drink, again, while she is under my roof. I have to keep her alive only until Friday. She won't die of thirst or starve to death by then, but she'll be very uncomfortable. And if you still persist in defying me, I'll allow Kyle to devise a fitting punishment for your sister."

It felt like a hammer slammed into Susannah's stomach. "You loathsome excuse for a man," she spat. "I'll play your sick little game. Now get away from me."

Fletcher straightened and adjusted his cuffs. "I would caution you to guard your tone when you speak to me, Susannah." He turned away from her and crossed to the massive mahogany wardrobe on the other side of the room. After flinging the doors open, he rifled through the clothes on the shelves within, finally selecting a garment. He shook it out, revealing an evening gown of royal blue silk. "This was made for you," he said.

Susannah stared in amazement. "I don't understand."

Fletcher waved an arm. "All of this was for you. The room, the furnishings, the clothes. You were to be my bride."

"You did all this without my consent? You just assumed I would do as you wished?" Susannah demanded incredulously.

"You would have had no choice." Fletcher threw the gown on the bed.

"But I did have a choice." Susannah shot up out of the chair. "There is always a choice. And that infuriates you, doesn't it, Fletcher? I made my choice, even before I knew Conor. Never would it have been you. Not under any circumstances."

Fletcher moved stiffly to the door. "Your sister will have no supper. Don't try my patience any further, Susannah, or your sister will suffer further."

Guilt-stricken, Susannah bit down on her bottom lip to stop the flow of angry words.

"You'll wear the blue dress when you join me for supper. We dine at nine o'clock." He turned the knob.

"Because of your threats to my sister, I *choose* to join you for supper, but I will wear my own clothes," Susannah said as politely as she could through clenched teeth.

Fletcher paused on his way out the door. "I suggest you also *choose* to wear that dress, or your dear sister will miss her breakfast as well. Present yourself in my drawing room at a quarter to nine." He closed the door and locked it.

Susannah stared at the door, her hands tightly clenched, fighting the urge to scream out her hatred and anger.

Later, the door opened again to admit Victoria and Lily Carolina. Although Victoria had softened her attitude toward Lily Carolina, she still resented Susannah, and was very clear about her feelings. She walked over to the window and stared out, her arms crossed over her chest, a sullen look on her young face.

Susannah gathered her sister in her arms and held her close.

"Oh, honey, it's good to see you," she whispered. "How is your arm?"

Lily Carolina hugged Susannah's neck. "It's fine, but 'Toria says the bandage is getting dirty."

Susannah examined her sister's small arm. "So it is."

"Can Dr. 'Xandra come and change it?"

"No, I'm afraid not. Mr. Banning won't let her come." Susannah lifted Lily Carolina up on the bed.

"Is Mr. Banning a bad man?" Lily Carolina asked in a troubled voice.

Susannah glanced at Victoria's back before she answered. "Yes, honey, he is."

"There's another bad man here, too, Susannah."

"And who is that?" Susannah sat next to her sister.

"I don't know his name, but he was at the cabin the day Papa was hurt, like Mr. Ben was. Only he was mean. His voice sounds funny now, but it's the same voice."

Victoria whirled to face them. Susannah watched nervously as she came over to sit in the chair by the bed. Would the girl tell her brothers that Lily Carolina could identify Kyle by his voice?

"Maybe we should talk about something else, honey. Tell me what you did today."

"No," Victoria interrupted. "I want to know how your papa was hurt."

Susannah stared at her. "You don't know?"

Victoria shook her head. Her brown eyes were wide and fearful. "Did my brothers hurt him?"

"Kyle did," Susannah said gently.

"But your father is an old man!" Victoria cried. "I remember meeting him in the mercantile last fall, the first time I met you. He was very nice to me, and talked funny, like you do. How could Kyle do that?"

Susannah hesitated, then decided to tell the truth. "Kyle enjoys hurting people, Victoria."

Victoria threw herself back in the chair, obviously disturbed. "But Fletcher is the bad one," she whispered.

Susannah took Lily Carolina's hand and stroked her tiny fingers. She said nothing. After a few minutes of uneasy silence, Victoria spoke again.

"Is your father all right now?"

Again, Susannah stared at her. "No, Victoria, he's not," she said quietly. "He's dead."

"He went to heaven to be with our mama and Uncle Walter," Lily Carolina added in a sad voice.

Tears welled in Victoria's eyes as she covered her mouth with one hand. "Oh, no." The tears spilled over and ran down her cheeks.

Susannah crossed to the bureau and pulled a dainty handkerchief from a drawer. She handed it to Victoria, then set Lily Carolina on the floor and took her hand. "Come over here to the window, Poppet. I want you to smell outside. It smells so good." She kept her sister occupied at the window, describing the view, for several minutes. Victoria quietly sobbed, then dried her eyes and blew her nose.

"I'm sorry, Susannah." She sniffed and blew her nose again. "I swear I didn't know. Fletcher makes me leave the room whenever he talks business with anyone. I knew he wanted your uncle's mine, but I didn't know he'd go this far. And Kyle." She jumped up out of the chair and paced, twisting the handkerchief in her hands. "I didn't know about Kyle, either. Did he kill your uncle, too?"

Susannah watched her curiously, holding Lily Carolina's hand. "No. Uncle Walter died of natural causes last winter."

The door suddenly flew open and Fletcher stood there. Victoria's eyes widened in fear. Susannah looked calmly at him while her mind raced. She had to find a way to talk to Victoria in private, to tell her about Fletcher refusing Lily Carolina her supper.

"It's time for you to begin dressing," Fletcher ordered. He looked at his sister. "You, too. Put on something nice, and for God's sake, do something with your hair. Go now. Get the brat out of here."

Susannah bent to kiss Lily Carolina's cheek. "Be quiet, honey, and do as Victoria tells you." She led the child to Victoria. "Fletcher, I'd like you to give Victoria permission to help me dress, if she wouldn't mind."

He scowled at her. "What for?"

"I don't mind," Victoria said quickly. She glanced at Susannah, then back to her brother. "Ladies always need help dressing, Fletcher, just like the maid helps me."

"Then the maid can help Susannah, too." Fletcher moved to the door.

Victoria's face fell. She started toward the door.

"Fletcher, I can help Victoria with her hair," Susannah pointed out.

"Oh, very well. Get the kid out of here and into bed, with no supper tonight."

"No supper?" Victoria repeated. "Fletcher—"

"Don't question me, you sniveling little bitch!" Fletcher thundered.

Victoria shrank back, pushing Lily Carolina behind her. Susannah stepped protectively to Victoria's side.

"Not one word from you," Fletcher warned, shaking his finger at her. He jerked his head in Victoria's direction. "Get out, now, and do as I tell you. Come for the key when the kid is in bed."

Victoria hurried Lily Carolina from the room. Fletcher slammed the door closed and locked it, leaving Susannah alone and shaking with fury.

* * *

"Thank you for smuggling some food up to Lily Carolina." Susannah stood behind Victoria, who was seated on the little stool in front of the dressing table. She ran a brush through Victoria's clean brown hair.

"I wouldn't let that child go to bed hungry." Victoria stared at her reflection in the mirror. "I hate Fletcher."

"I don't think much of him, either," Susannah admitted. She reached for a hairpin, which Victoria held up for her.

"You are so delicate with your words," Victoria said with an admiring smile. "I wish I could talk like a lady."

"I'm not always so delicate. It's my fault Fletcher sent Lily Carolina to bed with no supper. He said he'll withhold a meal from her each time I'm disrespectful to him, even if it means not feeding her for the rest of the week."

"That bastard!" Victoria spat vehemently. Her angry eyes met Susannah's in the mirror. "You be as disrespectful as you want. I'll make sure your sister gets plenty of food."

"Victoria, you must be very careful," Susannah cautioned. She placed the hairpin and reached for another. "He'll figure out what you're doing."

"No, he won't." Victoria's voice rang with confidence. "I've learned to let Fletcher *think* I'm doing as he wants, but I can get around him. He won't expect me to disobey him, because I never used to. Not like Kyle. Kyle is so stupid sometimes. It's like he deliberately makes Fletcher angry."

"I seem to suffer from a touch of the same affliction," Susannah commented dryly. "Fletcher makes me want to fight."

"You're not stupid. You just don't know Fletcher as well as I do."

Susannah silently vowed to remember Victoria's advice on how to handle Fletcher. It galled her to think of playing along with the brutal man, but for Lily Carolina's sake, she would. She would play convincingly.

A sadness settled over Victoria's young face. "I feel so bad about your father, Susannah. I don't know why I believe you when you say Kyle killed him, but I do." She sighed. "Kyle and me, we're, well, not friends, really, but . . ." She searched for the right word.

"Allies?" Susannah suggested. She reached for another hairpin.

"Yes, allies. The two of us against Fletcher, because Fletcher is always so mean to us. Kyle is never as nasty to me as Fletcher is. I even nursed him when Fletcher almost strangled him."

"Fletcher almost strangled Kyle? When?"

"That day Fletcher thought you died in the river. Kyle's voice has never been the same."

"I wondered what was wrong with him."

"I guess Fletcher broke something in his throat. It was awful, Susannah. Kyle could hardly breathe for days, his throat was so swollen. And bruised." She met Susannah's eyes again. "Did Kyle really attack you?"

"Yes, he did. When I fought him, he shot my dog, and tried to shoot me."

"Oh, no."

"Well, he didn't kill either one of us. A man named Conor O'Rourke pulled me out of the river and cared for me."

"Is he the man that came with you, besides Mr. McCleave, I mean? The one that Kyle shot?"

Susannah closed her eyes for a moment, stunned at the intense pain Victoria's words brought. "Yes," she whispered.

"Susannah." Victoria turned around on the stool, alarmed. Then comprehension dawned. "You loved him." She stood up, tears filling her eyes, and placed a tentative hand on Susannah's arm. "I'm so sorry."

"It's not your fault, Victoria." Susannah blinked her own tear-filled eyes. She did not dare mention the possibility that Conor could still be alive. "We have to hurry. We mustn't incur Fletcher's wrath by being late."

Victoria returned to her seat before the mirror, staring quietly at her reflection.

Susannah eyed that reflection, shocked at the sadness and bitterness she saw in Victoria's face. "How old are you?" she asked.

"Sixteen."

To Susannah, the pale face in the mirror looked much older than sixteen. She placed the final pin, then leaned down so that her own face appeared over Victoria's shoulder. "Sixteen-year-old young ladies should smile, not frown." She traced a gentle finger along the lines wrinkling Victoria's forehead. "Especially such pretty ones."

Victoria started. "You think I'm pretty?"

"Yes, I most certainly do. Look at yourself. Look at your eyes. You have beautiful eyes, Victoria. So big and such a warm, lovely brown. And your hair matches your eyes. You have been blessed with a perfect complexion, one that is complemented by the dark color of your eyes and your hair. And the rose color of this gown is just enchanting on you."

Victoria stared wonderingly at herself in the mirror. "No one has ever told me I was pretty," she whispered.

"Then everyone you've met is either blind or stupid." Susannah held out a hand mirror. "Now look at how I've arranged your hair. If we had a curling iron, I would have made curls, but it's always good to know how to fix your hair without an iron. I'll teach you to do it yourself."

Victoria accepted the mirror and turned on the stool so she could see the back of her head. She gasped, staring at the arrangement of rolls crisscrossed with narrow braids. "It's lovely," she breathed, then turned awed eyes to Susannah. "You can teach me to do that myself?"

"Yes, I can. It's not difficult. But now we must go. We'll be right on time. And just to let you know . . ." Susannah's voice dropped to a whisper, "ladies never call anyone a 'bastard.' We may think it, but we never say it." She winked.

Victoria stood up and impulsively threw her arms around Susannah. "Thank you."

Surprised, Susannah hugged her back. "You're welcome, Victoria. I was glad to fix your hair. And I thank you, from the bottom of my heart, for taking such good care of my sister."

Victoria stood back from her. "I hated you once," she admitted. "It shames me to say that. Fletcher just talked about how perfect you would be when he groomed you as his wife, how you would be his hostess when he went to Washington. I wanted to be his hostess. I wanted to be educated, like you are, and beautiful, like you are. But he said I was too thin, and ugly, and that no amount of education would change that."

Susannah flushed with anger. "He was horrible to say such things, and he is completely wrong. You listen to me, Victoria, not your brothers. You are beautiful now. You're young; you may fill out, you may stay thin, like Dr. Kennedy. You'll still be beautiful. And you can get an education, if you want one." She led the girl toward the door.

"I want to believe you, Susannah," Victoria said, her tone tinged with desperation.

"Then believe," Susannah said firmly. Victoria was silent as they went down the hall and the stairs. They entered the parlor to find Fletcher and Kyle waiting for them. Both men were dressed in formal evening attire. Fletcher looked right at home in his suit while Kyle was decidedly uncomfortable.

Susannah stood proudly, although she wished the shimmering blue gown did not expose so much of her shoulders; she was grateful she had found a lace shawl to wear. The weight of her pistol was noticeably missing; she thought longingly of it, hidden deep in one of the bureau drawers. She took note of the gleam of admiration and triumph in Fletcher's eyes, and the hot lust in Kyle's. The thought occurred to her that perhaps she should be thankful Fletcher kept her locked in her room. She couldn't get out, but Kyle couldn't get in.

"My, my," said Fletcher, raising his glass to Susannah and Victoria. "Such lovely dining companions. Don't you agree, Kyle? Susannah has even managed to transform our ugly duckling of a sister into something of a swan."

Victoria flushed, but held her head up.

"I believe that was a compliment to you, Victoria," Susannah said smoothly, "albeit a rather graceless one." She glared at Fletcher.

Fletcher chuckled. "Well done, Miss Duncan. She's right, little sister. You look very nice."

"Thank you, Fletcher." Victoria dropped a demure curtsy.

Fletcher set his sherry glass on the mantel. "Shall we dine?"

And so began a ritual that continued for the next few nights. Susannah worked patiently with Victoria, teaching her to arrange her hair, urging her to stand straight and tall, gently correcting her language. Victoria was an eager student, hungry, starving, in fact, for kind human contact. They were careful to maintain a cool politeness toward each other in front of the brothers, but grew close during the last days before Lucas McCleave's expected return. Susannah was gratified to see the love in Victoria's eyes when the girl looked at Lily Carolina. Her sister was in good hands. And Victoria had blossomed in one week's time.

The last night, Susannah sat at the dressing table and pulled the neckline of the blue gown up as high as she could. Fletcher had insisted she wear the dress again. She stared at her reflection in the mirror. *One more night.* Tomorrow she would learn if Conor was, indeed, still alive. The thought of seeing him again sent a thrill through her. She braced her elbows on the dressing table and hid her face in her hands, allowing her mind to wander over all the sweet memories of him. He was alive! She knew it, could feel it.

A knock at the door startled her. She looked up to see Victoria poke her head around the edge of the door.

"Are you ready?" Victoria asked.

"Yes." Susannah gave the dress one final tug, then stood and took the shawl from the bed. She joined Victoria at the door.

"What is it?" she asked, concerned by the sadness on Victoria's face.

"I'll miss you and Lily Carolina so much." Tears welled in Victoria's big eyes. "I know you must go. This has been terrible for you both, but I'll miss you."

"It hasn't been terrible, Victoria, thanks to you. And I know Lily Carolina has grown very fond of you."

"I love her," Victoria whispered.

"She has that effect on people." Susannah hooked her arm through Victoria's and they started down the hall. "If you remember nothing else that I've told you over these past few days, remember that as long as you have life in your body, you have choices. The choices are not always easy, or good, but you always have them. You don't have to stay here."

Victoria stared at her, a fragile hope in her eyes. "I'll remember."

When the supper was finished, rather than sending both women to their rooms as he usually did, Fletcher sent Victoria and Kyle away and insisted that Susannah accompany him to the drawing room. He saw her to a seat on the stiff, uncomfortable sofa and, without asking if she wanted it, poured her a glass of sherry.

"Thank you," she murmured as she accepted the delicate stemmed glass.

"Do you mind if I partake of some brandy?"

Knowing he could not see her from his position at the side table, Susannah rolled her eyes at Fletcher's pompous language, but her tone was cool and gracious when she replied, "Not at all." She heard the sound of liquid being poured into a glass, and sipped from her own glass. She had to admit the sherry was excellent, as the wine at supper had been, and the food. Fletcher Banning lived very well, even high in the Rocky Mountains, miles from the nearest railroad.

Fletcher moved in front of her, striking one of his ridiculous poses as he leaned against the fireplace mantel. He sipped from his snifter, then rolled the glass between his hands, deep in thought. His eyes seemed to devour her.

Susannah set her glass on the table at her elbow and met his gaze with calm directness.

Finally he spoke. "I had such plans for you, Susannah." He shook his head with regret. "All of this could have been yours." One hand waved in a grand gesture. "And so much more. My ambitions extend all the way to Washington."

"So I've heard," Susannah commented dryly. She folded her arms over her chest and waited for him to continue, cautioning herself to not act bored, which she most definitely was.

"Colorado will be granted statehood, Susannah. It's only a matter of time. Can you see me as one of her first two senators?" Fletcher threw his head back and hooked one thumb in his vest pocket.

The control that Susannah had exercised over her tongue the past few days fled. Lily Carolina would survive without breakfast. "Frankly, Fletcher, no, I can't."

Fletcher started. "What did you say?"

"I cannot envision you as a senator." Susannah shrugged apologetically. "And if I am to be truthful, which I'm sure you would wish, I must admit that I would find your attempts at civilized behavior comical, were they not so pathetic."

Fletcher's florid face turned an even darker shade of red. He set the snifter on the mantel with angry carelessness, slopping some of the amber liquid over his immaculate cuff. "I see the rose still has her thorns," he said curtly.

Susannah blinked, remembering Conor's comparison of her to a rose. *My mountain rose,* he had called her. The memory of his words filled her with warmth and gave her strength. *One more night.*

Fletcher took a step toward her. "These last few days have shown me that I wasn't wrong in my original assessment of you. You are a remarkable woman, Susannah Duncan, lovely and spirited. I would have greatly enjoyed breaking that spirit. And believe me, I would have broken you."

A flood of rage roared through Susannah. She rose from the sofa, her body held tall and proud. "You are wrong, Fletcher Banning."

Fletcher reached out and touched her cheek. "Still you defy me," he said in wonder. "Perhaps I am indeed wrong, giving up on you now."

Susannah pulled away from his touch.

"Such a pity." Fletcher shook his head. "You defiled yourself by taking Conor O'Rourke as your lover, Susannah. He was nothing, no one, could offer you nothing. I could have forgiven you almost anything, but not that." He held out his hands in regret. "Had you remained pure, I would have taken you, even now."

Something in Susannah snapped. Her hand lashed out, striking Fletcher full across one cheek. "You are not fit to clean the manure from Conor O'Rourke's boots." She gathered her skirts and turned to leave.

Fletcher grabbed her upper arm and pulled her around, hitting her across the face with a vicious backhand. She was thrown to the floor by the force of the blow.

"You *bitch!*" Fletcher shouted. "I warned you about lifting your hand to me! To think that I wanted you!"

Susannah rose up on one elbow and brought a shaking hand

to her bloody mouth. She shook her head in an attempt to clear it.

"Ben! Kyle!" Fletcher screamed into the hall. "Ben!"

She struggled to a sitting position as Ben rushed into the room. Kyle followed a few minutes later, misbuttoning his shirt as he came.

"What the hell is wrong, Fletcher?" Kyle demanded. "I was busy."

"Shut up!" Fletcher turned to Ben. "Get the brat. You and Kyle take her out now, tonight, up on the mountain. Make sure she's never found."

"No!" Susannah cried. She got to her feet.

"You want us to kill the kid?" Kyle asked. Ben's face remained impassive.

"That's right," Fletcher ground out. He reached for Susannah, taking her wrist in a cruel grip.

"Fletcher, no. I'll do anything you say. Just let my sister go. Our family no longer owns the mine. This whole thing has nothing to do with her."

"She's an heir of Walter Duncan." Fletcher dragged Susannah toward the door. "I never leave loose ends."

"For the love of God, Fletcher, she's a child!" Susannah frantically tried to pry his fingers from her wrist.

Fletcher suddenly whirled on her. "Do you honestly believe I ever intended either of you to live once I have the mine? Lucas McCleave will not survive tomorrow either."

Susannah gaped at him. "You'll not get away with it. People know what has happened. They know where we are."

"People can be silenced." Fletcher pulled her across the entryway. "Ben, Kyle. You heard me. Get going."

Susannah fought him when he started up the stairs, effectively enough that he had to enlist Kyle's help in getting her to the second floor and down the hall. She was battered and breathless when Fletcher slammed the door to her room and locked it. Still she pounded against the unmoving wood, bruising her hands, as she screamed her sister's name over and over again.

Kyle watched his brother go back down the stairs. Swearing under his breath, he stomped down the hall toward his room. "Shut up!" he shouted as he passed Susannah's door. He stuck his head in his room and ordered someone to stay there, then retraced his steps to Lily Carolina's door. He turned the key and stepped into the darkness. "Where's the goddamned lamp?" he muttered.

Lily Carolina instinctively covered her mouth with her hand. The shouting in the hall and her sister's screams had frightened her. She recognized the strange voice of the bad man. The lamp was hidden on the floor in the corner, and she was now under the bed, pressed as close to the wall as she could get.

She heard the sound of a match being struck, smelled the sulphur. After a minute, she heard swearing, then another match was struck.

"Where's the child?" Lily Carolina recognized Mr. Ben's voice.

"Hell if I know. I can't see a damned thing in here. Can't find the lamp."

Victoria came from her room, tying the belt of a wrapper around her waist. "What's going on?" she called to Ben.

He walked toward her.

"What's wrong with Susannah?" Victoria's gaze fell on the opened door to Lily Carolina's room. "Who's in there? Ben, tell me what's going on." She took two determined steps toward Lily Carolina's room. Susannah's cries had not abated.

Ben caught her arm. "Kyle's in there, Miss Victoria," he said in a low tone. "Fletcher has ordered us to take the child to the mountain and kill her."

Victoria's eyes widened in horror. She clutched at the front of his shirt. "No, Ben, you can't. I beg you, don't do it." Swearing and the sound of furniture being pushed around came from Lily Carolina's still-dark room.

Ben grabbed Victoria's hands and pulled her into her room. "No, miss, I won't. But Kyle will. I have to get the child away from him, and then away from here."

"Where's Fletcher?"

"Downstairs, in his study, I guess."

"What will you do with her?"

"Take her back to the doc's house, the place I took her from." His shoulders sagged. "I never thought he'd kill the kid."

Lily Carolina's terrified cry echoed down the hall. Victoria tensed, a fierce determination shining in her eyes. "I'm going with you, Ben. I'll help care for her. She trusts me."

Ben stared at her in surprise. "Yes, miss."

"Go now." Victoria pushed him toward the door. "Get her away from Kyle. Don't let him leave with her. I'll change and be out in a minute." She closed the door.

Ben strode the few paces to Lily Carolina's room, arriving at the door just as Kyle emerged with the child under his arm. Kyle's face was dark with anger, and he sucked at the back of his free hand.

"The brat bit me," he growled. Lily Carolina struggled against him, frightened whimpers coming from her throat. Susannah continued to scream against her door.

"Give me the child." Ben took Lily Carolina from Kyle. He cradled her in his arms. "She's got a broken wrist, for chrissakes."

"So what?" Kyle sneered. "She'll be dead soon."

"And she's not going to suffer beforehand," Ben vowed. "Why don't you just go join whoever's waiting in your room? I'll take care of this."

Kyle's eyes narrowed in suspicion. "Why? This ain't really your style, Ben, killing a kid."

"Better me than you."

"Why?"

"Because you'll enjoy it, Kyle, and I don't want you to." Ben's voice was heavy with disgust.

Kyle stared at him, then shrugged. "I'll enjoy poking the maid more," he said. He again pounded on Susannah's door. "Shut up!" He sauntered down the hall and disappeared into his room.

"Don't worry, little girl," Ben whispered to Lily Carolina. "I'm not gonna hurt you, no matter what I said. Just keep real quiet." Lily Carolina clung to him.

A minute later, Victoria stole out of her room, dressed and carrying a blanket. She pulled Lily Carolina's chemise down to cover her legs and wrapped the blanket around her.

"Do you want to get her dress?" Ben whispered.

Victoria shook her head. "There's no time. Just go. I'll be right behind you."

The screams from Susannah's room had stopped. Victoria put her ear to the wood. She could hear muffled sobs inside. She scratched at the door. "Susannah," she called in a whisper.

Lily Carolina's cry had driven Susannah over the edge. In crazed desperation, she had stumbled to the bureau and rummaged through the drawer until she found her gun. If she could not save Lily Carolina, she'd die trying. She whirled at the sound of scratching at her door, her gun in hand. The scratching came again, followed by a muffled voice. Susannah cocked the pistol and slowly approached the door. She realized someone was calling her name.

"Susannah."

Susannah recognized Victoria's voice and fell to her knees at the door. "Victoria," she whispered back.

"Ben and I have her. We'll take her to Dr. Kennedy. Keep yourself safe."

Susannah looked down and saw fingers wiggling under the door. With a sob, she touched Victoria's fingertips. "Thank you, thank you."

" 'Bye, Susannah." The fingers were gone, and so was Victoria.

Susannah leaned against the door and eased the cocked hammer back into place. Again the tears poured down her face, for a different reason. "Thank you," she whispered, over and over.

Twenty

"So the deputy marshal is staying at the Barton House?" Alexandra spoke from one of the chairs in the parlor. The fire in the fireplace had burned down, and the tall case clock had struck midnight only minutes earlier, yet the occupants of the room showed no signs of retiring for the night. The danger promised by the coming morning weighed heavy on them all.

Lucas nodded. "He'll be back at daybreak."

"He seems like a competent man," Conor remarked from the sofa.

"I'm impressed with him," said Lucas. "I had a chance to get to know him some on the trip from Denver. He's young, but I wouldn't underestimate Jeremiah Coulter. There's a core of steel in that man."

"With Neville bringing the copy of the mineral surveyor's report when he comes in the morning, we'll be all set." Conor shifted his position impatiently. "I wish we could go tonight. I'm ready to end this."

"Amen," Lucas agreed.

Joseph came in from the hall. "Hamilton is asleep." He looked at his father. "Do you mind if I stay up awhile longer? I'm just not sleepy."

"None of us are, son. Come on in."

Someone pounded on the front door. Alexandra rose from her chair. Jesse jumped up from his position on the rug and ran to

the door, barking. Then he began pawing at the door and whining.

"I'll see who it is," Joseph said. "Move on over there, Jess.
You're in the way." He pulled the door open and was astonished
to see Victoria Banning.

"Hello, Joseph," she said shyly. "We need to see Dr. Kennedy."

Joseph's eyes narrowed as he looked at the big man who stood
behind her. "You have a lot of nerve coming here, Hollister."

"Just let us in, boy. We've brought the doc something."

Joseph saw that Ben carried a blanket-wrapped bundle. He
stood back and motioned them into the house.

"Who is it?" Alexandra came from the parlor and stopped in
mid-stride. "Miss Banning." Her eyes fell on Ben, then on the
squirming bundle he held. Lily Carolina's sleepy little face
poked out of the blanket.

"Oh!" Alexandra cried. She grabbed Ben's sleeve and pulled
him into the parlor.

Ben came to an abrupt halt at the sight of Conor O'Rourke
on the sofa, with a gun in his hand. The bandages that were
wrapped around his chest showed through the gap in the opened
shirt draped over his shoulders. O'Rourke's face was pale, but
his gun hand did not waver, and his eyes burned with a dangerous
light.

"You can put the gun down, O'Rourke," Ben said. "You won't
need it tonight."

Conor realized Ben carried something, a squirming something with golden hair. His heart started pounding.

"Mr. Conor?" Lily Carolina's sweet voice reached his ears.
Conor returned the gun to the table and held out his arm as Ben
set Lily Carolina down on his lap.

"I'm here, honey." Conor hugged her tightly to his chest,
resting his cheek on the top of her head. He did not trust himself

to speak for a moment. Profound relief and overwhelming love filled him.

"Mr. Conor, Susannah told me you were hurt." Lily Carolina's small hand roamed over his bandages.

"I'll be fine, Lily Carolina. It's not serious." He glared up at Ben, but kept his voice calm. "Where is Susannah?"

"The bad man wouldn't let her come. Are you going to go get her?"

"Yes, honey, I am," Conor answered, not taking his eyes from Ben's face. "Is she all right?"

"She wasn't badly treated," Victoria assured him. "She was awful upset when we left, but she knows her sister is safe. I wish she knew you're still alive. I'm glad my brother didn't kill you."

"Thank you, Miss Banning. So am I." Conor dropped a kiss on Lily Carolina's head. A powerful longing for Susannah rushed through him, causing his stomach to tighten.

Jesse pushed his way to stand at Conor's knee, whimpering joyously, his tail wagging furiously. Lily Carolina giggled when the dog touched her hand with his wet tongue. "I missed you, Jesse," she said, patting his head.

"What's your game, Hollister?" Conor demanded. "I'm grateful you returned her, but I don't understand."

Ben nodded at Lily Carolina. "I'd rather discuss this privately."

"I'm just dying to hold that child, Conor." Alexandra stepped forward. "Let me get her washed and into her nightdress. I'll bring her back to say good night."

Conor nodded.

"I'm going to pick you up, Lily Carolina," said Lucas. He bent down and lifted her from Conor's lap. "I'll carry her up for you," he offered to Alexandra.

"No, I'll take her. I think you should learn what's going on. You can tell me later." She accepted Lily Carolina into her arms. "Well, hello, sweetie. I sure did miss you."

"I missed you, too. And I missed Amy." Lily Carolina yawned. "And 'Toria said my bandage is dirty. Will you change it, Dr. 'Xandra?" The child's voice faded as Alexandra carried her up the stairs.

Joseph led Victoria to one of the chairs and stood beside her. Lucas leaned against the doorjamb, his arms folded over his chest.

"Explain yourself, Hollister." Conor hunched his shoulder and pulled the shirt more closely around himself.

"Fletcher ordered me to kill the child."

"Kill her?" Conor stared at him. "Why?"

"He told Miss Duncan that he never meant for either of them to live. Said he don't leave loose ends." He glanced at Lucas. "I don't know what'll happen tomorrow, but you'd best watch your back."

"Why are you telling us this?" Conor demanded. "Are you changing sides?"

Ben drew himself up. "Don't insult me, O'Rourke. I brought the kid back because I don't believe in killing kids, just like I don't believe in killing women. I never thought Fletcher would want the kid killed. I was sorry as hell I took her. Bringing her back was the only thing I could do."

"And what about warning me?" asked Lucas.

"Mr. Banning said you wouldn't leave his place alive tomorrow. If that happens in a fair fight, so be it. But if he intends to murder you, that just ain't right."

"What are your plans?" Conor asked.

"I ride for the man, O'Rourke. I'm going back."

"But why do you ride for him? You know what he is."

Ben shrugged. "He saved my life. After the trouble in Texas, I went downhill fast, trying to kill myself with drink. Mr. Banning found me in a filthy cantina in El Paso, dried me out, and gave me a job. I owe him."

"I can't imagine Banning doing anything so noble," Conor commented dryly.

"Normally he wouldn't," Victoria quietly interjected. "But Ben saved Fletcher's life, when Fletcher was about my age. They were working for the same outfit. Ben risked his own life to pull my brother from a river. Although their lives took different paths for a while, Fletcher never forgot."

Ben twisted his hat in his hands. "That's all ancient history now. We'd best get back." He looked at Victoria. "Are you ready?"

"You don't have to go back, Miss Banning." Conor shifted his position, grimacing at the pain that shot through his shoulder when he moved.

Victoria stared at him. "That's what Susannah told me. She said there are always choices."

"There are. Bear in mind that it'll probably be dangerous to go back. Not only have you defied your brother, but Lucas and I are coming in the morning, and I think things are going to get ugly."

Ben nodded in agreement. "He's right, Miss Victoria. Maybe you should stay here."

Victoria did not hesitate. "I'm staying," she said firmly.

"I'll be heading out, then." Ben adjusted his hat.

"Thank you for bringing the child back, Hollister," said Conor.

"It was the least I could do." Ben stopped at the parlor door and looked back at Conor. "For what it's worth, I don't hold with shooting a man in the back. Kyle doing that was about the most cowardly thing I've ever seen. Like Miss Victoria, I'm glad he didn't kill you. I also hope Miss Duncan don't get hurt. I'll do what I can to watch out for her. You, though"—he nodded at Lucas, then at Conor—"once you step foot on Banning land, you two are on your own."

Conor met his gaze. "Fair enough. Thanks again."

Ben turned to go, then hesitated. "You know I'll tell him you're coming."

Conor nodded. "I know."

The morning dawned cool and clear. Conor had awakened before first light, after sleeping for only a few hours. He now sat at the kitchen table, sipping on a cup of hot coffee, while Alexandra checked his bandages. As usual of late, the kitchen was full of people. Lily Carolina sat on Horatio Potter's lap at the other end of the table, the center of attention in the cozy room. He watched the child's happy face. The intensity of the love he felt for her startled him.

"I am just so thankful Mr. Hollister brought our angel back," Minerva said from the stove. She speared a piece of frying bacon with a fork and deftly flipped it over. "And thanks to you, too, honey." She nodded at Victoria, who sat on another chair. "That was real brave of you to leave your brothers like that. Bless you for caring for Lily Carolina all those long days."

Victoria nodded, her large eyes roaming the room in confusion. There were so many people here! And they were all so nice!

"Polly, how's that biscuit dough coming?" Minerva boomed.

Polly peered doubtfully into the bowl she held. "I did everything you said, Minnie, but this doesn't look right."

"Well, bring it here, girl, and let me see. Joseph, get me a little more wood, will you?"

Conor smiled and took a sip of coffee. The only thing missing this morning was Susannah. He longed for the sight of her lovely, smiling face, with her hair piled on her head, her slim body wearing her green cotton dress, the dress that turned her eyes such a vivid green. He ached to hear her voice, with its charming accent, and her laugh. His fingers tightened on his cup. Then he became aware that Alexandra was wrapping the bandage around his shoulder and arm.

"Alexandra, you can't strap my arm down today. I need to be able to move it."

"Conor, you have to keep the arm as still as possible. I don't want you tearing out the stitches."

"I'd rather tear stitches than die," Conor said firmly. "I have to be able to move. If you strap the arm, I'll take the bandages off as soon as I'm out of your sight."

Alexandra sighed. "Oh, all right." She rearranged the bandages, leaving Conor's arm free.

A loud knock sounded at the front door. "Hamilton, please get the door," Alexandra shouted over the sound of Jesse barking. "And, Lucas, you could pour me a little more coffee, if you don't mind."

Lucas squeezed his way to the stove and Hamilton hurried down the hall. He returned a minute later, followed by Neville Thorpe and Jeremiah Coulter.

"Breakfast will be ready in just a few minutes," Minerva announced. "Since we don't have enough chairs or plates, we'll be eating in shifts. Conor, Lucas and Deputy Coulter, you three eat first, since you have to be leaving soon. Now you all hush while I say a prayer."

The room settled into silence.

"Dear Lord," Minerva began in a voice that was sure to get the Lord's attention. "We ask you to be with us today. Watch over the brave men who are going into the lion's den to rescue our beloved Susannah and to hold the Bannings accountable for their sinful deeds. Thank you for bringing our Lily Carolina safely home to us. Amen."

Conor looked around at the bowed heads of his friends as a chorus of "amen" filled the room. He was deeply touched by their concern for him, and for Susannah. He was going off to war today, along with Lucas and the deputy, and hopefully he would return alive, his woman at his side. It was comforting to know these people would be waiting for him and Susannah when they came back.

A half an hour later, Conor slid his loaded rifle into the scabbard. He checked the position of the extra gun he wore in a gunbelt buckled over his uninjured shoulder and across his chest. The butt stuck out just over the ribs on his left side, within easy reach of his right hand. Perhaps the presence of the deputy marshal would persuade Banning to surrender with no trouble, but Conor wasn't going to count on it. In fact, he doubted it very much.

He walked to where Lily Carolina stood on the porch, holding Polly's hand. Jesse sat at her other side.

"Lily Carolina, I'm leaving now to go get your sister. Will you give me a kiss goodbye?"

"I will, Mr. Conor." She lifted her face up and puckered her little lips.

Conor's heart lurched. How he loved this child! He kissed her lightly, then caressed her cheek. "From now on, I want you to call me 'Conor.' No more 'mister.' I'm going to bring your sister back and I'm going to marry her, and we'll be a family."

Lily Carolina's face lit up like the sun that had just come up over the mountaintop. She reached for him. "And you'll live with us forever?"

Conor bent down and hugged her with his good arm. "Forever." He kissed her again before he straightened.

" 'Bye, Conor." Lily Carolina waved at him.

"Be careful, Conor," said Polly.

"And watch your back," added Neville.

Alexandra and Lucas embraced tightly. He kissed her, then mounted his horse.

Conor gathered Charlie's reins and carefully climbed into the saddle, protecting his left arm. He lifted his hand in farewell, then touched his heels to the horse's sides. The waiting deputy followed him, and Lucas took up the rear.

Shouts of "goodbye" and "good luck" trailed after them.

Alexandra wrapped her arms around herself and watched until the riders could no longer be seen. Minerva came up beside her and circled Alexandra's waist with her arm.

"There goes three strong, smart men, Alexandra, and the Lord is riding with them. They'll be fine. That deputy will show the Bannings that they have to surrender. They won't buck the territory."

"But they will!" Victoria cried. "Isn't Conor meeting a posse or something?"

All eyes turned to the distraught girl standing off by herself.

"No, Victoria, they're not," Alexandra said, her forehead wrinkled with worry. "Fletcher told Lucas to come alone. They're running a risk taking even two other men."

"Oh, no." Victoria twisted her hands. "I know they have to go, because of Susannah. But you don't know Fletcher like I do. He's often sworn that nothing will stand in his way. He has a small army out there. Oh, why didn't they take more men?"

Alexandra moved closer to Victoria. "They felt they couldn't."

Victoria's eyes filled with tears. "Then we had all better pray for their lives. And Susannah's. She refused my brother, but accepted Conor. Fletcher will never forgive her for that. And when they learn that Conor is alive, both of my brothers will try to kill him."

Joseph stepped off the porch, his young face set with determination. "That's my father out there, and I'm going to do more than pray."

"Just a minute." Alexandra held her hands out in an attempt to calm the group that now surrounded her. "Let's not do anything crazy. We'll only make matters worse."

"Alexandra." Joseph straightened his shoulders and faced her squarely. "I have a great deal of respect for you, and am very fond of you as well. But my father may be riding into a trap. I'll not wait here for news of his death. I have to try to help, somehow."

Alexandra stared at the handsome, earnest boy-turned-man. With or without her blessing, he was going after his father.

"I'm going with Joe," Hamilton stated, pushing his spectacles up on his nose. "Mr. McCleave, he's been good to me, and so has Mr. O'Rourke. It ain't right, what those Bannings are doing."

"Give me a rifle," Polly demanded. "I used to be pretty good at bagging squirrels back home. I've got a score of my own to settle with Kyle Banning."

"Lucas McCleave is my friend," said Neville. "Count me in."

"And me," asserted Horatio Potter. "Mrs. Potter is also handy with a shotgun." A small, proud smile curved Minerva's lips.

Alexandra blinked suddenly full eyes. "Bless you all. I'm a decent shot myself. But we must make a plan, and we must be very careful. We're dealing with killers."

"I'll go, too," Lily Carolina announced. "I can throw rocks."

Joseph laughed and swung her up in his arms. "I'm sure you can, Lily Carolina, but then who'll take care of Jesse?"

Lily Carolina's forehead puckered in a frown. "Can't Jesse go? He can bite."

"But we have to sneak up on the bad men, and Jesse barks," Joseph pointed out.

"Yes, he does," Lily Carolina admitted.

"Someone has to stay with the child," said Alexandra.

"I will." Victoria's voice was soft. "I can't go with you. I despise them, but they're still my brothers."

Joseph was instantly contrite. "Victoria, I'm sorry. We've been insensitive."

"No, you've been honest. Go now. Help your friends. I promise I'll protect the child. Come on, Jesse." She took Lily Carolina from Joseph's arms and carried her into the house.

All eyes turned to Alexandra. She, in turn, looked at Joseph. "We'll need a farm wagon, something we can all fit into."

He nodded. "Ham and I will get it."

"Good. All right, who needs a weapon?"

Polly was the only one to raise her hand.

Alexandra turned to Neville. "Can you see to that? And pick up more ammunition?"

"Yes, ma'am, I can."

"What time is it?"

Neville pulled a watch from his pocket. "Eight-thirty."

"We'll meet back here in twenty minutes." Alexandra clapped her hands. "Hurry, people. There's not a moment to lose."

Susannah pulled the curtain back with one hand and breathed deeply of the fragrant air that came through the opened window. The sun had risen over the mountain, filling Fletcher Banning's land with golden light. Except for the noises of the horses in the corral, it was still. A lovely morning. It was difficult to believe that violent death threatened all who came to this place today.

She again wore her own dress, now clean and pressed. Her hair was neatly pinned up at the back of her head. The pistol snuggled in her pocket, its comforting weight reassuring. Somehow, she had to warn Lucas of Fletcher's plan to kill them. She had to survive this day. Lily Carolina waited for her, needed her. Hopefully, so did Conor. She pulled a chair to the window and settled down to wait.

Conor led the way under the Banning arch. "It's about a mile from here," he said over his shoulder to the deputy. Lucas spurred his horse forward. The deputy did likewise, until the three men rode abreast, with Conor in the middle.

"I reckon he'll have men waiting to escort us in, like the last time," Lucas commented.

"I reckon," Conor replied. He glanced at the deputy. "I hope you don't come to regret your decision to join us."

Jeremiah Coulter shrugged and smoothed his dark mustache. His lean, lanky body slouched carelessly in the saddle, but there was a relaxed confidence about the man. "Don't believe in regrets, myself," he said. "I know why I'm here."

Conor nodded in satisfaction. Deputy Coulter would do.

A few minutes passed in silence. No one was surprised when Ben Hollister guided his horse from the trees and met them in the road. He was not alone.

Ben pushed his hat back on his head and nodded at Jeremiah. "Who are you?"

Jeremiah pushed his lapel aside to expose his badge. "Jeremiah Coulter, Deputy Territorial Marshal."

Ben shook his head. "Mr. Banning isn't gonna like that, O'Rourke. He knows you're coming, but he specifically said no law."

"I invited myself along," Jeremiah said.

"You could invite yourself to leave," suggested Ben. "Would probably be better for you in the long run."

"No, thanks."

"Suit yourself." Ben adjusted his hat. "Shorty, make sure they weren't followed, then get up to the house."

One of the riders took off down the road at a gallop.

"This way, gentlemen." Ben turned his horse's head and led the way toward the estate. The rest of the escort closed around the three riders.

"Don't go too far into the yard," Conor said in a low voice. "If they attack, we'll have no room to maneuver if we're too close to the house. There'll be a corral on the left, Jeremiah, beyond that, the barn. If things get ugly, you can find cover there. Lucas, remember the carriage house is on the right. I'll see which way the wind blows; either one of you could have the pleasure of my company."

There was no time for further conversation. They entered the yard, and when they were about halfway across, Conor, Lucas and Jeremiah pulled their horses to a halt.

Ben rode up to the porch and dismounted. "Come on up!" he called.

"We'll talk from here," Conor replied.

Ben shrugged and disappeared into the house. The rest of the riders filed around them and let their horses into the corral, still saddled. They took up casual posts around the yard. Conor, Lucas, and Jeremiah waited patiently.

Susannah watched from her window, hardly able to believe her eyes. She was not surprised Conor was alive, only relieved and thankful. And he had come himself! Her gaze devoured him with loving concern. He sat easily in the saddle, relaxed as always, but alert, holding his left arm stiffly. His eyes were shaded by the brim of his hat. She had to get his attention, let him know where she was, warn him that Fletcher Banning intended to kill them all.

She snatched the lace shawl from the wardrobe and waved it out the window. Conor raised his head and lifted a hand in salute. Lucas touched the brim of his hat.

Susannah knelt on the floor and stuck her head out the window, cupping her hands around her mouth. "Go back, Conor!" she shouted. "Fletcher means to kill us all!"

"He's welcome to try! Get inside!"

That was all he had to say? Susannah stared at him, then remembered her promise to do as he said. Had that really been a week ago? She waved at him, then pulled her head back inside. She moved to one side of the window and waited.

Fletcher Banning stepped out onto the porch, Ben on one side, Kyle on the other.

"Well, O'Rourke, I see my brother has failed me yet again,"

said Fletcher. "And I warned you about involving the law, McCleave. You'll regret you didn't come alone."

"That remains to be seen, Banning," Lucas answered.

"Did you bring the deed?"

"I did, and I brought a few other things as well."

"In addition to the marshal?"

Shorty raced his mount into the yard and pulled up in front of the porch. "They weren't followed," he reported. "Didn't see anything but an old wagon on the main road, full of women and boys and old folks, out for a ride, they said."

Fletcher nodded and waved the man away.

"I have a copy of the U. S. deputy mineral surveyor's report on the Duncan mine, Banning," Lucas called. "I ordered the property surveyed as soon as I bought it." He pulled a folded wad of papers from his saddlebag and held it up. "There's no silver. The vein peters out about a hundred yards from the property line. If your miners had gone just a few more feet, they'd have discovered that for themselves. The lawsuit, the killing, the kidnapping, the extortion; you've done it all for nothing."

Fletcher stared at him, his faced stark white against his dark hair and mustache. "That can't be." He shook his head in shocked disbelief. "I couldn't have been wrong. You're lying, McCleave. You're lying!"

Lucas held out the papers. "See for yourself."

Fletcher jerked his head at Ben, who trotted to Lucas's side, took the papers, and returned to the porch. Fletcher snatched the papers from Ben's grasp. He unfolded them and looked at the top page, then the next, and the next. His face became more red with each page. Finally, with a furious roar, he tore the papers, again and again, until little scraps of paper floated to the porch floor. "That's what I think of your report, McCleave."

Lucas shrugged. "That was only a copy. Destroying it won't change the facts. Give it up, man."

"It's over, Banning," said Conor. "Bring Susannah out."

Fletcher stared at them.

"I suggest you bring the woman out, Mr. Banning." Jeremiah's tone was conversational and relaxed. "Don't make things worse for yourself than they already are."

Still Fletcher did not respond.

Kyle, with his hands hovering above the handles of his pistols, nervously looked at his brother. "What are we gonna do, Fletcher?"

"We can do this the easy way, Banning, or we can do this the hard way," Conor said harshly. "Either way, Susannah is coming with me."

Jeremiah stood up in his stirrups and looked at the men standing around the yard. "I am the deputy territorial marshal," he said in a firm, clear voice. "I have warrants for the arrests of Fletcher and Kyle Banning. Unless you men are interested in tangling with the territory, I suggest you lay down your weapons and surrender."

"Surrender?" Fletcher shrieked. "Never! You men stand your ground!" He jerked one of Kyle's pistols from the holster and fired at Jeremiah. "Your woman's dead, O'Rourke!"

Kyle pulled his other gun and began firing as well. Both brothers backed into the house, followed by Ben.

At the first shot, Conor whipped his rifle from its case and urged Charlie toward the wide, opened doors of the carriage house, right behind Lucas. Jeremiah dove from his mount in the direction of the corral. He hit the ground and rolled under the fence.

The Banning hands scattered for cover, drawing their weapons as they ran. Sporadic gunfire sounded around the yard.

Once inside the safety of the carriage house, Lucas and Conor slid from their saddles.

"You hit?" Lucas asked as he drew his pistol.

"Nope. You?"

"No." He moved to the side of the door. "I think Jeremiah's all right, too."

Conor came up behind him. "I have to get to the house."

"Any ideas on how you'll do that?"

"I'll get to the corral, then the barn, and work my way up past the bunkhouse."

"I can cover you for a distance, but not up where you'll have to cross the yard."

"I know. Hopefully Jeremiah can help me out there. Just try to keep the other men busy and pinned down. I'll handle the Bannings and Hollister."

Lucas nodded.

"Lucas, if anything happens to me, get Susannah out. See that she and Lily Carolina are taken care of."

"You know I would, but it won't be necessary. Like I told Susannah, you're a hard man to kill. Now go get your woman. I'll cover you." Lucas dropped to a crouch, peered around the edge of the door, and fired.

Conor patted his shoulder. "Watch your back," he murmured. Then he was gone.

Susannah heard the words from the yard, heard the gunshots, saw Conor and Lucas reach the safety of the carriage house, saw the deputy roll into the corral. The deputy's horse trotted off with a frightened whinny.

She sagged against the wall in momentary relief, then remembered Fletcher's furious vow. *Your woman's dead, O'Rourke!* She had to get out of the room. She pulled the pistol from her pocket and hurried to the door. Taking careful aim, she fired at the lock. The gunshot echoed loudly. She turned the knob and tugged with a strength born of desperation. With a grinding protest, the ruined latch gave way and the door flew open. She heard angry voices coming from the stairs. She raced down the hall, away from the approaching footsteps, and ducked into the first unlocked room she found. There was no sign of the key; she could not lock herself in.

"She's gone!" Fletcher's angry voice echoed down the hall. "Where the hell did she get a gun? Find her, Kyle, and bring her to me. I'll help Ben downstairs."

Susannah ran to the window. No escape that way. She whirled at the sound of the door opening, her gun up and cocked.

Kyle stood there, a gloating smile on his face. "How interesting that you came to my room, Susannah. Maybe you want me after all." He returned his gun to the holster and took a step forward.

"If you come near me, I'll shoot. I swear I will, Kyle." Susannah cupped her left hand under the butt of the pistol. A strange, determined calmness filled her as she took aim at Kyle's chest. Her finger tightened on the trigger.

"No, you won't," Kyle sneered. "You're no killer." He took another step.

"I'm no *murderer,*" Susannah corrected. "There's a difference. Conor's been teaching me. If I shoot, I'll shoot to kill."

Something in her voice, in her eyes, made Kyle stop. Her aim did not waver. Suddenly, he knew she would shoot, and at that distance, she would not miss. As fast as he was, he could not outdraw an already-drawn weapon. He backed up.

"You won't get out alive, Susannah. None of you will. You think about that while I go find your lover. You can go to hell together." He took the oil lamp off the table by the door and unscrewed the wick. Before her disbelieving eyes, he emptied the oil in a half circle around the door.

"You won't burn your own house."

Kyle set the lamp back on the table and stepped over the ring to the doorway. "It's Fletcher's house, and I never did like it." He pulled a match from his vest pocket.

Susannah steadied the gun. "Drop the match, Kyle, or I'll shoot."

With one hand on the half-closed door, he looked directly at her, an evil leer on his face. "Goodbye, Susannah. It's too bad I never got to ride you." In one smooth motion, he brushed the match down the doorjamb and threw it to the carpet.

Susannah fired. The bullet hit the closing door just as the oil ignited. She stared at the fire, heard Kyle's laugh from the hall, even over the leaping, crackling flames. There was no way out.

Joseph pulled the wagon to a stop at the Banning arch. The sounds of distant gunshots could be heard.

Alexandra turned on the seat. "We'll take the wagon in a little farther, then go on foot the rest of the way. We'll circle around the compound and try to take as many of Banning's men out of commission as we can. Don't kill unless you absolutely have to, but don't risk your own life." Everyone nodded. Alexandra looked at the grim, determined faces of her friends, and was filled with love and fear. "They'll never expect us, so we have the element of surprise on our side. But you all be careful. I expect to see every one of you at my house for supper tonight."

"We'll all be there, Alexandra," Minerva assured her. She adjusted her spectacles, then patted the small, outlandish hat that perched on the top of her head. Its bent feather waved in the breeze. "Let's go. Our friends need our help." She held her shotgun up.

Joseph slapped the reins against the horses' backs, and the wagon moved onto Banning land.

Conor looked around the corner of the bunkhouse. He estimated it to be a twenty-five-, maybe thirty-yard run to the main house. He glanced back to the corral. Jeremiah's dark head showed at the end of the water trough. Conor motioned toward the house. Jeremiah nodded, then disappeared. A rifle barrel emerged over the top of the trough.

Conor stared at the house. He decided to run for the middle window, which was opened. So far, he had seen no sign of life inside. Then something made him look up. Smoke billowed up over the roof, coming from the opposite side of the house. Too much smoke for a fireplace. The house was on fire! With Susannah inside. His heart slammed against his ribs. Memories of another fire filled his mind, a barn fire that had nearly killed his beloved cousin Alina the summer before. He saw the image of her limp body, felt the terror of not knowing if she was alive or dead. He could not go through that again. He sprinted for the house.

"O'Rourke!"

Conor came to an abrupt halt a short distance from his goal. Kyle Banning walked from behind the house, one pistol drawn.

"It's you and me, O'Rourke." Kyle waved at the man that had appeared in the doorway of the bunkhouse. The man withdrew.

In a detached part of his mind, Conor noticed something that looked suspiciously like a frying pan land on the man's head, and he caught a glimpse of a feather-decorated hat before the bunkhouse door closed. He didn't understand it, but he knew he wouldn't have to worry about the man in the bunkhouse.

Conor focused his attention on Kyle, holding his rifle in his hands, relaxed and ready. "I guess this has been coming since I saw you with Susannah on the mountain that day."

"You saw me?"

"Through a telescope. If I'd been closer, you'd have died then."

"You think you can best me?" Kyle taunted.

"I know I can, if we're facing each other."

Kyle's jaw tightened. "Then let's do it." He returned the pistol to its holster and took a stance, his hands over his hips.

Conor shrugged. "You're awful anxious to die, Banning." He

tossed the rifle to the ground under the window and walked farther into the yard. His mind instantly assimilated necessary information; the distance between him and Kyle, the position of the sun, the presence or lack of other people in the immediate area. There was not as much gunfire as there had been. He stopped.

"I've already sent Susannah to hell, O'Rourke," Kyle jeered. "She'll be burning by now."

Conor hardened his mind and his heart against Kyle's words. His eyes narrowed. "I don't need any more reasons to kill you, Banning. Quit jawing and get to it."

Kyle adjusted his stance.

Conor took a calming breath through his nose. He felt the familiar coldness settle over him, the eerie calm.

Kyle's hand moved.

Conor's gun was in his hand, belching fire, before Kyle brought his up to aim. Kyle stared at Conor in stunned amazement. He staggered, then looked down at the red stain spreading across his chest. The pistol fell from his hand. He brought his gaze back to Conor.

"You are faster," he admitted, and crumpled to the ground.

A shot whistled over Conor's head. He ran for the side of the house and dove through the opened window. He rolled and came up on one knee, gun ready, and saw that he was in an elaborate dining room, which, thankfully, was empty. Another shot sounded. Through the window, he saw a man topple from the roof of the bunkhouse. Lucas came around the corner of the building and waved. Conor raised his hand in acknowledgement, then turned back to the room. The smell of smoke was strong. He had to find Susannah.

Susannah stared at the flames that blocked the door. The door itself was on fire now, and thick smoke swirled through the room. After shoving the gun in her pocket, she ran to the window and opened it, although she knew the flames would welcome the fresh air as much as she did. Frantically she searched for an escape through the window, but the only way out was down. Down a long way. She'd do that only as a last resort.

She whirled around to face the room again, peering through the thickening smoke with watering eyes. Her desperate gaze fell on the oak wardrobe, saw the molding above it. The same type of molding that surrounded the burning door. Was this room connected to the next one? She ran to the wardrobe, pushed against it with all her strength, in vain.

Overcome by a fit of coughing, she staggered back to the window and breathed deeply. Because so much smoke poured out the window, the improvement was only moderate. She tore the covering from the bedside table, careless of the objects that fell to the floor, and fashioned a mask over her nose and mouth, tied at the back of her head.

"I must live," she muttered between clenched teeth. "I must live." With the images of Conor and Lily Carolina in her mind, she attacked the wardrobe with renewed determination. She grabbed the back edge and pulled. The wardrobe shifted. She pulled again. Another inch. She braced one foot on the wall and heaved. This time the wardrobe moved enough for her to see behind it. There was a door!

She pulled once more and managed to squeeze behind it. Settling her back against the solid oak of the wardrobe, she placed her hands on the wall and pushed with desperate strength. The piece of furniture scraped across the wooden floor.

Susannah stared at the door. There was no latch, no doorknob. She pushed against the unmoving wood, pounded at it with her fists. Finally she sank to the floor with a choking sob. And saw the floor latch. The metal easily slid up out of the floor. The door flew open and Susannah fell into the next room.

Smoke billowed around her. She slammed the door, leaning

against it as she took deep, choking breaths. Finally, she pulled
the cloth from her face. She was in another empty bedroom.
Out! You must get out! She struggled to her knees, then stumbled
out into the empty hall. Flames crackled as they fed on the walls
and the carpet. If there was a back stair, she wouldn't be able to
get to it.

She hurried toward the main staircase. Just as she came to
the top of the stairs, she met Fletcher, climbing toward her, a
pistol in his hand.

Susannah knew he saw her by the crazed light that flared in
his eyes. The heat of the fire breathed at her back. There was
nowhere to run.

"You set my home on fire!" he screamed.

"I did not." She slipped her hand into her pocket. Her fingers
closed around the comforting hardness of the pistol grip. "Kyle
did."

"Liar! Kyle would never fire my house."

"Like he would never assault your intended? I promise you,
he did."

Conor crept along the lower hall from the dining room, listening to the voices on the staircase. Now he knew where
Fletcher Banning was, and Susannah. Where was Ben Hollister?

"I said you wouldn't survive this day," Fletcher raved. "I
meant it. No mere woman will cause the downfall of Fletcher
Banning!" He raised his gun.

Susannah raised hers, within the confines of her pocket.

Twin gunshots echoed in the hall. Fletcher fell back against
the wall, clutching his thigh, then crashed down the stairs.
Susannah was knocked to the floor, spun around by the bullet
that grazed her upper arm. She lay in the smoke, stunned and
coughing, saw the flames advancing over the carpet, slowly, in-
exorably. Was this how it was all to end? *No!* It would not end
here, like this! She would live!

Downstairs, Conor raced around the corner, his heart in his

throat. Ben Hollister came from the opposite direction at the same moment. Both men stopped, their weapons trained on each other. Fletcher lay on the floor between them, facing Ben, struggling to rise.

"Ben," he gasped. "The stairs. Kill the woman."

Ben stared at Conor and motioned with his head up the stairs. "I will, Boss," he said. "You wait here."

Fletcher did not watch Ben go up the stairs. He managed to get to his feet and stumble into his office, clutching his wounded thigh. Movement outside the window caught his eye. He struggled over to the window and looked out. His jaw dropped.

His men milled about the yard, their hands in the air, surrounded by a strange assortment of armed people, including several women. The deputy was herding another man across the yard with a rifle. Lucas McCleave and Neville Thorpe carried a third man and laid his limp body next to two still men on the ground. With a start, Fletcher recognized Kyle. He stared for a moment, then raised his eyes to Blue Mountain, rising in silent majesty over the scene of defeat in the yard.

Fletcher sank into his chair and swiveled it to face away from the window.

Conor and Ben took the stairs two at a time. Susannah had managed to stand, hugging the wall. She reached for Conor with a happy cry. He wrapped his arms around her.

"I'm here," he whispered. "I'm here."

"Wait until I have Mr. Banning out of the way," Ben instructed. "Then get her out of the house."

Conor nodded. He glanced over his shoulder. "Banning's not there."

Ben started back down the stairs. He had not gone more than a few steps when a gunshot sounded from Fletcher's study.

"Get her out!" Ben shouted as he raced down the rest of the stairs. He flung the front doors open, then disappeared into Fletcher's study.

Jessica Wulf

Conor swept Susannah up into his arms, mindless of his injured shoulder and the pain that ripped through him as the stitches gave. He carried her down the stairs and out onto the porch, where an astonishing sight met his eyes. He gently set Susannah on her feet and they both stared.

The yard was filled with people, a good many of them unknown men with their hands held high. Their friends were all there: Alexandra and Lucas, Polly and Neville, Horatio and Minerva, Joseph and Hamilton, Jeremiah Coulter. Each held a weapons trained on the captured Banning hands. Conor hugged Susannah tightly against his side and led her into the yard.

Ben Hollister came from the house, carrying Fletcher Banning over one shoulder. He stepped off the porch and, with Jeremiah's help, laid Fletcher on the ground. A bloody table covering was wrapped around Fletcher's head, obscuring most of his face.

Susannah turned away.

Jeremiah looked at Ben. "By his own hand?"

"Yes, sir," Ben said. He took his hat off, his weatherbeaten face wrinkled with genuine sadness. "He always did say he'd never surrender."

A section of the roof collapsed with a loud crash. Instinctively, everyone took a step back. All watched as Fletcher Banning's mansion burned with the intensity of the fires of hell.

Twenty-one

Susannah awakened gradually, aware of a delicious warmth against the length of her body. She and Conor lay nestled under the blankets, her back to his chest, wearing nothing but their bandages. She rested quietly for several minutes, enjoying the feel of his strength against her, listening to his quiet breathing, rejoicing that they were both alive and together.

A week had passed since that terrible day at the Banning estate. Besides Fletcher and Kyle Banning, two other Banning men had been killed, and three more injured, one seriously, but he was expected to live.

Of their friends, none had been badly hurt. Aside from a few scrapes, bumps and bruises, everyone had returned to Alexandra's house for supper that night in fine shape. She and Lucas had been the most seriously injured, and they each had only been grazed by a passing bullet. She shivered. It could have been so much worse.

"What are you thinking about?" Conor planted a kiss on her bare shoulder.

"Good morning," she said, and leaned back against him. "I was just thinking how lucky we were that none of us were badly hurt last week. When I think of Hamilton going against armed men, and Polly, and Minerva . . ." She shuddered. "I think the Lord truly was watching over us, like Minerva said."

"Maybe He was, but I also think Jeremiah's little warning about firing on a territorial officer took a lot of the fight out of those men. Most of them aren't killers. It didn't take much to persuade them to give up. Of course, having Minerva hold a shotgun on me would persuade me to do whatever she wanted. I wouldn't argue with that woman."

Susannah laughed. "She is formidable, but she's also such a sweetheart. I just love her."

"And I love you." Conor nuzzled her neck.

Susannah enjoyed his caresses quietly for a moment, but she couldn't get the events of the past week out of her mind. She rolled over and faced him. "Do you think Jeremiah will press charges against any of the Banning men?"

"He's finished conducting all his interviews. Some of the men will go free and some will be charged with firing upon a territorial officer, but I think Ben is in the worst trouble. He did kidnap Lily Carolina."

"But he later saved her. He also kept Kyle from shooting me that day on the mountain." Susannah's brow furrowed in confusion. "I just don't understand Ben Hollister. He worked for Fletcher, but I don't think he's a truly bad man."

"He isn't. Maybe he has a strange idea of loyalty."

Susannah pondered that for a moment, then her thoughts jumped in another direction. "Do you realize this is Independence Day?"

"Yes. That's why we're leaving for Wyoming on Monday instead of today. Surely you remember Lucas's invitation to the celebration."

"Of course I remember. It's just that this Independence Day has a special meaning for us."

"And what is that?"

"We are free, Conor. Truly free. Free of the Bannings, free to plan a future. Without worrying about death."

"You're right. We are free." Conor kissed her soundly. "And I don't want to talk about the Bannings anymore."

Susannah smiled. "What do you want to talk about?"

"I'm not certain I want to talk about anything." His hand stroked her from neck to thigh.

"Mm." Susannah snuggled against him. "Do you mind terribly waiting a few weeks to get married?"

"Not *terribly*. I already think of you as my wife. Standing up before a preacher is just a formality."

Susannah stared at him, deeply moved by his words. "I feel the same way."

Conor kissed her again, light and teasing. "I understand that you want your friends at our wedding. I'm glad Jennifer wired that she'd be able to come. All the way from Philadelphia, too, just for a wedding."

"No, it's not just for the wedding. She and her uncle will be going farther west afterward, to Nevada and California. Her uncle wants to explore some investment opportunities. I think it was nice of him to arrange the trip so Jennie could come to the wedding."

Conor's hand moved from her back to her waist, then her ribs, then higher. "Very nice."

Susannah's breath caught as the familiar fire roared to life in her belly. "I wonder if I will ever get enough of you, Conor O'Rourke." Her hand moved over his chest, touching lightly when she encountered his bandage.

"I hope not." His fingers continued their magical work.

Susannah shifted against him, lifting her top leg over his legs. "One good thing I'll say about both of us being hurt and bandaged," she whispered.

Conor's hand wandered down her stomach. "What's that?"

Her eyes closed as his fingers moved lower, seeking, finding. "We are forced . . . to explore other, intriguing . . . paths to pleasure." Her own hand followed a similar trail down Conor's body.

He moaned when she found him. "True," he murmured. "We have become very . . . adventurous."

That morning they celebrated the Fourth of July with fireworks of their own making.

"We'll pick up the mares in Downieville, then stay in Denver for a day, then head up to Cheyenne and on to Laramie City." Conor placed Susannah's trunk in the back of the rented wagon. It was early Monday morning, and the wagon outside Alexandra's house was loaded. "We'll wire when we set the date for certain. Now, you all know you're invited." He looked at each member of the group gathered around the wagon. "Laramie City is not that far by train. We expect to see each of you there."

"You know Lucas and I will be there, and Joseph." Alexandra hugged Susannah. "Lordy, I'm going to miss you. All of you, especially that young one in my bed and that dog on top of it."

"Somehow I don't think your bed will be empty for long," Susannah whispered, with a conspiratorial glance at Lucas. "I think that man has marriage on his mind."

A tinge of pink colored Alexandra's cheeks, "You may be right."

Conor stood in front of Hamilton. "Are you going to come?"

"I don't know yet." The boy adjusted his spectacles.

"I know you need time, Hamilton. And I think you'll do well, living with Lucas and Joseph. I truly would like to have things at peace between us."

Hamilton nodded. "Yes, sir."

Conor turned to Victoria. "And what about you, young lady?"

Victoria smiled wanly. She had been subdued for the past week, trying to come to terms with the drastic changes in her life. "I'll stay with Aunt Minnie and Uncle Horatio for a while. Mr. McCleave is going to help me sort out my financial affairs. Fletcher's estate is a complicated one. But I'll be all right."

Minerva put an arm around the girl's waist. "We'll take good care of her, Conor."

Conor kissed Minerva's cheek. "I know you will."

"I'll come to the wedding, Conor." Polly smiled at him. "I may talk to that friend of yours, Katie, about a job at her saloon."

"You do that. She'll treat you good, Polly." Conor turned to Lily Carolina, who stood on the porch dressed in a travel outfit, clutching her doll. "Are you ready, Poppet?"

"Yes, Conor. So's Jesse and Amy."

"All right." Conor scooped her up into his arms and settled her on the seat. "Just sit tight for a minute. Your sister will be right there. Come on, Jess. Up in the wagon."

The big dog jumped easily to the wagon bed and Conor closed the tailgate. He tied Charlie's reins to the gate.

Susannah hugged Alexandra one last time, then allowed Lucas to help her up onto the seat. She adjusted her hat and scooted closer to Lily Carolina.

Conor held his hand out to Lucas. "Thank you for everything. That day I first met you in your office seems like a long time ago, doesn't it?"

Lucas shook his hand warmly. "It does. It's hard to believe we didn't trust each other at first."

Alexandra stepped up to the men. "Check with the doctor in Laramie City as soon as you get there," she ordered. "I think Lily Carolina's splint can come off in a week."

"Can Amy's splint come off, too?" the child asked from the seat.

"Only when yours does, honey," Alexandra answered.

Conor took Alexandra into an affectionate embrace. "Thank you for everything, Alexandra. You were a true friend in our time of need."

Alexandra tightened her arms around him. "I'm just glad everything worked out the way it did. You two take care of each other, and of that child. We'll see you in a few weeks." She kissed his cheek. "Go on, now. You'll have me blubbering like Minerva there."

Minerva removed her spectacles and dabbed at her eyes. "I'm not blubbering," she retorted. "Just got something in my eye." Horatio put a loving arm around his wife.

Conor climbed to the wagon seat and took up the reins. "We'll see you all in a few weeks." He shook the reins over the horses' backs, and the wagon rolled forward.

Susannah turned and waved. "Goodbye!"

" 'Bye," called Lily Carolina. Jesse barked excitedly.

When she could no longer see the group outside the little house, Susannah turned to face the road, dabbing at her own eyes.

Conor glanced at her. "How are you?"

Susannah took a shaky breath. "Oh, I'm sad to be leaving our friends, and at the same time I'm anxious to be on our way."

"You're sure you don't want to settle here?"

"No. There are too many painful memories here, Conor. Mixed in with pleasant memories, of course, but no, I don't want to stay here. I really want to raise horses, and like you said, it's too high here for that." She looked up at the towering mountains that surrounded the valley. "I love the mountains, but I need a little more open space. I'm anxious to see the land you want to buy."

"It's beautiful. Mountains and plains, rock outcroppings and trees. It's a wild, untamed land, with rough winters and pleasant summers. We could make a nice life there."

"It sounds good to me."

"Me, too," Lily Carolina chimed in.

Conor laughed. "That's good. It's settled, then." He looked at Susannah over Lily Carolina's head. "We're going home."

Susannah's breath caught at the warmth in his blue eyes. Her heart overflowed with love for him. "We're going home," she repeated.

Epilogue

Wyoming Territory, three weeks later

Alina Parker stood on the covered porch of her two-storied ranch house, one hand shading her eyes against the midday sun. The murmur of many cheerful voices washed over her from the open window. A light wind pressed the skirt of her dark blue day dress against her legs and coaxed a curl from the arrangement of her glossy black hair. She searched the yard, crowded with the buggies and wagons of her friends, her eyes at last finding a tall, familiar figure. With a smile, she stepped off the porch and started through the maze of vehicles.

Conor braced his elbows on the top rail of the corral fence and stared at the vista spread before him with deep satisfaction. The gentle downslope in front of the house led to the bunkhouse and the barn, then to a pasture, enclosed by the fence against which he rested. A cheerful creek gurgled and sang as it crossed the pasture. Beyond that stretched the wide expanse of Beau's land, covered with tall, waving grasses, golden-green in the sunlight, dotted with contented cattle and horses, as well as outcroppings of rock and stands of pine trees. In the distance, the Rocky Mountains paraded in ageless splendor, some of the towering peaks still white with snow, although it was late July.

It was a good land, he decided, a good place to build a life with Susannah and raise a family. It was home.

"I never grow tired of this view."

Conor turned at the sweet sound of his beloved cousin's voice. "Nor do I," he responded with a smile. He watched as the playful breeze teased Alina's cheek with an errant curl. His heart swelled with love for her.

"I'm so glad you came back, Conor." She turned to look at him, her blue eyes brilliant in the sunlight, her beautiful face soft with a tender smile. Curiosity arched one delicate eyebrow. "What brought you back? What has changed since April? You were welcome to stay all along. Surely Beau and I made that clear."

"Very clear." Conor affectionately poked her nose. "You practically begged me to stay."

"I did," she admitted. "I hated to see you leave."

Conor sighed and returned his gaze to the valley. "And I hated to leave. I ached to stay, Alina, truly I did. But this is *your* land, yours and Beau's." He waved an arm behind him toward the house. *"Your* home. *Your* dream. I needed to find my own." His features softened. "And I did. I found it in Susannah, and in Lily Carolina. Now it feels right to be here, with them." He shook his head in silent wonder. "I still find it hard to believe that Susannah and I have a thousand acres of our own, bordering your land."

"You worked hard for it, Conor."

"I did, but Walter Duncan's gold helped." He shook his head again. "Isn't it funny? The old guy was right all along. No silver, but there was gold, just enough to make a difference for Susannah and me, and Lily Carolina, and Lucas."

"It's too bad he didn't live long enough to find it himself."

Conor shrugged. "Maybe Walter didn't really care if he found the gold or not. Maybe he was satisfied with the search alone. It gave meaning to his life."

"Perhaps you're right." Alina's gaze traveled Conor's tall frame. He wore his black broadcloth suit and the brocade vest with the gray stock. His long hair was brushed back from his face and blew lightly in the wind. "You look real good in that suit, Cousin," she commented. "Susannah is a lucky woman."

Conor smiled. "I'm the lucky one, Alina. I sure am glad you told me to visit her." His eyes narrowed with sudden suspicion. "Were you playing matchmaker? Did you hope we'd like each other?"

"I *knew* you'd like each other," Alina answered, laughing. "But I swear I wasn't matchmaking. It didn't occur to me that you'd fall in love, although I'm glad you did."

"Alina!"

Both Conor and Alina turned toward the house. Beau stood on the porch, rocking a decidedly unhappy infant in his arms.

"It appears my daughter is hungry," Alina remarked as she waved to her husband. "I'd best see to her." After planting a quick kiss on Conor's cheek, she turned to go, but Conor drew her into his embrace.

They held each other tightly, without a word, then after a moment, Conor released her and pointed her in the direction of the house. "See to your daughter, Cousin."

She nodded and hurried away. Conor watched her go. The thought occurred to him that perhaps one day Susannah would be hurrying off to nurse their child. The picture that came to his mind filled him with pleasure. Not yet ready to go inside, he turned back to face the valley.

A short time later, Alina sat in the rocking chair in her upstairs bedroom, her infant daughter enthusiastically nursing at her breast, watching as Jennifer Mainwaring laced the back of Susannah's ivory wedding gown. The satin dress was elegant, but simple, with a high collar and long sleeves trimmed in lace, a pin-tucked bodice that came to a vee at Susannah's narrow waist, and a plain skirt swept up to a small bustle over an ivory lace underskirt. Jennifer had caught Susannah's golden locks back in a simple arrangement that left long curls flowing down to her waist. A modest wreath of tiny intertwined roses and leaves adorned her head, awaiting the attachment of the sheer veil that was draped over the finely carved oak footboard of Alina's bed. Susannah's eyes sparkled with anticipation and excitement, her cheeks touched with pink.

"You are beautiful, Susannah," Alina said quietly.

Susannah looked at her friend. Alina's thick black hair accented the creamy texture of her skin, and her blue eyes, so uncannily like Conor's, shone with love and contentment. "So are you," Susannah said softly. "I swear, you positively glow, Alina. Is that what motherhood will do for me?"

"You already glow yourself, Susannah." Jennifer gave the lacing one final adjustment and stepped back to examine her handiwork. "I think love is what gives a woman that glow. Even your friend Alexandra has it."

Susannah pressed her hands to her cheeks. "I glow?"

"Like a lamp," Jennifer said with a laugh.

Susannah turned to her and held out her hands. "I'm so glad you came. It's wonderful, the three of us together again. Isn't it amazing, the different roads our lives took after we came home from England?"

"Well, I never expected to be living in the wilds of Wyoming Territory, that's for certain," Alina commented. "And now I wouldn't consider living anywhere else."

"That has a lot to do with Beau, doesn't it?" Jennifer settled herself on the edge of the neatly made double bed.

"Oh, yes." Alina's features softened. "It has everything to do with him."

"And you'd follow Conor anywhere, too, wouldn't you?" Jennifer asked Susannah.

"I would, but he'd not insist I go somewhere I really didn't want to go." She sighed wonderingly. "I am so lucky to have found him. I consider our relationship a partnership. We each bring our own strengths and weaknesses to the union, and we'll work together to build a good life."

"That's what I want from my marriage," Jennifer announced.

Alina and Susannah both looked at her. "Is there something we should know?" Alina asked.

Jennifer shook her head. "Nothing definite. My uncle wants me to encourage the attentions of a young man at home. He's a decent fellow, and I like him well enough. But he doesn't make me glow."

Susannah eyed her friend. Jennifer was lovely in a green parlor gown, with her thick auburn hair arranged in a becoming style of rolls and curls. She was more slender than Susannah remembered, her beautiful face more pale. For the first time, Susannah noticed fine lines of worry and tension around Jennifer's striking green eyes, eyes that had taken on a pensive, melancholy expression.

"If I were you, I'd wait, then," Susannah advised. "Wait for a man who will make you glow." She hesitated. "Jennie, is everything all right?"

Jennifer met her gaze, startled. "Of course everything's all right. Why wouldn't it be?"

Susannah sat at Jennifer's side on the bed, taking her friend's hand. "I don't know. You just seem kind of . . . sad. I know it's only been a year since your parents died."

"And you didn't really know your uncle before he came to live with you and take over the management of your financial affairs," Alina added, her voice soft with concern. "I know that can be difficult; I went through a terrible time when my aunt tried to control my financial affairs." She glanced at the baby in her arms, then returned her gaze to Jennifer. "Susannah's right. You're trying to hide it, but you're troubled about something, Jen."

Jennifer looked from Alina to Susannah, a wry smile touching her lips. "I never could keep anything from the two of you." She sighed. "It has been difficult," she admitted.

"Tell us," Susannah encouraged.

Jennifer shrugged. "There's not much to tell. Uncle Edward is actually a lot like my father, which should not be surprising, as they were brothers. We disagree on some of the things I'd like to do, but that's nothing new. As you both well know, my parents weren't very supportive of most of my plans or wishes. Perhaps I hoped things would be different."

Susannah and Alina exchanged a glance.

"Are you displeased with this lengthy trip he has insisted you take?" Susannah asked.

"Not at all," Jennifer hastened to assure her. "I was anxious to get out of Philadelphia for a while; it can be miserable in the summer there. And you know I couldn't wait to see both of you." She smoothed her skirt with her free hand. "We'll visit my godfather on his ranch in California, and I am looking forward to it. I haven't seen Oliver Cantrell since I was a little girl. Of course, the real purpose of this trip is for Uncle Edward to explore investment opportunities in the West, but I'm glad he brought me along."

"I would have enjoyed getting to know your uncle better," Susannah said. "We didn't have much of an opportunity to talk when we met you at the train station. It's unfortunate he couldn't come out from town for the wedding."

"He could have come," Jennifer blurted, her voice bitter. "But he had nothing to gain from gracing a little country wedding with his presence. He's such a snob sometimes." Her cheeks colored and her grasp on Susannah's hand tightened. "I apologize. I shouldn't talk that way about him. Anyway, now is not the time to discuss my uncle." She smiled, an obviously forced smile. "This is your wedding day, Susannah, a happy, joyous day. My little concerns have no place here."

Susannah gave her a quick hug. "Maybe we can match you up with someone and you can live in Wyoming, too."

"If you find me a man like Beau or Conor, I'm all for it." Jennifer returned Susannah's hug, then stood up.

"I'll see what I can do," Alina said with a laugh. "After all, I'm responsible for Conor and Susannah meeting. Just remember to hold out for a man who makes you glow." She dabbed at her daughter's mouth with a cloth. "Have you had enough for now, sweetheart?" she cooed. She closed the front of her dress, then, after draping the cloth over her shoulder, held the baby against her and patted its back.

A knock sounded on the door. Susannah called to enter, and the door flew open to admit Lily Carolina pulling Alexandra Kennedy into the room.

"Lily Carolina, you look so pretty!" Susannah cried. She moved from the bed to take the little girl's hand, crouching down beside her. Lily Carolina wore a blue bodice and overskirt, trimmed with blue silk ruches, over a white underskirt. Matching blue ribbons were woven through her golden hair.

"Are you almost ready?" the child asked. "Conor is ready." Her voice dropped to a conspiratorial whisper. "There's a lot of people downstairs."

Susannah smiled. "All we have to do is attach my veil. Then Lucas will bring me down."

"Susannah, you are absolutely beautiful in that dress," said Alexandra.

"Of course she is," Lily Carolina said loyally, her free hand searching for and finding Susannah's cheek. "Conor said she's always beautiful, even when she's not wearing anything at all."

Susannah felt her face heat to a fiery red as she grabbed her sister's hand. Ignoring the light titter of laughter from her friends, she stroked Lily Carolina's wrist. "Aren't you glad to have that splint off?" she asked, desperate to steer the conversation in a different direction.

"Yes, 'cause now I can go riding. Mr. Pike said that as soon as the preacher is finished jawing over you and Conor, he'll change out of his fancy clothes and take me on a ride. Can I go, Susannah?"

Now Alina laughed out loud. "I can hear Pike saying exactly that, Susannah."

"So can I," Susannah agreed. She straightened. "Yes, honey, you can go for a ride with Mr. Pike when the ceremony is over."

"Good." Lily Carolina abruptly changed the subject. "Is Cousin Elizabeth here?"

"Yes, she is," Alina answered. "She's over here in the rocking chair with me. Just follow the footboard and come about four steps beyond the end of it."

Susannah guided Lily Carolina's hand to the oak footboard and released her. The child carefully made her way to the rocking chair. She reached out with a gentle hand to caress the baby's soft head.

"I *love* babies," Lily Carolina said reverently. "Conor said he would give Susannah a baby."

Susannah blushed again. "Conor has evidently been saying a lot," she grumbled. She stood still as Jennifer attached the veil to her headpiece and arranged the folds that fell to the floor.

Elizabeth closed her tiny hand around Lily Carolina's finger while the child innocently continued her conversation with no one in particular. "When I asked how he would give her a baby, he said it was magic."

Alina and Susannah shared a knowing, contented glance.

"It certainly is magic," Susannah said softly, a thrill of excitement chasing itself around her belly just at the thought. Tonight she and Conor would share the big bed in his old room downstairs as husband and wife, and tomorrow work would begin on their own house, on their own land. And one day his child would grow in her, if it wasn't growing already. Unconsciously her hand moved to her flat stomach.

Susannah noticed the look of wistful longing that flashed across Jennifer's face. She grabbed her friend's hand again. "Wait for a man who makes you glow, Jennie," she urged in a whisper. "He'll be worth the wait."

Jennifer nodded, her mouth curved in a small, hopeful smile.

Lucas McCleave knocked lightly on the opened door. "Hello, ladies. Is the bride ready?"

"I am," Susannah answered. She felt that her heart would overflow with happiness.

"Lily Carolina, you come with me," Alexandra ordered. "We'll wait downstairs. Alina, shall I take that darling baby with me so you and Susannah and Jennifer can have a moment alone?"

"Yes, thank you, Alexandra." She rose from the rocker, kissed her daughter on the cheek, and gave her into Alexandra's capable hands.

"Give me a hug, Lily Carolina." Susannah crouched down, holding her arms out. The child found her and the sisters clung tightly to each other. After a moment, Susannah straightened and guided Lily Carolina to Alexandra's side.

"Hold onto my skirt, Lily Carolina," Alexandra instructed. "And be real careful going down the stairs." They went out into the hall and Lucas pulled the door closed, leaving the three friends alone.

The women formed a circle, their arms at each other's waists.

"Welcome to my family, Susannah," Alina said softly. "Now we truly are sisters."

"Be happy, Susannah." Jennifer kissed her cheek.

Susannah blinked back threatening tears. "I love you both," she whispered.

After a moment of emotional silence, Alina said, "Let's not keep my cousin waiting for you any longer." She and Jennifer left the room and Lucas entered. He idly stroked his beard as his sharp gray eyes traveled over her.

"You are radiant, Susannah," he said, his voice warm with sincerity.

"Thank you, Lucas, and thank you for giving me away."

"It's my honor. I only wish your father were here to exercise that privilege himself." He extended his arm to her.

"I feel he is here, in some way," Susannah said softly.

"Perhaps he is, my dear."

She laid her hand on Lucas's arm and he led her out of the room.

Downstairs, Conor stood in front of the fireplace with Beau Parker and Sebastian Pike. "I sure do appreciate you holding the wedding here, Beau," he said.

Beau laughed, a deep, rich sound. "As if I had anything to do with it. Alina would not have considered anything else. When that woman sets her mind on something, there's no budging her." He smoothed the edges of his full, dark mustache. "Ask Pike here. He wasn't going to wear a suit today, but she insisted."

Pike snorted in disgust and crossed his arms over his chest.

Conor looked at the older man, determined not to smile. He took in Pike's neatly combed gray hair, his trimmed beard, his new suit. "Sorry to make you wear that get-up, Pike." His gaze dropped down further to the wooden peg that extended from Pike's right knee to the floor. "You're even wearing your fancy carved leg. This *is* an honor."

Pike only snorted again.

Beau leaned over and straightened Pike's shoestring tie. "A wedding is a good reason to get dressed up, although Pike would not agree with me."

Pike slapped Beau's hand away and finally spoke, gruffly. "Ya're right about that, Beau Parker. The only time I wanta be all gussied up like this is at my own funeral."

"But you look so pretty, Pike," Conor said, at last breaking into a broad grin.

"Ya just wipe that silly smile off your face this minute, Conor O'Rourke, or ya ain't gonna be too pretty your ownself by the time your woman gets down here." Pike dug at his collar in a futile attempt to loosen it.

Conor laughed out loud. "I'm glad you didn't change in the months I was gone, Pike. It would get awful boring around here."

"Laugh all ya want," Pike grumbled. "As soon as ya and that lovely Susannah are hitched, this here suit is goin' in the fireplace. Just see if it don't."

Beau held up his hands in protest. "No, Pike, not the fireplace. Alina will have your head."

"For what?" Alina asked sweetly as she and Jennifer joined the men.

"Nothing," Pike muttered. He pulled at his collar again.

Alexandra, with Elizabeth in her arms, guided Lily Carolina to Jennifer's side, then stepped back to stand with the crowd.

As she descended the stairs at Lucas's side, Susannah saw that the main room of Alina's home was indeed filled with people. All their friends had come from Georgetown, including Hamilton Grant, who stood stiffly in a new suit. Minerva Potter lifted her spectacles to dab at her eyes, while Horatio awkwardly patted her shoulder. Polly, Neville, Joseph, Victoria, they were all there. And Conor's friends; David and Cynthia Freeman and their four children, who lived on a neighboring ranch; Katie Davenport, the flamboyant red-haired saloon owner, her friends Emerald and Moses, and Sam Trudeau, the deputy marshal, all of whom had come from Laramie City; Michael and Ian Rafferty, the Parker ranch hands; they were all there.

The room quieted and all heads turned toward the stairs. Conor watched, seeing first the ivory satin skirt. Then she came into view. His breath caught and his heart started hammering. The lovely, spirited woman coming toward him had given herself to him, her body and her life, her heart and her soul. She belonged to him, as he did to her. A deep, satisfying pride settled comfortably next to the bottomless well of love he felt for her.

Susannah descended the last step and turned. A clear path lined with dear, happy friends led to the stone fireplace, in front of which the justice of the peace waited, with Alina, Jennifer and Lily Carolina on one side, Beau and Pike on the other. And there in the middle was Conor.

At the sight of him, Susannah felt that her breath was taken away. He was tall and elegant, again wearing his black broadcloth suit. His long hair was brushed back from his handsome face, and his blue eyes shone with love and pride.

Conor watched her approach, resplendent in the dress they had bought for her in Denver. Her gray-green eyes were shining, her cheeks kissed with a tinge of pink, her lips curved in a smile. She looked so happy! Had he made her happy? He fervently hoped so, for she had given him joy, the like of which he had never known. Yes, she had given him joy, and love, and peace. He silently vowed to spend the rest of his life returning her gifts to her tenfold.

Lucas led Susannah closer. Conor held his hand out to her. She left Lucas's side and stepped forward, reaching for him. His strong fingers closed on hers, drawing her to him. He kissed her hand before he tucked her arm securely in his. She looked up at him, letting her love pour over him with silent warmth. He touched her cheek in response, then they faced the justice of the peace the same way they would face the rest of their lives: together.

Dear Reader:

One of the things I love about writing historical novels is the research. I read history books for pleasure. And when I am concentrating my research on a specific town, area, and year, I read the old newspapers. They are fascinating, and often give my stories directions I never expected.

I knew all along that a doctor would play an important role in *The Mountain Rose,* but I had no idea that doctor would be a woman until I read the Georgetown *Daily Colorado Miner* of May 27, 1873, and saw the advertisement for the services of Mrs. Helene Anderson, Female Physician and Midwife. The fact that there was a female physician in Georgetown at that time opened up a whole world of possibilities, and the character of Alexandra Kennedy, M.D., was born.

The situation with the mining lawsuits is also historically accurate, as was the incident of a man being killed on Alpine Street in front of many witnesses. Armed men terrorized the town for several days afterward, and I could find no evidence that the murderer was ever brought to justice. As this actually happened in 1875, two years after the setting of *The Mountain Rose,* I took a little historical license by including a similar incident in my novel, and I changed the names of the concerned parties. Still, the essence of the times remains.

My third novel, titled *The Wild Rose,* is the story of Jennifer Mainwaring, whom you met at Conor and Susannah's wedding, and John Cantrell, the handsome, dangerous, half-Mexican son of a powerful California landowner. The story of the cool, lovely lady from Philadelphia and the hot-blooded, blue-eyed warrior known as El Lobo, who fought for Juarez against Maximillian, should prove fascinating to research and a great deal of fun to write. *The Wild Rose* is scheduled for a September 1995 release.

I sincerely hope you find my novels entertaining, and that, for a while, they take you to a different time and place. I believe in the power of love, and its ultimate triumph in the world, and I write my books to reflect that belief. Hopefully, my stories will leave you with a good feeling. You may write to me at P.O. Box 461212, Aurora, Colorado, 80046. A self-addressed stamped envelope would be greatly appreciated.

With my warmest regards,
Jessica Wulf

About the Author

Jessica Wulf is a native of North Dakota and has spent most of her life in Colorado, where she now lives with her husband and two dogs. She has a B.A. in History, as well as a passion and fascination for it, and often feels that she was born in the wrong century. *The Mountain Rose* is her second novel.